PUFFIN BOOKS
Editor: Kaye Webb

COLLECTED STORIES FOR CHILDREN

These seventeen strange tales offer, you might say, seventeen gateways into the country of Walter de la Mare, a place like nowhere else in story or in poetry. It shares a border with fairytale, where witches, ogres, ghosts are regular citizens, where a fish may be really a boy, where everyone ready to risk it has a chance of a wish coming true. Yet it is recognizably England, with its valleys, meadows and orchards, its villages, woods and churchyards, and the sandy edge of the sea. It is far; it is also near. Sometimes it seems exactly where we are now. Those who have met it first by way of de la Mare's poetry (*John Mouldy, Nod, The Little Green Orchard* and, needless to say, all of *Come Hither*) will find the same landscape and people here: the forests and phantoms, dwarfs and wizards, the tree-shadowed houses where you may go from room to room for ever, the echoes and silences, the comedy and the dark. And of course, the children – safe among all the mysteries because de la Mare is on their side.

Open the book: a girl comes to an ancient mansion for her great-great-great-great grandmother's 350th birthday. She is offered a fateful secret. Three orphan boys fall into a long charmed slumber. What will make them wake? The story is sharp as spring hail, shining as a poem by Blake, who also wrote about orphan chimney sweeps. And seven orphans, brothers and sisters, appear in that short and marvellous tale, *The Riddle*, which seems to solve itself every time, yet always lures its readers back to ask the question again.

Turn more pages and an old woman recalls an April when angels were seen on the hilltops over London. A boy perceives that some of the birds around are ghost birds, carrying messages from yesterday or tomorrow. Another boy comes on an age-old dried-out beanstalk leading up higher than eye can see. He climbs. 'He found himself (we read) in a country of low, smooth but very wide hills and of wide, gentle valleys ... and far, far to the north, rising dark and lowering in the distance above the blur and pallor of snow, showed the turrets of a Castle.'

That Castle waits for all of us if we wish to find it. Step carefully, though. The country of de la Mare is easy to enter; it is here in these very pages, but it is not so easy to leave. Something stays with us always when we move on – a rare piece of landscape in the mind. We come away, too, knowing more than we did about the nature of spells: here and there, even, the recipes themselves. But for the right sort of reader, this book may cast the most potent and rewarding spell of all.

Walter de la Mare

Collected Stories for Children

Illustrated by ROBIN JACQUES

Puffin Books
in association with Faber and Faber Ltd

Puffin Books, Penguin Books Ltd, Harmondsworth, Middlesex, England
Penguin Books, 625 Madison Avenue, New York, New York 10022, U.S.A.
Penguin Books Australia Ltd, Ringwood, Victoria, Australia
Penguin Books Canada Ltd, 2801 John Street, Markham, Ontario, Canada L3R 1B4
Penguin Books (N.Z.) Ltd, 182–190 Wairau Road, Auckland 10, New Zealand

—

This collected edition first published by Faber and Faber Ltd 1947

—

Published in Puffin Books 1977

—

Copyright © Estate of Walter de la Mare, 1947
Illustrations copyright © Faber and Faber Ltd, 1947

—

Made and printed in Great Britain
by Richard Clay (The Chaucer Press) Ltd,
Bungay, Suffolk
Set in Linotype Times

Contents

Dick and the Beanstalk

In the county of Gloucestershire there lived with his father, who was a farmer, a boy called Dick. Their farm was not one of the biggest of the Gloucestershire farms thereabouts. It was of the middle size, between large and small. But the old house had stood there, quiet and peaceful, for at least two hundred years, and it was built of sound Cotswold stone. It had fine chimney stacks and a great roof. From his window under one of its gables Dick looked out across its ploughland and meadows to distant hills, while nearer at hand its barns, stables and pigsties clustered around it, like chicks round a hen.

Dick was an only son and had no mother. His father – chiefly for company's sake – had never sent him to school. But being a boy pretty quick in his wits, Dick had all but taught himself, with his father's help, to read and write and figure a little. And, by keeping his eyes and his ears open wherever he went, by asking questions and, if need be, finding out the answers for himself, he had learned a good deal else besides.

When he was a child he had been sung all the old rhymes and told most of the country tales of those parts by his mother, and by an old woman who came to the farm when there was sewing to be done, sheets to be hemmed, or shirts to be made. She was a deaf, poring old woman, but very skilful with her needle; and he never wearied of listening to the tales she told him; though at times, and particularly on dark windy nights in the winter, he would at last creep off rather anxious and shuddering to bed.

These tales not only stayed in Dick's head, but *lived* there. He not only remembered them, but thought about them; and he sometimes dreamed about them. He not only knew almost by heart what they told, but would please himself by fancying what else had happened to the people in them after the tales were over or before they had begun. He could not only find his way about in a story-book, chapter by chapter, page by page, but if it told only about the inside of a house he would begin to wonder what its garden was like – and in imagination would find his way into it and then perhaps try to explore even further. It was in this way, for example, that Dick had come to his own conclusions on which finger Aladdin wore his ring, and the colour of his uncle the Magician's eyes; on what too at last had happened to the old Fairy Woman in *The Sleeping Beauty*. After, that is, she had ridden off on her white ass into the forest when the magic spindle had begun to spread the deathly slumber over her enemies that was not to be broken for a hundred years. *He* knew why she didn't afterwards come to the Wedding!

And as for Blue-beard's stone-turreted and many-windowed castle, with its chestnut gallery to the east, and its muddy moat with its carp, under the cypresses, Dick knew a good deal more about *that* than even Fatima did! So again, if he found out that Old Mother Hubbard had a *cat*, he could tell you the cat's name. And he could describe the crown that Molly Whuppie was crowned with when she became Queen, even to its last emerald. He was what is called a *lively* reader.

Dick often wished he had been born the youngest of three brothers, for then he would have gone out into the world early to seek his fortune. And in a few years, and after many adventures, he would have come back again, his pockets crammed with money, a magic Table on his back or a Cap of Invisibility in his pocket, and have lived happily with his father ever afterwards. He had long been certain too that if only he could spruce up his courage and be off if but a little way, even if only into one of the next counties, Warwickshire or Wiltshire, Monmouthshire or Somerset, adventures would be sure to come. He itched to try his luck.

But there was a hindrance. His father would hardly let him out of his sight. And this was natural. Poor man, he had no daughters, so Dick was his only child as well as his only son. And his mother was dead. Apart then from his farm, the farmer had but one thought in the world – Dick himself. Still, he would at times give him leave to jog off alone to the nearest market town on an errand or two. And going alone for Dick was not the same thing as *not* going alone.

Sometimes Dick went further. He had an uncle, a very fat man, who was a mason at Moreton-in-the-Marsh, and an old widowed aunt who had a windmill and seven cats at Stow-on-the-Wold. He would visit *them*. He had also been to the Saffron Fair at Cirencester; and had stayed till the lights came out and the flares of the gingerbread stalls and Merry-go-rounds. But as for the great cities of Gloucestershire – Gloucester itself, or Bristol; or further still, Exeter, or further the other way, London (where his old friend and namesake Dick Whittington had been Lord Mayor three-and-a-half times) – Dick had never walked the streets of any of them, except in his story-books or in dreams. However, those who wait long enough seldom wait in vain.

On his next birthday after the one on which he had gone to the Saffron Fair, his father bought him for a birthday present a rough-coated pony. It was hog-maned – short and bristly; it was docktailed, stood about eleven hands high, and was called Jock. His father gave Dick leave to ride about the country when his morning's work was done, 'just to see the world a bit', as he said, and to learn to fend for himself. And it was a bargain and promise between them that unless any mischance or uncommon piece of good fortune should keep him late, Dick would always be home again before night came down. Great talks of the afternoon's and evening's doings the two of them would have over their supper together in the farmhouse kitchen. His father began to look forward to them as much as Dick looked forward to them himself. Very good friends they were together, Dick and his father.

Now one winter morning – in the middle of January – of the next year, Dick asked leave of his father to have the next whole fine day all to himself. The weather had been frosty, the evening skies a fine shepherd's red, and everything promised well. He told his father he wanted to press on further afield than he had before – 'beyond those hills over there'. And as the days were now short, he must be off early, since there were few hours after noon before dark. His father gave him leave, but warned him to be careful of what company he got into and against any folly or foolhardiness. 'Don't run into mischief, my son,' he said, 'nor let mischief run into you!' Dick laughed and promised.

Next day, before dawn, while the stars were shining, he got up, put on his clothes, crept downstairs, ate a hurried breakfast and cut himself off a hunch of bread and meat in the larder to put in his pocket. Then he scribbled a few lines to his father to tell him that he had gone, pinned the paper to the kitchen table, and having saddled up his pony set out due north-west into the morning.

There had been a very sharp frost during the night. It was as though a gigantic miller had stalked over the fields scattering his meal as he went. The farm ruts were hard and sharp as stone, and, as they jogged along, Jock's hoofs splintered the frozen puddles lying between them as if they were fine thin glass. Soon the sun rose, clear as a furnace, though with so little heat yet that its beams were not strong enough even to melt the rime that lay in the hollows and under the woods.

Now on the Friday before this, Dick had come to a valley between two round hills, and had looked out beyond it. But it had been too late in the day to go further. He reached this valley again about ten o'clock of the morning, and pushed on, trotting steadily along between its wooded slopes, following a faint overgrown grass-track until at last the track died away, and he came out on the other side. Here was much emptier, flatter country, though not many miles distant snow-topped hills began again. These hills were strange to him, and he had no notion where he was.

The unploughed fields were larger here than any he was accustomed to, and were overgrown with weeds. In these a multitude of winter birds were feeding. The hedges were ragged and untended, and there was not a house to be seen. Dick got off Jock's back and took out his lunch. Uncommonly good it tasted in the sharp cold air. And as he ate – sitting on a green knoll in the thin pale sunshine – he looked about him. And he saw a long way off what at first sight he took to be a column of smoke mounting up into the sky. He watched it awhile, marvelling. But there was no show of fire or of motion in it. It hung still and glimmering between the frosty earth and the blue of space. If not smoke, what could it be? Dick pondered in vain.

Having hastily finished his bread and meat, and feeling much the better for it, he mounted again and set off as fast as Jock could carry him in its direction. About three o'clock in the afternoon he drew near. And he found him-

11

self at last in a hollow where was an old tumbledown cottage, its thatch broken, its chimney fallen, its garden run wild. And growing within a few paces of this old cottage – towering up high above it, its top beyond view – was a huge withered tangle of what looked like a coarse kind of withy-wind or creeper. It went twisting and writhing corkscrew-fashion straight up into the air and so out of sight. Dick could not guess how far, because the sunlight so dazzled his eyes. But when he examined this great growth closely, and its gigantic pods of dried-up seeds as big as large kidney-shaped pebble-stones that still clung to its stem, he decided that it must be beans.

Never had he seen anything to match these beans. Who could have planted them, and when, and for what purpose? And where was he gone to? And then, in a flash, Dick realized at last where he himself *was*, and what he was looking at. There could be no doubt in the world. This was *Jack's* old cottage. This was where Jack had lived with his mother – before he met the friendly butcher on his way to market. And this huge tangled ladder here – which must have sprung up again as mighty as ever after Jack had cut it down and the Giant had fallen headlong – was Jack's famous Beanstalk.

Poor old woman, thought Dick. Jack's mother must be dead and gone ages and ages ago. And Jack too. He spied through the broken wall where a window had been. The hearth was full of old nettles. The thatch was riddled with abandoned bird-nests and rat-holes. There was not a sound in earth or sky; nor any trace of human being. He sat down on a hummock in the sun not far from the walls, and once more gazed up at the Beanstalk; and down again; and in his mind Dick went through all Jack's strange adventures. He knew them by heart.

The turf at his foot had been nibbled close by rabbits.

His seat, though smooth, was freckled with tiny holes, and it rounded up out of the turf like a huge grey stone. Near at hand, ivy and bramble had grown over it, but there showed another smaller hummock in the turf about three or four paces away. And as he eyed it he suddenly realized that he must be sitting on the big knuckle end of one of Jack's Giant's larger bones, probably his thigh bone, now partly sunken and buried and hidden in the ground. At thought of this he sprang to his feet again, and glanced sharply about him. Where, he wondered, lay the Giant's skull. Then he took another long look at the vast faded Beanstalk, and another at the bone. It was still early afternoon, but it was winter; and at about four o'clock, he reckoned, the sun would be set.

The more Dick looked at the Beanstalk, the more he itched to climb it – even if he got only as high as the cottage chimney. Farther up, much farther up, he would be able to see for miles. And still farther, he might even, if his sight carried, catch a glimpse of Old Bowley – a lofty hill which on days when rain was coming he could see from his bedroom window.

And he began arguing with himself: 'Now, surely, my father would never forgive me if he heard that I had actually discovered Jack's Beanstalk, and had come away again without daring to climb an inch of it!' And his other self answered him: 'Aye, that's all very well, my friend! But an inch, if it bears you, will be as good as a mile. What of *that*?'

What of *that*? thought Dick. He went close and tugged with all his might at the tangle of stalks. A few hollow cockled-up bean seeds peppered down from out of their dry shucks. He ducked his head. Once more he tugged; the stalks were tough as leather. And he began to climb.

But he made slow progress. The harsh withered strands

13

of the bean-bines not only cut into his hands but were crusted with rime, and his hands and feet were soon numb with cold. He stayed breathless and panting, not venturing yet to look down. On he went, and after perhaps a full hour's steady climbing, he stayed again and gazed about him. And a marvellous scene now met his eyes. His head swam with the strangeness of it.

Low in the heavens hung the red globe of the sun, and beneath him lay the vast saucer of the world. And there, sure enough, was Old Bowley! Jack's cottage seemingly no bigger than a doll's house showed plumb under his feet. And an inch or so away from it stood Jock, no bigger than a mole, cropping the grass in Jack's mother's garden.

Having come so high, Dick could not resist climbing higher. So on he went. Bruised with the beans that continually rattled down on him, breathless and smoking hot though powdered white with hoarfrost, at last he reached the top of the Beanstalk. There he sat down to rest. He found himself in a country of low, smooth, but very wide hills and of wide gentle valleys. Here too a thin snow had fallen. In this clear blue light it looked much more like the strange kind of place he had sometimes explored in his dreams than anything he had ever seen down below. And, far, far to the north, rising dark and lowering in the distance above the blur and pallor of the snow, showed the turrets of a Castle. Dick watched that Castle; and the longer he watched it, the less he liked the look of it.

Still, where Jack had led, Dick soon decided to follow. And best be quick! Thinking no more whether or not he would be able to get home that night, and believing his father would forgive him for not this time keeping to the bargain between them, since it was certain Dick would have plenty to tell him in the morning, he set off towards the Castle as fast as he could trudge. The frozen snow was scarcely an inch deep, but it was numbing cold up here in this high country; and the crystals being dry and powdery he could not get along fast.

Indeed, Dick did not reach the great Castle's gates under their cavernous, echoing, stone archway until a three-quarters moon had risen bright behind him. It shone with a dazzling lustre over the snow – on the square-headed iron nails in the gates, and on the grim bare walls of the

Castle itself. A rusty bell-chain hung high over his head beside the gates. Dick stood there eyeing it, his heart thumping against his ribs as it had never thumped before. But having come so far he was ashamed to turn back. He gave a jump, clutched at the iron handle with both hands, and tugged with all his might.

He heard nothing, not a sound. But in a few minutes – and slow they seemed – a wicket that had been cut out of the timbers of the huge gate, turned on its hinges, and a leaden-faced woman, her head and shoulders muffled up in a shawl, and, to Dick's astonishment, only about nine feet high, looked out on him and asked him what he wanted.

Following Jack's example, Dick told her that he had lost his way – as indeed he had, though he had found Jack's! He said he was tired out and hungry, and afraid of perishing in the cold. He implored the woman to give him a drink of water and a crust of bread, and perhaps to let him warm himself if only for a few minutes by her fire. 'Else, ma'am,' he said, 'the only thing I can do is to lie down under the wall here and maybe die. I can go no further.'

Not the faintest change showed in the woman's long narrow bony face. She merely continued to peer down at him. Then she asked him his name. Dick told her his name, and at that her eyes sharpened as if she had expected it.

'Step out there into the moonlight a little,' she told him, 'so that I can see your face. So it's *Dick*, is it?' she repeated after him. ' "Dick"! And you have come begging, eh? I have heard that tale before. And how, pray, am I to tell that you aren't from the same place, wherever that may be, as that villainous *Jack* who came here years and years and years ago with just such a tale as you have told me, and then ran off, first with my great-grandfather's moneybags, then with his Little Hen, and last with his Harp? How am I to know *that*? Why! – from what I've heard – you look to me as like as two peas!'

Dick stared up in wonder into her face. Jack's Giant, he thought, could not have been nearly so far back as the story had made out if this woman was only his great-granddaughter. He himself would have guessed a round dozen of *greats* at least. It was a mystery.

'Jack?' he said, as if he were puzzled. 'And who was Jack, ma'am? There are so many Jacks where I come from. Nobody of mine. What became of him, then?'

'Ah,' said the woman, 'you may well ask that. If my great-grandfather had caught him he would have ground his bones to powder in his mortar, and made soup of what was left. He was in the flower of his age, was my great-grandfather then, but he never came back. Never. And a kinder gentler soul never walked! "*And who was* JACK," says he!' she muttered to herself, and Dick little liked the sound of it.

'Well, I wonder!' said he, wishing he could hide his face from the glare of the moon. 'I mean, I wonder if your great-grandfather ever found his Harp again. Or his Little Hen either. There are plenty of hens where I come from. And harps too, as I have heard. It sounds a dreadful story, I mean; but what could that bad boy you mention have wanted with a harp?'

'Aye,' said the leaden-faced woman, blinking once but no more as she stared at him. 'What?'

'Anyhow,' said Dick, 'that must have been more years ago than I could count. And if I *were* Jack, ma'am, or even his great-grandson either, I couldn't be the size I am now. I should have grown a grey beard as long as your arm, and be dead and done with long ago. I am sorry about your great-grandfather. It is a sad story. And I don't know *what* end that Jack mustn't have come to. But if you would give me only a sip of water and a bit of bread and a warm by the fire, I wouldn't ask for *anything* more.'

'Nor did Jack, so they say,' said the woman sourly; and looked him over, top to toe again.

But she led him in none the less through the great gates of the Castle and down into the kitchen, where a fire was burning on the hearth. This kitchen, Dick reckoned, was about the size of (but not much bigger than) a little church. It was warm and cosy after the dark and cold. A shaded lamp stood burning on the table, and there were pewter candlesticks three feet high for fat tallow candles on the dresser. Dick looked covertly about him, while he stood warming his hands a few paces from the huge open hearth. Here, beside him, was the very cupboard in which in terror Jack had hidden himself. The shut oven door was like the door of a dungeon. Through a stone archway to the right of him he could spy out the copper. A chair stood beside the table. And on the table, as if waiting for somebody, was a tub-sized soup tureen. There was a bowl beside it, and a spoon to fit. And next the spoon was a hunch of bread of about the size of a quartern loaf. Even though he stood at some distance, it was only by craning his neck that Dick could spy out what was on the table.

He looked at all this with astonished eyes. He had fancied Jack's Giant's kitchen was a darker and gloomier place. But in Jack's day there was perhaps a fire less fierce burning in the hearth and no lamp alight; perhaps too in summer the shadows of the Castle walls hung coldly over its windows. Not that he felt very comfortable himself. Now that he had managed to get into the Castle, he began to be anxious as to what might happen to him before he could get out again. The ways and looks of this woman were not at all to his fancy and whoever was going to sup at that table might look even worse!

She had taken off her shawl now, and after rummaging in a high green cupboard had come back with a common-sized platter and an earthenware mug – mere dolls' china by comparison with the tureen on the table. She filled the mug with milk.

'Now get you up on to that stool,' she said to Dick, bringing the mug and a platter of bread over to him. 'Sit you up there and eat and drink and warm yourself while you can. My husband will be home at any moment. Then you can tell him who you are, what you want, why you have come, and where from.'

Dick quaked in his shoes – not so much at the words, as at the woman's mouth when she said them. But he looked back at her as boldly as he dared, and climbed up on to the stool. There, clumsy mug in one hand and crust in the other, he set to on his bread and milk. It was pleasant enough, he thought to himself, to sit here in the warm eating his supper, though a scrape of butter would have helped. But what kind of dainty might not this woman's husband fancy for *his* when *he* came home!

So, as he sipped, he peeped about him for a way of escape. But except for the door that stood ajar, some great pots on the pot-board under the dresser, and a mouse's hole in the wainscot that was not much bigger than a fox's in a hedgerow, there was no crack or cranny to be seen. Besides, the woman was watching him as closely as a cat. And he decided that for the present it would be wiser to keep his eyes to himself, and to stay harmless where he was.

At last there came the sound of what Dick took for foot-steps, from out of the back parts of the Castle. It was as if a man were pounding with a mallet on a tub. They came nearer. In a moment or two the kitchen door opened, and framed in the opening stood the woman's husband. Dick could not keep from squinting a little as he looked at him.

He guessed him to be about eighteen to twenty feet high – not more. Apart from this, he was not, thought Dick, what you could call a fine or large-sized giant. He was lean and bony; his loose unbuttoned leather jacket hung slack from his shoulders; and his legs in his stockings were no thicker than large scaffolding poles. There was a long nose in his long pale face, and on either side of his flat hat dangled dingy straw-coloured hair, hanging down from the mop above it.

When his glance fell on Dick enjoying himself on his stool by the kitchen fire, his watery green-grey eyes looked as if they might drop at any moment from out of his head.

'Head and choker! what have we here, wife?' he said at last to the leaden-faced woman. 'What have we here! *Hm, hm.*'

Before she could answer, Dick spoke up as boldly as he knew how, and told the young giant (for though Dick could not be certain, he *looked* to be not above thirty) – he told the young giant how he had lost his way, and chancing on the withered Beanstalk had climbed to the top of it to have a look round him. He told him, too, how grieved he had been to hear that the woman's great-grandfather had never come back to the Castle after he had chased the boy called Jack away, and how much he wondered whether the Little Hen was buried, and what had become of the Harp. Dick went on talking because it was easier to do so than to keep silent, seeing that the two of them continued to stare at him, and in a far from friendly fashion.

'I expect it played its last tune,' he ended up, 'ages and ages before I was born.'

'Aye,' said the woman. 'That's all pretty enough. But

what *I* say is that unless the tale I have heard is all fable, this ugly imp here must be little short of the very spit of that wicked thief himself. Anywise, he looks to me as if he had come from the same place. What's more –' she turned on Dick, 'if you can tell us where that is, you shall take my husband there and show it him. And he can look for the grave of my great-grandfather. And perhaps,' and her thin dark lips went arch-shaped as she said it, 'perhaps if you find it, you shall learn to play a tune on his Harp!'

Dick, as has been said, liked neither the looks nor the sound of this woman. She was, he decided, as sly and perhaps as treacherous as a fox. 'I can show you where *I* came from easily enough,' he answered. 'But I know no more about Jack than I have – than I have heard.'

'Nor don't we,' said the woman. 'Well, well, well! When he has supped you shall take my husband the way you came, and we shall see what we *shall* see.'

Dick glanced at the giant, who all this while had been glinting at him out of his wide and almost colourless eyes. So, not knowing whether he followed his great-grandfather's habits, or how long his wife would remain with them, he thought it best to say no more. He smiled, first at one of them, and then at the other, took a sip of milk, and rank greasy goat's milk it was, and said, 'When you are ready, I am ready too.' The difficulty was to keep his tongue from showing how fast his heart was beating.

At this the giant sat down to table and began the supper his wife had prepared for him. Spoon in hand he noisily supped up his huge basin of soup, picking out gingerly with his fingers, and as greedily as a starling, the hot steaming lumps of meat in it. He ate like a grampus. His soup finished, he fell to work on what looked like a shepherd's pie that had been sizzling in the oven. Then having sliced off a great lump of greenish cheese, he washed it all down with what was in his mug. But whether wine, ale, cider or water, Jack could not tell.

Having eaten his fill, the young giant sat back in his chair, as if to think his supper over. And soon he fell asleep. Not so did the woman. She had seated herself on the other side of the hearth in a great rocking-chair, a good deal closer to him than Dick fancied, and she had begun to knit. Like the clanking of fire-irons her needles sounded on and on in the kitchen, while the young giant, his mouth wide open, now and again shuddered in his slumbers or began or ceased to snore. Whereas if Dick even so much as opened his mouth to yawn, or shifted his legs out of the blaze of the fire, the woman's slow heavy face turned round on him, and stared at him as if she had been made of stone.

At last, much to Dick's comfort, the young giant awoke and stretched himself. He seemed to be in a good humour after his nap, and not sulky or sharp as some people are. 'What *I* say,' he said with a laugh on seeing Dick again, 'what *I* say is, there's more than one kind of supper!'

'Ha, ha, ha!' echoed Dick, but not very merrily. The giant then fumbled for a great club of blackthorn that stood behind the kitchen door. He put on his flat hat again, wound a scarf of sheep's wool round his neck, and said he was ready. Never had Dick, inside a book or out, heard before of a giant that wore a scarf. He clambered down from his stool and stood waiting. Her hand over her mouth, and her narrow sallow face showing less friendly than ever, the woman took another long look at him. Then she turned to her husband, and looked him over too.

'Well, it's a cold night,' she said, 'but you will soon get warm walking, and won't need your sheepskins.' At mention of *cold* her husband stepped back and lifted the curtain that concealed the kitchen window. He screened his eyes with his hands and looked out.

22

'Cold!' he said. 'It's perishing. There's a moon like a lump of silver, and a frost like iron. Besides,' he grumbled, 'a nap's no sleep, and I don't stir a step until the morning.'

The two of them wrangled together for a while and Dick listened. But at last after drawing iron bars across the shutters and locking him in, leaving him nothing to make him comfortable, and only the flames of the fire for company, they left him – as Dick hoped, for good. But presently after, the woman came back again, dangling a chain in her hand.

'So and *so*!' she said, snapping together the ring at the end of it on his ankle. 'There! That kept safe my old Poll parrot for many a year, so it may keep even *you* safe until daybreak!'

She stooped to fix the other end of the chain round a leg of the great table. Then, 'Take what sleep you can, young man,' she said, 'while you can, and as best you can. You'll need all your wits in the morning.'

Her footsteps died away. But long afterwards Dick could hear the voices of the two of them, the giant and his wife, mumbling on out of the depths of the night overhead, though he himself had other things to think about. After striving in vain to free his leg from the ring of the chain, he examined as best he could with the help of his stool the locks and bolts of the shutters over the windows – stout oak or solid iron every one of them. He reckoned the walls of this kitchen must be twelve feet thick at least and the bolts were to match.

And while more and more anxiously he was still in search of a way out, he heard a sudden scuffling behind him, and a squeak as shrill as a bugle. He turned in a flash, and in the glow of the fire saw what he took to be a mouse that had come out of its hole, though it was an animal of queer shape, lean and dark, and half as large again as a

full-sized English rat. Next moment, a score or more of
these creatures had crept out of the wainscot. They gam-
bolled about on the kitchen floor, disporting themselves
and looking for supper.

By good fortune, when the squeak sounded, Dick had
been standing on his stool by the window. He held his
breath at sight of them, and perhaps had held it too long,
or the giant's pepper had got into his nose, for he suddenly
sneezed. At which a jubilee indeed went up in the kitchen.
And if, in spite of his chain, by a prodigious leap from the
stool to the table he had not managed to land on it safely,
it might well have been the last of him. Luckily too, the
margins of the table jutted out far beyond its legs, so that
though the sharp-nosed hungry animals scrabbled up the
legs in hopes to get him, they could climb no further.

Now and again, squatting there, through the long hours
that followed – half-hidden between the giant's tureen and
mug – Dick drowsed off, in spite of these greedy noisy
rodents, and in spite too of the crickets in the outer cracks
of the oven, which kept up a continuous din like a covey
of willow-wrens. He was pestered also by the cunning and
curiosity of a wakeful housefly, though others like it,
straddling as big as cockroaches on the walls in the dusky
light of the fire, remained asleep. It must be a fusty airless
place, Dick thought, that had flies in winter. And so he
passed a sorry night.

It was five by the clock when the giant and his wife came
down again, Grackel still grumbling, and she pressing him
to be gone. At last he was ready. She looked him up and
down. 'What's to be done is best done quickly,' she said to
him. 'You can get breakfast at a tavern maybe. And leave
your aunt's watch behind you, husband. It will be safer
at home.'

The giant sullenly did as his wife had bidden, drew out

of his pocket a fine gold watch, its back embedded with what looked to Dick like sapphires and emeralds and other precious stones, and laid it on the table.

'That looks a fine watch,' said Dick, shivering in his breeches, for he was stiff and cold.

'Aye, so it is,' said the woman, and she put it away on a shelf in the cupboard. 'Now look you here, Grackel,' she added, when they had all three come together to the gates of the Castle, 'if you are not home before sundown the day after tomorrow, I shall send for your uncles, and they shall come and look for you.'

Dick raised his hat to the woman as he left her there by the Castle gates, but there was so much mistrust of him in her eye that he feigned he had done so only in order to scratch his head, and he couldn't manage even to say the Good day that was in his mouth.

So he and the giant went off together into the snow, shining white in the light of the moon. The moon was still far from her setting. But they had not gone much above a mile – one of Dick's miles – before the giant began to be impatient at the slow pace he had to move in order that Dick might keep up with him, even though for every stride *he* took Dick trotted three. So at last he stooped down in the snow and told Dick to climb up over his back on to his shoulders. Up went Dick like a cat up a tree, clutched on to his coarse yellow hair, and away they went.

Perched up on high like this, a good twenty feet above the snow, and tossing along on Grackel's shoulders, the giant's great bony hand clutched round his knees, Dick thought he had never seen a more magical sight than these strange hills and valleys sparkling cold and still in the glare of the moonlight. No, not even in his dreams. He might have been an Arab on the hump of his camel in the desert of Gobi.

It was easy for the giant to find his way. For though there were many prints of wild creatures and of long-clawed birds in the snow, Dick's footmarks were clearer than any. Now and then they passed a great clump of trees – their bare twigs brushing the starry sky – which looked like enormous faggots of kindling wood. And in less than a quarter of the time that Dick had spent on his journey to the Castle, they came to the top of the Beanstalk. And Dick shouted in the giant's ear that he wanted to be put down.

'Here we are,' he shouted, when he was on his own feet again. The giant in the last few minutes had been ambling on very warily as if he knew he was on dangerous ground. As soon as Dick had stamped life into his legs again, he pointed to the huge tangle of frosty bine and withy that jutted high above the edge of the abyss. 'See there!' he shouted at the top of his voice, in the sharp frosty air. 'That's the Beanstalk. Down *there* is where I come from. But I doubt if it will bear *you*.'

He almost laughed out loud to see with what caution Grackel crept out on hands and knees to peer out over the brink at the world below. But the giant could see nothing in the sombre shadow of the moon except the dried-up Beanstalk twisting and writhing down below him into space. 'Hm, hm,' he kept stupidly muttering.

And Dick understood at last how it was that the Beanstalk had never been discovered before. These giants, it seemed, were by nature a stupid race. So scared was Grackel at last at sight of the abyss that his teeth began to chatter like millstones, and his face was as white as a sheet. Dick rejoiced. It seemed he would never dare even to set foot on the Beanstalk.

Grackel peered round at him. 'So this,' he said, 'is where my great-grandad climbed down when he was chasing after that thief and vagabond Jack! I can't see to the bottom of it!'

Dick shook his head. 'No, nor, I suppose, could he! Though why you should be so fond of your *wife*'s grandad I can't think!'

'Aye,' said the giant leering at him, 'and supposing she and I are first cousins and he was grandad to both, what then?'

'Well,' said Dick, 'I know nothing of that. But Jack or no Jack, this is not only the only way down I know, but it's the way I climbed *up*. Once, I suppose, it must have been green and fresh and full of sap. Now it's all dried and withered away. And every yard I climbed I supposed it would come tumbling down over my head.'

'Aye,' said the giant. 'But what did you want to come *for*?'

'Oh, just to see,' said Dick, as airily as he could. The giant with a sigh rose to his feet.

'Well,' he said, 'I'm not so weighty as was my great-grandad, not at least according to his portrait in the gallery. And if he managed to climb down in safety when this ladder was young and green, what is there to prevent my doing the same, now that it is old and tough and dry?'

With that, he thrust his long lean arm over the edge and, clutching the tangle of withered shoots, violently shook the Beanstalk. It trembled like a spider's web in all its fibres, and Dick could hear the parched seeds clattering down from out of their pods towards the earth below.

'Well,' said he, looking up at the giant in the moonlight, 'what may be, may be. My only fear is that once down there, you may find it impossible to get back again. Or supposing it breaks in the middle?'

Grackel stared into his face, and then at the snow. 'He's

thinking of the Little Hen,' thought Dick to himself, 'and the Harp.'

'Yes, it would be a dreadful thing,' Dick repeated, 'if it broke in the middle.'

'Aye,' leered the giant, 'and so it would! But what about my great-grandad? It didn't break in the middle with him.' Dick made no answer to this. He held his peace.

'We'll have no more words about it,' said the giant. 'I'm never so stupid as when folks talk at me. You shall go first, being no more than an atomy, and I will follow after. I'll wait no longer.'

And with that, he flung his cudgel over the edge and began to pull up his wristbands. Dick listened in vain to hear the crash of the cudgel on the earth below. He feared for poor Jock.

There was no help in waiting. So Dick began to climb down the Beanstalk, and the giant followed after him so close with his lank scissor-legs that Dick had to keep dodging his head to avoid his great shoes, with their shining metal hooks instead of laces. Beanseeds came scampering down over Dick's head and shoulders like hailstones. It was lucky for him they were hollow and dry.

'Now,' said Dick at last, when they reached the bottom and he had seen the cudgel sticking up out of the ground beyond the broken wall. 'Here we are. This is where I come from. This is England. And *you* will want to be off at once to look for your great-grandfather's grave. Now that way is the way you should go. I go this. My father is expecting me and I must get home as soon as I can.'

It was so he hoped to slip away. But Grackel was at least too crafty for that. He stood leaning his sharp elbows on the broken roof of the cottage, leering down at Dick so steadily that he was mortally afraid the giant might notice the bulge of his great-grandad's leg-bone in the rabbit-nibbled turf of the garden.

'No, no, my young master,' said he at last. 'Fair and easy! Good friends keep together. You have had bite and sup in my house, now you shall give me bite and sup in yours. And it may be your father has heard of that Jack. The cackling of my great-grandad's Hen, let alone the strumming of his Harp, must have reached a long way among stubby hills in a little country like this! England!'

The rose and grey of daybreak was stirring in the eastern sky. Dick, though angry, reasoned with the giant as best he could, but the great oaf could not be dissuaded from keeping him company. It was bitter cold in this early morning, and Dick longed to let his father know that nothing was amiss with him.

'Well,' he said at last, 'I have told you nine times over that no travellers come this way. It is over there the big cities are.' And he pointed west. 'But if come you must, why come! And I can only hope my father will be pleased to see you.'

He put two fingers into his mouth and whistled. There came an answering whinny. And from a lean-to or out-house behind the cottage where it had found shelter during the night and a bite or two of old hay to munch, Jock answered his summons. This time Grackel had no reason to complain of Dick's lagging behind. Jock cantered away up the valley with his young master on his back, and the giant like a gallows strode on beside them.

When they came at length to a drift of woodland near the farm, Dick dismounted; and, having pointed out the chimneys of the farmhouse in the hollow below, he told the giant to hide himself among the trees, while he went to prepare his father for the guest he had brought home with him. So Grackel edged down as best he could among the trees, and Dick, leading Jock by his bridle, went on to the house.

In spite of the cold, the back door was ajar, and on an old horsehair sofa beside the burnt-out fire Dick found his father fast asleep, the stable lantern with which he had been out in the night looking for his son still burning beside him. Dick called him softly and touched his hand. His father stirred, muttering in his dreams; then his eyes opened. And at sight of Dick a light came into them as if he had found an unspeakable treasure.

Safely come home again, Dick was soon forgiven for being so long away. As quickly as he could he told his father his adventures. But when the farmer heard that the giant was actually in hiding not more than a quarter of a mile away from the house, and greedy for bed and board, he opened his eyes a good deal wider.

'Is that so?' he said at last. 'Twenty-foot in his shoes and all! Lorramussy! Well, well! And his great-grandad and all! That don't seem so *very* far back, now do it? Still, if there he is, my son, why, there he *is*; and we must do the best we can. And I don't see myself,' he added, glancing at Dick's troubled face, 'being what and where you were, you could have done much else. But who'd have guessed it, now? Who *would*? That Beanstalk!'

'The worst of all, father,' said Dick, 'is that woman up there. She'd freeze your blood even to look at her. What *she* wants is the Little Hen. And if *she* came down ... !'

'Fox or vixen, one thing at a time, my son,' said the farmer. 'Your friend out in the cold, if we keep him waiting, may get restless. So we'll be off at once to see what we can do to keep him quiet. The other must come after.'

The shining of the wintry sun lay all over the frosty fields when they went back together to the giant. And sour and fretful they found him. He only scowled at the farmer's polite Good morning, grumbled that he was famished and wanted breakfast. 'And plenty of it!' he muttered, leering at Dick.

The farmer eyed him up and down for the twentieth time, and wished more than ever that Dick could have persuaded him to stay in his own country. He liked neither his pasty peevish face nor his manners. And his blood boiled to think of Dick tied up like a monkey to the leg of a table. Still, it had always been the farmer's rule in life to make the best of a bad job. With worry, what's wrong waxes worse, he would say. So he decided then and there to lodge the giant for the time being in his great barn; and to keep him in a good temper with plenty of victuals. The sooner they could pack him off the better. But they must be cautious.

So Dick and his father led the giant off to the barn, the sheepdogs following behind them. They threw open the wide double doors, and stooping low, Grackel went in and stretched his long shins in the hay at the other end of it. After which they shut-to the doors again and hastened off to the farm to fetch him breakfast.

By good chance there was not only a side of green bacon but a cold roast leg of mutton in the larder that had been prepared for dinner the day before, though then the farmer had no stomach for it. With this, a tub of porridge, half a dozen loaves of bread, a basketful of boiled hens' eggs and a couple of buckets of tea, they went back to the barn. Two or three journeys the giant gave them before he licked the last taste out of his last broken honey-pot, wiped his mouth with the back of his hand, and said he had had enough. Indeed, he had gorged himself silly.

'My son tells me,' bawled the farmer, 'that you have had a broken night. *His* friends are *my* friends. Maybe you'd enjoy a nap in the hay now. Make yourself easy; we'll be back anon.'

They closed behind them the great doors of the barn again, and went off themselves to breakfast, staying their talk and munching every now and again to listen to what sounded like distant thunder, but which, Dick explained to his father, was only the giant's snoring.

For the next day or two their guest was good-humoured and easy-going enough but, like some conceited people far less than half his size, he was by nature both crafty *and* stupid. And since he had now found himself in lodgings where he had nothing to do, no wife to make him mind and keep him busy, and he could eat and guzzle and sleep and idle the whole day long, he had little wish to be off in search of his great-grandfather, and none to go home again.

He knew well, the cunning creature, that even if his wife sent out his uncles in search of him and they discovered the Beanstalk, neither of them would venture to set foot on it. It would be certain death! For these were ordinary-sized giants, while he himself was laughed at in his own country for a weakling and nicknamed Pygmy Grackel. But this Dick did not know till afterwards.

When evening came, and the farm hands had gone home from their work, Grackel would take a walk in the fields, though Dick's father, after once accompanying him, did not do so again. He had kept the great bumpkin out of the meadows and the turnips because it was lambing season. But it enraged him to see Grackel's clod-hopper footprints in his winter wheat, and the ricks in his stack-yard ruined by Grackel's leaning upon them to rest. And it enraged him even more when the giant crept up to the farmhouse one midnight to stare in at him as he lay in his bed, and kicked over the water-butt on his way. The great lubber grew more and more mischievous.

In less than a week both Dick and his father were at their wits' end to know what to do with their guest. The good woman who cooked for them had to toil continually the best part of the day to prepare his food. A couple of ducks and three or four fat hens he accounted no more than a snack; he would gollop up half a roasted sheep for supper and ask for more. Indeed his appetite was far beyond his size, and he seemed to think of nothing but his belly.

Apart from this too, and the good home-brewed ale and cider they had to waste on him, he lay on their minds like a thunder cloud. And when he had eaten and guzzled to gluttony, as like as not he would grow sulky and malicious. He could do more damage in five minutes than an angry bull in half an hour. And when in a bad humour he would do it on purpose. Besides, tongues soon began to get busy about him in the villages round about. The shepherd complained that his lambs began to be missing; the ploughman's wife that her two small children had not been out of doors for a week. It was reported that the farmer had caught a cruel and ravenous ogre in his fields, and had chained him up in his barn. Some said it was not an ogre but a monster that trumpeted like an elephant and had claws like a bird.

Though the great doors of the barn were usually kept shut on the giant all day until dusk, and the farmer had stuffed up every hole he could find in its roof and timbers – and Grackel was as sensitive as any female to draughts – the roar of his snoring could be heard a full mile away, and when he laughed – which luckily was seldom – it was like a house falling down. At least so it seemed, though perhaps Dick made worse of it than was the truth. He had not yet seen Grackel's uncles.

There was at any rate no hope of keeping the giant secret. For some reason too there was always a host of birds – rooks, daws, starlings and the like, hovering about the barn. The horses and cattle, and even the pigs, were never at peace while the giant was near; but pawing and lowing and neighing and wuffing the whole day long. And well any pig *might* wuff, since Grackel could devour him at a meal.

The result of all this was that the farmer would now often find strangers lurking in his fields. They had come in hope to get a glimpse of the giant. And whether they succeeded or not, talk of his size, his appetite, his strength and his fury spread far and wide. Worse even than this : two urchins from a neighbouring village had managed by hiding themselves in a ditch until it was evening to creep up close to the barn and, peeping through a hole in the wood where a knot had fallen out, found themselves peering into the great staring still watery eye of the giant fixed on them as he lay in the hay on the other side. Cold as stone with terror, they had rushed away home to their mothers, been seized with fits, and one of them had nearly died.

Dick could hardly get a wink of sleep for thinking of the giant and how to be rid of him. To see the trouble and care in his father's kindly face filled him with remorse. He searched his story-books again and again but could find no help in them. Nor could he discover any advice, not a single word, about giants in *The Farmer's Friend* or *The Countryman's Companion* – books which belonged to his father.

On the next Sunday afternoon his father walked off to the vicarage, six miles away by the field paths, to ask the advice of the old parson. He was the most learned man the farmer knew. But though the old gentleman listened to him very attentively, and was sorry for the trouble he was in, his chief fear was that the giant might find his way to the church. Once in, how without damage could he be coaxed out again?

There were giants in days of old, he told the farmer, who lived for centuries; and at a hundred or more were as hale and lusty as an ordinary man of less than forty. One such in Carmarthenshire had stolen all the millstones for thirty miles around and amused himself by flinging them into the sea. There had been a dearth of meal for months. Giants can be as cunning as a fox, the parson told the farmer, and as surly as a bear, and are great gluttons. But this the farmer knew already.

At last, one night, a little less than a fortnight after he had climbed the Beanstalk, having fallen asleep after hours of vain thinking, Dick suddenly woke up with so bright a notion in his head that it might have been whispered to him straight out of a dream.

There could be no waiting for the morning. He went off at once to his father's bedroom, woke him up, and, having made sure the giant was not listening at the window, shared it with him then and there. And the farmer thought almost as well of the notion as Dick did himself. They sat together there, Dick hooded up in a blanket at the foot of his father's bed, and for a full hour talked Dick's plan over. To and fro and up and down they discussed it, and could think of nothing better.

So as soon as light had begun to show next morning, Dick mounted his pony, and keeping him awhile on thick grass to muffle his hoofs, he galloped off by the way he had gone before.

This time he had brought with him an old pair of leathern pruning gloves and climbing irons, and he reached the top of the Beanstalk before noon. He arrived at the

Castle gates while it was still full daylight. Till this moment all had gone well with him, though he had hated leaving his father alone to all the troubles of the day.

But now, as Dick was on the point of leaping up to clutch the rusty bell-chain, a distant bombilation fell on his ear – such a rumbling and bumbling as is made by huge puncheons of rum being rolled about over the hollow stones of a cellar. He had not listened long before he guessed this must be the voices of Grackel's uncles colloguing together. At sound of them he shook in his shoes. What was worse, they seemed to be in an ill humour. But whether it was anger or mere argument in their voices, there was nothing in the music that boded much good for Dick!

At last they ceased, and Dick (who was by now bitterly cold, for an icy wind was whiffling round the Castle walls) decided to give a tug at the bell only just strong enough for a single ding. He then hid himself behind a buttress of the wall. The woman presently looked out of the wicket in the great gates. And Dick, peeping, and seeing that she was alone, showed himself and came nearer.

'Aha,' she called at sight of him, 'so you have come back! Aye, and a fortnight late! And where, my fine young man, is my husband? Answer me that! *Grackel!*' she wailed aloud, as if beside herself, 'Where are you? Where *are* you, Grackel?

'Not here, eh!' she went on, watching Dick out of her black eyes as closely as a cat a bird. 'So you have come back to ...' – and with that she pounced on him. She gripped him by the slack of his coat, and stooped low over his face. 'Eh, eh, eh! So now I have you, my fine young man!' Her teeth chattered as she spoke. 'Step you in, and you shall see what you *shall* see!'

Dick had scarcely breath left to speak with. He thought his end was come at last. And then, suddenly, the woman drew back, let go of him, turned her head away and began to cry.

Then Dick knew that what had seemed only anger was chiefly grief, that she supposed her husband must be dead and would never come back to her. And he rejoiced. His plan was turning out even better than he had hoped for. As best he could he tried to comfort the poor woman. He took the long hand that hung down beside her, and assured her that her husband was in the best of health, better far than when he had started, and in such ease and comfort at his father's farm that nothing would persuade him to go on his travels in search of the Little Hen and the Harp, or induce him to come home again. 'It's no use your crying,' he said. 'That won't bring him back!'

At last the woman dried her eyes and began to listen to him. She took him into a little room this side of the kitchen, hung with smoked carcasses of beasts for the table, a room, which, though cold, was secret.

'I kept on telling your husband,' Dick said, 'that he need but send you word that he is well, that he is comfortable. I thought of you, ma'am, and kept on. For though I haven't a wife myself, I know they want news of their husbands. So would my mother of my father, if she had not died when I was four. And perhaps she does even now. But your husband has grown fatter and won't stir out of the house even to take a little exercise. He eats and eats, and at a mention of *home* only flies into a rage.

' "But," I said to him, "your wife will be weeping for you to come!" And all he answered was to bawl for another bucket of cider. So I came along by myself and am nearly dead-beat and starved with cold.'

All this Dick said, and, it being chiefly lies, he said it much too boldly. But the woman was overjoyed at his news and believed him. Her one thought now was to get her husband home again, and to keep her wrath against him till then.

She told Dick she would go at once and wake her husband's uncles. 'They are taking a nap,' she said. Then he himself could go along with them, and they would soon persuade her husband to come home. 'And if he won't, they'll make him,' she said.

But this plan was by no means to Dick's liking. He asked the woman how long the giants would be sleeping and in what room they lay. 'I am too tired to talk to them just now,' he said, 'frozen. I couldn't bear the din they make. Leave them at peace awhile and take me into the kitchen, ma'am, else I shall soon perish of cold. Give me some food and a mug of milk, and I'll tell you a better plan – a far better plan – than that. But quietly!'

Now by good fortune the giants were napping in a room at the other end of the Castle where they were accustomed to play cards – *Dumps*, *Frogbite*, and other old games. And Dick sat up once more on his stool by the kitchen fire, and after refreshing himself, he explained to the woman his plan.

'What I want to say, ma'am, is this,' he said. And he told her that the people of his country were utterly weary of having her idle husband loafing about in their villages and doing nothing for his keep. 'Down there, we are all little like me,' he said, 'and though my father – who wouldn't hurt a fly – has done his utmost to put your husband at ease, to feed him and keep him happy, it is all wasted. He has no more thanks in him than a flea.

'He wanders about, scares the women, frightens the children, steals from the shops, and shouts and sings at dead of night when all honest folk are asleep in their beds. And now the King's soldiers are coming, and as soon as they catch him, ma'am, they will drag him off to some great dismal underground dungeon, and he will never see daylight again. For little though we may be, there's a cage in my country that would hold nine or more giants together, and every one of them twice as big as your husband, and every one of them loaded groaning up with chains. You see, ma'am, we don't mean them any harm, but can't keep them safe else. So I came to tell you.' He took another slow sip of his greasy buttermilk, and glanced back into the fire.

'Then again,' he went on, 'if these two uncles of your husband's, who you say are big heavy men, ventured to go my way home, and that must be ten thousand feet from top to bottom, they would only come to grief. They would topple down and break every bone in their bodies. And even if they did climb safely down and came into my country, what good would that be to them? I agree, ma'am, that in mere size and shape they are much larger than we are where I come from. But for wits and quickness and cunning – why, they are no better than rabbits!

'Just think, ma'am, though I have no wish to hurt your feelings, with your husband gone and all, how a mere boy of my size and not much older, came sneaking again and again into this huge Castle of yours, and ran off with your great-grandad's treasures three times over without losing a hair of his head. I agree it was not fair dealings, between equals, as you might say. I agree that that Jack borrowed the Harp without leave. But boy to giant, ma'am, *you* can't but agree he had his wits about him and was no coward.

'Besides, down there we have great cannon and what is called gunpowder, which would blow fifty giants to pieces before they could sneeze. I mean,' cried Dick, 'there would be a noise like that,' and he clapped his hands together, 'and the next minute there wouldn't be a scrap of your husband's uncles to be seen. Except perhaps for a button here and there for a keepsake ten miles off. You must give me something to prove I have seen you.'

Dick spoke with such a zest and earnestness that this poor woman began once more to be afraid that she would never see her husband again, alive or dead, for she dearly loved him even though he had given her his word of honour and not kept it. She would talk to him about that, all in good time.

'Now see here,' said Dick at last, 'your husband has been gobbling and guzzling so much that he is almost too stupid now to understand good sense when he hears it. It's true I could make a fortune out of him by leading him round from town to town and charging a piece of silver for every peep at him. But I haven't a heart as hard as that, ma'am; and if you want your husband back, there is only one thing to do.'

So after they had talked the matter over a little longer the woman fetched out from her bosom on a ribbon a locket in which was a twine of her husband's hair when he was a little boy. The hair though very coarse was almost as pale as gold. And in the back of the locket was a glass in which, said the woman, you could see your dearest friend. But she herself did not much believe in it, because when *she* looked into it she could see only herself.

So Dick peeped in, and there he saw what looked very much like his father. His cheeks grew red and he smiled into the locket; and his father seemed to give him a look back. 'And what,' Dick said to the woman, turning the locket over, 'what is this *milky* side for?'

'Oh, in that,' said the woman, 'you can see what you are dreaming about. But it's nothing but black dreams come to me.'

Dick looked; and sure enough the milkiness cleared away in a moment, and he saw a tiny image there of Jack's

Beanstalk, but fresh and green. He slipped the bauble into his jacket pocket and told the woman that it would do very well for a proof to her husband that he himself had seen and talked with her. 'For you see,' he said, 'if I had nothing to show him, he might not believe me.'

And the message the woman sent Grackel was that she had heard with joy he was happy in the place he had come to, that he must remember to behave himself, and that his uncles would not come out in search of him so long as she knew he was safe. All she desired was to have but one more glimpse of him, and that he should come back if but for one night, because a feast was preparing, the feast they had every year on his long-lost great-grandfather's birthday.

'He'll remember that,' the woman said to Dick. 'And tell him that his uncles and his nephew and his cousins and his neighbours and his friends from afar off will all be at the feast, and will never forgive him if he is absent. Tell him I haven't missed him so much as I thought I should. Tell him I cried a little when I thought he was dead, and laughed when I knew he was safe. If he thinks I don't much want him back he will come. If he settles for good in your country, I am a lost woman.'

'Ah,' said Dick, 'leave that to me. But what am I to have for my trouble?'

The woman offered him a bag of money. There it was in the cupboard.

'Too heavy,' said Dick.

She brought out her family's Seven-League boots.

Dick laughed. He could almost have gone to bed in one of them. She showed him her husband's drinking cup.

Dick laughed again. He said it was too big for a wash-basin and not big enough for a bath. 'Besides,' he said, 'it's only silver.'

Dick and the Beanstalk

At last the woman, as Dick hoped she would, remembered her husband's watch – the watch that had belonged to one of his aunts. This of course was but a little watch compared with the giant's father's watch, which was safe upstairs. Dick's mouth watered as he took hold of the chain and lifted the watch out of the woman's hand. What he had supposed were sapphires and emeralds were not common stones like these at all. There was a toadstone, a thunderstone, an Arabian crystal and a blagroon – though Dick didn't then know the names of them.

'But I had hoped,' he said, eyeing it and pretending to be disappointed, 'that it was not a mere pocket watch, but a watch with a little magic in it. I think perhaps, after all, I should get more money by taking your husband round to show him off at some of our country fairs. You see, as I keep on saying, he doesn't *want* to come back.'

But the woman showed him with her finger that if he pressed a secret spring at the edge of the watch near the guard-ring he could make time seem to go much slower – whenever, that is, he was truly happy; and that if he pressed the secret spring on the left he could make time seem to go much quicker – say, when he was feeling miserable, or was tired or waiting for anything or anybody. And not only this; there was a third spring. 'If you press that,' the woman said, 'you can't tell what will happen next.'

Dick was mightily pleased with the watch, and just to test it, pressed the left-hand spring. And it seemed not a moment had passed by when there came a prodigious stamping and thumping and clattering from out of the back parts of the Castle, and he knew that Grackel's two uncles had woken up. So loud was the din they were making that it sounded as if a volcano had broken out, and it scared Dick more than he liked to show. So – though he pretended to be in no hurry – he let the spring go, fixed the chain round his waist, and slipped the watch in under the front of his breeches.

'If your husband isn't with you again by sundown to-morrow evening,' he told the woman, 'then send his uncles after me. The Beanstalk, of course, *might* bear them; and even though they might never come back again, they would at least have a chance to make an end of *me*.'

'If you come along with me now,' said the woman, 'you shall have a peep at them, and they won't see you. But quietly! They have ears like the east wind!'

So, treading mimsey as a cat, Dick followed after the woman, and she led him up a flight of stairs so steep he might have been climbing a pyramid, and took him into a gallery overlooking the room in which the giants sat. Dick crept forward, and, leaning out a little between the bases of the balusters of the gallery, peeped down. They were intent on a game that looked like common dominoes, though the pieces or men they played with were almost as big as tombstones. In no story-book he had ever read had Dick chanced on the like of these giants. They sat like human mountains at their game, and the noise of the dominoes was like Pharaoh's chariots. And when one of them, laying down a domino on the table, mumbled, *Double!*, it was like the coughing of a lion. Dick didn't need to watch them long. But as soon as he was out of earshot of them again, he burst out laughing, though it was only feigned.

'It's a good thing,' he said to the woman, 'I thought of what I told you. They are fine men, your husband's uncles, and no beanstalk I have ever seen would bear even half the weight of either. I'll keep the locket safe, you can trust me, ma'am, and if my father will let me, perhaps I might come back with your husband to the feast.'

The woman was by nature mean and close, but seeing how little by comparison Dick would be likely to eat and drink, she said he would be welcome. So he bade her good-bye and off he went.

It was pitch-black when he got home again, but his father was waiting up for him. They were so anxious for the giant to be gone that they couldn't stay till morning. They went off together with a lantern to the barn, and having gone in, shouted at the top of their voices in Grackel's ear. They managed to wake him at last, and gave him his wife's message. He was so stupid after his first sleep, and he had eaten so vast a supper, that they might as well have been conversing with a mule. Even when he understood what they were saying, he sat blinking, morose and sullen at being disturbed.

'And how can I tell,' said he, 'that what you say is true? A fine story, a pretty story, but I don't believe a word of it.'

But when Dick told him of the feast that was being prepared, that all his wife wanted was to see him once again, that else his uncles might come to look for him; and when at last he showed the giant his wife's locket – then Grackel believed what was said to him (though Dick kept the watch to himself). And the very next morning the two of them set out together for the Beanstalk. And the farmer, eyes shining and all smiles, saw them off.

It was a morning fine and bright. A little hard snow had fallen in the small hours and lay on the grass like lumps of sago. The ponds were frozen hard as crystal. And as he cantered along on his pony – the giant's lank legs keeping pace with him on his right side like the arms of a wind-mill – Dick was so happy at the thought of at last getting rid of his guest that he whistled away like a starling as he rode.

And Grackel said, 'Why are you whistling?'

' "Why?" ' said Dick. 'Why, to think what a happy evening you are going to have, and how pleased your wife will be to see you, and what a feast they are making for you up there. I could almost smell the oxen roasting for the cold meats on the side table; and there must have been seven score of fat pigs being driven in for the black puddings.'

This only made Grackel the more eager to press on.

'And now,' said Dick, when in the height of the morning they came to the foot of the Beanstalk, which was masked thick with hoarfrost smouldering in the sun, 'here we part for a while. When you are come up to the top, give a loud *hullabaloo*, and I shall know you are safe. Then I shall ride off home again, and I will come to meet you here the day after tomorrow, about two.'

Now, though it was a great folly, Dick had not been able to resist bringing Grackel's watch with him. He had hooked the chain round his waist under his breeches, and the watch bulged out like a hump in the wrong place. By good luck the giant was on the further side away from the watch, so that he had not noticed this hump. But now that they were at a standstill, and all was quiet, he detected the ticking.

And he said, 'What is that sound I hear?'

And Dick said, 'That is my heart beating.'

'Why is it beating so loud?' said Grackel.

'Ah,' said Dick, in a doleful tone, 'it must be for sadness that you are going away, even if only for a little while! We have had our little disagreements together, you and me, about the sheep and the snoring and the cider. But now we are friends, and that is all over. Isn't there any

45

little keepsake you could give me by which to remember you till you come back?'

At this the giant drew in his lips, and none too eagerly felt in his pockets. He brought out at last from beneath the leather flap of his side pocket a discoloured stub of candle in a box.

'It's not much to look at,' he grumbled, 'but once it's lit it will never go out till you say, *Out, candle, out!* even if it's left burning in a hurricane for a hundred years.' Dick kept this candle until the day he met his sweetheart and lit it then. It may be lighting his great-grandchildren to sleep this very evening. But that came afterwards.

'There,' said Grackel, 'take great care of it, and you shall give it me back when we meet again. Aye, and then I am sure to be hungry. So have plenty of hot supper waiting for me in my house – legs of pork soused in apples, and kids in batter, and drink to wash it down! And get in for me too some more hay and blankets and horse-cloths. I could scarcely sleep a wink last night for the cold.'

Dick nodded and laughed, and the giant began to climb the Beanstalk. Dick watched him till first he was as small to look up to as an ordinary man, and next no bigger than a dwarf, and not long after that he was out of sight. About an hour or so afterwards, for Grackel being lean and sinewy was a nimble climber, Dick heard a rumbling in the higher skies. He knew that it was the giant's hullabalooing, and that he was safe. Then as quick as lightning he set about gathering together a great heap of the last year's bracken and dead wood and dry grass, and piled it round the parched-up roots of the Beanstalk. Then he felt in his pocket for his flint and tinder-box that his father had laid out for him overnight. He felt – and felt again; and his beating heart gave one dull thump and almost stood still.

In the heat and haste of getting away he had left them both on the kitchen table!

Dick hauled out Grackel's watch to see the time. It was seven minutes to twelve. It would now be impossible for him to get home before nightfall and back again much before morning. It was a long journey, and the way would be difficult to follow in the dark. And how was he to be certain that the giant, having come to the Castle and found that his watch was gone, would not climb down the Beanstalk again to fetch it? Dick pressed the right-hand spring of the watch, for though he was in great trouble of mind, he wanted to think hard and to make the time go slowly. And as, brooding on there under the Beanstalk, he stared at the second hand, though it was not much bigger than a darning needle, it was jerking so sluggishly that he could have counted twenty between every beat. The sun, that was now come to the top of his winter arch in the sky, and was glistening like a tiny furnace on the crystal of the watch, danced in his eyes so fiercely that at last he could scarcely see.

'Why,' thought Dick suddenly, 'the glass magnifies. It's a *burning*-glass!'

Instantly, after but one sharp upward glance towards the top of the Beanstalk, he took out his pocket-knife and heaved up the watch lid. The glass was as thick as half the nail-width of his little finger. He held it close down over the dried-up leaves and bracken in the full beams of the noonday sun. And in a few moments, to his great joy, a faint twirling wreath of grey smoke appeared on the buff of the bracken frond. Then there came a black pin-prick circle that rapidly began to ring out larger. Then a little red appeared at the edge of the circle. And at this Dick began to puff very very softly, still tilting the glass into the direct rays of the sun. The frond began to smoulder, and the smoulder began to spread, and now Dick blew with all his might.

Presently a thin reek of vapour appeared, and the bracken broke into flames. And when once these parched-up leaves and grasses had fairly taken fire, the Beanstalk itself was soon ablaze. The flames – and theirs was a strange music – roared loud in the wintry air – red, greenish, copper and gold – licking and leaping their way from strand to strand up and up, while a huge pale-umber tower of smoke rose billowing into the blue air of the morning.

Dick gazed at the flames in delight and terror. Never in all his born days had he seen such a bonfire. Even Jock, who had been quietly browsing by the ruinous cottage walls, lifted his head and whinnied. Indeed, the flaming Beanstalk must have been visible to all Gloucestershire's seven neighbour counties round. And the fire burned up and up, and the pods and red-hot bean-seeds came hailing down, with wisps of fire and smoke. And the roaring gradually grew more and more distant, until at last the blaze up above was dwindled to little more than a red spark, like a tiny second sun, far far up in the vacancy of the heavens. And then it vanished and was gone.

And Dick with a deep sigh, partly of regret and partly of relief, knew that Jack's old Beanstalk was gone for ever. At least this might be so, though he had been wise enough before he had begun gathering together the fuel for his fire to put two or three of the dry bean-seeds into his pocket. Some day he meant to plant them; just to see.

He broke the ice over a little spring that was frozen near the cottage, took a sip or two of the biting cold water underneath, and dabbled his hot cheeks and eyelids. Then he whistled for Jock, and jumped into the saddle. Yet again he dragged out Grackel's watch, pressed down the left spring, and with one last glance up over his shoulder, set off for home. And pleased beyond all words was his father the farmer to see him.

The Dutch Cheese

Once – once upon a time there lived, with his sister
Griselda, in a little cottage near the Great Forest, a young
farmer whose name was John. Brother and sister, they
lived alone, except for their sheep-dog, Sly, their flock of
sheep, the numberless birds of the forest, and the 'fairies'.
John loved his sister beyond telling; he loved Sly; and he
delighted to listen to the birds singing at twilight round the
darkening margin of the forest. But he feared and hated the
fairies. And, having a very stubborn heart, the more he
feared, the more he hated them; and the more he hated
them, the more they pestered him.

Now these were a tribe of fairies, sly, small, gay-hearted
and mischievous, and not of the race of fairies noble, silent,
beautiful and remote from man. They were a sort of gipsy-
fairies, very nimble and of aery and prankish company,
and partly for mischief and partly for love of her they were
always trying to charm John's dear sister Griselda away,
with their music and fruits and trickery. He more than half
believed it was they who years ago had decoyed into the
forest not only his poor old father, who had gone out
faggot-cutting in his sheepskin hat with his ass; but his
mother too, who soon after had gone out to look for him.

But fairies, even of this small tribe, hate no man. They
mocked him and mischiefed him; they spilt his milk, rode
astraddle on his rams, garlanded his old ewes with sow-
thistle and briony, sprinkled water on his kindling wood,
loosed his bucket into the well, and hid his great leather

shoes. But all this they did, not for hate – for they came and went like evening moths about Griselda – but because in his fear and fury he shut up his sister from them, and because he was sullen and stupid. Yet he did nothing but fret himself. He set traps for them, and caught starlings; he fired his blunderbuss at them under the moon, and scared his sheep; he set dishes of sour milk in their way, and sticky leaves and brambles where their rings were green in the meadows; but all to no purpose. When at dusk, too, he heard their faint, elfin music, he would sit in the door blowing into his father's great bassoon till the black forest re-echoed with its sad, solemn, wooden voice. But that was of no help either. At last he grew so surly that he made Griselda utterly miserable. Her cheeks lost their scarlet and her eyes their sparkling. Then the fairies began to plague John in earnest – lest their lovely, loved child of man, Griselda, should die.

Now one summer's evening – and most nights are cold in the Great Forest – John, having put away his mournful bassoon and bolted the door, was squatting, moody and gloomy, with Griselda, on his hearth beside the fire. And he leaned back his great hairy head and stared straight up the chimney to where high in the heavens glittered a host of stars. And suddenly, while he lolled there on his stool moodily watching them, there appeared against the dark sky a mischievous elvish head secretly peeping down at him; and busy fingers began sprinkling dew on his wide upturned face. He heard the laughter too of the fairies miching and gambolling on his thatch, and in a rage he started up, seized a round Dutch cheese that lay on a platter, and with all his force threw it clean and straight up the sooty chimney at the faces of mockery clustered above. And after that, though Griselda sighed at her spinning wheel, he heard no more. Even the cricket that had been whistling all through the evening fell silent, and John supped on his black bread and onions alone.

Next day Griselda woke at dawn and put her head out of the little window beneath the thatch, and the day was white with mist.

' 'Twill be another hot day,' she said to herself, combing her beautiful hair.

But when John went down, so white and dense with mist were the fields, that even the green borders of the forest were invisible, and the whiteness went to the sky. Swathing and wreathing itself, opal and white as milk, all the morning the mist grew thicker and thicker about the little house. When John went out about nine o'clock to peer about him, nothing was to be seen at all. He could hear his sheep bleating, the kettle singing, Griselda sweeping, but straight up above him hung only, like a small round fruit, a little cheese-red beamless sun – straight up above him, though the hands of the clock were not yet come to ten. He clenched his fists and stamped in sheer rage. But no one answered him, no voice mocked him but his own. For when these idle, mischievous fairies have played a trick on an enemy they soon weary of it.

All day long that little sullen lantern burned above the mist, sometimes red, so that the white mist was dyed to amber, and sometimes milky pale. The trees dripped water from every leaf. Every flower asleep in the garden was neckleted with beads; and nothing but a drenched old forest crow visited the lonely cottage that afternoon to cry: 'Kah, Kah, Kah!' and fly away.

But Griselda knew her brother's mood too well to speak of it, or to complain. And she sang on gaily in the house, though she was more sorrowful than ever.

Next day John went out to tend his flocks. And wherever he went the red sun seemed to follow. When at last he found his sheep they were drenched with the clinging mist and were huddled together in dismay. And when they saw him it seemed that they cried out with one unanimous bleating voice:

'O ma-a-a-ster!'

And he stood counting them. And a little apart from the rest stood his old ram Soll, with a face as black as soot; and there, perched on his back, impish and sharp and scarlet, rode and tossed and sang just such another fairy as had mocked John from the chimney-top. A fire seemed to break out in his body, and, picking up a handful of stones, he rushed at Soll through the flock. They scattered, bleating, out into the mist. And the fairy, all-acockahoop on the old ram's back, took its small ears between finger and thumb, and as fast as John ran, so fast jogged Soll, till all the young farmer's stones were thrown, and he found himself alone in a quagmire so sticky and befogged that it took him till afternoon to grope his way out. And only Griselda's singing over her broth-pot guided him at last home.

Next day he sought his sheep far and wide, but not one could he find. To and fro he wandered, shouting and calling and whistling to Sly, till, heartsick and thirsty, they were both wearied out. Yet bleatings seemed to fill the air, and a faint, beautiful bell tolled on out of the mist; and John knew the fairies had hidden his sheep, and he hated them more than ever.

After that he went no more into the fields, brightly green beneath the enchanted mist. He sat and sulked, staring out of the door at the dim forests far away, glimmering faintly red beneath the small red sun. Griselda could not sing any more, she was too tired and hungry. And just before twilight she went out and gathered the last few pods of peas from the garden for their supper.

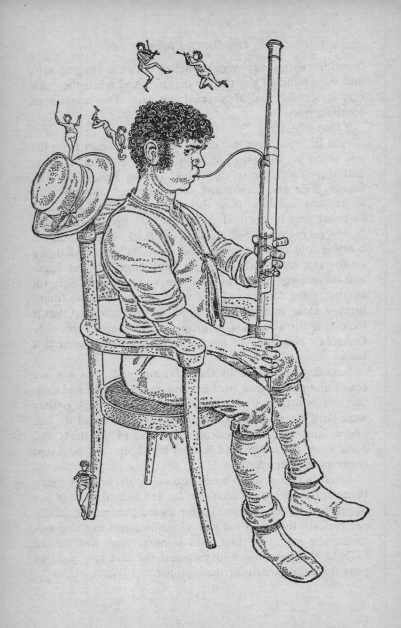

And while she was shelling them, John, within doors in the cottage, heard again the tiny timbrels and the distant horns, and the odd, clear, grasshopper voices calling and calling her, and he knew in his heart that, unless he relented and made friends with the fairies, Griselda would surely one day run away to them and leave him forlorn. He scratched his great head, and gnawed his broad thumb. They had taken his father, they had taken his mother, they might take his sister – but he *wouldn't* give in.

So he shouted, and Griselda in fear and trembling came in out of the garden with her basket and basin and sat down in the gloaming to finish shelling her peas.

And as the shadows thickened and the stars began to shine, the malevolent singing came nearer, and presently there was a groping and stirring in the thatch, a tapping at the window, and John knew the fairies had come – not alone, not one or two or three, but in their company and bands – to plague him, and to entice away Griselda. He shut his mouth and stopped up his ears with his fingers, but when, with great staring eyes, he saw them capering like bubbles in a glass, like flames along straw, on his very doorstep, he could contain himself no longer. He caught up Griselda's bowl and flung it – peas, water and all – full in the snickering faces of the Little Folk! There came a shrill, faint twitter of laughter, a scampering of feet, and then all again was utterly still.

Griselda tried in vain to keep back her tears. She put her arms round John's neck and hid her face in his sleeve. 'Let me go!' she said, 'let me go, John, just a day and a night, and I'll come back to you. They are angry with us. But they love me; and if I sit on the hillside under the boughs of the trees beside the pool and listen to their music just a little while, they will make the sun shine again and drive back the flocks, and we shall be as happy as ever. Look at poor Sly, John dear, he is hungrier even than I am.' John heard only the mocking laughter and the tap-tapping and the rustling and crying of the fairies and he wouldn't let his sister go.

And it began to be marvellously dark and still in the cottage. No stars moved across the casement, no water-drops glittered in the candleshine. John could hear only one low, faint, unceasing stir and rustling all around him. So utterly dark and still it was that even Sly woke from his hungry dreams and gazed up into his mistress's face and whined.

They went to bed; but still, all night long, while John lay tossing on his mattress, the rustling never ceased. The old kitchen clock ticked on and on, but there came no hint of dawn. All was pitch-black and now all was utterly silent. There wasn't a whisper, not a creak, not a sigh of air, not a footfall of mouse, not a flutter of moth, not a settling of dust to be heard at all. Only desolate silence. And John at last could endure his fears and suspicions no longer. He got out of bed and stared from his square casement. He could see nothing. He tried to thrust it open; it would not move. He went downstairs and unbarred the door and looked out. He saw, as it were, a deep, clear, green shade, from behind which the songs of the birds rose faint as in a dream.

And then he sighed like a grampus and sat down, and knew that the fairies had beaten him. Like Jack's bean-stalk, in one night had grown up a dense wall of peas. He pushed and pulled and hacked with his axe, and kicked with his shoes, and buffeted with his blunderbuss. But it was all in vain. He sat down once more in his chair beside the hearth and covered his face with his hands. And at last Griselda, too, awoke, and came down with her candle. And she comforted her brother, and told him if he would do what she bade she would soon make all right again. And he promised her.

So with a scarf she bound tight his hands behind him; and with a rope she bound his feet together, so that he could neither run nor throw stones, peas or cheeses. She bound his eyes and ears and mouth with a napkin, so that he could neither see, hear, smell, nor cry out. And, that done, she pushed and pulled him like a great bundle, and at last rolled him out of sight into the chimney-corner against the wall. Then she took a small sharp pair of needlework scissors that her godmother had given her, and snipped and snipped, till at last there came a little hole in the thick green hedge of peas. And putting her mouth there she called softly through the little hole. And the fairies drew near the doorstep and nodded and nodded and listened.

And then and there Griselda made a bargain with them for the forgiveness of John – a lock of her golden hair; seven dishes of ewes' milk; three and thirty bunches of currants, red, white and black; a bag of thistledown; three handkerchiefs full of lambs' wool; nine jars of honey; a peppercorn of spice. All these (except the hair) John was to bring himself to their secret places as soon as he was able. Above all, the bargain between them was that Griselda would sit one full hour each evening of summer on the hillside in the shadow and greenness that slope down from the great forest towards the valley, where the fairies' mounds are, and where their tiny brindled cattle graze.

Her brother lay blind and deaf and dumb as a log of wood. She promised everything.

And then, instead of a rustling and a creeping, there came a rending and a crashing. Instead of green shade, light of amber; then white. And as the thick hedge withered and shrank, and the merry and furious dancing sun scorched and scorched and scorched, there came, above the singing of the birds, the bleatings of sheep – and behold sooty Soll and hungry Sly met square upon the doorstep; and all John's sheep shone white as hoarfrost on his pastures; and every lamb was garlanded with pimpernel and eyebright; and the old fat ewes stood still, with saddles of moss; and their laughing riders sat and saw Griselda standing in the doorway in her beautiful yellow hair.

As for John, tied up like a sack in the chimney-corner, down came his cheese again crash upon his head, and, not being able to say anything, he said nothing.

A Penny a Day

Once upon a time, there lived in a cottage that had been
built out of the stones of a ruinous Castle and stood within
its very walls, an old woman, and her granddaughter –
whose name also was Griselda. Here they lived quite alone,
being the only two left of a family of farmers who had once
owned a wide track of land around them – fields, meadows,
heath and moorland – skirting the cliffs and the sea.

But all this was long ago. Now Griselda and her old
grandmother had little left but the roof over their heads and
a long garden whose apples and cherries and plum-trees
flowered in spring under the very walls of the Castle. Many
birds nested in this quiet hollow; and the murmur of the sea
on the beach beyond it was never hushed to rest.

The old woman tended the garden. And Griselda had
very little time wherein to be idle. After her day's work in
the farms and fields, she went so weary to bed that however
much she tried to keep awake in order to enjoy the company of her own thoughts, she was usually fast asleep before
the wick of her tallow candle had ceased to smoulder. Yet
for reasons not known even to herself she was as happy
as she was good-natured. In looks she resembled a mermaid.
Her fair face was unusually gentle and solemn, which may
in part have come from her love and delight in gazing at
and listening to the sea.

Whenever she had time to herself, which was very seldom,
she would climb up by the broken weed-grown steps to the
very top of the Castle tower, and sit there – like Fatima's

sister – looking out over the green cliffs and the vast flat blue of the ocean. She sat as small as a manikin there. When the sea-winds had blown themselves out she would search the beach for driftwood – the only human creature to be seen – in the thin salt spray blown in on the wind. And the sea-birds would scream around her while the slow toppling Atlantic breakers shook the earth with their thunder. In still evenings, too, when storms had been raging far out over the ocean, and only a slow ground-swell poured in its heavy waters upon the shore, it seemed that sunken bells were ringing from a belfry submerged and hidden for ever in the deeps.

But no humans, except Griselda, were there to listen. It was seldom, even, that the people in the nearest village came down to the sea-strand; and never when night was falling. For the Castle was a place forbidden. It was the haunt, it was said, of the Strange Folk. On calm summer evenings unearthly dancers had been seen dancing between the dusk and the moonlight on the short green turf at the verge of the sands, where bugloss and sea-lavender bloomed, and the gulls had their meeting place, gabbling softly together as they preened their wings in the twilight.

Griselda had often heard these tales. But, as she had lived under the walls of the Castle, and had played alone in its ruins ever since she could remember anything at all, she listened to them with delight. What was there to be afraid of? She longed to see these dancers; and kept watch. And when the full moon was ablaze in the sky, she would slip out of her grandmother's cottage and dance alone in its dazzling light on the hard, sea-laid sands of the beach; or sit, half-dreaming, in some green knoll of the cliffs. She would listen to the voices of the sea among the rocks and in the caves; and could not believe that what she heard was only the lully and music of its waters.

Often, too, when sitting on her sun-warmed doorstep, morning or evening, mending her clothes, or peeling potatoes, or shelling peas, or scouring out some copper pot, she would feel, all in an instant, that she was no longer alone. Then she would stoop her head a little lower over her needle or basin, pretending not to notice that anything was different. As you can hear the notes of an unseen bird or in the darkness can smell a flower past the finding, so it was with Griselda. She had company beyond hearing, touch or sight.

Now and again, too, as she slid her downcast eyes to right or left, she had actually caught a fleeting glimpse of a shape, not *quite* real perhaps, but more real than nothing – though it might be half-hidden behind the bushes, or peering down at her from an ivy-shadowed hollow in the thick stone walls.

Such things did not alarm Griselda – no more than would the wind in the keyhole, or the cry of flighting swans at night. They were part of her life, just as the rarer birds and beetles and moths and butterflies are part of the Earth's life. And whatever these shadowy creatures were, she was certain they meant her no harm.

So the happy days went by, spring on to winter, though Griselda had to work nearly all her waking hours to keep herself and her old grandmother from want. Then, one day, the old woman fell ill. She had fallen on the narrow stairs as she was shuffling down in the morning, and there, at the foot of them, looking no more alive than a bundle of old clothes, Griselda found her when she came in with her driftwood.

She was old, and worn and weary, and Griselda knew well that unless great care was taken of her, she might get worse; and even die. The thought of this terrified her. 'Oh, Grannie, Grannie!' she kept whispering to herself as she went about her work, 'I'll do anything – anything in the world – I don't mind what happens – if only you'll promise not to *die!*' But she soon began to take courage again, and kept such a cheerful face that the old woman hadn't an inkling of how sick with care and foreboding Griselda's small head often was, or how near her heart came to despair.

She scarcely had time now to wash her face or comb her hair, or even to sleep and eat. She seldom sat down to a meal, and even when she did, there was but a minute or two in which to gobble it up. She was so tired she could scarcely drag her feet up the steep narrow staircase; the colour began to fade out of her cheeks, and her face to grow haggard and wan.

Still, she toiled on, still sang over her work, and simply refused to be miserable. And however sick and hungry and anxious she might feel, she never let her grandmother see that she was. The old soul lay helpless and in pain on her bed, and had troubles enough of her own. So Griselda had nobody to share hers with; and instead of their getting better they got worse.

And when – after a hot breathless night during which she had lain between waking and dreaming while the lightning flared at her window, and the thunder raved over the sea – when, next morning she came down very early to find that the hungry mice had stolen more than half of the handful of oatmeal she had left in the cupboard, and that her little crock of milk had turned sour, her heart all but failed her. She sat down on the doorstep and she began to cry.

It was early in May; the flashing dark blue sea was tumbling among the rocks of the beach, its surf like snow. The sun blazed in the east, and all around her the trees in their new leaves were blossoming, and the birds singing, and the air was cool and fragrant with flowers after the rain.

In a little while Griselda stopped crying – and very few

tears had trickled down from her eyes – and with her chin propped on her hands, she sat staring out across the bright green grass, her eyes fixed vacantly on three butterflies that were chasing one another in the calm sweet air. This way, that way, they glided, fluttered, dipped and soared; then suddenly swooped up into the dazzling blue of the sky above the high broken wall and vanished from sight.

Griselda sighed. It was as if they had been mocking her misery. And with that sigh, there was no more breath left in her body. So she had to take a much deeper breath to make up for it. After that she sighed no more – since she had suddenly become aware again that she was being watched. And this time she knew by what. Not twelve paces away, at the top of a flight of tumbledown stone steps that corkscrewed up to one of the Castle turrets, stood what seemed to be an old wizened pygmy hunched-up old man.

He was the height of a child of five; he had pointed ears, narrow shoulders, and a hump on his back. And he wore a coat made of a patchwork of moleskins. He stood there – as stock-still as the stones themselves – his bright colourless eyes under his moleskin cap fixed on her, as if Griselda was as outlandish an object to him as he was to Griselda.

She shut her own for a moment, supposing he might have come out of her fancy; then looked again. But already, his crooked staff in his hand, this dwarf had come rapidly shuffling along over the turf towards her. And yet again he stayed – a few paces away. Then, fixing his small bright gaze on her face, he asked her in a shrill, cracked, rusty voice why she was crying. In spite of their lightness, his eyes were piercingly sharp in his dried-up face. And Griselda, as she watched him, marvelled how any living creature could look so old.

Gnarled, wind-shorn trees – hawthorn and scrub oak – grew here and there in the moorland above the sea, and had stood there for centuries among the yellow gorse and sea-pinks. He looked older even than these. She told him she had nothing to cry about, except only that the mice had been at her oatmeal, the milk had turned sour, and she didn't know where to turn next. He asked her what she had to do, and she told him that too.

At this he crinkled up his pin-sharp eyes, as if he were thinking, and glanced back at the turret from which he had come. Then, as if he had made up his mind, he shuffled a step or two nearer and asked Griselda what wages she would pay him if he worked for her for nine days. 'For three days, and three days, and three days,' he said, 'and that's all. How much?'

Griselda all but laughed out loud at this. She told the dwarf that far from being able to pay anyone to work for her, there wasn't a farthing in the house – and not even food enough to offer him a taste of breakfast. 'Unless,' she said, 'you would care for a cold potato. There's one or two of *them* left over from supper.'

'Ay, nay, nay,' said the dwarf. 'I won't work without wages, and I can get my own food. But hark now: if you'll promise to give me a penny a day for nine days, I will work here for you from dawn to dark. Then you yourself will be able to be off to the farms and the fields. But it must be a penny a day and no less; it must be paid every evening at sunset before I go to my own parts again; the old woman up there must never see me, and shall hardly know that I have come.'

Griselda sat looking at him – as softly and easily as she could; but she had never in all her days seen any human being like this before. Though his face was wizened and cockled up like a winter apple, yet it seemed as if he could

64

never have been any different. He looked as old as the
stones around him and yet no older than the snapdragons
that grew in them. To meet his eyes was like peering through
a rusty keyhole into a long empty room. She expected at any

instant he would vanish away, or be changed into something utterly different – a flowering thistle or a heap of
stones!

Long before this very morning, indeed, Griselda had often

caught sight of what looked like living shapes and creatures
– on the moorland or the beach – which, when she had
looked again, were clean gone; or, when she had come
close, proved to be only a furze-bush, or a rock jutting out of
the turf, or a scangle of sheep's wool caught on a thorn.
This is the way of these strangers. While then she was
not in the least afraid of the dwarf, she felt uneasy and
bewildered in his company.

But she continued to smile at him, and answered that
though she could not promise to pay him a penny until she
had a penny to pay, she would do her best to earn some.
Now nothing was left. And she had already made up her
mind to be off at once to a farm along the sea-cliffs, where
she would be almost sure to get work. If the dwarf would
wait but one day, she told him, she would ask the farmer
to pay her her wages before she came home again. 'Then I
could give you the penny,' she said.

Old Moleskins continued to blink at her. 'Well,' he said,
'be off then now. And be back before sunset.'

But first Griselda made her grandmother a bowl of water-
porridge, using up for it the last pinch of meal she had in
the house. This she carried up to the old woman, with a sprig
of apple blossom in a gallipot to put beside it and make it
taste better. Since she had so promised him, and felt sure he
meant no harm, she said nothing to her grandmother about
the dwarf. She tidied the room, tucked in the bedclothes,
gave the old woman some water to wash in, beat up her
pillow, pinned a shawl over her shoulders, and, having
made her as comfortable as she could manage, left her
to herself, promising to be home again as soon as she could.

'And be sure, Grannie,' she said, 'whatever happens, not
to stir from your bed.'

By good fortune, the farmer's wife whom she went off to
see along the sea-cliffs was making butter that morning. The

farmer knew Griselda well, and when she had finished helping his wife and the dairymaid with the churning, he not
only paid her two pennies for her pains, but a third, 'For
the sake', as he said, 'of your goldilocks, my dear; and
they're worth a king's ransom! ... What say you, Si?' he
called to his son, who had just come in with the calves.
Simon, his face all red, and he was a good deal uglier
(though pleasant in face) than his father, glanced up at
Griselda, but the gold must have dazzled his eyes, for he
turned away and said nothing.

At this moment the farmer's wife came bustling out into
the yard again. She had brought Griselda not only a pitcher
of new milk and a couple of hen's eggs to take to her grandmother, but some lardy-cakes and a jar of honey for herself.
So Griselda, feeling ten times happier than she had been
for many a long day, hurried off home.

Now there was a duck-pond under a willow on the way
she took home, and there, remembering what the farmer
had said, she paused, stopped over, and looked at herself
in the muddy water. But the sky was of the brightest blue
above her head; and there were so many smooth oily
ripples on the surface of the water made by the ducks as
they swam and preened and gossiped together that Griselda
couldn't see herself clearly, or be sure from its reflection
even if her hair was still gold! She got up, laughed to herself,
waved her hand to the ducks and hastened on.

When, carrying her pitcher, she had come in under
the high snapdragon-tufted gateway of the Castle, and so
home again, a marvel it was to see. The kitchen was as neat
as a new pin. The table had been scoured; the fire-irons
twinkled like silver; the crockery on the dresser looked as
if it had been newly painted; a brown jar of wallflowers
bloomed sweet on the sill, and even the brass pendulum of
the cuckoo-clock, that hadn't ticked for years, shone round

as the sun at noonday, and was swinging away as if it meant to catch up before nightfall all the time it had ever lost.

Beside the hearth, too, lay a pile of broken driftwood, a fire was merrily dancing in the grate, there was a fish cooking in the pan in the brick oven, the old iron kettle hung singing from its hook; and a great saucepan, brimful of peeled potatoes, sat in the hearth beneath it to keep it company. And not only this, for there lay on the table a dish of fresh-pulled salad – lettuces, radishes, and young sorrel and dandelion leaves. But of Old Moleskins, not a sign.

Griselda herself was a good housewife, but in all her days she had never seen the kitchen look like this. It was as fresh as a daisy. And Griselda began to sing – to keep the kettle company. Having made a custard out of one of the eggs and the milk she had brought home with her, she climbed upstairs again to see her grandmother.

'Well, Grannie,' she said, 'how are you now? I've been away and come back. I haven't wasted a moment; but you must be nearly starving.'

The old woman told her she had spent the morning between dozing and dreaming and looking from her bed out of the window at the sea. This she could do because immediately opposite her window was the broken opening of what had once been a window in the walls of the Castle. It was a kind of spy-hole into the world for the old woman.

'And what else were you going to tell me, Grannie?' said Griselda.

The old woman spied about her from her pillow as if she were afraid she might be overheard. Then she warned Griselda that next time she went out she must make sure to latch the door. Some strange animal must have been prowling about in the house, she said. She had heard it not only under her open window, but even stirring about in the room below. 'Though I must say,' she added, 'I had to listen pretty hard!'

Griselda glanced up out of the lattice window and, since her head was a good deal higher than her grandmother's pillow, she could see down into the green courtyard below. And there stood Old Moleskins, looking up at her.

An hour or two afterwards, when the sun was dipping behind the green hills beyond the village, and Griselda sat alone, beside the fire, her sewing in her lap, she heard shuffling footsteps on the cobbles outside, and the dwarf appeared at the window. Griselda thanked him with all her heart for what he had done for her, and took out of her grandmother's old leather purse one of the three pennies she had earned at the farm.

The dwarf eyed it greedily, then, pointing with his thumb at an old pewter pot that stood on the chimneyshelf, told Griselda to put the penny in it and to keep it safe for him until he asked for it.

'Nine days,' he said, 'I will work for you – three and three and three – and no more, for the same wages. And then you must pay me all you owe me. And I will come every evening to see it into the pot.'

So Griselda tiptoed on the kitchen fender, put the penny in the pot, and shut down the lid. When she turned round again Old Moleskins was gone.

Before she went to bed that night, she peeped out of the door. There was no colour left in the sky except the dark blue of night; but a slip of moon, as thin as an egg-shell, hung in the west above the hill, and would soon be following the sun beyond it. Griselda solemnly bowed to the moon seven times, and shook the old purse in her pocket.

When she came down the next morning, the kitchen had been swept, a fire was dancing up the chimney, her mug and plate and spoon had been laid on the table, and a smoking bowl of milk-porridge was warming itself on the hearth. When Griselda took the porridge up to her grandmother, the old woman's eyes nearly popped out of her head, for Griselda had been but a minute gone. She took a sup of the porridge, smacked her lips, tasted it again, and asked Griselda what she had put in it to flavour it. It was a taste she had never tasted before. And Griselda told the old woman it was a secret.

That day the farmer gave Griselda some old gold-brown Cochin-China hens to pluck for market. 'They've seen better days, but will do for the pot,' he said. And having heard that her grandmother was better, he kept her working for him till late in the afternoon. So Griselda plucked and singed busily on, grieved for the old hens, but happy to think of her wages. Then once more the farmer paid her twopence; and, once more, a penny over; this time not for the sake of her gold hair, but for her 'glass-grey eyes'. So now there was fivepence in her purse, and as yet there had been no need, beyond last night's penny for the dwarf, to spend any of them.

When Griselda came home, not only was everything in the kitchen polished up brighter than ever, but a pot of broth was simmering on the hob, which, to judge by the savour of it, contained not only carrots and onions and pot-herbs but a young rabbit. Besides which, a strip of the garden had been freshly dug; three rows of brisk young cabbages had been planted, and, as Griselda guessed, two more each of broad beans and peas. Whatever the dwarf had set his hand to was a job well done.

Sharp to his time – the sun had but that very moment dipped beneath the hills – he came to the kitchen door for his wages. Griselda smiled at him, thanked him, and took out a penny. He gazed at it earnestly; then at her. And he said, 'Put that in the pot, too.' So now there were two pennies in his pewter pot and four pennies in Griselda's purse.

And so the days went by. Her grandmother grew steadily better, and on the next Sunday – muffled up in a shawl like an old tortoiseshell cat – she sat up a little while beside her window. On most mornings Griselda had gone out to work at the farm or in the village; on one or two she had stayed in the house and sat with her grandmother to finish her sewing and mending or any other work she had found to do.

While she was in the cottage she never saw the dwarf, though he might be hidden away in the garden. But still her grandmother talked of the strange stirrings and noises she heard when Griselda was away. 'You'd have thought,' the old woman said, 'there was a whole litter of young pigs in the kitchen, and the old sow, too!'

On the eighth day, the farmer not only gave Griselda her tuppence for her wages and another for the sake of 'the dimple in her cheek', but the third penny had a hole in it. 'And that's for luck,' said the farmer. She went home rejoicing. And seeing no reason why she shouldn't share her luck with the dwarf, she put the penny with the hole in it into the pewter pot when he came that evening. And as usual he said not a word. He merely watched Griselda's face with his colourless eyes while she thanked him for what he had done, and then watched her put his penny into the pot. Then in an instant he was gone.

'That maid Griselda, from the Castle yonder,' said the farmer to his wife that night as, candlestick in hand, the two of them were going up to bed, 'she seems to me as willing as she's neat and pretty. And if she takes as good care of the pence as she seems to, my dear, there's never a doubt, I warrant, but as she will take as good care of the pounds!'

And he was right. Griselda had taken such good care of

the pence that at this very moment she was sitting alone in the kitchen in the light of her solitary candle and slowly putting down on paper every penny that she had been paid and every penny that she had spent:

Acounts

receeved		Spent	
from Farmer for wages	10	oatmeel	2
prezants	5	bones for soop	2
wages for Missus Jakes	2	shuger	2
wages for piggs	1	hair ribon	1
	—	wole	1
	18	doll	1
		money for Moalskins	8
			—
			17

The doll had been a present for the cowman's little daughter. And though Griselda had made many mistakes before she got her sum right, it was right *now*; and here was the penny over in her purse to prove it.

The next evening, a little before sunset, Griselda sat waiting for the dwarf to come. Never had she felt so happy and light-hearted. It was the last of his nine days; she had all his nine pennies ready for him – one in her purse and eight in the pewter pot; the farmer had promised her as much work as she could manage; her old grandmother was nearly well again; the cupboard was no longer bare, and she was thankful beyond all words. It seemed as if her body could not possibly contain her happiness.

The trees stood in the last sunshine of evening as though they had borrowed their green coats from Paradise; the paths were weeded; the stones had a fresh coat of whitewash; there was not a patch of soil without its plants or seedlings. From every clump of ivy on the old walls of the

Castle a thrush seemed to be singing; and every one of them seemed to be singing louder than the rest.

Her sewing idle in her lap, Griselda sat on the doorstep, drinking everything in with her clear grey eyes, and at the same time she was thinking too. Not only of Moleskins and of all he had done for her, but of the farmer's son also, who had come part of the way home with her the evening before. And then she began to day-dream.

But it seemed her spirit had been but a moment gone out of her body into this far-away when the tiny sound of stone knocking on stone recalled her to herself again, and there – in the very last beam of the setting sun – stood the dwarf on the cobbles of the garden path. He told Griselda that his nine days' work for her was done, and that he had come for his wages.

Griselda beckoned him into the kitchen, and there she whispered her thanks again and again for all his help and kindness. She took her last penny out of her purse and put it on the table, then tiptoeing, reached up to the chimney-shelf and lifted down the pewter pot. Even as she did so, her heart turned cold inside her. Not the faintest jingle sounded when she shook it. It seemed light as a feather. With trembling fingers she managed at last to lift the lid and look in. 'Oh!' she whispered. 'Someone . . .' A dark cloud came over her eyes. The pot was empty.

The dwarf stood in the doorway, his eager cold bright eyes fixed on her face. 'Well,' he croaked. 'Where is my money? Why am I to be kept waiting, young woman? Answer me that!'

Griselda could only stare back at him, the empty pot in her hand. His eyebrows began to jerk up and down as if with rage, like an orang-outang's. 'So it's gone, eh? My pennies are all gone, eh? So you have cheated me! Eh? Eh? *Cheated* me?'

Nothing Griselda could say was of any avail. He refused to listen to her. The more she entreated him only to have patience and she would pay him all she owed him, the more sourly and angrily he stormed at her. And to see the tears rolling down her cheeks on either side of her small nose only worsened his rage.

'I will give you one more day,' he bawled at last. 'One! I will come back tomorrow at sunset, and every single penny must be ready for me. What I do, I can undo! What I make, I can break! Hai, hai! we shall see!' With that he stumped out into the garden and was gone.

Griselda was so miserable and her mind was in such a whirl that she could do nothing for a while but sit, cold and vacant, staring out of the open door. Where could the pennies have gone to? Mice don't eat pennies. Had she been walking in her sleep? Who could have stolen them? And how was she to earn as many more in only one day's work?

And while she sat brooding, there came a *thump, thump, thump* on the floor over her head. She sprang to her feet, lit a candle by the fire-flames, dabbed her eyes in the bucket of cold water that Old Moleskins had brought in from the well, and took up her grandmother's supper.

'Did you hear any noises in the house today, Grannie?' she asked cautiously as she put the bowl of broth into her skinny old hands. At this question the old woman, who was very hungry, fell into a temper. Every single evening, she told Griselda, she had warned her that some strange animal had come rummaging into the house below when she was away working at the farm. 'You never kept watch, you never even answered me,' she said. 'And now it's too late. Today I have heard nothing.'

It was all but dark when, having made the old woman comfortable for the night, Griselda hastened down into the kitchen again. She could not bear to wait until morning. She had made up her mind what to do. Leaving her grandmother drowsy after her broth and nodding off to sleep, she stole out of the house and shut the door gently behind her. Groping her way under the ivied walls into the open she hastened on in the quiet moonlight, climbing as swiftly as she could the steep grassy slope at the cliff's edge. An owl called. From far below she could hear the tide softly gushing on the stones of the beach; and over the sea the sky was alive with stars.

A light was still glimmering at an upper window when she reached the farm. She watched it a while and the shadows moving to and fro across the blind, and at last timidly lifted the knocker and knocked on the door. The farmer himself answered her knock. A candlestick in his hand, he stood there in his shirt sleeves looking out at her over his candle, astonished to find so late a visitor standing there in the starlight, muffled up in a shawl. But he spoke kindly to her. And then and there Griselda poured out her story, though she said not a word about the dwarf.

She told the farmer that she was in great trouble; that, though she couldn't give him any reasons, she must have eight pennies by the next evening. And if only he would lend her them and trust her, she promised him faithfully she would work for just as long as he wanted her to in exchange.

'Well,' said the farmer. 'That's a queer tale, *that* is! But why not work for four days, and I'll give 'ee the eightpence then.' But Griselda shook her head. She told him that this was impossible; that she could not wait, not even for one day.

'See here, then,' said the farmer, smiling to himself, though not openly, for he was curious to know what use she was going to make of the money. 'I can't give you any work tomorrow, nor be sure of the next day. But supposing there's none for a whole week, if you promise to cut off that gold hair of yours and give me that *then*, you shall have the eight pennies now – this very moment – and no questions asked.'

Griselda stood quite still in the doorway, her face pale and grave in the light of the farmer's candle. It seemed that every separate hair she had was stirring upon her head. This all came, she thought, of admiring herself in the duck-pond; and not being more careful with her money; and doing what the dwarf told her to do and not what she thought best. But as it seemed that at any moment the farmer might run in and fetch a pair of shears to cut off her hair there and then, she made her promise; and he himself went back laughing to his wife, and told her what had happened. 'She turned as white as a sheet,' he said. 'And what I'd dearly like to know is what's worriting the poor dear. She's as gentle as the day is long, and her word's as good as her bond. Well, well! But I'll see to it. And we'll have just one lock of that hair, my dear, if only for a keepsake.'

'It looks to *me*,' said the farmer's wife, '*that*'ll be for our Simon to say.'

When Griselda reached home again – and a sad and solitary walk it had been through the dewy fields above the sea – she went to an old wooden coffer in which she kept her few 'treasures'. Many of them were remembrances of her mother. And she took out a net for the hair that her mother herself had worn when she was a girl of about the same age as Griselda. Then she sat down in front of a little bare square of looking-glass, braided her hair as close as she could to her head, and drew the net tightly over it. Then she put her purse with the nine pennies in it under her pillow, said her prayers, and got into bed.

For hours she lay listening to the breakers on the shore,

solemnly drumming the night away, and watched her own particular star as moment by moment it sparkled on from diamond pane to pane across her lattice window. But when at last she fell asleep, her dreams were scarcely less sorrowful than her waking.

She stayed at home the next day in case the dwarf should come early, but not until sunset did she hear the furtive clatter of his shoes as usual on the stones. She took out her purse to pay him his pennies. He asked her where they had come from. 'And why,' said he, 'have you braided your hair so close and caged it up in a net? Are you frightened the birds will be after it?'

Griselda laughed at this in spite of herself. And she told him that she had promised her hair to a friend, and that she had wound it up tight to her head in order to remind herself that it was not her own any longer, and to keep it safe. At this Old Moleskins himself burst out laughing under the green-berried gooseberry bush – for Griselda had taken him out into the garden lest her grandmother should hear them talking.

'A pretty bargain *that* was!' he said. 'But *I* know one even better!' And he promised Griselda that if she would let him snip off but one small lock of her hair he would transport her into the grottoes of the Urchin People under the sea. 'And *there*,' he said, 'if you will work for us for only one hour a day for seven days, you shall have seven times the weight of all your hair in fine solid gold. If, after that, I mean,' and he eyed her craftily, 'you will promise to come back and stay with us always. And then you shall have a basket of fruit from our secret orchards.'

Griselda looked at the dwarf, and then at the small green ripening gooseberries on the bush, and then stared a while in silence at the daisies on the ground. Then she told the dwarf she could not give him a lock of her hair because that was all promised. Instead, she would work for him every day for nine days, free. It was the least she could do, she thought, in return for what he had done for her.

'Well then,' said Moleskins, 'if it can't be hair it must be an eyelash. Else you will never see the grottoes. An eyelash for your journey-money!'

To this she agreed, and knelt down beside the gooseberry bush, shutting her eyes tight so that he might more easily pluck out one of the lashes that fringed their lids. She felt his stumpy earthy fingers brush across them, and nothing beside.

But when she opened them, and looked out of her body, a change had come upon the scene around her – garden, cottage, castle walls and ruined turrets, cliffs, sea and caves – all had vanished. No evening ray of sun shone here, not the faintest sea-breeze stirred the air. It was a place utterly still, and lay bathed in a half-light pale and green, rilling in from she knew not where. And around her, and above her head, faint colours shimmered in the quarried quartz of the grottoes. And the only sound to be heard was a distant sighing, as of the tide.

There were many trees here, too, in the orchards of the Urchin People, their slim stems rooted in sands as fine and white as hoarfrost. And their branches were laden with fruits of as many colours as there are precious stones. And there was a charm of birds singing, though Griselda could see none. The very air seemed thin and fine in this dim and sea-green light: the only other sound to be heard was a faint babbling of water among the rocks, water which lost itself in the sands of the orchard.

The dwarf had brought out some little rush baskets, and told Griselda what she must do. 'Gather up the fallen fruit,' he said, 'but pick none from the branches, and sort it out each according to its kind and colour, one colour into each of the baskets. But be sure not to climb into the trees or shake them. And when your hour is finished I will come again.'

Griselda at once set to work. Though the branches over-head were thick with fruit, there were as yet not many that had fallen, and it seemed at first it would take her but a few moments to sort them out into their baskets. But the thin air and twilight of the grotto made her drowsy, and as she stooped again and yet again to pick up the fruit, her eye-lids drooped so heavily that at any moment she feared she would fall asleep. And if once she fell asleep what might not happen then? Would she ever win back to earth again? Was this all nothing but a dream? She refreshed her eyes in the trickle of snow-cold water rilling down from the rocks; and now she fancied she heard a faint metallic noise as of knocking and hammering and small voices in the distance. But even when all the fallen fruits had been sorted out into her baskets, emerald-green, orange, amethyst, crystal and blue, her work was not done. For the moment she sat down to rest, yet another of the fruits would plump down softly as an apple into deep grass upon the sand beneath it, and she had to hasten away to put it into its basket.

When the dwarf came back he looked about him to see that no fruits had been left lying in the sand. He squinnied here, he squinnied there, and even turned over the fruits in the baskets to see that they had been sorted right. 'Well, Griselda,' he said at last, and it was the first time he had used her name, 'what's well done is done for good. And here's the penny for your wages.'

There was a stealthy gleam in his eyes as he softly fumbled with his fingers in the old moleskin pouch that hung at his side, and fetched out his penny. Griselda held out her hand, and he put the penny into its palm, still watching her. She looked at it – and looked again. It was an old, thick, battered penny, and the king's image on it had been worn very faint. It had a slightly crooked edge, too, and there was a hole in it. There could be no doubt of it – this was the penny the farmer had given her, 'for luck'. Until now Griselda had not realized that she had for a moment suspected it might be Old Moleskins himself who had stolen his pennies out of the pewter pot. Now she was sure of it. She continued to stare at the penny, yet said nothing. After all, she was thinking to herself, the money in the pot belonged to him. He had a right to it. You cannot steal what is yours already! But then, a lie is almost as bad as stealing. Perhaps he hadn't meant it to be a lie. Perhaps he merely wanted to see what she might say and do. That would still be a lie but not such a wicked lie. Perhaps since he wasn't *quite* human he couldn't in any case tell *quite* a lie. Perhaps it was only a dwarf lie, though his kindness to her had certainly not been only dwarf kindness! She smiled to herself at this; lifted up her face again, and seeing the dwarf still watching her, smiled at him also. And she thanked him.

At this he burst out laughing, till the roof and walls of the grotto echoed with the cackle of it, and at least half a dozen of the grotto fruits dropped from their twigs and thumped softly down into the sand. 'Aha,' he cried, 'what did I tell you? Weep no more, Griselda. That is one penny, and here are the others.' He took them out of his pouch, and counted them into her hand, and the eight pennies too that she had given him but a little while before; and as he did so, he sang out in a high quavering voice like a child's :

'Never whatever the *humans* say
Have the Urchin Folk worked for any man's pay.

Ah, Griselda,' he said, 'if we could keep you, you would scarcely ever have to work at all. No churning and weed-ing, no sewing and scrubbing, no cooking or polishing, sighing or sobbing; you should be for ever happy and for ever young. And you wouldn't have to scissor off a single snippet of your silk-soft hair!'

Griselda looked at him in the still green light and faintly shook her head. But she made a bargain with him none the less that every year she would work in the grottoes for the Urchin People – if he could come to fetch her – for one whole summer's day. So this was the bargain between them.

And he took out of his breeches' pocket a thick gold piece, about the size of an English crown-piece, and put it into her hand. On the one side of it the image of a mermaid was stamped, on the other a little fruit tree growing out of a mound of sand and knobbed with tiny fruits. 'That's for a keepsake,' he said. And he himself took one of each kind of the orchard fruits out of their baskets and put them into another. 'And since "no pay" is *no* pay,' he went on, 'stoop, Griselda, and I'll give you your eyelash back again.'

Griselda knelt down in the sand, and once more the earthy fingers brushed over her eyelids. The next instant all was dark; and a thin chill wind was stirring on her cheek. She opened her eyes to find herself alone again under the night-sky, and – as though she had been overtaken by the strangeness of a dream – kneeling on the dew-damped mould of her familiar garden under the stars. But for proof that what had happened was no dream, the gold piece stamped with the images of the mermaid and the leafy tree was still clasped in her hand, and in the other was the basket of fruits.

As for the eyelash, since Griselda had never counted how many she had before Old Moleskins plucked one out, she could never tell for certain if it had been put back. But when she told Simon, the farmer's son, that there *might* be one missing – and she could tell him no more because of her promise to the dwarf – he counted them over again and again. And though he failed to make the total come to the same number twice, he assured Griselda that there couldn't possibly ever have been room for another. And Griselda gave him the green one of the grotto fruits she had brought him for a present from out of the dwarf's basket. This too was for a keepsake. 'It's as hard as a stone,' he said. 'Do we eat it, Griselda?' But hard though it was, there must have been a curious magic in it, for as they sat there together under the willow tree by the duck-pond, it was as if they had been transported not into the grottoes of the Urchin People under the sea, but clean back into the Garden of Eden.

As for Griselda's hair, there it shone as thick as ever on her head. And as for the farmer, he refused every single penny of the eightpence.

'It's a queer thing to me, mother,' he was saying to his wife at this very moment, as they sat together on either side of the kitchen fire – just as they were accustomed to sit even in the height of summertime – 'it's a queer thing to me that this very farm of ours once belonged to that young woman's great-great-grandfather!' He took a long whiff of his pipe. 'And what *I* says is that them who once had, when they gets again, should know how to *keep*.'

'Ay, George,' said she, and she said no more.

The Scarecrow

The house in which old Mr Bolsover lived was a faded yellow primrose colour; it was a long house, but of only two storeys. Yet even its lower windows looked out far away over the meadows lying at this moment spread out beneath them, bright green in the morning sunshine. A narrow veranda shaded the windows, its sloping canopy of copper now a pale grey-green; and around its slim wooden pillars clematis and jessamine clambered. At either end of it was a low weather-worn stone pedestal. On these stood two leaden fauns – the one ever soundlessly piping to the other across the wall-flowers and the pinks. And it was the pinks that were now in flower, white as snow, and filling the air with their musky fragrance.

A little clock had just chimed ten, and old Mr Bolsover, in his cool white jacket, was coming out of the french windows of the breakfast-room with his small niece, Letitia. Letitia had a quick nimble way of walking and talking and turning her head that was like a bird's. And old Mr Bolsover, with his eyes and his nose, was rather like a bird himself, but of the long-legged, tall, solemn kind – the flamingos and the storks. They came to a standstill together looking out over the meadows.

'Oh, Uncle Tim, what a *perfectly* lovely morning!' said Letitia.

'A *perfectly* lovely morning,' said Uncle Tim. 'Just as if it had been ordered all complete and to match for a certain small friend of mine!

83

The Scarecrow

Lettie's like a lovely day:
She comes; and then – she goes away.'

'Ah, Uncle Tim,' said Letitia, 'that's called *flattery*.'

'Bless me, my dear,' replied her uncle, squinnying at her from under the glasses of his spectacles, 'it doesn't matter a pin what it's called!'

'Ah, I know all about that!' said Letitia. 'And to think it is exactly a whole year since I was here before! Yet you wouldn't believe a single pink was different. Isn't that funny, Uncle Tim? *We* are. And why, yes,' she went on hastily, twisting her head on her slender neck, 'there's that curious old Guy Fawkes creature over there by the willows. He's not changed a single bit either.'

'So it is, so it is,' said Uncle Tim, peering out over the meadows. 'Though as a matter of fact, my dear, it's not quite true to say he hasn't changed a *bit*. He has changed his hat. Last year it was an old hat, and now it's a very old hat, a shocking hat. No wonder he covers up one eye under its brim. But it doesn't matter how long you stare at him, he'll stare longer.'

Letitia none the less continued to gaze at the scarecrow – and with a peculiar little frown between her eyes. 'You know, he *is* a little queer, Uncle Tim – if you look at him long enough. And you can easily pretend you are not *quite* looking at him. You don't seem to remember either,' she went on solemnly, 'that the very last morning I was here you promised me faithfully to tell me all about him. But you didn't, because Mother came in just when I was asking you, and you forgot all about it.'

'Why, so I did,' said Mr Bolsover. 'That's what comes of having a memory like a bag with a hole in it. That's what comes of the piecrust promises are made of—they just melt in your mouth ... Still, that's Old Joe right enough. *So* old, my dear, you could hardly tell us apart!'

'You're please not to say that, Uncle Tim – it isn't true. You are the youngest oldest kindest Uncle Tim that ever was. So there. But what *were* you going to tell me about Old Joe? Where did he come from? What is he for – except the rooks, I mean? Isn't there a tune about Old Joe? Is that him? Tell me *now*?' cried Letitia. 'Let's sit down here comfily on the stones. Feel! they are as warm as toast with the sun! And now go straight on. *Please*.'

Down sat old Mr Bolsover; down sat Letitia – side by side like Mr Punch and his dog Toby. And this is the story he told of Old Joe ...

'I must begin, Letitia,' he began, 'at the beginning. It is much the best place from which to get to the end. Now when I was about your age – not quite 129 years ago – I used sometimes to go and stay with an old friend of my mother's – your grandmother's, that is – whose name was Sara Lumb. She was a very stout woman, with black sleek hair, round red cheeks, and dimples for knuckles. And she used, I remember, to wear an amethyst-coloured velvet cap, flat over her ears, and a lace thingummy over her shoulders. I can see her now – her wide face all creased up in smiles, and her fat fingers with their emeralds and their amethysts, and even the large emerald brooch she wore at her neck. She wasn't an aunt of mine, she wasn't even so much as my godmother, but she was extremely kind to me. *Almost* as kind as I am to you! She was very fond of eatables and drinkables too and had a cook that could make every sort of cake that is worth talking about – seven sultanas and nine currants to the square inch. Jams, jellies, raspberry fool, fritters, pancakes, tipsy-cake – they were the best I have ever tasted. So were her stuffed eggs and oyster patties at Christmas parties. My eye!'

'Oh, Uncle Tim,' said Letitia, 'you *were* a greedy thing.'

'And what's worse,' said her uncle, 'I have never grown out of it. You shall see for yourself at lunch. And if I'm not an unprophetic Double-Dutchman I can already smell apple charlotte. But never mind about that. It's no good – until it's ready. But in any case I am sure you will agree, Letitia, that my old friend Mrs Lumb was just the kind of old friend for a small boy with a large appetite to stay *with*. This of course was always during the holidays; and, in those days, while there was plenty of hard tack at school, "impots", canings, cabbage stalks, cod, suet-duff, castor oil, bread-and-scrape and what not, there was no such horror as a holiday task. Holiday tasks always remind me, my dear, of the young lady who wanted to go out to swim:

> Mother may I go out to swim?
> Yes, my darling daughter.
> Fold your clothes up neat and trim,
> And don't go near the water.'

'The rhyme *I* know,' said Letitia, 'is "Hang your clothes on a hickory limb".'

'That's all very well,' said her uncle, 'but just you show me one! Let's have it both ways then:

> Mother, may I go out to swim?
> Yes, my darling daughter.
> Fold your clothes up neat and trim,
> (So at least says Uncle Tim),
> Or hang them up on a hickory limb,
> (That's what Letitia said to him),
> And don't go near the water.

What – before this violent quarrel – I *meant* was, my dear, that in those days *no* good little boy had to stew indoors in his holidays and simply *detest* reading a book which he would have given half his pocket money to read for its own sake *if* he had never been made to. Q.E.D. But that's quite between ourselves. We must never, never criticize our elders. And anyhow, at my old friend's Mrs Lumb's there was no need to. It was bliss.

'First, hers was a queer old rambling house, much older than this one, and at least three and a half times as big again. Next, there was beautiful country round it too; fields stretching down their sunny slopes, and little woods and copses on the crests and in the folds and valleys; and a stream – with reeds and rushes and all sorts of water birds – that came brawling over the stones at the foot of her long sloping garden. But I hate descriptions, don't you, Letitia? And *there*, an orchard so full of cherry trees that in springtime it looked as if it were thick with snow. Well well, if ever I got to heaven, my child, I hope to see that house and garden again.'

'But isn't it still *there*?' said Letitia. 'I mean, you know, where it used to be?'

'Alas, my dear, no,' said old Mr Bolsover. 'It is gone for ever. There came a cook – *not* Mrs Lumb's. She was frying dabs – Brighton dabs – for breakfast one morning; the cat squealed and scratched her leg; she upset the pan; there was one huge blaze; she ran screeching into the garden instead of – well, doing what she ought to have done; and the old house was burned down clean to the ground. Clean. Think of that, Letitia. Always keep your eye on cats and fat. But this, I am thankful to say, was *after* my dear old friend Mrs Lumb had left the house and had gone out to live with her younger brother in Ceylon, where the bad cook's strong tea had come from.

'Now in those far-away days *birds* were all my fancy. The wonder is I never sprouted feathers. I loved them too much to carry a catapult, but not enough to refrain from setting traps for them, to catch them for pets. Brick traps and sieve traps. But how would you like to be a linnet or

a lark or a thrush or a bullfinch caged up in one tiny room
with bars for windows just to amuse a wretch of a boy
like me when I was nine or ten or eleven or thereabouts?'

'I shouldn't,' said Letitia. 'But I'd *much* much rather be
in your cage than in any other horrid little boy's.'

'Thank you, my dear,' said Mr Bolsover. 'That's a bargain. Still, the wilder the bird the worse the cage. But then
as I was a boy, I did as boys do – bless their little hearts!
And I used to weep tears like a crocodile when the sparrows
or finches I caught moped off and died. After the funeral
I'd stick a bit of wood in the ground to mark the grave –
and go off to set another trap.

'My traps were everywhere, and sometimes in places
where they had no business to be. But first you must understand what I was after, really *after*.' Mr Bolsover all but
whispered it. 'It was rare birds – hoopoes, golden orioles,
honey buzzards – the lovely and seldom. Deep down in me
I pined for a bird unspeakably marvellous in plumage and
song; a bird that nobody else had ever even seen; a bird
that had flown clean out of the window of some magician's
mind. Which means of course that I had become a little
cracked on birds. I used even to dream of that bird sometimes – but then it was usually me myself that was in the
cage!

'Well, there was one particular covert that I kept in
memory to set a trap in for days before I ventured to make
the attempt. This was at the edge of a field where a great
many birds of all kinds and sizes were accustomed to haunt,
though I never found out why. I watched them again and
again, hosts of them – their wings shimmering in the light.
It seemed it was their happy secret meeting place – and in
spite of Old Joe!'

'*That* Old Joe *there*?' cried Letitia, pointing at the mute
lank ungainly figure over against the grey-green willows,

with its ragged arms, and battered old hat on one side, that stood blankly gazing at them from out of the field beyond the garden.

'Yes,' said her uncle, 'that Old Joe *there*. You see, between you and me, Letitia, and don't let us look his way for a moment in case we should hurt his feelings, that Old Joe there (as perhaps you've guessed) is a scarecrow. He is nothing but a dumb, tumbledown hugger-mugger antiquated old hodmadod. He has never really been anything else; though after all the years he and I have been together, and not a single unkind word said on either side, he is now a sort of twin brother. Like Joseph and Benjamin, you know. Why, if we changed places, I don't suppose you would be able to tell us apart.'

'How can you dare to say such things, Uncle Tim?' cried Letitia, pushing her hand in under his elbow. 'You know perfectly well that that's a sort of a kind of flattery – of yourself, you bad thing.'

'All I can say to that, Miss Tomtit,' replied Uncle Tim, 'is, ask Old Joe. Still, we are old friends now, he and I, whereas the first time I saw him he gave me a pretty bad fright. I had come creeping along on the other side of the hedge, keeping a very wary eye open for anybody that might be in the fields – because I was trespassing. When they were not being ploughed or harrowed or rolled or sown or hoed or cropped, there never was anybody; except perhaps on Sunday, when the farmer, Mr Jones, a large stout man with a red face and a thick stick, came round to have a look at his crops.

'It was a wide, sloping, odd-shaped field of about forty acres running down to a point, rather like the map of England turned upside down, and with a little wood of larch on one side of it. This particular morning was in April. It was sunny but cold, and the field was bare except for its flints glinting in the sunbeams. It had been sown, but nothing green was showing.

'Well, I was skirting along the hedge, as I say, but on this side of it, carrying the bird snare I had with me under my jacket, and hardly able to breathe for excitement. I knew exactly – as I peered through the hedge, on which the thorn buds were just breaking green as emeralds – which was the place for me. There was a ditch beyond the hedge, and I could see only a narrow strip of the field at the moment, because of the hedge and bushes in between. But it was truly a little paradise of birds, my dear, and particularly when spring was on its way.

'Well, on I went until I came to the corner by the rickety old gate, which was tied up with a piece of chain. Between you and me it was a shameful old gate. But that is not *our* business. And all of a sudden I caught sight of what I supposed was Farmer Jones himself, glaring straight at me across the field, and not thirty yards away. I fairly jumped in my skin at sight of him, turned hot, then cold, and waited, staring back. For that one instant it seemed as if I could see the very colour of his eyeballs moving in his head.

'But all this was only in the flicker of a moment. No Farmer Jones that, and not even one of his men! It was just Old Joe; *our* Old Joe. That Old Joe there! Come alive. And after all, what *is* life, Letitia?'

'That's perfectly true, Uncle Tim,' Letitia whispered, edging a little closer to him. 'He might be alive at this very instant.'

'And not only that, you must remember,' went on Mr Bolsover, 'this was in Old Joe's better days. He was young then. He has been peacocked up in many a fine new suit of old clothes since then, and more hats than I could count on twice my fingers. But *then* he was in his hey-day, in the very bloom of his youth, the glass of fashion and the knave of trumps. And now I wouldn't part with him for a bag of golden guineas. No, not for twenty bags. And though I am very fond of guineas, the reason for that is, first, that I love him for his own sweet sake alone, and next, my dear Letitia, because one doesn't very often see – *see*, I mean – real fairies in this world.'

Letitia burst out laughing. 'Real live fairies, Uncle Tim!' she cried, stooping forward in her amusement and dragging her skirts tight down over her knees. 'Why, you can't mean to say, you poor dear, that Old Joe's a *fairy*?'

'No,' said Mr Bolsover, 'I didn't mean to say quite that. Then, as now, Old Joe was the scaringest of scaring scarecrows I have ever set eyes on. But, like the primrose in the poem, he was nothing more. No, it wasn't Old Joe himself who was the fairy, no more than the house behind us *is* you and me. Old Joe was merely one of this particular fairy's rendyvouses, as the old word goes. He was where she *was*.

'That morning, I remember, he was wearing a pair of slack black-and-white check trousers and a greenish black coat, very wide at the shoulders. Apart from the stick for his arm, another had been pushed into one of his coat-sleeves for a cudgel. Another with a lump at the top made his head and on that was a hat, hard, battered, square black hat – like the hats farmers and churchwardens used to wear in those days. He was stooping forward a little, staring across at me as I crouched by the gate. As I say, I hugged the wire snare under my jacket closer, and stared back.

'Whether it was because of the hot air that was eddying up from the stony soil under the sun, or because of some cheating effect of the light on the chalky field, I can't say, Letitia. But even while I stood watching him, his head seemed to be ever so gently turning on his shoulders as if he were secretly trying to get a better view of me without my noticing it. Yet all the time I fancied this, I knew it wasn't true.

'Still, I was a good deal startled. Quite apart from crows and such riff-raff, he had certainly scared *me* – for in those days young trespassers (not to mention the old double-toothed mantraps, which were a little before my time) might find themselves in for a smart walloping if they were caught. But even when I had recovered my wits I continued to watch him, and at the same time kept glancing from side to side at the birds that were flighting about me, or feeding, or preening and sunning themselves in the dust. And though by this time I knew him for what he was, I wasn't by any means at ease.

'For even if there were no real eyes in his own head, I was perfectly certain that somebody or something was actually looking at me from under that old black hat, or from out of his sleeve – from *some*where about him. The birds were already used to my being there, simply because I remained so still. After perhaps five whole minutes of this, I squatted down at the edge of the field and began to set my trap.

'But the whole time I was stooping over it, and softly hammering the wooden peg in with a large flint, I was thinking of the old scarecrow – though without looking at him – and knew I was being watched. I say without looking at him, but whenever I got a chance I would snatch a little secret glance at him from between my legs or over my shoulder or from under my arm, pretending that I was doing nothing of the kind. And then at last, the trap finished, I sat down on the grass under the hedge and steadily fixed my eyes on him again.

'The sun climbed slowly up the blue sky, his rays twinkling from sharp-cut stone to stone and scrap of glass. The hot air rilled on at his feet. The birds went about their business, and nothing else happened. I watched so hard that my eyes began to water, but whatever was hiding there, if anything *was* hiding there, could be as patient as I was. And at last I turned home again.

'At the far corner of the field under an old thorn tree I stooped down once more as if I were tying up my shoe lace, and had another long look, and *then* I was perfectly certain I had caught a glimpse of something moving there. It was as

if a face had very stealthily peered out of the shadow of
the old scarecrow, and, on sighting me under the thorn tree,
had as swiftly withdrawn into hiding again.

'All the rest of that day I could think of nothing else but
Old Joe, assuring myself that my eyes had deceived me, or
that a bird perched on his shoulder had fluttered down, or
that a very faint breeze from over the open upland had
moved in his sleeve. Or that I had made it all up. Yet I knew
deep down inside me that this wasn't true. It was easy to
invent explanations, but none of them fitted.'

'It might, of course, Uncle Tim, you know,' said Letitia,
'it might have been not a bird but some little animal,
mightn't it? I once saw a hare skipping about in the middle
of a field, and then suddenly, though there wasn't even the
tip of his ear showing before, there was another hare. And
then another : would you believe it? And they went racing
over the field one after the other until they went right out of
sight. Or might it have been a bird, do you think, which was
building its nest in Old Joe? Robins, you know, build their
nests anywhere, even in an old boot. And I have seen a
tit's nest with I don't know how many eggs in it in an old
pump. And look, Uncle Tim, there is a bird actually perched
on Old Joe's shoulder now! That's what it might have been,
I think – some little animal, or bird nesting.'

'Well, you shall hear,' said Uncle Tim. 'But I am quite
certain that if you had been with me that morning, hundreds
of years ago, you would have agreed that there was something different about Old Joe; different, I mean, from what
he looks like now. He looked *queer*. I can't quite explain;
but it was the difference between an empty furnished house
and the same house with its family in it. It was the difference
between fishing in a millpond which has fish in it and in one
which has none. It was the difference between you yourself
when you are really asleep and when you are only foxing

and pretending to be. And what's more, sure enough, I was right.

'Now I had my proper bedtime at Mrs Lumb's; and before it, always, an apple and a glass of milk. My old friend was not only a great believer in apples, but she had seven beautiful Jersey cows, which are a great help, my dear, not only at bedtime, but with gooseberry tart or apple pie. But she wasn't one of those Uncle Tims who want everything done exactly at the right moment. She didn't wait till the clock struck eight (which just shows how easy it is to rhyme if you don't try to) and then come peeping in to see if I was safe in bed.'

'Why, you know very well,' said Letitia, 'you don't do that yourself.'

'Aha!' said Mr Bolsover, 'I wonder. People who sleep with one eye open grow as wise as old King Solomon. I creep and I creep and I creep, and every door has a keyhole. But never mind that. That very evening after my first sight of Old Joe, and when if I had been a nice honest boy I should have been in bed, I made my way down to his field again – slipping on from bush to bush, tree to tree, as cautiously as I could, so cautiously that I trod on the scut of a bunny, Esmeralda by name, that happened to be enjoying a dandelion for her supper on the other side of a bramble bush.

'When I reached my hawthorn tree – and hundreds of years old *that* looked – I stooped down beside its roots very low to the ground, having made up my mind to watch until evening grew too dark to see across the field. It was getting into May, and the air was so sweet and still and fresh that your eyes almost shut with bliss of themselves every time you breathed. And in those days, Letitia, we kept clocks by the sun. We didn't cheat him in the morning and pay him back in the evenings, as we do now. So there was faded gold and rose in the sky, though he himself was gone down.

'But apart from the birds and the bunnies, nothing happened except this great Transformation Scene of day turning into night, until it began to be dark. And then it seemed that almost every moment Old Joe, inch by inch, was steadily moving nearer. Seemed, mind you. And then, at the very instant when I noticed the first star – which by its mellow brightness and by where it was, must have been the planet Venus – I saw – well, now, what do you think I saw?'

'The fairy!' said Letitia, and sighed.

'Full marks, my dear,' said Mr Bolsover, squeezing her hand under his elbow. 'The fairy. And the odd thing is that I can't – can't possibly – describe her. This is perhaps partly because the light wasn't very good, and partly because my eyes were strained with watching. But mostly for other reasons. I seemed, you see, to be seeing her as *if* I were imagining her, even though I knew quite well she was there.

'You must just take my word for it – I knew she was there. She was stooping forward a little, and the top of her call Old Joe's waist. There he is – say the third button down of that old black coat he has on. Her face seemed to be a little long and narrow, but perhaps this was because her fair long and narrow, but perhaps this was because her fair hair was hanging down on either cheek, straight and fine as combed silk, and in colour between gold and grey – rather like the colour of a phosphorescent fish in the dark, but much more gold than silver. It looks to me, now I come to think of it, that since it was now gloaming I must have been seeing her in part as if by her own light.

'She stood lovely and motionless as a flower. And merely to gaze at her filled me with a happiness I shall not forget but cannot describe. It was as though I had come without knowing it into the middle of a dream in another world; and cold prickles went down my back, as if at the sound of enchanted music.

'There was not a breath of wind stirring. Everything around me seemed to have grown much more sharp and clear, even though the light was dim. The flowers were different, the trees, the birds. I seemed to know within me what the flowers were feeling – what it is like to be a plant with green pointed leaves and tiny caterpillar feet, like ivy, climbing from its white creeping roots in the dark earth by fractions of an inch, up the stem of a tree; or to have feathers all over me, and to float lighter than air, and to be looking out from two small bright round eyes at my bird-world. I can't explain it, Letitia, but I am sure you will understand.'

Letitia gave two solemn nods. 'I *think* so, Uncle Tim – a little. Though I never should have guessed, you know, that any *boy* was like that.'

'Boys, my dear, are mainly animals,' Uncle Tim agreed heartily, 'and so was I – nine and three-quarter tenths. But it was the other bit, I suppose, that was looking at Old Joe.

'And I firmly believe that the fairy knew I was there, but that in spite of knowing it, she could not delay doing what she wished to do any longer. For presently, after a minute or two, she drew very gently backwards and out of sight, and then began to hasten away over the field towards the corner of it furthest away from me, keeping all the time as far as she was able so that Old Joe stood in between us, and so prevented me from seeing her clearly, however much I dodged my head from side to side in the attempt to do so. Now that, Letitia, considering that she had her back turned to me, and was flitting along as swiftly as a shadow – *that* was a very difficult thing to do; and I don't quite see how she managed it. I am perfectly certain *I* couldn't – without once looking back, I mean.'

'And what,' said Letitia, 'was she like from behind?'

Old Mr Bolsover narrowed his eyes, and shut his lips. 'She was like,' he said slowly, 'a wraith of wood smoke from a bonfire. She was like what, if you could see it, you might suppose a puff of wind would be in the light over snow. She was like the ghost of a little waterfall. She moved, I mean, my dear, as if she were hovering on her way; and yet she never left the ground. Far, far more lightly than any gazelle she stepped; and it was so entrancing to watch her in the quiet and dusk of that great field, it fairly took my breath away. And mind you, I was only a clod-hopping boy of about ten.'

Mr Bolsover took a large coloured silk handkerchief out of his pocket and, as if in triumph, blew his nose. 'I ought to add at once,' he continued, pushing the handkerchief back into his pocket again except for one bright coloured corner, 'that this is not a story at all. Not a story, Letitia.'

'But *I* think, Uncle Tim, it *is* a story,' said Letitia. 'It doesn't make stories any worse if they are *true*. I mean, don't you think, that all *real* stories seem better than true? Don't you think so yourself, Uncle Tim? Just think of the Seven Swans, and Snow White! Oh, all those. At least I do. Please, please go on.'

'What *I* mean, my dear, is that a story ought really to be like a piece of music. It should have a beginning and a middle and an end, though you could hardly say which is which when it all comes out together. It ought to be like a whiting with its tail in its mouth – but a live whiting, of course. This one, you see, this one I am telling you, begins – and then goes off into nothing.'

'I don't think,' said Letitia, 'that matters one atom. Just please go on with the fairy, Uncle Tim.'

'Well, as soon as she was gone out of sight, my one and only desire was to steal into the field and take a look at Old Joe at close quarters. But upon my word, Letitia, I hadn't the courage. He was *her* dwelling-place, her hiding-place, her habitation: at least whenever she needed one. That was certain. Now that she was absent, had forsaken it, had gone away, the very look of him had changed. He was empty, merely a husk; he was just nothing but a hodmadod – Old Joe. Though we won't think a bit the worse of him for that. Bless me, no! When *you* have gone daydreaming, your face, Letitia, I assure you, looks still and quiet and happy. But I am afraid you must be thinking I was an exceedingly stupid boy. You see, I *was*. And I confess that I simply could not make up my mind to go a step nearer.

'Old Joe was quite alone now. I wasn't afraid of *him*. But after what I had seen I felt a curious strangeness all about me. I was afraid because I felt I had been spying, and that every living thing within view under the quiet sky knew of this and wanted to be rid of my company. I didn't – which was worse – even go to look at my bird snare. And when I went to the field again it had vanished.

'Next morning after breakfast with my old friend Mrs Lumb, I talked my way round until at last we came to fairies. "I sometimes wonder if they *can* be true," I said to her airily – as if I had just thought of it. Alas, Letitia, what deceivers we may be! But yes. My old friend believed in fairies all right. I never felt any doubt about that. But she had never seen one. I asked her what she thought a fairy would be like if she ever did see one. She sat in her chair – with her cup in her hand – looking out of the window and munching her toast.

' "Well, between you and me, my dear Tim," she said (*crunch, crunch*), "I never much cared about the flibberti-gibbety little creatures which are supposed to find a water-lily as comfortable a place to sleep in as you might a four-post bed. That, I think, is all my eye and Betty Martin. And I don't believe myself that any fairy would pay much attention to *me* (*crunch, crunch*). I expect (*crunch, crunch*) they prefer people, if they care for human beings at all, with less *of* and *to* them. And probably there are not many of them left in England now. Fairies, I mean. There are too many of *us*. Mr Lumb, as you know, was an entomologist. Perhaps he would have been able to tell you more about it. Besides (*crunch, crunch*), he had once seen a ghost." '

'Do you really mean,' said Letitia, 'that your friend Mrs Lumb's *husband* had once seen a ghost, and that *he* was – was dead too?'

'That's what Mrs Lumb meant, my dear, and I asked her what the ghost her husband saw was like. "Well," she said, "it was like (*crunch, crunch*) it was like, he told me, seeing something with your eyes shut. It made him feel very cold; the bedroom went black; but he wasn't frightened." '

Letitia sidled yet a little closer to her uncle. 'Between you and me, Uncle Tim,' she said, 'I believe that ghost would have given *me* the shudders. Don't you? But please let's go back to your fairy. Did you tell Mrs Lumb about that?'

'I never breathed so much as a single syllable, though if you were to ask me why, I couldn't say. It's just like small boys, I suppose; and small girls too, eh? They are dumplings, but keep the apple to themselves.'

'I think I'd have told just you, Uncle Tim,' said Letitia. 'And what happened then?'

'Two whole days went by before I ventured near the field again, though I doubt if an hour passed without my thinking of it. The birds in my memory seemed now to be stranger, wilder and lovelier creatures than I had ever realized. I even set free the two I had in small wooden cages – a linnet and a chaffinch – and for a while thought no more of traps and snaring. I loafed about wondering if all that I had seen might not have been mere fancy.

'And then on the third evening, I was so ashamed of myself that I determined to go down to the edge of the woods again and keep watch. This time I made my way to the upper corner of the field by the larch plantation, all in its fresh young green. It was there, as I supposed, I had seen the fairy vanish. The pheasants were crowing in their coverts, and the last birds were at evensong. I crept in between some elder bushes, and having made myself comfortable took out a little red and brass pocket telescope which my father had given me. Through this I hoped to be able to see clearly everything that might happen near Old Joe. It would bring him as close as if I could touch him with my hand. But when I came to put the telescope to my eye I found that one of the lenses was broken.

'It was a little later in the evening than on my first visit, and though the skies were still burning, the sun had set. But my legs were all pins and needles, and my eyes nearly gone black with staring on and on, before I saw anything out of the common.

'And then, Letitia, all of a sudden I knew not only that the fairy was there again but also that again she was aware she was being watched. Yes, and though I had seen not the least stir or motion in Old Joe, she had already stolen out of her hiding-place and was steadily and *openly* gazing across the first faint green flush of the sprouting wheat in my direction. I held my breath and tried in vain to keep myself from shivering.

'For a moment or two she hesitated, then turned as before, and sped away, but now towards the very thorn tree from which I had first spied out on her. I was bitterly disappointed, *angry* and – well, I suppose it would be a queer boy who had nothing of the old hunter in him. It was clear she was pitting her wits against mine. And just as, though I was devoted to the wild birds, I would sometimes shake my fist at them and almost howl with rage when I saw one steal my bait without falling into the trap I had set, so I felt now.

'But I was stiff and aching, and it was too late to attempt to try and intercept her now. *You wait!* thought I to myself, next time we'll see who's craftiest. So I shut up my telescope, brushed the dead leaves from my clothes, stayed till life came back into my leg, and then rather sulkily went home.

'That night was still and warm though April was not over yet. And while I was undressing a full moon began to rise. In spite of the candlelight I could see it shining through my bedroom blind. I blew out my candle, drew up the blind and looked out of the window, and the world looked as if it were enchanted – like an old serpent that has sloughed its skin. It seemed the moon shed silence as well as light. And though I was there in my old friend Mrs Lumb's familiar house – wood and brick and stone – it was as if no human being had ever looked out of her window like this before. And – even better, Letitia. The same feeling came over me when I had first caught sight of that Old Joe there. Just as the fairy had been aware of me watching her in the fields, so I was sure now that she was concealing herself not very far from the house and – watching my window.'

'It *does* seem odd, Uncle Tim,' said Letitia. 'Isn't that *curious*! I know exactly what you mean. It's just as if there were things in the air, *telling* people, isn't it! And did – did you go out?'

'To tell you the truth, Letitia, no. I didn't. I didn't dare to, though it was not because I was afraid. No; I stood watching at the window until presently a bird began to sing, out of the warm hollow darkness away from the moon. It may have been a nightingale, as there was a hurst or thicket

of common land not far from the house which was the resort
of nightingales in the summer. Still, it was very early in
the year. The song I heard was fully as sweet and musical
as theirs, and yet it seemed less the song of a bird than –
well, than even the song of a nightingale seems. A strange
happiness and mournfulness came over me, listening to it.
And even when I got to bed it was a long time before the
echo of it had faded out in memory, and I fell asleep.

'Can it have been, do you think, that the fairy was beseeching me not to come to her haunts any more? I can't
tell. But in my stupidity I persisted in persecuting her, just
as I had persisted in persecuting the birds. I was too stupid,
you see, to realize that my company in her field might be as
disquieting to her as it would be for us if, when we had a few
nice solid friends to tea, *she* came too.'

'Oh, Uncle Tim, if only she would! Then we wouldn't ask
a single soul to tea for months and months and months.
Would we?'

'No,' said Mr Bolsover. 'But it's no good denying it, *she*
wouldn't. They don't. We ourselves may wish, even pine, to
see them; but I don't think, Letitia, they pine to see us. And
I am quite sure she didn't want a clod-hopping, bird-
trapping boy spying about in her field. Old Joe was not only
roof and house, but company enough; and her own solitude.

'None the less, my dear, I met her face to face. And this
is how it happened. It was the day before I had to go home
again, and two or three other visits to the field had been
entirely in vain. I could tell by now almost at a glance at
Old Joe whether she was here or not. Just as you could tell
at a glance at me if *I* were here or not. I don't mean merely
my body and bones – eyes, nose, boots and so on; but the
me which is really and truly – well, just me.'

'Yes,' said Letitia.

'Well, she never was. And this particular evening I was

in as black and sullen a temper as a small boy can be. I was
full of aches and pains owing no doubt to my being so stupid
as to lie on the ground under the bushes after rain. Night
after night too, I had lain awake for hours. It seemed that the
fairy had forsaken the field. It seemed that all my cunning
and curiosity and hope and longing had been in vain. I
scowled at Old Joe as if he were to blame. Just vanity and
stupidity.

'Besides, my old friend Mrs Lumb had discovered somehow that I was creeping late into the house while she was at
dinner; and though she never scolded me, it was quite easy
to know when she was displeased at anything. And she could
smile at you with her nice red apple-dumpling cheeks and
black eyes, and be pretty tart of tongue at the same time.'

'There's a mistress at school,' cried Letitia, 'called Miss
Jennings that's just like that; though she's not very fat.
At least, not yet. And then? ... You saw her, Uncle Tim?'

'Yes, I saw her – face to face. I was making my way back
through the copse at the upper corner of the field where two
hedges met at the end of a narrow green lane. And as I
came stumping along I suddenly went cold all over, and I
firmly believe my cap had pushed itself up a little on the
top of my head, owing to the hair underneath it trying to
stand on end.

'I can't even tell you what she was wearing, but as I
recall her at this moment it was as if she were veiled about
with a haze like that of a full moon – like bluebells at a little
distance in a dingle of a wood. That may or may not be, but
I quite clearly saw her face, for I was staring steadily into
her eyes. They too were blue, like the blue flames in a wood
fire, especially when there is salt in it, or the wood has come
from some old ship, with copper in it. Her hair was hanging
on either side her head in a long strand from brow to chin,
and down the narrow shoulder. All else in the world I had

completely forgotten. I was alone, an ugly small awkward human animal looking, as if into a dream, into those strange unearthly eyes.

'There was not the smallest movement between us; not the least stir in her face that she knew me or recognized me or reproached me or feared me. But as I looked – how can I possibly describe it? – there did come a faint far-away change in her eyes. It was as though while you might be looking out to sea some summer's evening from a high window or from the edge of a cliff, a flight of distant sea-birds should appear out of the blue and vanish into it again. We poor mortals can smile with our eyes only – and that's a much better smile than with the lips only. But not like that. This was *her* way of smiling at *me*. Just as the angels on the ladder might have had their way of smiling at Jacob – with his sleeping head on the stone. And I doubt if they smile often. It told me in my heart of hearts that she was not unfriendly to me; and yet that she was entreating me to come no more and trespass near her lair. What she was doing in this world, how much alone she was, and where and with whom she was when not in my parts, near Mrs Lumb's, I can't say. All she was *telling* me was that she meant me no harm but begged me not to spy on her or watch her any more. After all, what right had I to do so – quite apart from manners? And then she was gone.'

'Oh, *gone!*' said Letitia, and stooped her head suddenly.

'You see, it was easy to take hiding in the evening shadow of the woods, and the field hedges were dense. Yes, she was gone, my dear, and I have never seen her since, nor anything resembling her ... But there, as I have said already,' added old Mr Bolsover, 'you can't call *that* a story.' He was blinking at his small niece like an owl caught out in the morning sun. Letitia remained silent for a few moments.

'But I *do* call it a story, Uncle Tim,' she said at last. 'And oh, how I wish ... Still, it's no good saying that. But then what about Old Joe, that Old Joe *there*, Uncle Tim?'

'Ah, Old Joe! Him, the old rascal! The fact of the matter is I never forgot that evening. Years and years afterwards – and I must have been a young man by then – say twenty or so – I stayed a night or two with my old friend Mrs Lumb again. She, alas, was older too; and so no doubt was her cook. But that was the only difference. The first walk I took alone was to the field under the woods, and about the time of sunset. Would you believe it, there was Old Joe in his usual place, though the barley crop he was watching over that particular summer was now well above his knees. And whether it was because I myself was changed, or whether the fairy had long since forsaken her hiding-place, or whether really and truly he was merely her way of getting into and out of *our* world, who can say?

'However that may be, Old Joe looked' – Mr Bolsover lowered his voice – 'well precisely, Letitia, between you and me, as he looks now: a little vacant-like, empty, accustomed to being alone. He had brand-new clothes on then, too, standing up there in his barley, and an immeasurably old wide-brimmed hat, just the kind of hat that might once have belonged to old Mr Hiawatha Longfellow – the kind of hat, I mean, that nobody but a poet would wear, and not unless he had a long white beard to match. And what do you think I did?'

'You didn't go and *steal* him, Uncle Tim?' whispered Letitia.

'No, Letitia. What I can't help thinking was much worse, I went and bought him,' said Uncle Tim; 'though "bought" is not the word I should say out loud. I went straight off to the old farmer – old Farmer Jones – still as stout as he used to be, but with his whiskers all gone grey, and asked him how much he would take for his hodmadod in the barley field, just as a curiosity. I told him I had known Old Joe as a boy, that there was an old friendship between us. There sat the old farmer in his great wheel-back chair in his kitchen – as fat as a porpoise, with his large mulberry-red face and eyes like bits of agate. He sat there merely staring at me for a time, as if he thought I was a lunatic.

' "Well, that's a good 'un," he said at last. And what do you think he charged?'

Letitia pondered, her eyes fixed on the grass at her feet, though they were blinking so fast she couldn't have been thinking very clearly. 'I suppose,' she said, 'five pounds would be a good deal, wouldn't it, Uncle Tim? Even for Old Joe? Though of course,' she added, as if old Mr Bolsover had suddenly gone much further off, 'even then it would be *'strordinarily* cheap.'

'No. Guess again, my dear. Nothing like five pounds! Nothing like tuppence, even. "Give me a pipe of that plug baccy of yours," said the old farmer, "and he's yours for ever."'

'So mine he was. And I'm glad it wasn't money.'

'So am I,' said Letitia. 'Baccy doesn't hurt your feelings, Uncle Tim, I suppose; does it? And ... and you never saw the – the fairy again?'

'In a way of speaking,' old Mr Bolsover replied, 'I have never, Letitia, really *seen* anything else. It's a question of what one means exactly by "seeing", I suppose. Words are no use. It can't be done, can it?'

Letitia shook her head violently. 'No, Uncle Tim, it can't be done,' she said, and fell silent again.

The low wide-windowed house, with its jasmine and clematis, crouched in the light and heat of the sun, as if it had been listening all this while. Tiny butterflies, like pale scraps of the blue sky, were circling and flitting over the flowers. The bells from their belfry in the stone tower of the village church, muffled by the leafy woods between, sounded sweet and solemn in the summer air. It was so still the great world might have stopped spinning.

And there, half in shadow of his grey-green willows, black in his old clothes, shocking hat over one eyebrow and one lank arm aloft, stood the scarecrow; and never stirred. Nor did he seem to be wishing for company. Hiding-place he may have been once (as might a bee long ago have taken possession of old Mr Bolsover's bonnet), but whatever visitor had come, had gone. Letitia turned her head at last to look up into the old man's face.

'What I believe myself, Uncle Tim,' she began again, in a voice so low it was almost as if she were talking to herself, 'what I believe myself, and I am sure you won't mind my saying so – I believe it was almost as if you must have fallen in love with that fairy. Was that it, Uncle Tim, do you think?'

'Ah!' replied old Mr Bolsover, and sat there blinking in the sunlight. Then, 'Goodness me!' he muttered almost as if to *him*self, 'I can smell that apple charlotte now, even above the pinks! ... I'll tell you what, Letitia. It's high time we stirred our stumps. We'll go over and ask Old Joe! ...'

The Three Sleeping Boys of Warwickshire

In a long, low-ceiled, white-washed room on the upper floor
of a red-brick building in Pleasant Street, Cheriton, ranged
there in their glazed cases, is a collection of shells, conchs,
seaweeds, sea-flowers, corals, fossils, goggling fish, stuffed
birds – sea and land – and 'mermaids'. Coffers, chests and
anchors, and old guns, and lumps of amber and ore and
quartz. All sorts of outlandish oddities, too, curiosities
and junk. And there for years and years – the narrow windows, with their carved brick fruits and flowers and old
leaden gutters, showering the day's light upon their still
retreat – there for years and years slumbered on in their
great glass case the Three Sleeping Boys of Warkwickshire.
The tale of them goes a long way back. But so, too, do most
tales, sad or merry, if only you will follow them up.

About the year 1600, when Queen Elizabeth was sixty-
seven, and William Shakespeare was writing his play called
Julius Caesar, there died, twenty-four miles from Stratford-
on-Avon, a rich miller – John James Nollykins by name.
His was the handsomest mill in Warwickshire. But none of
his neighbours – or none at least of his poorer neighbours
– could abide the sight of him. He was a morose, close-
fisted, pitiless old man. He cheated his customers and had
no mercy for those whom he enticed into his clutches.

As he grew older he had grown ever more mean and
churlish until at last he had even begun to starve his own
horses. Though he died rich, then, few of his neighbours
mourned him much. And as soon as he was gone his money

began to go too. His three sons gobbled up what he had left behind him, as jackals gobble up a lion's left supper-bones. It slipped through their fingers like sand through a sieve. They drank, they diced, they gambled high and low. They danced, and capered and feasted in their finery; but they hardly knew offal from grain. Pretty soon they began to lose not only their father's trade but also all his savings. Their customers said that there was not only dust but stones in the flour; and tares too. It was fusty; it smelt mousy. What cared they? They took their terriers rat-hunting, but that was for the sake of the sport and not of the flour. Everything about the Mill got shabbier and shabbier – went to rack and ruin. The sails were patched. They clacked in the wind. The rain drove in. There were blossoming weeds in the millstream and dam where should have been nothing but crystal water. And when their poorer customers complained, they were greeted with drunken jeers and mockery.

At length, three or four years after the death of the miller's last poor half-starved mare, his sons were ruined. They would have been ruined just the same if, as one foul windy night they sat drinking and singing together in the Mill-house, the youngest of them had not knocked over the smoking lamp on the table, and so burned the Mill to the ground.

The eldest – with what he could pick up – went off to Sea, and to foreign parts, and died of yellow fever in Tobago. The second son was taken in by an uncle who was a goldsmith in London. But he was so stupid and indolent that he broke more than he mended; and at last, by swallowing an exquisitely carved peachstone from China, which had been brought back to Italy by Marco Polo, so enraged his master that he turned him off then and there. He went East and became a fishmonger in Ratcliff Highway, with a shop like a booth, and a long board in front of it. But he neglected this trade too, and at last became a man-of-all-work (or of none) at the old Globe Theatre in Southwark, where he saw Shakespeare dressed up as the ghost in *Hamlet* and was all but killed as if by accident while taking the part of the Second Murderer in *Macbeth*.

The youngest son, named Jeremy, married the rich widow of a saddler. She was the owner of a fine gabled house in the High Street of the flourishing town of Cheriton – some eight miles from Bishops Hitchingworth. He had all the few good looks of the family, but he was sly and crafty and hard. The first thing he did after he came home from his honeymoon was to paint in a long red nose to the portrait of the saddler. The next thing he did was to drown his wife's cat in the water-butt, because he said the starveling had stolen the cheese. The third thing he did was to burn her best Sunday bonnet, then her wig – to keep it company. How she could bear to go on living with him is a mystery. Nevertheless she did.

This Jeremy had three sons: Job, John and (another) Jeremy. But he did not flourish. Far from it. The family went 'down the ladder', rung by rung, until at long last it reached the bottom. Then it began to climb up again. But Jeremy's children did best. His youngest daughter married a well-to-do knacker, and *their* only son (yet another Jeremy), though he ran away from home because he hated water-gruel and suet pudding, went into business as assistant to the chief sweep in Cheriton. And, at last, having by his craft and cunning and early rising and hard-working inherited his master's business, he bought his great-uncle's fine gabled house, and became Master Chimney-Sweep and 'Sweep by Appointment', to the Mayor and Corporation and the Lords of three neighbouring Manors. And *he* never married at all. In spite of his hard childhood, in spite of the kindness shown him by his master, in spite of his good fortune with the three Lords of the Manor, he was a skinflint and a pick-halfpenny. He had an enormous brush over his door, a fine brass knocker, and – though considering all things, he had mighty few friends – he was the best, as well as the richest master-sweep in those parts.

But a good deal of his money and in later years most of his praise was due to his three small orphan 'prentices – Tom, Dick and Harry. In those days, hearths and fireplaces were as large as little rooms or chambers, or at any rate, as large as large cupboards or closets. They had wide warm comfortable ingle-nooks, and the chimneys were like deep wells running up to the roof, sometimes narrowing or angling off towards the top. And these chimneys were swept by hand.

Jeremy's 'prentices, then, had to climb up and up, from sooty brick to brick with a brush, and sweep till they were as black as blackest blackamoors, inside and out. Soot, soot, soot! Eyes, mouth, ears and nose. And now and then the bricks were scorching hot, and their hands got blistered. And now and then they were all but suffocated in the narrow juts. And once in a while were nearly wedged there, to dry like mummies in the dark. And sometimes, in the midst of the smother, a leg would slip, and down they would come tumbling like apples out of a tree or hailstones out of a cloud in April.

And Jeremy Nollykins, after tying up all the money they brought him in fat canvas and leather bags, served them out water-gruel for supper, and water-gruel for breakfast. For dinner on Tuesdays and Thursdays he gave them slabs of suet-pudding with lumps of suet in it like pale amber beads; what he called soup on Mondays and Wednesdays and Fridays; and a bit of catsmeat (bought cheap from his second cousin) on Sundays. But then you can't climb chimneys on *no* meat. On Saturdays they had piping-hot pease-pudding and pottage: because on Saturdays the Mayor's man might look in. You would hardly believe it: but in spite of such poor mean living, in spite of their burns and their bruises, and the soot in their eyes and lungs and in their close lint-coloured hair, these three small boys, Tom, Dick and Harry, managed to keep their spirits up. They even rubbed their cheeks rosy after the week's soot had been washed off under the pump on a Saturday night.

They were like Tom Dacre in the poem:

> ... There's little Tom Dacre, who cried when his head
> That curled like a lamb's back was shav'd: so I said
> 'Hush, Tom! never mind it for when your head's bare
> You know that the soot cannot spoil your white hair.'
>
> And so he was quiet, and that very night
> As Tom was a-sleeping, he had such a sight!
> That thousands of sleepers, Dick, Joe, Ned, and Jack
> Were all of them lock'd up in coffins of black ...

Still, they always said 'Mum' to the great ladies and 'Mistress' to the maids, and they kept their manners even when some crabbed old woman said they were owdacious, or imperent, or mischeevious. And sometimes a goodwife would give them a slice of bread pudding, or a mug of milk, or a baked potato, or perhaps a pocket-full of cookies or a slice of white bread (which did not remain white for very long). And now and then, even a sip of elderberry wine. After all, even half-starved sparrows sometimes find tit-bits, and it's not the hungry who enjoy their victuals least.

When they *could* scuttle away too, they would bolt off between their jobs to go paddling in the river, or bird-nesting in the woods, or climbing in an old stone quarry not very far from the town. It was lovely wooded country thereabouts – near ancient Cheriton.

Whether they played truant or not, Jeremy Nollykins the

Fourth – Old Noll, as his neighbours called him – used to beat them morning, noon and night. He believed in the rod. He spared nobody, neither man nor beast. Tom, Dick and Harry pretty well hated old Noll: and that's a bad thing enough. But, on the other hand, they were far too much alive and hearty and happy when they were not being beaten, and they were much too hungry even over their water-gruel to *think* or to brood over how much they hated him: which would have been very much worse.

In sober fact – with their bright glittering eyes and round cheeks and sharp white teeth, and in spite of their skinny ribs and blistered hands, they were a merry trio. As soon as ever their teeth stopped chattering with the cold, and their bodies stopped smarting from Old Noll's sauce, and their eyes from the soot, they were laughing and talking and whistling and champing, like grasshoppers in June or starlings in September. And though they sometimes quarrelled and fought together, bit and scratched too, never having been taught to fight fair, they were very good friends. Now and again too they shinned up a farmer's fruit-trees to have a taste of his green apples. Now and again they played tricks on old women. But what lively little chimney-sweeps wouldn't?

They were three young ragamuffins, as wild as colts, as nimble as kids, though a good deal blacker. And, however hard he tried, Old Noll never managed to break them in. Never. And at night they slept as calm and deep as cradled babies – all three of them laid in a row up in an attic under the roof on an immense wide palliasse or mattress of straw, with a straw bolster and a couple of pieces of old sacking each.

Now Old Noll, simply perhaps because he was – both by nature as well as by long practice – a mean old curmudgeonly miser, hated to see anybody merry, or happy, or

even fat. There were moments when he would have liked
to skin his three 'prentices alive. But then he wanted to
get out of them all the work he could. So he was compelled
to give them *that* much to eat. He had to keep them alive
– or the Mayor's man would ask why. Still, it enraged him
that he could not keep their natural spirits down; that however much he beat them they 'came up smiling'. It enraged
him to know in his heart (or whatever took its place) that
though – when they had nothing better to do, or were
smarting from his rod in pickle – they detested him, they
yet had never done him an ill-turn.

Every day he would gloat on them as they came clattering down to their water-gruel just as Giant Despair gloated
on Faithful and Christian in the dungeon. And sometimes
at night he would creep up to their bare draughty attic, and
the stars or the moon would show him the three of them
lying there fast asleep on their straw mattress, the sacking
kicked off, and on their faces a faint far-away smile as if
their dreams were as peaceful as the swans in the Islands of
the Blest. It enraged him. What could the little urchins be
dreaming about? What made ugly little blackamoors grin
even in their sleep? You can thwack a wake boy, but you
can't thwack a dreamer; not at least while he *is* dreaming.
So here Old Noll was helpless. He could only grind his teeth
at the sight of them. Poor Old Noll.

He ground his teeth more than ever when he first heard
the music in the night. And he might never have heard it at
all if hunger hadn't made him a mighty bad sleeper himself.
A few restless hours was the most he got, even in winter.
And if Tom, Dick and Harry had ever peeped in on *him*
as he lay in his four-post bed, they would have seen no
smile on his old sunken face, with its long nose and long
chin and straggling hair – but only a sort of horrifying
darkness. They might even have pitied him, stretched out

there, with nightmare twisting and contorting his sharp features, and his bony fingers continually on the twitch.

Because, then, Old Noll could not sleep of nights, he would sometimes let himself out of his silent house to walk the streets. And while so walking, he would look up at his neighbours' windows, glossily dark beneath the night-sky, and he would curse them for being more comfortable than he. It was as if instead of marrow he had malice in his bones, and there is no fattening on that.

Now one night, for the first time in his life, except when he broke his leg at eighteen, Old Noll had been unable to sleep at all. It was a clear mild night with no wind, and a fine mild scrap of a moon was in the West, and the stars shone bright. There was always a sweet balmy air in Cheriton, borne in from the meadows that then stretched in within a few furlongs of the town; and so silent was the hour you almost hear the rippling of the river among its osiers that far away.

And as Old Nollykins was sitting like a gaunt shadow all by himself on the first milestone that comes into the town – and he was too niggardly even to smoke a pipe of tobacco – a faint easy wind came drifting along the street. And then on the wind a fainter music – a music which at first scarcely seemed to be a music at all. None the less it continued on and on, and at last so rilled and trembled in the air that even Old Nollykins, who was now pretty hard of hearing, caught the strains and recognized the melody. It came steadily nearer, that music – a twangling and toot-ling and a horning, a breathing as of shawms, waxing mer-rier and merrier in the quick mild night October air:

> Girls and boys, come out to play!
> The moon doth shine as bright as day;
> Leave your supper, and leave your sleep,
> And come with your playfellows into the street! ...

The Three Sleeping Boys of Warwickshire

Girls and boys come out to play: on and on and on, now
faint now shrill, now in a sudden rallying burst of sound
as if it came from out of the skies. Not that the moon just
then was shining as bright as day. It was but barely in its
first quarter. It resembled a bent bit of intensely shining
copper down low among the stars : or a gold basin, of
which little more than the edge showed, resting a-tilt. But
little moon or none, the shapes that were now hastening
along the street, running and hopping and skipping and
skirring and dancing, had heard the summons, had obeyed
the call. From by-lane and alley, court, porch and house-
door the children of Cheriton had come pouring out like
water-streams in spring-time. Running, skipping, hopping,
dancing, they kept time to the tune. Old Noll fairly gasped
with astonishment as he watched them. What a dreadful
tale to tell – and all the comfortable and respectable folks
of Cheriton fast asleep in their beds! To think such in-
nocents could be such wicked deceivers! To think that
gluttonous and grubby errand and shop and boot-and-shoe
and pot boys could look so clean and nimble and happy
and free. He shivered; partly because of his age and the
night air, and part with rage.

But real enough though these young skip-by-nights appeared to be, there were three queer things about them. First,
there was not the faintest sound of doors opening or shutting, or casement windows being thrust open with a squeal
of the iron rod. Next, there was not the faintest rumour of
footsteps even, though at least half the children of Cheriton
were now bounding along the street, like autumn leaves in
the wind, and all with their faces towards the East and the
water-meadows. And last, though Noll could see the very
eyes in their faces in the faint luminousness of starshine
and a little moon, not a single one of that mad young company turned head to look at him, or showed the least sign

117

of knowing that he was there. Clockwork images of wood or wax could not have ignored him more completely.

Old Noll, after feeling at first startled, flabbergasted, a little frightened even, was now in a fury. His few old teeth began to grind together as lustily as had the millstones of

Jeremy the First when he was rich and prosperous. Nor was his rage diminished when, lo and behold, even as he turned his head, out of his own narrow porch with its three rounded steps and fluted shell of wood above it, came leaping along who but his own three half-starved 'prentices, Tom, Dick and Harry – now seemingly nine-year-olds as plump and comely to see as if they had been fed on the fat of the land, as if they had never never in the whole of their lives so much as tasted rod-sauce. Their mouths were opening and shutting, too, as if they were whooping calls one to the other

118

and to their other street-mates, though no sound came from them. They snapped their fingers in the air. They came cavorting and skirling along in their naked feet to the strains of the music as if bruised elbows, scorched shins, cramped muscles and iron-bound clogs had never once pestered their young souls. Yet not a sound, not a whisper, not a footfall could the deaf old man hear – nothing but that sweet, shrill and infuriating music.

In a few minutes the streets were empty, a thin fleece of cloud had drawn across the moon, and only one small straggler was still in sight, a grandson of the Mayor. He was last merely because he was least, and had nobody to take care of him. And Old Noll, having watched this last night-truant out of sight, staring at him with eyes like marbles beneath his bony brows, hobbled back across the street to his own house, and after pausing a while at the nearest doorpost to gnaw his beard and think what next was to be done, climbed his three flights of shallow oak stairs until he came to the uppermost landing under the roof. There at last with infinite caution he lifted the pin of the door of the attic and peered in on what he supposed would be an empty bed. Empty! Not a bit of it! Lying there asleep, in the dim starlight of the dusty dormer window, he could see as plain as can be the motionless shapes of his three 'prentices, breathing on so calmly in midnight's deepmost slumber that he even ventured to fetch in a tallow candle in a pewter stick in order that he might examine them more closely.

In its smoky beams he searched the three young slumbering faces. They showed no sign that the old skinflint was stooping as close over them as a bird-snarer over his nets. There were smears of soot even on their eye-lids and the fine dust of it lay thick on the flaxen lambs'-wool of their close-shorn heads. They were smiling away, gently and distantly as if they were sitting in their dreams in some wonderful orchard, supping up strawberries and cream; as though the spirits within them were untellably happy though their bodies were as fast asleep as humming-tops or honey-bees in winter.

Stair by stair Old Nollykins crept down again, blew out his candle, and sat down on his bed to think. He was a cunning old miser, which is as far away from being generous and wise as the full moon is from a farthing dip. His fingers had itched to wake his three sleeping chimney-boys with a smart taste of his rod, just to 'larn them a lesson'. He hated to think of the quiet happy smile resting upon their faces while the shadow-shapes or ghosts of them were out and away, pranking and gallivanting in the green water-meadows beyond the town. How was he to know that his dimming eyes had not deluded him? Supposing he went off to the Mayor himself in the morning and told his midnight tale, who would believe it? High and low, everybody hated him, and as like as not they would shut him up in the town jail for a madman, or burn his house about his ears supposing him to be a wizard. 'No, no, no!' he muttered to himself. 'We must watch and wait, friend Jeremy, and see what we *shall* see.'

Next morning his three 'prentices, Tom, Dick and Harry, were up and about as sprightly as ever, a full hour before daybreak. You might have supposed from their shining eyes and apple cheeks that they had just come back from a long holiday on the blissful plains of paradise. Away they tumbled – merry as frogs – to work, with their brushes and bags, still munching away at their gritty oat-cakes – three parts bran to one of meal.

So intent had Old Noll been on watching from his chimney-corner what he could see in their faces at break-fast, and on trying to overhear what they were whispering to each other, that he forgot to give them their usual morning dose of stick. But not a word had been uttered about the music or the dancing or the merry-making at the water-meadows. They just chattered their usual scatter-brained gibberish to one another – except when they saw that the old creature was watching them; and he was speedily convinced that whatever adventures their dream-shapes may have had in the night-hours, these had left no impression on their waking minds.

Poor Old Noll. An echo of that music and the sight he had seen kept him awake for many a night after, and his body was already shrunken by age and by his miserly habits to nothing much more substantial than a bag of animated bones. And yet all his watching was in vain. So weary and hungry for sleep did he become, that when at last the hunter's moon shone at its brightest and roundest over the roofs of Cheriton, he nodded off in his chair. He was roused a few hours afterwards by a faint glow in his room that was certainly not moonlight, for it came from out of the black dingy staircase passage. Instantly he was wide awake – but too late. For, even as he peeped through the door-crack, there flitted past three small 'prentices – just the ghosts or the spirits or the dream-shapes of them – faring happily away. They passed him softer than a breeze through a willow tree and were out of sight down the staircase before he could stir.

The morning after the morning after that, when Tom, Dick and Harry woke up at dawn on their mattress, there was a wonderful rare smell in the air. They sniffed it greedily as they looked at one another in the creeping light of daybreak. And sure enough, as soon as they were in their ragged jackets and had got down to their breakfast, the old woman who came to the house every morning to do an hour or two's charing for Old Nollykins, came wadd-

ling up to the kitchen table with a frying-pan of bacon
frizzling in its fat.

'There, me boys,' said Old Noll, rubbing his hands together with a cringing smile, 'there's a rasher of bacon for
ye all, and sop in the pan to keep the cold out, after that
long night-run in the moonlight.'

He creaked up his eyes at them finger on nose; but all
three of them, perched up there on their wooden stools
the other side of the table, only paused an instant in the
first polishing up of their plates with a crust of bread to
stare at him with such an innocent astonishment on their
young faces that he was perfectly sure they had no notion
of what he meant.

'Aha,' says he, 'do ye never dream, me boys, tucked up
snug under the roof in that comfortable bed of yours?
D'ye never dream? – never hear a bit of a tune calling, or
maybe see what's called a nightmare? Lordee, when I was
young there never went a night but had summat of a dream
to it.'

'Dream!' said they, and looked at one another with
their mouths half open. 'Why, if you ax me, Master,' says
Tom, 'I dreamed last night it was all bright moonshine, and
me sitting at supper with the gentry.'

'And I,' says Dick, 'I dreamed I was dancing under trees
and bushes all covered over with flowers. And I could hear
'em playing on harps and whistles.'

'And me,' says Harry, 'I dreamed I was by a river, and
a leddy came out by a green place near the water and took
hold of my hand. I suppose, Master, it must have been
my mammie, though I never seed her as I knows on.'

At all this the cringing smile on Old Nollykins' face set
like grease in a dish, because of the rage in his mind underneath. And he leaped up from where he sat beside the
skinny little fire in the immense kitchen hearth. ' "Gentry"!

"Harps"! "Mammie"!' he shouted, 'you brazen, ungrateful, greedy little deevils. Be off with ye, or ye shall have such a taste of the stick as will put ye to sleep for good and all.'

And almost before they had time to snatch up their bags and their besoms, he had chased them out of the house. So there in the little alley beside the garden, sheltering as close to its wall as they could from the cold rain that was falling, they must needs stand chattering together like drenched jackdaws, waiting for the angry old man to come out and send them about the business of the day.

But Old Nollykins' dish of bacon fat had not been altogether wasted. He knew now that the young rapscallions only *dreamed* their nocturnal adventures, and were not in the least aware that they themselves in actual shadow-shape went off by night to the trysting-place of all Cheriton's children to dance and feast and find delight. But he continued to keep watch, and would again and again spy in on his three 'prentices lying asleep together on their mattress up in the attic, in the hope of catching them in the act of stealing out. But although at times he discerned the same gentle smile upon their faces, shining none the less serenely for the white gutter-marks of tears on their sooty cheeks, for weeks together he failed to catch any repetition of the strains of the strange music or the faintest whisper of their dream-shapes coming and going on the wooden stairs.

Nevertheless, the more he brooded on what he had seen, the more he hated the three urchins, and the more bitterly he resented their merry ways. The one thing he could not decide in his mind was whether when next, if ever, he caught them at their midnight tricks, he should at once set about their slumbering bodies with his stick or should wait until their dream-wraiths were safely away and then try to prevent them from coming back. Then indeed they might be at his mercy.

Now there was an old crone in Cheriton who was reputed to be a witch. She lived in a stone hovel at the far end of a crooked alley that ran beside the very walls of Old Nollykins' fine gabled house. And Old Nollykins, almost worn to a shadow, knocked one dark evening at her door. She might have been the old man's grandmother as she sat there, hunched up in her corner beside the great iron pot simmering over the fire. He mumbled out his story about his three 'thieving, godless little brats', and then sat haggling over the price he should pay for her counsel. And even then he hoped to cheat her. At last he put his crown in her shrunken paw.

Waken a sleeper, she told him, before his dream-shape can get back into his mortal frame, it's as like as not to be sudden death. But keep the wandering dream-shape out *without* rousing his sleeping body, then he may for ever more be your slave, and will never grow any older. And what may keep a human's dream-shape out – or animal's either – she said, is a love-knot of iron the wrong way up or a rusty horseshoe upside down, or a twisted wreath of elder and ash fastened up with an iron nail over the keyhole – and every window shut. Brick walls and stone and wood are nothing to such wanderers. But they can't abide iron. And what she said was partly true and partly false; and it was in part false because the foolish old man had refused to pay the crone her full price.

He knew well, and so did she, that there was only a wooden latch to his door, because he had been too much of a skinflint to pay for one of the new iron locks to be fixed on. He had no fear of thieves, because he had so hidden his money that no thief on earth would be able to find it, not if he searched for a week. So he asked the old woman again, to make doubly sure, how long a natural human creature would live and work if his dream-shape never came back. 'Why, that,' she cheepered, leering up at him out of her wizened old face, 'that depends how young they be; what's the blood, and what's the heart. Take 'em in the first bloom,' she said, 'and so they keeps.' She had long ago seen what the old man was after, and had no more love for him than for his three noisy whooping chimney-sweeps.

Very unwillingly he dropped another piece of money into her skinny palm and went back to his house, not knowing that the old woman, to avenge herself on his skinflint ways, had told him only half the story. That evening his three 'prentices had a rare game of hide-and-seek together in the many-roomed old rat-holed house; for their master had gone out. The moment they heard his shuffling footsteps in the porch they scampered off to bed, and were to all appearance fast asleep before he could look in on them.

He had brought back with him a bundle of switches of elder and ash, a tenpenny nail, a great key, and a cracked horseshoe. And, strange to say, the iron key which he had bought from a dealer in broken metal had once been the key of the Mill of rich old Jeremy the First at Stratford-on-Avon! He pondered half that night on what the old woman had said, and 'surely', said he to himself, 'their blood's fresh enough, my old stick keeps them out of mischief, and what is better for a green young body than a long day's work and not too much to eat, and an airy lodging for the night?' The cunning old creature supposed indeed, that if only by this sorcery and hugger-mugger he could keep their wandering dream-shapes from their bodies for good and all, his three young 'prentices would never age, never weary, but stay lusty and nimble perhaps for a century. Ay, he would use them as long as he wanted them, and sell them before he died. *He'd* teach them to play truant at night, when honest folk were snoring in their beds. For the first time for weeks his mingy supper off a crust and a ham-bone and a mug of water had tasted like manna come down from the skies.

The very next day chanced to be St Nicholas's Day. And those were the times of old English winters. Already a fine scattering of snow was on the ground, like tiny white lumps of sago, and the rivers and ponds were frozen hard as iron. Better still, there was all but a fine full moon that night, and the puddles in Cheriton High Street shone like Chinese crystal in the beams slanting down on them from between the eaves of the houses.

For five long hours of dark, after his seven o'clock supper, Old Nollykins managed to keep himself awake. Then, a little before midnight, having assured himself that his three 'prentices were sound asleep in their bed, he groped downstairs again, gently lifted the latch and looked out. There was never such a shining scene before. The snow on the roofs and gables and carved stonework of the houses gleamed white and smooth as the finest millers' meal. There was not a soul, not even a cat, to be seen in the long stretch of the lampless street. And the stars in the grey-blue sky gleamed like dewdrops on a thorn.

Sure enough, as soon as ever the last stroke of midnight had sounded from St Andrew's tower, there came faintly wreathing its way out of the distance the same shrill penetrating strains of the ancient tune. Lord bless me, if Old Nollykins had had but one sole drop of the blood of his own youth left in his veins he could not have resisted dancing his old bones out of his body down his steps and into the crudded High Street at the sound of it:

Girls and boys, come out to play!
The moon doth shine as bright as day;
Leave your supper, and leave your sleep,
And come with your playfellows into the street! ...

But, instead, he shuffled like a rat hastily back into the
house again; pushed himself in close under the staircase;
and waited – leaving the door ajar.

Ho, ho, what's that? Faint flitting lights were now showing in the street, and a sound as of little unhuman cries,
and in a minute or two the music loudened so that an old
glass case on a table near by containing the model of a brig
which had belonged to Old Nollykins' wicked grandfather
who had died in Tobago, fairly rang to the marvellous stirrings on the air. And down helter-skelter from their bed,
just as they had slipped in under its sacking – in their
breeches and rags of day-shirts, barefoot, came whiffling
from stair to stair the ghosts of his three small 'prentices.
Old Nollykins hardly had time enough to see the wonderful smile on them, to catch the gleam of the grinning white
teeth shining beneath their parted lips, before they were
out and away.

Shivering all over, as if with palsy, the old man hastened
up the staircase, and in a minute or two the vacant house
resounded with the strokes of his hammer as he drove
in the ten-penny nail into the keyhole above the attic
door, and hung up key and horseshoe by their strings. This
done, he lowered his hammer and listened. Not the faintest
whisper, sigh or squeak came from within. But in dread
of what he might see he dared not open the door.

Instead, curiosity overcame him. Wrapping a cloak round
his skinny shoulders he hurried out into the street. Sure
enough, here, there, everywhere in the snow and hoarfrost
were footprints – traces at any rate distinct enough for *his*
envious eyes, though they were hardly more than those of

127

the skirring of a hungry bird's wing on the surface of the snow. And fondly supposing in his simplicity that he had now safely cheated his 'prentices, that for ever more their poor young empty bodies would be at his beck and call, Old Noll determined to follow away out of the town and into the water-meadows the dream shapes of the children now all of them out of sight. On and on he went till his breath was whistling in his lungs and he could scarcely drag one foot after the other.

And he came at last to where, in a loop of the Itchen, its waters shining like glass in the moon, there was a circle of pollard and stunted willows. And there, in the lush and frosty grasses was a wonderful company assembled, and unearthly music ascending, it seemed, from out of the bowels of a mound near by, called Caesar's Camp. And he heard a multitude of voices and singing from within. And all about the meadow wandered in joy the sleep-shapes not only of the children from Cheriton, but from the farms and cottages and gipsy camps for miles around. Sheep were there too, their yellow eyes gleaming in the moon as he trod past them. But none paid heed to the children or to the 'strangers' who had called them out of their dreams.

Strange indeed were these strangers: of middle height, with garments like spider-web, their straight hair of the colour of straw falling gently on either side their narrow cheeks, so that it looked at first glimpse as if they were grey-beards. And as they trod on their narrow feet, the frozen grasses scarcely stirring beneath them, they turned their faces from side to side, looking at the children. And then a fairness that knows no change showed in their features, and their eyes were a faint flame like that of sea-water on nights of thunder when the tide gently lays its incoming ripples on some wide flat sandy strand of the sea.

And at sight of them Old Nollykins began to be mortally

afraid. Not a sign was there of Tom, Dick or Harry. They must have gone into the sonorous mound – maybe were feasting there, if dream-shapes feast. The twangling and trumpeting and incessant music made his head spin round. He peered about for a hiding-place, and at length made his way to one of the old gnarled willows beside the icy stream. There he might have remained safe and sound till morning, if the frost, as he dragged himself up a little way into the lower branches of the tree, had not risen into his nostrils and made him sneeze. There indeed he might have remained safe and sound if he had *merely* sneezed, for an old man's sneeze is not much unlike an old sheep's wheezy winter cough. But such was this poor old man's alarm and terror at the company he had stumbled into that he cried, 'God bless us!' after his sneeze – just as his mother had taught him to do.

That was the end of wicked old Nollykins; as it was his first step on the long road of repentance. For the next thing he remembered was opening his eyes in the half-light of stealing dawn and finding himself perched up in the boughs of a leafless willow-tree, a thin mist swathing the low-lying water-meadows, the sheep gently browsing in the grasses, leaving green marks in the frosty grass as they munched onwards. And such an ache and ague was in Old Noll's bones as he had never, since he was swaddled, felt before. It was as if every frosty switch of every un-polled willow in that gaunt fairy circle by the Itchen had been belabouring him of its own free will the whole night long. His heart and courage were gone. Sighing and groaning, he lowered himself into the meadow, and by the help of a fallen branch for staff made his way at last back into the town.

It was early yet even for the milkmaids, though cocks were crowing from their frosty perches, and the red of the coming sun inflamed the eastern skies. He groped into his house and shut the door. With many rests on the way from stair to stair he hoisted himself up, though every movement seemed to wrench him joint from joint, until at last he reached the attic door. He pressed his long ear against the panel and listened a moment. Not a sound. Then stealthily pushing it open inch by inch, he thrust forward his shuddering head and looked in.

The ruddy light in the East was steadily increasing, and had even pierced through the grimy panes of the dormer window as though to light up the slumbers of his small chimney-sweeps. It was a Sunday morning and their fair skins and lamb's-wool heads showed no trace of the week's soot. But while at other times on spying in at them it looked to Old Nollykins as if their smiling faces were made of wax, now they might be of alabaster. For each one of the three – Tom, Dick, and Harry – was lying on his back, their chapped, soot-roughened hands with the torn and broken nails resting on either side of their bodies. No smile now touched their features, but only a solemn quietude as of images eternally at rest. And such was the aspect of the three children that even Old Nollykins dared not attempt to waken them because he knew in his heart that no earthly rod would ever now bestir them out of this sound slumber. Not at least until their spirits had won home again. And the soured old crone was not likely to aid him in that.

He cursed the old woman, battering on her crazy door, but she paid him no heed. And at last, when the Cheriton Church bells began ringing the people to morning service, there was nothing for it, if there was any hope of saving his neck, but to go off to the Mayor's man, dragging himself along the street on a couple of sticks, to tell him that his 'prentices were dead.

Dead they were not, however. The Mayor's man fetched

a doctor, and the doctor, after putting a sort of wooden trumpet to their chests, asseverated that there was a stirring under the cage of their ribs. They were fallen into a trance, he said. What is called a *catalepsy*. It was a dreamlike seizure that would presently pass away. But though the old midwife the doctor called in heated up salt, for salt-bags, and hour by hour put a hot brick fresh from the fire to each 'prentice's stone-cold feet, by not a flutter of an eyelid nor the faintest of sighs did any one of the three prove that he was alive or could heed.

There they lay, on their straw pallet, motionless as mummies, still and serene, lovely as any mother might wish, with their solemn Sunday-morning soap-polished cheeks and noses and foreheads and chins, and as irresponsive as cherubs made of stone.

And the Mayor of the Town, after listening to all Old Nollykins could say, fined him Five Bags of Guineas for allowing his three 'prentices to fall into a catalepsy for want of decent food and nourishment. And with the pain of his joints and the anguish of having strangers tramping all over his house, and of pleading with the Mayor, and of seeing his money fetched out from its hiding-places and counted out on the table, the miserable old man was so much dazed and confused that he never thought to take down the wreath of ash and elder and the horseshoe and the key. That is why, when a week or two had gone by and no sign had shown how long this trance would continue, the Mayor and Councillors decided that as Tom, Dick and Harry could be of no further use to the town as chimney-sweeps, they might perhaps earn an honest penny for it as the 'Marvels of the Age'.

So the Mayor's man with a flowing white muslin band round his black hat, and his two mutes – carrying bouquets of lilies in their hands – came with his handcart and fetched the three bodies away. A roomy glass case had been made for them of solid Warwickshire oak, with a fine chased lock and key. And by the time the Waits had begun to sing their Christmas carols in the snow, the three children had been installed in this case on the upper floor of the Cheriton Museum, and there lay slumbering on and on, quiet as Snow-White in the dwarfs' coffin, the gentle daylight falling fairly on their quiet faces – though during the long summer days a dark blind was customarily drawn over the glass whenever the sun shone in too fiercely at the window.

News of this wonder spread fast, and by the following Spring visitors from all over the world – even from cities as remote as Guanojuato and Seringapatam – came flocking into Warwickshire merely to gaze a while at the sleeping Chimney-Sweeps: at 6d. a time. After which a fair proportion of them went on to Stratford to view the church where lie William Shakespeare's honoured bones. Indeed Mrs Giles, the old woman who set up an apple and ginger-bread stall beside the Museum, in a few years made so much money out of her wares that she was able to bring up her nine orphaned grandchildren all but in comfort, and to retire at last at the age of sixty to a four-roomed cottage not a hundred yards from that of Ann Hathaway's herself.

In course of time the Lord-Lieutenant and the Sheriffs and the Justices of the Peace and the Bishop and the mayors of the neighbouring towns, jealous no doubt of this fame and miracle in their midst, did their utmost to persuade and compel the Mayor and Corporation of Cheriton to remove the Boys to the county-town – the Earl himself promising to lodge them in an old house not a stone's-throw distant from the lovely shrine of his ancestors, Beauchamp Chapel. But all in vain. The people of Cheriton held tight to their rights: and the Lord Chief Justice after soberly hearing both sides at full length wagged his wigged head in their favour.

For fifty-three years the Sleeping Boys slept on. During this period the Town Council had received One Hundred and Twenty Three Thousand, Five Hundred and Fifty-Five sixpence in fees alone (i.e. £3,088 17s. 6d.). And nearly every penny of this vast sum was almost clear profit. They spent it wisely too – widened their narrow chimneys, planted lime-trees in the High Street and ash and willow beside the river, built a fountain and a large stone dovecot, and set apart a wooded meadowland with every comfort wild creatures can hope to have bestowed on them by their taskmaster, Man.

Then, one fine day, the curator – the caretaker – of the Museum, who for forty years had never once missed dusting the 'prentices' glass case first thing in the morning, fell ill and had to take to his bed. And his niece, a pretty young thing, nimble and high-spirited, came as his deputy for a while, looked after the Museum, sold the tickets, and kept an eye on the visitors in his stead. She was only seventeen; and was the very first person who had ever been heard to sing in the Museum – though of course it was only singing with her lips all but closed, and never during show-hours.

And it was Summer-time, or rather the very first of May. And as each morning she opened the great door of the Museum and ascended the wide carved staircase and drew up the blinds of the tall windows on the upper floor, and then turned – as she always turned – to gaze at the Three Sleepers (and not even a brass farthing to pay), she would utter a deep sigh as if out of the midst of a happy dream.

'You lovely things!' she would whisper to herself. 'You lovely, lovely things!' She had a motherly heart; and the wisps of her hair were as transparent as the E-string of a fiddle in the morning light. And the glance of her blue eyes rested on the glass case with such compassion and tenderness that if mere looking could have awakened the children they would have been dancing an Irish jig with her every blessed morning.

Being young, too, she was inclined to be careless, and had even at times broken off a tiny horn of coral, or a half-hidden scale from the mermaid's tail for a souvenir of Cheriton to any young stranger that particularly took her fancy. Moreover, she had never been told anything about the magicry of keys or horseshoes or iron or ash or elder, having been brought up at a School where wizardry and witchcraft were never so much as mentioned during school hours. How could she realize then that the little key of the glass case and the great key of the Museum door (which, after opening both, she had dropped out of her pocket by accident plump into the garden well) could keep anybody or anything out, or in, even when the doors were wide open? Or that water can wash even witchcraft away?

That very morning there had been such a pomp of sunshine in the sky, and the thrushes were singing so shrilly in the new-leafed lime trees as she came along to her work, that she could resist her pity and yearning no longer. Having drawn up the blinds on the upper floor, in the silence she gently raised the three glass lids of the great glass case and propped them back fully open. And one by one – after first listening at their lips as stealthily as if in hope of hearing what their small talk might be in their dreams – she kissed the slumbering creatures on their stone-cold mouths. And as she kissed Harry she fancied she heard a step upon the stair. And she ran out at once to see.

No one. Instead, as she stood on the wide staircase listening, her young face tilted and intent, there came a waft up it as of spiced breezes from the open spaces of Damascus. Not a sound, no more than a breath, faint and yet almost unendurably sweet of Spring – straight across from the bird-haunted, sheep-grazed meadows skirting the winding river: the perfume of a whisper. It was as if a distant memory had taken presence and swept in delight across her eyes. Then stillness again, broken by the sounding as of a voice smaller than the horn of a gnat. And then a terrible sharp crash of glass. And out pell-mell came rushing our three young friends, the chimney-sweeps, their dream-shapes home at last.

Now Old Nollykins by this time had long been laid in his grave. So even if anyone had been able to catch them, Tom, Dick, and Harry would have swept no more chimneys for him. Nor could even the new Mayor manage it. Nor the complete Town Council. Nor the Town Crier, though he cried twice a day to the end of the year: 'O-yess! O-yess!! O-yess!!! Lost, stolen, or strayed: Three World-Famous and Notorious Sleeping Boys of Warwickshire.' Nor even the Lord-Lieutenant. Nor even the mighty Earl.

As for the mound by the pollard willows – well, what clever Wide-awake would ever be able to give any news of that?

The Lovely Myfanwy

In an old castle under the forested mountains of the Welsh Marches there lived long ago Owen ap Gwythock, Lord of Eggleyseg. He was a short, burly, stooping man with thick black hair on head and face, large ears, and small restless eyes. And he lived in his great castle alone, except for one only daughter, the lovely Myfanwy.

Lovely indeed was she. Her hair, red as red gold, hung in plaits to her knees. When she laughed, it was like bells in a faraway steeple. When she sang, Echo forgot to reply. And her spirit would sit gently looking out of her blue eyes like cushats out of their nest in an ivy bush.

Myfanwy was happy, too – in most things. All that her father could give her for her ease and pleasure was hers – everything indeed but her freedom. She might sing, dance, think and say; eat, drink, and delight in whatsoever she wished or willed. Indeed her father loved her so dearly that he would sit for hours together merely watching her – as you may watch wind over wheat, reflections in water, or clouds in the heavens. So long as she was safely and solely his all was well.

But ever since Myfanwy had been a child, a miserable foreboding had haunted his mind. Supposing she should some day leave him? Supposing she were lost or decoyed away? Supposing she fell ill and died? What then? The dread of this haunted his mind day and night. His dark brows loured at the very thought of it. It made him morose and sullen; it tied up the tongue in his head.

For this sole reason he had expressly forbidden Myfanwy even to stray but a few paces beyond the precincts of his castle; with its battlemented towers, its galleries and corridors and multitudinous apartments, its high garden and courtyard, its alleys, fountains, fish-pools and orchards. He could trust nobody. He couldn't bear her out of his sight. He spied, he watched, he walked in his sleep, he listened and peeped; and all for fear of losing Myfanwy.

So although she might have for company the doves and swans and peacocks, the bees and butterflies, the swallows and swifts and jackdaws and the multitude of birds of every song and flight and feather that haunted the castle; humans, except her father, she had none. The birds and butterflies could fly away at will wherever their wings could carry them. Even the fishes in the fish-pools and in the fountains had their narrow alleys of marble and alabaster through which on nimble fin they could win back to the great river at last. Not so Myfanwy.

She was her father's unransomable prisoner; she was a bird in a cage. She might feast her longing eyes on the distant horizon beyond whose forests lay the sea, but knew she could not journey thither. While as for the neighbouring township, with its busy streets and marketplace – not more than seven country miles away – she had only dreamed of its marvels and dreamed in vain. A curious darkness at such times came into her eyes, and her spirit would look out of them not like a dove but as might a dumb nightingale out of its nest – a nightingale that has had its tongue cut out for a delicacy to feed some greedy prince.

How criss-cross a thing is the heart of man. Solely because this lord loved his daughter so dearly, if ever she so much as sighed for change or adventure, like stubborn beast of burden he would set his feet together and refuse to budge an inch. Beneath his heavy brows he would gaze at the brightness of her unringleted hair as if mere looking could keep that gold secure; as if earth were innocent of moth and rust and change and chance, and had never had course to dread and tremble at sound of the unrelenting footfall of Time.

All he could think of that would keep her his own was hers without the asking: delicate raiment and meats and strange fruits and far-fetched toys and devices and pastimes, and as many books as would serve a happy scholar a long life through. He never tired of telling her how much he loved and treasured her. But there is a hunger of the heart no *thing* in the world can ever satisfy. And Myfanwy listened, and sighed.

Besides which, Myfanwy grew up and grew older as a green-tressed willow grows from a sapling; and now that she had come to her eighteenth spring she was lovelier than words could tell. This only added yet another and sharper dread and foreboding to her father's mind. It sat like a skeleton at his table whenever he broke bread or sipped wine. Even the twittering of a happy swallow from distant Africa reminded him of it like a knell. It was this: that some day a lover, a suitor, would come and carry her off.

Why, merely to *see* her, even with her back turned – to catch a glimpse of her slim shoulders, of her head stooping over a rosebush would be enough. Let her but laugh – two notes – and you listened! Nobody – prince nor peasant, knight nor squire – brave, foolish, young or weary, would be able to resist her. Owen ap Gwythock knew it in his bones. But one look, and instantly the looker's heart would be stolen out of his body. He would fall in love with her – fall as deep and irrevocably as the dark sparkling foaming water crashing over into the gorge of Modwr-Eggleyseg, scarcely an arrow's flight beyond his walls.

And supposing any such suitor should *tell* Myfanwy that

he loved her, might she not – forgetting all his own care
and loving-kindness – be persuaded to flee away and leave
him to his solitude? Solitude – now that old age was close
upon him! At thought of this, for fear of it, he would sigh
and groan within: and he would bid the locksmiths double
their locks and bolts and bars; and he would sit for hours
watching the highroad that swept up past his walls, and
scowling at sight of every stranger who passed that way.

He even at last forbade Myfanwy to walk in the garden
except with an immense round mushroom hat on her head, a
hat so wide in the brim that it concealed from any trespasser
who might be spying over the wall even the glinting of her
hair – everything of her indeed except her two velvet shoes
beneath the hem of her dress as they stepped in turn –
and softly as moles – one after the other from blossoming
alley to alley and from lawn to lawn.

And because Myfanwy loved her father almost as dearly
as he loved her, she tried her utmost to be gay and happy
and not to fret or complain or grow pale and thin and pine.
But as a caged bird with a kind mistress may hop and
sing and flutter behind its bars as if it were felicity itself,
and yet be sickening at heart for the wild wood and its green
haunts, so it was with Myfanwy.

If only she might but just once venture into the town,
she would think to herself; but just to see the people in the
streets, and the pedlars in the market-place, and the cakes
and sweet-meats and honey-jars in the shops, and strangers
passing to and fro, and the sunshine in the high gables, and
the talking and the laughing and the bargaining and the
dancing – the horses, the travellers, the bells, the starshine.

Above all, it made her heart ache to think her father
should have so little faith in her duty and love for him that
he would not consent to let her wander even a snail's journey out of his sight. When, supper over, she leaned over

his great chair as he sat there in his crimson – his black hair dangling on his shoulders, his beard hunched up on his chest – to kiss him good night, this thought would be in her eyes even if not on the tip of her tongue. And at such times he himself – as if he knew in his heart what he would never dare to confess – invariably shut down his eyelids or looked the other way.

Now servants usually have long tongues, and gossip flits from place to place like seeds of thistledown. Simply because Myfanwy was never seen abroad, the fame of her beauty had long since spread through all the countryside. Minstrels sang of it, and had even carried their ballads to countries and kingdoms and principalities far beyond Wales.

Indeed, however secret and silent men may be concerning rare beauty and goodness, somehow news of it sows itself over the wide world. A saint may sit in his cave or his cell, scarcely ever seen by mortal eye, quiet as sunshine in a dingle of the woods or seabirds in the hollows of the Atlantic, doing his deeds of pity and loving-kindness, and praying his silent prayers. And he may live to be a withered-up, hollow-cheeked old man with a long white beard, and die, and his body be shut up in a tomb. But nevertheless, little by little, the fame of his charity, and of the miracles of his compassion will spread abroad, and at last you may even chance on his image in a shrine thousands of leagues distant from the hermitage where he lived and died, and centuries after he has gone on his way.

Like this it was with the loveliness and gentleness of Myfanwy. That is why, when the Lord of Eggleyseg himself rode through the streets of the neighbouring town, he perceived out of the corner of his eye strangers in outlandish disguise who he suspected at once must be princes and noblemen from foreign climes come thither even if merely to set eyes on his daughter. That is why the streets were so

full of music and singing that of a summer evening you could
scarcely hear the roar of its cataracts. That is why its towns-
folk were entertained with tumblers and acrobats and
fortune-tellers and soothsayers and tale-tellers almost the
whole year long. Ever and again, indeed, grandees visited
it *without* disguise. They lived for weeks there, with their
retinues of servants, their hawks and hounds and tasselled
horses in some one of its high ancient houses. And their
one sole hope and desire was to catch but a glimpse of the
far-famed Myfanwy.

But as they came, so they went away. However they might
plot and scheme to gain a footing in the castle – it was in
vain. The portcullis was always down; there were watchmen
perpetually on the look-out in its turrets; and the gates of
the garden were festooned with heavy chains. There was
not in its frowning ancient walls a single window less than
twenty feet above the ground that was not thickly, rustily,
and securely barred.

None the less, Myfanwy occasionally found herself in the
garden alone. Occasionally she stole out if but for one breath
of freedom, sweeter by far to those who pine for it than
that of pink, or mint, or jasmine, or honeysuckle. And one
such early evening in May, when her father – having nodded off to sleep, wearied out after so much watching and
listening and prying and peering – was snoring in an arbour
or summerhouse, she came to its western gates, and having
for a moment lifted the brim of her immense hat to look
at the sunset, she gazed wistfully a while through its bars out
into the green woods beyond.

The leafy boughs in the rosy light hung still as pictures
in deep water. The skies resembled a tent of silk, blue as
the sea. Deer were browsing over the dark turf; and a
wonderful charm and carolling of birds was rising out of
the glades and coverts of the woods.

But what Myfanwy had now fixed her dark eyes on was none of these, but the figure of a young man leaning there, erect but fast asleep, against the bole of a gigantic beech tree, not twenty paces distant from the gate at which she stood. He must, she fancied, have been keeping watch there for some little time. His eyelids were dark with watching; his face pale. Slim and gentle does were treading close beside him; the birds had clean forgotten his presence; and a squirrel was cracking the nut it held between its clawed forepaws not a yard above his head.

Myfanwy had never before set eyes on human stranger in this valley beyond the gates. Her father's serving men were ancients who had been in his service in the castle years before she was born. This young man looked, she imagined, like a woodman, or a forester, or a swine-herd. She had read of them in a hand-written book of fantastic tales which she had chanced on among her mother's belongings.

And as Myfanwy, finger on brim of her hat, stood intently gazing, a voice in her heart told her that whoever and whatever this stranger might be, he was someone she had been waiting for, and even dreaming about, ever since she was a child. All else vanished out of her mind and her memory. It was as if her eyes were intent on some such old story itself, and one well known to her. This unconscious stranger was that story. Yet he himself – stiff as a baulk of wood against the beech-trunk, as if indeed he had been nailed to its bark – slumbered on.

So he might have continued to do, now so blessedly asleep, until she had vanished as she had come. But at that moment the squirrel there, tail for parasol immediately above his head, having suddenly espied Myfanwy beyond the bars of the gate, in sheer astonishment let fall its nut, and the young man – as if at a tiny knock on the door of his mind – opened his eyes.

For Myfanwy it was like the opening of a door into a strange and wonderful house. Her heart all but ceased to beat. She went cold to her fingertips. And the stranger too continued to gaze at Myfanwy – as if out of a dream.

And if everything could be expressed in words, that this one quiet look between them told Myfanwy of things strange that yet seemed more familiar to her than the peebles on the path and the thorns on the rose-bushes and the notes of the birds in the air and the first few drops of dew that were falling in the evening air, then it would take a book ten times as long as this in which to print it.

But even as she gazed Myfanwy suddenly remembered her father. She sighed; her fingers let fall the wide brim of her hat; she turned away. And oddly enough, by reason of this immense ridiculous hat, her father who but a few moments before had awakened in his arbour and was now hastening along the path of the rosery in pursuit of her, caught not a single glimpse of the stranger under the beech-tree. Indeed, before the squirrel could scamper off into hiding, the young man had himself vanished round the trunk of the tree and out of sight like a serpent into the grass.

In nothing except in this, however, did he resemble a serpent. For that very evening at supper her father told Myfanwy that yet another letter had been delivered at the castle, from some accursed Nick Nobody, asking permission to lay before him his suit for her hand. His rage was beyond words. He spilt his wine and crumbled his bread – his face a storm of darkness; his eyes like smouldering coals.

Myfanwy sat pale and trembling. Hitherto, such epistles, though even from princes of renowned estate and of realms even of the Orient, had carried much less meaning to her heart than the cuckooing of a cuckoo, or the whispering of the wind. Indeed, the cuckoo of those Welsh mountains and the wind from over their seas were voices of a language which, though secret, was not one past the heart's understanding. Not so these pompous declarations. Myfanwy would laugh at them – as though at the clumsy gambollings of a bear. She would touch her father's hand, and smile into his face, to assure him they had no meaning, that she was still as safe as safe could be.

But *this* letter – not for a single moment had the face of the young stranger been out of her mind. Her one sole longing and despair was the wonder whether she would ever in this world look upon him again. She sat like stone.

'Ay, ay, my dear,' said her father at last, laying his thick, square hand on hers as she sat beside him in her high-backed velvet chair – 'ay, ay, my gentle one. It shows us yet again how full the world is of insolence and adventurers. This is a *cave*, a warning, an *alarum*, my dear – maledictions on his bones! We must be ten times more cautious; we must be wary; we must be lynx and fox and Argus – all eyes! And remember, my all, my precious one, remember this, that while I, your father, am alive, no harm, no ill can approach or touch you. Believe only in my love, beloved, and all is well with us.'

Her cold lips refused to speak. Myfanwy could find no words with which to answer him. With face averted she sat in a woeful daydream, clutching her father's thumb, and only vaguely listening to his transports of fury and affection, revenge and adoration. For her mind and heart now welled over with such a medley of thoughts and hopes and fears and sorrows that she could find no other way but this dumb clutch of expressing that she loved her father too.

At length, his rage not one whit abated, he rose from his chair, and having torn the insolent letter into thirty-two tiny pieces he flung them into the huge log fire burning in the stone chimney. 'Let me but lay a finger on the shameless popinjay,' he muttered to himself; 'I'll – I'll cut his tongue out!'

Now the first thing Myfanwy did when the chance offered was to hasten off towards the Western Gate if only to warn the stranger of her father's rage and menaces, and bid him go hide himself away and never, never, never come back again.

But when once more she approached its bars the deer were still grazing in the forest, the squirrel was nibbling another nut, the beech had unfolded yet a few more of its needle-pointed leaves into the calm evening light; but of the stranger – not a sign. Where he had stood was now only the assurance that he was indeed gone for ever. And Myfanwy turned from the quiet scene, from the forest, its sunlight faded, all its beauty made forlorn. Try as she might in the days that followed to keep her mind and her thoughts fixed on her needle and her silks, her lute and her psalter, she could see nothing else but that long look of his.

And now indeed she began to pine and languish in body, haunted by the constant fear that her stranger might have met with some disaster. And simply because her father loved her so jealously, he knew at once what worm was in her mind, and he never ceased to watch and spy upon her, and to follow her every movement.

Now Myfanwy's bed-chamber was in the southern tower of this lord's castle, beneath which a road from the town to the eastward wound round towards the forests and distant mountains. And it being set so high above the ground beneath, there was no need for bars to its windows. While then, from these window-slits Myfanwy could see little more than the tops of the wayfarers' heads on the turf below, they were wide and lofty enough to let the setting sun in its due hour pour in its beams upon her walls and pictures and cur-

tained Arabian bed. But the stone walls being so thick, in
order to see out of her chamber at all, she must needs lie
along a little on the cold inward sill, and peer out over the
wide verdant countryside as if through the port-hole of a
ship.

And one evening, as Myfanwy sat sewing a seam –
and singing the while a soft tune to herself, if only to keep
her thoughts from pining – she heard the murmur of many
voices. And, though at first she knew not why, her heart for
an instant or two stopped beating. Laying her slip of linen
down, she rose, stole over the mats on the flagstones, and
gently pushing her narrow shoulders onwards, peeped
out down at last through the window to look at the world
below. And this was what she saw. In an old velvet cloak,
his black hair dangling low upon his shoulders, there in the
evening light beneath her window was a juggler standing,
and in a circle round and about him was gathered a throng
of gaping country-folk and idlers and children, some of
whom must even have followed him out of the town. And
one and all they were lost in wonder at his grace and skill.

Myfanwy herself indeed could not have imagined such
things could be, and so engrossed did she become in
watching him that she did not catch the whisper of a
long-drawn secret sigh at her keyhole; nor did she hear her
father as he turned away on tip-toe to descend the staircase again into the room below.

Indeed one swift glance from Myfanwy's no longer sorrowful eyes had pierced the disguise – wig, cloak, hat, and
hose – of the juggler. And as she watched him she all but
laughed aloud. Who would have imagined that the young
stranger, whom she had seen for the first time leaning
dumb, blind and fast asleep against the trunk of a beech-
tree could be possessed of such courage and craft and cunning as this!

146

His head was at the moment surrounded by a halo of glittering steel – so fast the daggers with which he was juggling whisked on from hand to hand. And suddenly the throng around him broke into a roar, for in glancing up and aside he had missed a dagger. It was falling – falling: but no, in a flash he had twisted back the sole of his shoe, and the point had stuck quivering in his heel, while he continued to whirl its companions into the golden air.

In that instant, however, his upward glance had detected the one thing in the world he had come out in hope to see – Myfanwy. He flung his daggers aside and fetched out of his travelling box a netful of coloured balls. Holloing out a string of outlandish gibberish to the people, he straightaway began to juggle with these. Higher and higher the seven of them soared into the mellow air, but one of the colour of gold soared on ever higher and higher than any. So high, indeed, that at last the people could watch it no longer because of the dazzle of the setting sun in their eyes. Presently, indeed, it swooped so loftily into the air that Myfanwy need but thrust out her hand to catch it as it paused for a breath of an instant before falling, and hung within reach of her stone window-sill.

And even as she watched, enthralled, a whispering voice within her cried, 'Take it!' She breathed a deep breath, shut her eyes, paused, and the next instant she had stretched out her hand into the air. The ball was hers.

Once more she peeped down and over, and once more the juggler was at his tricks. This time with what appeared to be a medley of all kinds of varieties of fruits; pomegranates, quinces, citrons, lemons, oranges and nectarines, and soaring high above them, nothing more unusual than an English apple. Once again the whisperer in Myfanwy's mind cried, 'Take it!' And she put out her hand and took the apple too.

Yet again she peeped and peered over, and this time it seemed that the juggler was flinging serpents into the air, for they writhed and looped and coiled around him as they whirled whiffling on from hand to hand. There was a hissing, too, and the people drew back a little, and a few of the timider children ran off to the other side of the high-road. And now, yet again, one of the serpents was soaring higher and higher above the rest. And Myfanwy could see from her coign of vantage that it was no live serpent but a strand of silken rope. And yet again and for the third time the whisperer whispered, 'Take it!' And Myfanwy put out her hand and took that too.

And, it happening that a little cloud was straying across the sun at this moment, the throng below had actually seen the highestmost of the serpents thus mysteriously disappear and they cried out as if with one voice, 'Gone!' 'Vanished!' 'Vanished!' 'Gone!' 'Magician, magician!' And the coins that came dancing into the juggler's tambourine in the moments that followed were enough to make him for that one minute the richest man in the world.

And now the juggler was solemnly doffing his hat to the people. He gathered his cloak around him more closely, put away his daggers, his balls, his fruits, his serpents, and all that was his, into a long green narrow box. Then he hoisted its strap over his shoulder, and doffing his cap once more, he clasped his tambourine under his elbow and seizing his staff, turned straight from the castle tower towards the hazy sun-bathed mountains. And, it beginning to be towards nightfall, the throng of people soon dispersed and melted away; the maids and scullions, wooed out by this spectacle from the castle, returned to their work; and the children ran off home to tell their mothers of these marvels and to mimic the juggler's tricks as they gobbled up their supper-crusts and were packed off to bed.

In the stillness that followed after the jugglers's depar-ture, Myfanwy found herself kneeling in her chamber in the tranquil golden twilight beside a wooden chair, her hands folded in her lap and her dark eyes fixed in wonderment and anxiety on the ball, and the apple and the rope; while in another such narrow stone chamber only ten or twelve stone steps beneath, her father was crouching at his window shaken with fury, and seeing in his imagination these strange gifts from the air almost as clearly as Myfanwy could see them with her naked eye.

For though the sun had been as much a dazzle to himself as to the common people in the highway, he had kept them fastened on the juggler's trickeries none the less, and had counted every coloured ball and every fruit and every ser-pent as they rose and fell in their rhythmical maze-like net-work of circlings in the air. And when each marvellous piece of juggling in turn was over, he knew that in the first place a golden ball was missing, and that in the second place a fruit like an English apple was missing, and that in the third place a silken cord with a buckle-hook to it like the head of a serpent had been flung into the air but had never come down to earth again. And at the cries and the laughter and the applause of the roaring common people and children beneath his walls, tears of rage and despair had burst from his eyes. Myfanwy was deceiving him. His dreaded hour was come.

But there again he was wrong. The truth is, his eyes were so green with jealousy and his heart so black with rage that his wits had become almost useless. Not only his wits either, but his courtesy and his spirit; for the next moment he was actually creeping up again like a thief from stair to stair, and presently had fallen once more on to his knees outside his beloved Myfanwy's chamber door and had fixed on her one of those green dark eyes of his at its little gaping cut-out pin-hole. And there he saw a strange sight indeed.

The evening being now well advanced, and the light of the afterglow too feeble to make more than a glimmer through her narrow stone window-slits, Myfanwy had lit with her tinder box (for of all things she loved light) no less than seven wax candles on a seven-branched candlestick. This she had stood on a table beside a high narrow mirror. And at the moment when the Baron fixed his eye to the pin-hole, she was standing, a little astoop, the apple in her hand, looking first at it, and then into the glass at the bright-lit reflected picture of herself holding the apple in her hand.

So now there were two Myfanwys to be seen – herself and her image in the glass. And which was the lovelier not even the juggler could have declared. Crouching there at the door-crack, her father could all but catch the words she was softly repeating to herself as she gazed at the reflected apple: 'Shall I, shan't I? Shall I, shan't I?' And then suddenly – and he dared not stir or cry out – she had raised the fruit to her lips and had nibbled its rind.

What happened then he could not tell, for the secret and sovereign part of that was deep in Myfanwy herself. The sharp juice of the fruit seemed to dart about in her veins like flashing fishes in her father's crystal fountains and water-conduits. It was as if happiness had begun gently to fall out of the skies around her, like dazzling flakes of snow. They rested on her hair, on her shoulders, on her hands, all over her. And yet not snow, for there was no coldness, but a scent as it were of shadowed woods at noonday, or of a garden when a shower has fallen. Even her bright eyes grew brighter, a radiance lit her cheek; her lips parted in a smile.

And it is quite certain if Myfanwy had been the Princess of Anywhere-in-the-World-at-All, she would then and there – like Narcissus stooping over his lilied water-pool – have fallen head over ears in love with herself! 'Wonder of wonders!' cried she in the quiet; 'but if this is what a mere nibble of my brave juggler's apple can do, then it were wiser indeed to nibble no more.' So she laid the apple down.

The Baron gloated on through the pin-hole – watching her as she stood transfixed like some lovely flower growing in the inmost silent solitude of a forest and blossoming before his very eyes.

And then, as if at a sudden thought, Myfanwy turned and took up the golden ball, which – as she had suspected and now discovered – was no ball, but a small orb-shaped box of rare inlaid woods, covered with golden thread. At touch of the tiny spring that showed itself in the midst, its lid at once sprang open, and Myfanwy put in finger and thumb and drew out into the crystal light a silken veil – but of a gossamer silk so finely spun that when its exquisite meshes had wreathed themselves downward to the floor the veil looked to be nothing more than a silvery grey mist in the candlelight.

It filmed down from her fingers to the flagstones beneath, almost as light as the air in which it floated. Marvellous that what would easily cover her, head to heel, could have been packed into so close a room as that two-inch ball! She gazed in admiration of this exquisite handiwork. Then, with a flick of her thumb, she had cast its cloudlike folds over her shoulders.

And lo! – as the jealous lord gloated on – of a sudden there was nothing to be seen where Myfanwy had stood but seven candles burning in their stick, and seven more in the mirror. She had vanished.

She was not gone very far, however. For presently he

heard – as if out of nowhere – a low chuckling childlike peal of laughter which willy-nilly had broken from her lips at seeing that this Veil of Invisibility had blanked her very glass. She gazed steadily on into its clear vacancy, lost in wonder. Nothing at all of her whatsoever was now reflected there! – not the tip of her nose, not a thumb, not so much as a button or a silver tag. Myfanwy had vanished; and yet, as she well knew, here she truly was in her own body and no other, though tented in beneath the folds of the veil, as happy as flocks on April hills, or mermaids in the deep blue sea. It was a magic thing indeed, to be there and yet not there; to hear herself and yet remain transparent as water.

Motionless though she stood, her thoughts were at the same time flitting about like quick and nimble birds in her mind. This veil, too, was the gift of the juggler; her young sleeping stranger of the beech-tree in a strange disguise. And she could guess in her heart what use he intended her to make of it, even though at thought of it that heart misgave her. A moment after and as swiftly as she had gone, she had come back again – the veil in her fingers. Laughing softly to herself she folded and refolded it and replaced it in its narrow box. Then turning, she took up from the chair the silken cord, and as if in idle fancy twined it twice about her slender neck. And it seemed the cord took life into itself, for lo, showing there in the mirror, calm now as a statue of coloured ivory, stood Myfanwy; and couched over her left temple the swaying head of the Serpent of Wisdom, whispering in her ear.

Owen ap Gwythock could watch no more. Groping his way with trembling fingers through the thick gloom of the staircase he crept down to the Banqueting Hall where already his Chief Steward awaited his coming to announce that supper was prepared.

To think that his Lovely One, his pearl of price, his gentle innocent, *his* Myfanwy – the one thing on earth he treasured most, and renowned for her gentleness and beauty in all countries of the world – had even for an instant forgotten their loves, forgotten her service and duty, was in danger of leaving and forsaking him for ever! In his jealousy and despair tears rolled down his furrowed cheeks as he ground his teeth together, thinking of the crafty enemy that was decoying her away.

Worse still; he knew in his mind's mind that in certain things in this world even the most powerful are powerless. He knew that against true love all resistance, all craft, all cunning at last prove of no avail. But in this grief and despair the bitterest of all the thoughts that were now busy in his brain was the thought that Myfanwy should be cheating and deceiving him, want only beguiling him; keeping things secret that should at once be told.

A dark and dismal mind was his indeed. To distrust one so lovely! – *that* might be forgiven him. But to creep about in pursuit of her like a weasel; to spy on her like a spy; to believe her guilty before she could prove her innocence! Could *that* be forgiven? And even at this very moment the avenger was at his heels.

For here was Myfanwy herself. Lovely as a convolvulus wreathing a withered stake, she was looking in at him from the doorpost, searching his face. For an instant she shut her eyes as if to breathe a prayer, then she advanced into the room, and, with her own hand, laid before him on the oak table beside his silver platter, first the nibbled apple, next the golden ball, and last the silken cord. And looking at him with all her usual love in her eyes and in her voice, she told him how these things had chanced into her hands, and whence they had come.

Her father listened; but durst not raise his eyes from

his plate. The scowl on his low forehead grew blacker and blacker; even his beard seemed to bristle. But he heard her in silence to the end.

'So you see, dear father,' she was saying, 'how can I but be grateful and with all my heart to one who takes so much thought for me? And if you had seen the kindness and courtesy of his looks, even you yourself could not be angry. There never was, as you well know, anybody else in the whole wide world whom I wished to speak to but to you. And now there is none other than you except this stranger. I know nothing but that. Can you suppose indeed he meant these marvellous gifts for me? And why for me and no other, father dear? And what would you counsel me to do with them?'

Owen ap Gwythock stooped his head lower. Even the sight of his eyes had dimmed. The torches faintly crackled in their sconces, the candles on the table burned unfalteringly on.

He turned his cheek aside at last like a snarling dog. 'My dear,' he said, 'I have lived long enough in this world to know the perils that beset the young and fair. I grant you that this low mountebank must be a creature of infinite cunning. I grant you that his tricks, if harmless, would be worth a charitable groat. If, that is, he were only what he seems to be. But that is not so. For this most deadly stranger is a Deceiver and a Cheat. His lair, as I guess well, is in the cruel and mysterious East, and his one desire and stratagem is to snare you into his company. Once within reach of his claws, his infamous slaves will seize on you and bear you away to some evil felucca moored in the river. It seems, beloved, that your gentle charms are being whispered of in this wicked world. Even the beauty of the gentlest of flowers may be sullied by idle tongues. But once securely in the hands of this nefarious mountebank, he will put off to

Barbary, perchance, or to the horrid regions of the Turk,
perchance, there to set you up in the scorching market-place
and to sell you for a slave. My child, the danger, the peril is
gross and imminent. Dismiss at once this evil wretch from
your mind and let his vile and dangerous devices be flung
into the fire. The apple is pure delusion; the veil which you
describe is a mere toy; and the cord is a device of the devil.'

Myfanwy looked at her father, stooping there, with sorrow in her eyes, in spite of the gladness sparkling and
dancing in her heart. Why, if all that he was saying he
thought true – why could he not lift his eyes and meet her
face to face?

'Well then, that being so, dear father,' she said softly at
last, 'and you knowing ten thousand times more of God's
world than I have ever had opportunity of knowing, whatever my desire, I must ask you but this one small thing.
Will you promise me not to have these pretty baubles des-
troyed at once, before, I mean, you have thought once
more of *me*? If I had deceived you, then indeed I should
be grieved beyond endurance. But try as I may to darken
my thoughts of him, the light slips in, and I see in my very
heart that this stranger cannot by any possibility of nature
or heaven be all that you tell me of him. I have a voice at
times that whispers me yes or no: and I obey. And of him
it has said only yes. But I am young, and the walls of this
great house are narrow, and you, dear father, as you have
told me so often, are wise. Do but then invite this young
man into your presence! Question him, test him, gaze on
him, hearken to him. And that being done, you will
believe in him as I do. As I know I am happy, I know he is
honest. It would afflict me beyond all telling to swerve by
a hair's-breadth from my dear obedience to you. But, alas,
if I never see him again, I shall wither up and die. And
that – would it not –' she added smilingly – 'that would

be a worse disobedience yet? If you love me, then, as from
my first hour in the world I *know* you have loved me, and
I have loved you, I pray you think of me with grace and
kindness – and in compassion too.'

And with that, not attempting to brush away the tears
that had sprung into her eyes, and leaving the juggler's
three gifts amid the flowers and fruit of the long table
before him, Myfanwy hastened out of the room and returned to her chamber, leaving her father alone.

For a while her words lay like a cold refreshing dew
on the dark weeds in his mind. For a while he pondered
them, even; while his own gross fables appeared in all their
ugly falseness.

But alas for himself and his pride and stubbornness,
these gentler ruminations soon passed away. At thought
once more of the juggler – of whom his spies had long since
brought him far other tidings than he had expressed – rage,
hatred and envy again boiled up in him and drowned
everything else. He forgot his courtesy, his love for Myfanwy, his desire even to keep her love for him. Instead,
on and on he sipped and sipped, and sat fuming and plotting
and scheming with but one notion in his head – by hook or
by crook to defeat this juggler and so murder the love of
his innocent Myfanwy.

'Lo, now,' broke out at last a small shrill voice inside
him. 'Lo, now, if thou taste of the magic apple, may it not
be that it will give thee courage and skill to contend against
him, and so bring all his hopes to ruin? Remember what
a marvel but one merest nibble of the outer rind of it
wrought in thy Myfanwy!'

And the foolish creature listened heedfully to this crafty
voice, not realizing that the sole virtue of the apple was
that of making any human who tasted it more like himself
than ever. He sat there – his fist over his mouth – staring

intently at the harmless-looking fruit. Then he tiptoed like a humpback across the room and listened at the entry. Then having poured out, and drained at a draught, yet another cup of wine, he cautiously picked up the apple by its stalk between finger and ringed thumb and once more squinted close and steadily at its red and green, and at the very spot where Myfanwy's small teeth had rasped away the skin.

It is in a *moment* that cities fall in earthquake, stars collide in the wastes of space, and men choose between good and evil. For suddenly – his mind made up, his face all turned a reddish purple – this foolish lord lifted the apple to his mouth and, stalk to dried blossom, bit it clean in half. And he munched and he munched and he munched.

He had chawed for but a few moments, however, when a dreadful and continuous change and transformation began to appear upon him. It seemed to him that his whole body and frame was being kneaded and twisted and wrung in much the same fashion as dough being made into bread, or clay in a modeller's fingers. Not knowing what these aches and stabbings and wrenchings meant, he had dropped as if by instinct upon his hands and knees, and thus stood munching, while gazing blankly and blindly, lost in some inward horror, into the great fire on the hearth.

And meanwhile, though he knew it not in full, there had been sprouting upon him grey coarse hairs – a full thick coat and hide of them – in abundance. There had come a tail to him with a sleek, dangling tassel; long hairy ears had jutted out upon his temples; the purple face turned grey, lengthening as it did so until it was at least full eighteen inches long, with a great jawful of large teeth. Hoofs for his hands, hoofs where his feet used to be, and behold! – standing there in his own banqueting hall –

this poor deluded Owen ap Gwythock, Lord of Eggleyseg, transmogrified into an ass!

For minutes together the dazed creature stood in utter dismay – the self within unable to realize the change that had come over its outer shape. But, happening to stretch his shaggy and unfamiliar neck a little outward, he perceived his own image in a scoured and polished suit of armour that stood on one side of the great chimney. He shook his head, the ass's head replied. He shook himself, the long ears flapped together like a wood-pigeon's wings. He lifted his hand – a hoof clawed at nowhere!

At this the poor creature's very flesh seemed to creep upon his bones as he turned in horror and dismay in search of an escape from the fate that had overtaken him. That ass *he*? he *himself*? His poor wits in vain endeavoured to remain calm and cool. A panic of fear all but swept him away. And at this moment his full, lustrous, long-lashed, asinine eyes fell by chance upon the golden ball lying ajar on the table beside his wine-cup – the Veil of Invisibility glinting like money-spider's web from within.

Now no ass is quite such a donkey as he looks. And this Owen ap Gwythock, though now completely shut up in this uncouth hairy body, was in his *mind* no more (though as much) of a donkey than he had ever been. His one thought, then, was to conceal his dreadful condition from any servant that might at any moment come that way, while he himself could seek out a quiet secluded corner in the dark wherein to consider how to rid himself of his ass's frame and to regain his own usual shape. And there lay the veil! What thing sweeter could there be than to defeat the juggler with his own devices.

Seizing the veil with his huge front teeth, he jerked it out of the ball and flung it as far as he could over his shaggy shoulders. But alas, his donkey's muzzle was far from being as deft as Myfanwy's delicate fingers. The veil but half concealed him. Tail, rump and back legs were now vanished from view; head, neck, shoulders and fore-legs remained in sight. In vain he tugged; in vain he wriggled and wrenched; his hard hoofs thumping on the hollow flagstones beneath. One half of him stubbornly remained in sight; the rest had vanished. For the time being he was no more even than half an ass.

At last, breathless and wearied out with these exertions, trembling and shuddering, and with not a vestige of sense left in his poor donkey's noddle, he wheeled himself about once more and caught up with his teeth the silken cord. It was his last hope.

But this having been woven of wisdom – it being indeed itself the Serpent of Wisdom in disguise – at touch of his teeth it at once converted itself into a strong hempen halter, and, before he could so much as rear out of the way to escape its noose or even bray for help, it had tethered him to a large steel hook in his own chimneypiece.

Bray he did, none the less: 'Hee-haw! Hee-haw!! Hee-ee-ee-ee Haw-aw-aw!!!' His prolonged, see-saw, dismal lamentations shattered the silence so harshly and so hoarsely that the sound rose up through the echoing stone walls and even pierced into Myfanwy's own bedchamber, where she sat in the darkness at her window, looking out half in sorrow, half in unspeakable happiness, at the stars.

Filled with alarm at this dreadful summons, in an instant or two she had descended the winding stone steps; and a strange scene met her eyes.

There, before her, in the full red light of the flaming brands in the hearth and the torches on the walls, stood the forelegs, the neck, head, and ears of a fine, full-grown ass, and a yard or so behind them just nothing at all. Only vacancy!

Poor Myfanwy – she could but wring her hands in grief and despair; for there could be no doubt in her mind of who it was in truth now stood before her – her own dear father. And on his face such a look of rage, entreaty, shame and stupefaction as never man has seen on ass's countenance before. At sight of her the creature tugged even more furiously at his halter, and shook his shaggy shoulders; but still in vain. His mouth opened and a voice beyond words to describe, brayed out upon the silence these words: 'Oh, Myfanwy, see into what a pass your sorceries and deceits have reduced me!'

'Oh, my dear father,' she cried in horror, 'speak no more, I beseech you – not one syllable – or we shall be discovered. Or, if you utter a sound, let it be but in a whisper.'

She was at the creature's side in an instant, had flung her arms about his neck, and was whispering into his long hairy ear all the comfort and endearments and assurances that loving and tender heart could conceive. 'Listen, listen, dear father,' she was entreating him, 'I see indeed that you have been meddling with the apple, and the ball, and the cord. And I do assure you, with all my heart and soul, that I am thinking of nothing else but how to help you in this calamity that has overtaken us. Have patience. Struggle no more. All will be well. But oh, beloved, was it quite just to me to speak of my deceits?'

Her bright eyes melted with compassion as she looked upon one whom she had loved ever since she could remember, so dismally transmogrified.

'How can you hesitate, ungrateful creature?' the see-saw voice once more broke out. 'Relieve me of this awful shape, or I shall be strangled on my own hearthstone in this pestilent halter.'

But now, alas, footsteps were sounding outside the door. Without an instant's hesitation Myfanwy drew the delicate veil completely over the trembling creature's head, neck and forequarters and thus altogether concealed him from view. So – though it was not an instant too soon – when the Lord of Eggleyseg's Chief Steward appeared in the doorway, nothing whatever was charged within, except that his master no longer sat in his customary chair. Myfanwy stood solitary at the table, and a mysterious cord was stretched out between her hand and the hook in the chimney-piece.

'My father,' said Myfanwy, 'has withdrawn for a while. He is indisposed, and bids me tell you that not even a whisper must disturb his rest. Have a hot posset prepared at once, and see that the room beneath is left vacant.'

The moment the Steward had gone to do her bidding Myfanwy turned at once to her father, and lifting the veil, whispered into the long hairy ear again that he must be of good cheer. 'For you see, dear father, the only thing now to be done is that we set out together at once in search of the juggler who, meaning no unkindness, presented me with these strange gifts. He alone can and will, I am assured, restore you to your own dear natural shape. So I pray you to be utterly silent – not a word, not a murmur – while I lead you gently forth into the forest. Once there I have no doubt I shall be able to find our way to where he is. Indeed he may be already expectant of my coming.'

Stubborn and foolish though the Baron might be, he realized, even in his present shape, that this was his only wisdom. Whereupon, withdrawing the end of the bridle from the hook to which it was tethered, Myfanwy softly led the now invisible creature to the door, and so, gently onward down the winding stone staircase, on the stones of which his shambling hoofs sounded like the hollow beating of a drum.

The vast room beneath was already deserted by its usual

occupants, and without more ado the two of them, father and daughter, were soon abroad in the faint moonlight that now by good fortune bathed the narrow bridle-path that led into the forest.

Never before in all her years on earth had Myfanwy strayed beyond the Castle walls; never before had she stood lost in wonder beneath the dark emptiness of the starry skies. She breathed in the sweet fresh night air, her heart blossoming within her like an evening primrose, refusing to be afraid. For she knew well that the safety of them both – this poor quaking animal's and her own – depended now solely on her own courage and resource, and that to be afraid would almost certainly lead them only from one disaster into another.

Simply, however, because a mere ownerless ass wandering by itself in the moonlit gloom of the forest would be a spectacle less strange than that of a solitary damsel like herself, she once more drew down her father's ear to her lips and whispered into it, explaining to him that it was she who must now be veiled, and that if he would forgive her such boldness – for after all, he had frequently carried her pickaback when she was a child – she would mount upon his back and in this way they would together make better progress on their journey.

Her father dared not take offence at her words, whatever his secret feelings might be. 'So long as you hasten, my child,' he gruffed out in the hush, striving in vain to keep his tones no louder than a human whisper, 'I will forgive you all.' In a moment then there might be seen jogging along the bridle-path, now in moonlight, now in shadow, a sleek and handsome ass, a halter over its nose, making no stay to browse the dewy grass at the wayside, but apparently obeying its own whim as it wandered steadily onward.

Now it chanced that night there was a wild band of

mountain robbers encamped within the forest. And when of a sudden this strange and pompous animal unwittingly turned out of a thicket into the light of their camp fire, and raised its eyes like glowing balls of emerald to gaze in horror at its flames, they lifted their voices together in an uproarious peal of laughter. And one of them at once started up from where he lay in the bracken, to seize the creature's halter and so make it his prize.

Their merriment, however, was quickly changed into dismay when the robbers saw the strange creature being guided, as was evident, by an invisible and mysterious hand. He turned this way, he turned that, with an intelligence that was clearly not his own and not natural even to his kind, and so eluded every effort made by his enemy to get hold on his halter, his teeth and eyeballs gleaming in the firelight.

At this, awe and astonishment fell upon these outlaws. Assuredly sorcery alone could account for such ungainly and unasslike antics and manoeuvres. Assuredly some divine being must have the beast in keeping, and to meddle with it further might only prove their own undoing.

Fortunate indeed was it that Myfanwy's right foot, which by mischance remained uncovered by the veil, happened to be on the side of the animal away from the beams of the camp fire. For certainly had these malefactors seen the precious stones blazing in its buckle, their superstitions would have melted away like morning mist, their fears have given place to cupidity, and they would speedily have made the ass their own and held its rider to an incalculable ransom.

Before, however, the moon had glided more than a soundless pace or two on her night journey, Myfanwy and her incomparable ass were safely out of sight: and the robbers had returned to their carousals. What impulse

bade her turn first this way, then that, in the wandering
and labyrinthine glades and tracks of the forest, she could
not tell. But even though her father – not daring to raise
his voice in the deep silence – ever and again stubbornly
tugged upon his halter in the belief that the travellers had
taken a wrong turning and were irrevocably lost, Myfanwy
kept steadily on her way.

With a touch of her heel or a gentle persuasive pat of her
hand on his hairy neck she did her best to reassure and to
soothe him. 'Only trust in me, dear father: I am sure all
will be well.'

Yet she was haunted with misgivings. So that when at
last a twinkling light, sprinkling its beams between the
boughs, showed in the forest, it refreshed her heart beyond
words to tell. She was reaching her journey's end. It was as
if that familiar voice in the secrecy of her heart had murmured, 'Hst! He draws near!'

There and then she dismounted from off her father's
hairy back and once more communed with him through
that long twitching ear. 'Remain here in patience a while,
dear father,' she besought him, 'without straying by a
hair's-breadth from where you are; for everything tells
me our Stranger is not far distant now, and no human
being on earth, no living creature, even, must see you in
this sad and unseemly disguise. I will hasten on to assure
myself that the light which I perceive beaming through
the thicket yonder is his, and no other's. Meanwhile –
and this veil shall go with me in case of misadventure –
meanwhile do you remain quietly beneath this spreading
beech-tree, nor even stir unless you are over-wearied after
our long night journey and you should feel inclined to
rest a while on the softer turf in the shadow there under
that bush of fragrant roses, or to refresh yourself at the
brook whose brawling I hear welling up from that dingle

in the hollow. In that case, return here, I pray you; contain yourself in patience, and be your tongue as dumb as a stone. For though you may *design* to speak softly, dearest father, that long sleek throat and those great handsome teeth will not admit of it.'

And her father, as if not even the thick hairy hide he wore could endure his troubles longer, opened his mouth as if to groan aloud. But restraining himself, he only sighed, while an owl out of the quiet breathed its mellow night-call as if in response. For having passed the last hour in a profound and afflicted reverie, this poor ass had now regained in part his natural human sense and sagacity. But pitiful was the eye, however asinine the grin, which he now bestowed as if in promise on Myfanwy who, with veil held delicately in her fingers stood there, radiant as snow, beside him in the moonlight.

And whether it was because of her grief for his own condition or because of the expectancy in her face at the thought of her meeting with the Stranger, or because maybe the ass feared in his despair and dejection that he might never see her again, he could not tell; but true it was that she had never appeared in a guise so brave and gay and passionate and tender. It might indeed be a youthful divinity gently treading the green sward beside this uncouth beast in the chequered light and shadow of that unearthly moonshine.

Having thus assured herself that all would be well until her return, Myfanwy kissed her father on his flat hairy brow, and veil in hand withdrew softly in the direction of the twinkling light.

Alas, though the Baron thirsted indeed for the chill dark waters whose song rose in the air from the hollow beneath, he could not contain himself in her absence, but unmindful of his mute promise followed after his daughter at a distance as she made her way to the light, his hoofs scarce sounding in the turf. Having come near, by peering through the dense bushes that encircled the juggler's nocturnal retreat in the forest, he could see and hear all that passed.

As soon as Myfanwy had made sure that this stranger sitting by his glowing watch-fire was indeed the juggler and no man else – and one strange leap of her heart assured her of this even before her eyes could carry their message – she veiled herself once more, and so, all her loveliness made thus invisible, she drew stealthily near and a little behind him, as he crouched over the embers. Then pausing, she called gently and in a still low voice, 'I beseech you, Stranger, to take pity on one in great distress.'

The juggler lifted his dreaming face, ruddied and shadowed in the light of his fire, and peered cautiously but in happy astonishment all around him.

'I beseech you, Stranger,' cried again the voice from the unseen, 'to take pity on one in great distress.'

And at this it seemed to the juggler that now ice was running through his veins and now fire. For he knew well that this was the voice of one compared with whom all else in the world to him was nought. He knew also that she must be standing near, though made utterly invisible to him by the veil of his own enchantments.

'Draw near, traveller. Have no fear,' he cried out softly into the darkness. 'All will be well. Tell me only how I may help you.'

But Myfanwy drew not a hair's-breadth nearer. Far from it. Instead, she flitted a little across the air of the glade, and now her voice came to him from up the wind towards the south, and fainter in the distance.

'There is one with me,' she replied, 'who by an evil stratagem has been transformed into the shape of a beast, and that beast a poor patient ass. Tell me this, sorcerer – how I may restore him to his natural shape, and mine shall be an everlasting gratitude. For it is my own father of whom I speak.'

Her voice paused and faltered on the word. She longed almost beyond bearing to reveal herself to this unknown one, trusting without the least doubt or misgiving that he would serve her faithfully in all she asked of him.

'But *that*, gentle lady,' replied the juggler, 'is not within my power, unless he of whom you speak draws near to show himself. Nor – though the voice with which you speak to me is sweeter than the music of harp-strings twangling on the air – nor is it within my power to make promises to a bodiless sound only. For how am I to be assured that the shape who utters the words I hear is not some dangerous demon of the darkness who is bent on mocking and deluding me, and who will bring sorcery on myself?'

There was silence for a while in the glade, and then 'No, no!' cried the juggler. 'Loveliest and bravest of all that is, I need not see thy shape to know thee. Thou art most assuredly the lovely Myfanwy, and all that I am, have ever been, and ever shall be is at thy service. Tell me, then, where is this poor ass that was once thy noble father?'

And at this, and at one and the same moment, Myfanwy, withdrawing the veil from her head and shoulders, disclosed her fair self standing there in the faint rosy glow of the slumbering fire, and there broke also from the neighbouring thicket so dreadful and hideous a noise of rage and anguish – through the hoarse and unpractised throat of the eavesdropper near by – that it might be supposed the clamour was not of one but of a chorus of demons – though it was merely our poor ass complaining of his fate.

The Lovely Myfanwy

'Oh, sir,' sighed Myfanwy, 'my dear father, I fear, in his grief and anxiety has been listening to what has passed between us. See, here he comes.'

Galloping hoofs were indeed now audible as the Lord of Eggleyseg in ass's skin and shape drew near to wreak his vengeance on the young magician. But being at this moment in his stubborn rage and folly more ass than human, the glaring of the watch-fire dismayed his heavy wits, and he could do no else but paw with his fore-legs, lifting his smooth nose with its gleaming teeth into the night air, snuffing his rage and defiance some twenty paces distant from the fire.

The young magician, being of a nature as courteous as he was bold, did not so much as turn his head to scan the angry shivering creature, but once more addressed Myfanwy. She stood bowed down a little, tears in her eyes; in part for grief at her father's broken promise and the humiliation he had brought upon himself, in part for joy that their troubles would soon be over and that she was now in the very company of the stranger who unwittingly had been the cause of them all.

'Have no fear,' he said, 'the magic that has changed the noble Baron your father into a creature more blest in its docility, patience, and humbleness than any other in the wide world, can as swiftly restore him to his natural shape.'

'Ah then, sir,' replied the maid, 'it is very certain that my father will wish to bear witness to your kindness with any small gift that is in our power. For, as he well knows, it was not by any design but his own that he ate of the little green apple of enchantment. I pray you, sir, moreover, to forgive me for first stealing that apple, and also the marvellous golden ball, *and* the silken cord from out of the air.'

The juggler turned and gazed strangely at Myfanwy. 'There is only one thing I desire in all this starry universe,' he answered. 'But I ask it not of him – for it is not of his giving. It is for your own forgiveness, lady.'

'*I* forgive you!' she cried. 'Alas, my poor father!'

But even as she spoke a faint smile was on her face, and her eyes wandered to the animal standing a few paces beyond the margin of the glow cast by the watch-fire, sniffing the night air the while, and twitching dismally the coarse grey mane behind his ears. For now that her father was so near his deliverance her young heart grew entirely happy again, and the future seemed as sweet with promise as wild flowers in May.

Without further word the juggler drew from out of his pouch, as if he always carried about with him a little privy store of vegetables, a fine, tapering, ripe, red carrot.

'This, lady,' said he, 'is my only wizardry. I make no bargain. My love for you will never languish, even if I never more again refresh my sleepless eyes with the vision of your presence in this solitary glade. Let your noble father the Lord of Eggleyseg draw near without distrust. There is but little difference, it might be imagined, between a wild apple and a carrot. But then, when all is said, there is little difference in the long sum between any living thing and another in this strange world. There are creatures in the world whose destiny it is in spite of their gentleness and humility and lowly duty and obedience to go upon four legs and to be in service of masters who deserve far less than *they* deserve, while there are men in high places of whom the reverse might truly be said. It is a mystery beyond my unravelling. But now all I ask is that you bid the ass who you tell me is hearkening at this moment to all that passes between us to nibble of this humble but useful and wholesome root. It will instantly restore him to his proper shape. Meanwhile, if you bid, I will myself be gone.'

Without further speech between them, Myfanwy accepted the magic carrot, and returned once more to the ass.

'Dear father,' she cried softly, 'here is a root that seems to be only a carrot; yet nibble of it and you will be at once restored, and will forget you were ever an – as you are. For many days to come, I fear, you will not wish to look upon the daughter that has been the unwilling cause of this night's woeful experience. There lives, as I have been told, in a little green arbour of the forest yonder, a hermit. This young magician will, I am truly certain, place me in his care a while until all griefs are forgotten between us. You will of your kindness consent, dear father, will you not?' she pleaded.

A long prodigious bray resounded dolefully in the hollows of the far-spread forest's dells and thickets. The Lord of Eggleyseg had spoken.

'Indeed, father,' smiled Myfanwy, 'I have never before heard you say "Yes" so heartily. What further speech is needed?'

Whereupon the ass, with more dispatch than gratitude, munched up the carrot, and in a few hours Owen ap Gwythock, once more restored to his former, though hardly his more appropriate shape, returned in safety to his Castle. There for many a day he mourned his woeful solitude, but learned, too, not only how true and faithful a daughter he had used so ill, but the folly of a love that is fenced about with mistrust and suspicion and is poisoned with jealousy.

And when May was come again, a prince, no longer in the disguise of a wandering juggler, drew near with his adored Myfanwy to the Lord of Eggleyseg's ancient castle. And Owen ap Gwythock, a little older but a far wiser man, greeted them with such rejoicings and entertainment, with such feastings and dancing and minstrelsy and jubilations as had never been heard of before. Indeed he would have been ass unadulterated if he had done else.

Lucy

Once upon a time there were three sisters, the Misses MacKnackery – or, better still, the Miss MacKnackeries. They lived in a large, white, square house called Stoneyhouse; and their names were Euphemia, Tabitha, and Jean Elspeth. They were known over Scotland for miles and miles, from the Tay to the Grampians – from the Tay to the Grumpy Ones, as a cousin who did not like Euphemia and Tabitha used to say.

Stoneyhouse had been built by the Miss MacKnackeries's grandfather, Mr Angus MacKnackery, who, from being a poor boy with scarcely a bawbee in his breeches pocket, had risen up to be a wealthy manufacturer of the best Scotch burlap, which is a kind of sacking. He made twine, too, for tying up parcels. He would have made almost anything to make money. But at last, when he was sixty-six, he felt he would like to be a gentleman living in the country with a large garden to walk about in, flowers in beds, cucumbers in frames, pigs in sties, and one or two cows for milk, cream, and butter.

So he sold his huge, smoky works and warehouse, and all the twine and burlap, hemp, jute, and whalebone still in it, for £80,000. With this £80,000 he built Stoneyhouse, purchased some fine furniture and some carriages and horses, and invested what was over.

Jean Elspeth, when she was learning sums, and when she had come to Interest – having sometimes heard her father and mother speak of her grandfather and of his

173

fortune, and how he had *invested* it – just to please her governess, Miss Gimp, thought she would make a sum of it. So she wrote down in her rather straggly figures in an exercise book:

$$£80,000 \text{ @ } £4 \text{ per centum per annum}$$
$$= £80,000 \times 4 \div 100 = £3,200.$$

It was the first really enjoyable sum she had ever done. And yet Miss Gimp was a little put about when Jean Elspeth showed it to her father. Still, Mr MacKnackery, senior, had been a really rich man, and regretted that the gentleman who bought his factory could never afterwards make such fine burlap as himself, nor even such durable twine.

He lived to be eighty, and then he died, leaving his money to his son, Robert Duncan Donald David, Jean Elspeth's father. And when *he* died, his dear wife Euphemia Tabitha being dead too, he left all that was over of the £80,000 (for, alas and alas! he had lost a good part of it) to his three daughters: Euphemia, Tabitha, and Jean Elspeth.

When Jean Elspeth was old enough to breakfast with the family in the big dining-room with the four immense windows, she used to sit opposite the portraits of her grandfather, her father, and her mother. They hung in heavy handsome gilt frames on the wall opposite the windows. And while in her high chair she gobbled up her porridge – and gobbled it up quickly, not so much because she liked it as because she hated being put in the corner for not eating it – she would sit and look at them.

Her grandfather's was by far the largest of the three portraits, and it hung in the very middle of the lofty wall, under the moulded ceiling. He was a stout and imposing man, with bushy whiskers and cold bright blue eyes. The thumb and first finger of his right hand held a fine thick

174

Albert watch-chain, which the painter had painted so skil-
fully that you could see it was eighteen-carat gold at a single
glance. So he hung: for ever boldly staring down on his
own great dining-room and all that was in it – yet not
appearing to enjoy it very much.

What was more, her grandfather always looked exactly
as if he were on the point of taking out his watch to see
the time; and Jean Elspeth had the odd notion that, if he
ever did succeed in so doing, its hands would undoubtedly
point to a quarter to twelve. But she could no more have
told you why, than she could tell you why she used to
count each spoonful of her porridge, or why she felt happier when the last spoonful was an odd number.

The portrait of her father was that of a man much
less stout and imposing than her grandfather. He was dark,
and smiling, and he had no whiskers. And Jean Elspeth
had loved him dearly. Every morning when she had
finished her breakfast (and if nobody was looking) she
would give a tiny little secret wave of the spoon towards
him, as if he might be pleased at seeing her empty plate.

On the other side of her grandfather's portrait hung a
picture of her mother. And the odd thing about this picture
was that, if you looked long enough, you could not help
seeing – as if it were almost the ghost of Jean Elspeth –
her very own small face, peeping out of the paint at you,
just like a tiny little green marmoset out of a cage all to
itself in the Zoo. Jean Elspeth had discovered this when
she was only seven; but Euphemia and Tabitha had never
noticed it at all.

They knew they were far less like their mother (who had
been a Miss Reeks MacGillicuddy of Kelso) than their
grandfather. Still they were exceedingly proud of *that*. As
for Jean Elspeth, they didn't think she was like any of the
family at all. Indeed, Euphemia had more than once re-

marked that Jean Elspeth had 'nae deegnity', and Tabitha that 'she micht jist as weel ha' been a changeling'. Even now, when they were elderly ladies, they always treated her as if she were still not very far from being a child, though, after all, Jean Elspeth was only five years younger than Tabitha.

But then, how different she was in looks! For while Tabitha had a long pale face a little like a unicorn's, with mouse-coloured hair and green-grey eyes, Jean Elspeth was dark and small, with red in her cheek and a tip to her nose. And while Tabitha's face changed very little, Jean Elspeth's was like a dark little glancing pool on an April morning. Sometimes it looked almost centuries older than either of her sisters', and then, again, sometimes it looked simply no age at all.

It depended on what she was doing – whether she was sitting at seven o'clock dinner on Great Occasions, when the Bults, and the McGaskins, and Dr Menzies were guests, or merely basking idly in the sunshine at her bedroom window. Jean Elspeth would sometimes, too, go wandering off by herself over the hills a mile or two away from the house. And *then* she looked not a minute older than looks a harebell, or a whinchat, perched with his white eyebrow on a fuzz-bush near a lichenous half-hidden rock among the heather.

However sad, too, she looked, she never looked grim. And even though (at dinner parties) she parted her hair straight down the middle, and smoothed the sides over as sleek as satin, she simply could not look what is called 'superior'. Besides, she had lips that were the colour of cherries, and curious quick hands that she was sometimes compelled to clasp together lest they should talk even more rapidly than her tongue.

Now in Stoneyhouse nobody – except perhaps the

tweeny-maid and the scullery-maid, Sally and Nancy McGullie, who were cousins – ever talked *much*. It was difficult even to tell exactly how wise and sagacious and full of useful knowledge Euphemia and Tabitha were, simply because except at meals they so seldom opened their mouths. And never to sing.

This, perhaps, was because it is impossible to keep order if everybody's tongue keeps wagging. It wastes time, too; for only very few people can work hard and talk hard both at the same moment. And in Stoneyhouse everything was in apple-pie order (except the beds), and nobody ever wasted *any* time (except kissing-time).

And yet, although time was never wasted, nobody seemed to be very much the better off for any that was actually 'saved'. Nobody had ever managed to pack some of it up in neat brown-paper parcels, or to put it in a bank as Mr MacKnackery, senior, had put his money, or to pour it into jars like home-made jam. It just went. And in Stoneyhouse (until, at least, Euphemia one morning received a certain letter) it went very very slowly. The big hands of its clocks seemed to be envious of the little ones. They crept like shadows. And between their 'tick' and their 'tock' at times yawned a huge hole, as dark as a cellar. So, at least, Jean Elspeth fancied.

One glance at Stoneyhouse, even from the outside, would tell you how orderly it was. The four high white walls, with their large square slate roof fixed firmly on top of them, stood stiff as bombardiers on extremely solid foundations, and they on even solider rock. No tree dared cast a shadow upon them, no creeper crept. The glossy windows, with their straight lines of curtains behind them, just stared down on you as if they said, 'Find the faintest speck or smear or flaw in us if you can!' And you hadn't the courage even to try.

It was just so inside. Everything was frozen in its place.
Not only the great solid pieces of furniture which Mr
MacKnackery had purchased with his burlap money –
wardrobes, coffers, presses, four-posters, highboys, sideboards, tables, sofas, and oak chairs – but even all the little
things, bead-mats, foot-stools, candle-snuffers, boot-trees,
ornaments, knick-knacks, Euphemia's silks and Tabitha's
water-colours. There was a place for everything, and everything was in its place. Yes, and it was kept there.

Except in Jean Elspeth's room. She had never never
learned to be tidy, not even in her sums. She was constantly
taking things out, and either forgetting to put them away
again or putting them away again in their wrong places.
And do you suppose she blamed herself for this? Not at
all. When she lost anything and had been looking for it
for hours and hours – a book, or a brooch, or a ribbon, or
a shoe – she would say to herself, laughing all over, 'Well
now, there! That *Lucy* must have hidden it!' And presently
there it would be, right in the middle of her dressing-table
or under a chair, as if a moment before it had been put back
there; just for fun.

And who was this '*Lucy*'? There couldn't be a more
difficult question; and Jean Elspeth had never attempted
to answer it. It was one of those questions she never even
asked herself. At least, not out loud. This, perhaps, was
because she hated the thought of hurting anybody's feelings. As if Lucy ... but never mind!

It was Lucy, at any rate, who so unfortunately came into
that dreadful talk over the porridge on the morning when
the fatal letter came to Euphemia. It arrived just like
any other letter. The butler, with his mouth as closely shut
as usual, had laid it beside Euphemia's plate. Judging from
its large white envelope, nobody could possibly have thought
it was as deadly as a poison and sharper than a serpent's

tooth. Euphemia opened it, too, just as usual – with her long, lean forefinger, and her eyebrows lifted a little under her grey front of hair. Then she read it – and turned to ice.

It was from her lawyer, or rather from her Four Lawyers, for they all shared the same office, and at the foot of the letter one of them had signed all their four names. It was a pitch-black letter – a thunderbolt. It said at the beginning that the Miss MacKnackeries must expect in future to be a little less well off than they had been in the past, and it said at the end that they were ruined.

You see, Euphemia's grandfather had lent what remained of his £80,000 (after building his great mansion) to the British Government, for the use of the British nation. The British Government of that day put the money into what were called the Consolidated Funds. And to show how much obliged they were to Mr MacKnackery for the loan of it, they used every year to pay him interest on it – so many shillings for every hundred pounds. Not so much as £4 per annum, as Jean Elspeth had put down in her sum, but as much as they could afford – and that was at least 1,000,000 bawbees. There couldn't have been a safer money-box; nor could Mr MacKnackery's income have 'come in' more regularly if it had come in by clockwork. So far the British Government resembled Stoneyhouse itself.

But the Miss MacKnackeries's father was not only a less imposing man than their grandfather, he had been much less careful of his money. He enjoyed *helping* the nation to use the Funds. He delighted in *buying* things and giving presents, and the more he bought the more he wanted to buy. So he had gradually asked for his money back from the British Government, spending most of it and lending the rest to persons making railways and gasworks in foreign parts, and digging up gold and diamonds, and making scent out of tar, and paint which they said would never wear off or change colour, and everything like that.

These persons paid him for helping them like this a good deal more than the Consolidated Funds could pay him. But then gasworks are not always so *safe* as the British nation. It is what is called a speculation to lend gentlemen money to help them to dig up diamonds or to make water-works in Armenia, which means that you cannot be perfectly sure of getting it back again. Often and often, indeed, the Miss MacKnackeries's father had not got *his* money back again.

And now – these long years after his death – the worst had befallen. The Four Lawyers had been suddenly compelled to tell the Miss MacKnackeries that nearly every bit left of their grandfather's savings was gone; that their solid gold had vanished like the glinting mists of a June morning. They had for some time been accustomed to growing less and less rich; but that's a very different thing from becoming alarmingly poor. It is the difference between a mouse with a fat nugget of cheese and a mouse with a bread-crumb.

Euphemia, before opening the letter, had put on her pince-nez. As she read, the very life seemed to ebb out of her poor old face, leaving it cold and grey. She finished it to the last word, then with a trembling hand took the glasses off her nose and passed the letter to Tabitha. Tabitha could still read without spectacles. Her light eyes angled rapidly to and fro across the letter, then she, too, put it down, her face not pale, but red and a little swollen. 'It is the end, Euphemia,' she said.

Jean Elspeth was sitting that morning with her back to the portraits, and at the moment was gently munching a slice of dry toast and Scotch marmalade (made by the Miss MacKnackeries's cook, Mrs O'Phrump). She had been watching a pied wagtail flitting after flies across the smooth shorn lawn on the white stone terrace. Then her gaze had wandered off to the blue outline of the lovely distant hills, the Grumpy Ones, and her mind had slid into a kind of day-dream.

Into the very middle of this day-dream had broken the sound of Tabitha's words, 'It is the end, Euphemia'; and it was as if a trumpet had sounded.

She looked round in dismay, and saw her sisters, Euphemia and Tabitha, sitting there in their chairs at the table, as stiff and cold as statues of stone. Not only this, which was not so very unusual, but they both of them looked extremely unwell. *Then* she noticed the letter. And she knew at once that this must be the serpent that had suddenly bitten her sisters' minds. The blood rushed up into her cheeks, and she said – feeling more intensely sorry for them both than she could possibly express – 'Is there anything wrong, Euphemia?'

And Euphemia, in a voice Jean Elspeth would certainly not have recognized if she had heard it from outside the door, replied, 'You may well ask it.' And then in a rush Jean Elspeth remembered her strange dream of the night before and at once went blundering on: 'Well, you know, Euphemia, I had a dream last night, all dark and awful, and, in it, *there* was *Lucy* looking out of a crooked stone window over some water. And she said to me –'

But Tabitha interrupted her: 'I think, Elspeth, neither myself nor Euphemia at this moment wishes to hear what Lucy, as you call her, said in your dream. We have received exceedingly bad news this morning, that very closely concerns not only Euphemia and me, but even yourself also. And this is *no* time for frivolity.' And it sounded even more tragic in her Scots tongue.

Jean Elspeth had not meant to be frivolous. She had hoped merely, and if but for a moment, to turn her sisters' minds away from this dreadful news that had come with the postman, and to explain what her dream had seemed to promise. But no. It was just her way. Whenever she said anything to anyone – anything that came from the very bottom of her heart – she always made a muddle of it. It sounded as small and meaningless as the echo of a sparrow's cheeping against a bare stone wall. They would look at her out of their green-grey eyes, down their long pale noses, with an expression either grim or superior, or both. Of course, too, at such a moment, any mention of Lucy was a dreadfully silly mistake. Even at the best of times they despised Jean Elspeth for her 'childishness'. What must they think of her now!

For there never was and there never could be any *real* Lucy. It was only a name. And yet Jean Elspeth still longed to find *some* word of hope or comfort that would bring back a little colour into poor Euphemia's cheeks, and make her look a little less like an image in marble. But no word came. She had even failed to hear what her sisters were saying. At last she could bear herself no longer.

'I am sure, Euphemia, that you would like to talk the letter over with Tabitha in quiet, and that you will tell me if I can be of any help. I think I will go out into the garden.'

Euphemia bowed her head. And though, by trying to move with as little noise as possible, Jean Elspeth made her heavy chair give a loud screech on the polished floor, she managed to escape at last.

It was a cold, clear, spring morning, and the trees in the distance were now tipped with their first green buds. The gardeners were already mapping out their rows of plants in the 'arbaceous borders', in preparation for the summer. There never was a garden 'kept' so well. The angles of the flower-beds on the lawn – diamonds and lozenges, octagons, squares, and oblongs – were as sharp as if they had been cut out of cardboard with a pair of scissors. Not a blade of grass was out of place.

If even one little round pebble pushed up a shoulder in the gravel path, up came a vast cast-iron roller and ground him back into his place. As for a weed, let but one poke its little green bonnet above the black mould, it would soon see what happened.

The wide light from the sky streamed down upon the house, and every single window in the high white wall of it seemed to be scornfully watching Jean Elspeth as she made her way down to a little straight green seat under the terrace. Here, at least, she would be out of their sight.

She sat down, folded her hands in her lap, and looked straight in front of her. She always so sat when she was in trouble. In vain she tried to compose and fix her mind and to *think*. It was impossible. For she had not been there more than a moment or two before her heart knew that Lucy was haunting somewhere close beside her. So close and so much on purpose, it seemed, that it was almost as if she wanted to whisper something in her ear ...

Now it has been said that Lucy was only a name. Yet, after all, she was a little more than that. Years and years ago, when Jean Elspeth was only seven, she had 'sort of' made Lucy up. It was simply because there was no one else to play with, for Tabitha was five years older, and at least fifty-five times more sensible and intelligent and grown-up. So Jean Elspeth had pretended.

In those days she would sometimes sit on one flowerpot on the long hot or windy terrace, and she would put another flowerpot for Lucy. And they would talk, or rather she would talk, and Lucy would look. Or sometimes they sat together in a corner of the great bare nursery. And sometimes Jean Elspeth would pretend she was holding Lucy's hand when she fell asleep.

And the really odd thing was that the less in those days she tried to 'pretend', the more often Lucy came. And though Jean Elspeth had never seen her with what is called her naked eye, she must have seen her with some other kind of eye, for she knew that her hair and skin were fairer than the fairest of flax, and that she was dressed in very light and queer-fashioned clothes, though she could not say *how* queer.

Another odd thing was that Lucy always seemed to appear without warning entirely out of nothing, and entirely of herself, when anything mysterious or unexpected or sad or very beautiful happened, and sometimes just before it happened. That had been why she told Euphemia of her dream of the night before. For though everything else in the dream had been dark and dismal, and the water had roared furiously over its rocks, breaking into foam like snow, and Jean Elspeth had been shaken with terror, Lucy herself appearing at the window had been more beautiful than moonlight and as consoling as a star.

It was a pity, of course, that Jean Elspeth had ever even so much as mentioned Lucy at all. But that had been years and years ago, and then she could not really help doing so. For Tabitha had crept up behind her one morning – it was on her eighth birthday – while she herself was sitting in a corner by the large cupboard, with her back to the nursery door, and had overheard her talking to someone.

'Aha! little Miss Toad-in-the-hole! So here you are! And who are *you* talking to?' Tabitha had asked.

Jean Elspeth had turned cold all over. 'Nobody,' she said.

'Oh, Nobody, is it? Then you just tell me, Madam Skulker, Nobody's name!'

And Jean Elspeth had refused. Unfortunately, she had been wearing that morning a high-waisted frock, with sleeves that came down only to the elbow, and though Tabitha, with nips and pinches of her bare skinny arm, could not make Jean Elspeth cry, she had at least made her tell.

'Oh, so its name's Lucy, is it?' said Tabitha. 'You horrid

185

little frump. Then you tell her from me that if *I* catch her anywhere about, I'll scratch her eyes out.'

After another pinch or two, and a good 'ring-of-the-bells' at Jean Elspeth's plait, Tabitha had gone downstairs to her father.

'Papa,' she said, 'I am sorry to interrupt you, but I think poor Elspeth must be ill or in a fever. She is "rambling". Had we better give her some Gregory's powder, or some castor-oil, do you think?'

Mr MacKnackery had been worried that morning by a letter about a Gold Mine, something like that which poor Euphemia so many years afterwards was to receive from the Four Lawyers. But when *he* was worried he at once tried to forget his worry. Indeed, even at sight of what looked like an ugly letter, he would begin softly whistling and smiling. So it was almost with a sigh of relief that he pushed the uncomfortable letter into a drawer and climbed the stairs to the nursery.

And when Jean Elspeth, after crying a little as she sat on his knee, had told him about Lucy, he merely smiled out of his dark eyes, and, poking his finger and thumb into a waistcoat pocket, had pulled out, just as if it had been waiting there especially for this occasion, a tiny little gold locket with a picture of a moss-rose inside, which he asked Jean Elspeth to give to Lucy the very next time she came again. 'My dear,' he had said, 'I have my Lucy, too, though I never, never talk about her. I keep her "for best".'

As for Tabitha, he thanked her most gratefully that morning at luncheon for having been so thoughtful about her sister. 'But I fear, my child,' he said, 'you must be fretting yourself without need. And for fretting there is nothing as good as Gregory's powder. So I have asked Alison to mix a good dose for you at bedtime, and if you are very generous, perhaps Jenny would like to lick the spoon.'

The very moment he turned his face away, with as dreadful a grimace as she could manage, Tabitha had put out her long pale tongue at Jean Elspeth – which was about as much use as it would have been to put out her tongue for their old doctor, Dr Menzies – *after* he had gone out of the room ...

Even now, years and years after she had become completely grown up, whenever Jean Elspeth thought of those far-away times she always began wool-gathering. And whenever she began wool-gathering Lucy was sure to seem more real to her than at any other time. The gravel path, the green lawn, the distant hills vanished away before her eyes. She was lost as if in a region of light and happiness. There she was happy to be lost. But spattering raindrops on her cheeks soon called her back to herself. A dark cloud had come over the world, and for the first time a foreboding came into her mind of what Euphemia's letter might really mean.

She turned sharply on the little green seat almost as if she had been caught trespassing. And at that instant she could have vowed that she actually saw – this time with her real naked eye – a child standing and looking at her a few paces beyond. It could not have been so, of course; but what most surprised Jean Elspeth was that there should be such a peculiar smile on the child's face – as if she were saying: 'Never mind, my dear. Whatever happens, whatever they say, I promise to be with you more than *ever* before. You just see!'

And then, for the very first time in her life, Jean Elspeth felt ashamed of Lucy; and then, still more ashamed of being ashamed. When they were all in such trouble, was it quite fair to Euphemia and Tabitha? She actually went so far as to turn away in the opposite direction and would have hastened straight back to the house if, at that moment, she had not heard a small, curious fluttering behind her. She glanced swiftly over her shoulder, but it was to find only that a robin had stolen in on her to share her company, and was now eyeing her with his bead-black eye from his perch on the green seat which she had just vacated.

And now, of course, there was no Lucy. Not a trace. She had been 'dismissed' – would never come back.

For lunch that day the butler carried in a small soup-tureen of porridge. When he had attended to each of the ladies, and had withdrawn, Euphemia explained to Jean Elspeth precisely what the lawyers' letter meant. It was a long letter, not only about the gentlemen who had failed to find water enough for their waterworks in Armenia, but also about some other gentlemen in Madagascar whose crops of manioc and caoutchouc had been seized with chor-blight. Jean Elspeth did not quite grasp the details; she did not quite understand why the lawyers had ever taken such a fancy to caoutchouc; but she did perfectly understand Euphemia's last sentence: 'So you see, Elspeth, we – that is Us – are ruined!'

And would you believe it? Once more Jean Elspeth said the wrong thing. Or rather it was her voice that was wrong. For far away in it was the sound as of a bugle rejoicing at break of day. 'And does that mean, Euphemia, that we shall have to *leave* Stoneyhouse?'

'It means,' said Tabitha tartly, 'that Stoneyhouse may have to leave *us*.'

'In either case we are powerless,' added Euphemia. And the tone in which Euphemia uttered these words – sitting there straight and erect, with her long white face, in her sleek grey silk morning-gown with its pattern of tiny mauve flowers – brought tears, not to Jean Elspeth's eyes but to somewhere deep down inside her. It was as if somebody was drawing water out of the very well of her heart.

'It is the *disgrace*,' said Tabitha. 'To have to turn our backs, to run away. We shall be the talk, the laughing-stock of the county.'

'What! Laugh at us because we are ruined!' cried Jean Elspeth.

But this time Tabitha ignored her. 'This is the house,' she said, 'our noble grandfather built for us. And here I will die, unless I am positively driven out of it by these systematic blood-suckers.'

'Tabitha!' pleaded Euphemia. 'Surely we should not demean ourselves so far as even to call them by their right name.'

'Systematic blood-suckers,' cried Tabitha fiercely. 'I will sell the very rings off my fingers rather than be an exile from the house where I was born. And *he – he* at least shall never witness the ruin into which our father's folly has betrayed us.'

She rose from the table, and mounting one of the expensive damask chairs that, unless guests were present, were accustomed to stand in a stately row along the wall, she succeeded, after one or two vain attempts, in turning the immense gilt-framed portrait of her grandfather with its face to the wall.

Then tears really came into Jean Elspeth's eyes. But they were tears of anger rather than of pity. 'I think,' she said, 'that is being dreadfully unkind to Father.'

'By this time,' said Tabitha sternly, 'I should have supposed that you would have given up the notion that you are capable of "thinking". What right have you to defend your father, pray, simply because you take after him?'

Jean Elspeth made no answer. Her father at any rate continued to smile at her from *his* nail – though it was not a very good portrait, because the painter had been unable to get the hair and the waistcoat quite right. And if – even at this unhappy moment – Jean Elspeth had had her porridge spoon in her hand, she would certainly have given it a little secret wave in his direction.

But he was not to smile down for very long. The Miss MacKnackeries's grandfather continued to hang with his face to the wall. But the two other portraits, together with the wardrobes, coffers, presses, sideboards, bead-mats, samplers, and even the Indian workboxes, were all taken off in a few weeks, to be sold for what they would fetch. And Euphemia now, instead of five, wore but one ring, and that of turquoises.

In a month all the servants, from the butler to Sally McGullie, and all the gardeners were gone. Mrs O'Phrump alone remained – first because she was too stout to be likely to be comfortable in any new place, and next, because she wasn't greedy about wages. That was all. Just Mrs O'Phrump and the gardener's boy, Tom Piper, whose mother lived in the village, and who slept at home. But he was a lazy boy, was Tom Piper, and when he was not fast asleep in the tool-shed, he was loafing in the deserted orchard.

Nevertheless, it was from this moment that Jean Elspeth seemed to have become completely alive.

It was extraordinary to find herself so much herself in so empty a house. The echoes! Why, if you but walked alone along a corridor, you heard your own footsteps pit-a-pattering after you all the way down. If by yourself, in 'your ain, ain companie', you but laughed out in a room, it was like being the muffled clapper of a huge hollow bell. All Stoneyhouse seemed endlessly empty now; and perhaps the emptiest place of all was the coach-house.

And then the stables. It was simply astonishing how quickly stray oats, that had fallen by chance into the crannies, sprang up green among the cobble-stones in front of their walls. And if for a little while you actually stood in the stables beside one of the empty mangers, the call of a bird was as shrill as early cock-crow. And you could almost see ghostly horses with their dark eyes looking round at you out of their long narrow heads, as if to say: 'So this is what you have done for us!'

Not that Jean Elspeth had very much time to linger over such little experiences. No; and she seemed to have grown even smaller in the empty house. But she was ten times more active. And, though she tried not to be selfish by showing it, she was more than ten times happier. Between Jean Elspeth herself and the eagle-surmounted gateposts, indeed, she now secretly confessed that she had always hated Stoneyhouse. How very odd, then, that the moment it ceased to be a place in which *any* fine personage would be proud to be offered a pillow, she began to be friends with it. She began to pity it.

No doubt Tabitha was right. Their grandfather would assuredly have 'turned in his grave', poor creature, at the sound of those enormous vans, those hideous pantechnicons, as their wheels ground down the gravel in the lingering twilight evenings. And yet, after all, that grandfather had been born – a fact that very much shocked Tabitha, whenever her father had smilingly related it – their grandfather had been born in a two-roomed cottage so cramped that, if only you could have got it through the window, it would have fitted quite comfortably even into the breakfast-room of the great house he had lived to build.

Then there had been not two bawbees in his breeches pocket, and – having been such a good man, as both Euphemia and Tabitha agreed – he did not need a bawbee now. *Would* he then – once the pantechnicons were out of the way – would he, thought Jean Elspeth, have been so very miserable to see all this light and sunshine in the house and to listen to these entrancing echoes.

There were other advantages, too. It was easy to sweep the dining-room now; and much easier to dust it. And one day, more out of kindness than curiosity, after busily whisking over its gilt frame with her feather cornice-broom, Jean Elspeth climbed on to a chair, and, tilting it, looked in at the portrait. A spider had spun its web in one corner, but otherwise (it was almost disappointing) the picture was unchanged. Nor had Mr MacKnackery yet taken his watch out of his pocket, even though (for his three granddaughters at any rate) the time was now – well, a good way past a quarter to twelve.

Jean Elspeth had had ridiculous thoughts like these as long as she could remember. But now they came swarming into her head like midsummer bees into a hive. Try as she might, she could not keep them all to herself, and though on this account alone Tabitha seemed to dislike her more than ever, Euphemia seemed sometimes to wish for her company. But then Euphemia was by no means well. She had begun to stoop a little, and sometimes did not hear what was said to her. To watch her visibly grow older like this gave Jean Elspeth dreadful anxiety. Still, in most things – and she all but said it out loud every morning at her first early look out of her upper window – she was far happier than when Stoneyhouse stood in all its glory. It seemed rather peculiar, but it was true.

Also, there was no time to be anything else; and even if there had been a complete cupboard *full* of neat packages of time *saved*, she would have used them all up in week. Euphemia, being so poorly, did very little. She helped to make the beds and with the mending. Only the mending, for, fortunately, the making of any new clothes would be unnecessary for years and years to come; they had so many old ones. Tabitha did what she could manage of the lighter work, but although she had a quick tongue, she had slow, clumsy hands. And it is quite certain, though nobody, naturally, would have been so unkind as to say so, that she would never have got even as low wages as Sally McGullie, if she had been in need of a place.

Mrs O'Phrump did the cooking; but sat on a chair in the kitchen for so many hours together that she became almost like a piece of furniture herself – the heaviest piece in the house. For the cooking of water-porridge and potatoes does not require very much time, and these were now pretty much all that the Miss MacKnackeries had to eat, except for the eggs from Jean Elspeth's three Cochin-Chinas. And Mrs O'Phrump needed most of these, as there was so much of her to sustain. As for the apples and pears in the orchard, since Mrs O'Phrump was too stout to stoop to make dumplings, Jean Elspeth, having two wonderful rows of small sharp teeth, shared these raw with Tom Piper – though *he* had all the stomach-aches.

All the rest of the work fell to Jean Elspeth. She slaved from morning till night. And to slave the more merrily, she had taught herself to whistle. She never asked herself why she was so happy. And no doubt it was chiefly by contrast with having been so cramped in, and kept under, and passed over in days gone by.

Still, certain things did now happen in Stoneyhouse that had not happened before, and some of these may have helped. For one thing, Jean Elspeth had always dreaded 'company'. Dressing-up made her feel awkward. The simplest stranger made her shy. She much preferred the company even of her two sisters. None came now, except Dr Menzies, who of his kindness sometimes called to feel Euphemia's pulse and mutter, 'H'm h'm' – though he did not charge for it.

Jean Elspeth, too, had never liked servants, not because

they were servants, but because Euphemia and Tabitha seemed to think they oughtn't to be talked to much. Just given their orders. Now Jean Elspeth could easily have given everything else in the world: but not orders. And if there ever *had* been an interesting creature in Stoneyhouse, even though she was so stupid in some things, it was Sally McGullie.

Then, again, Jean Elspeth, being by nature desperately untidy, never showed it now. For it's all but impossible to be untidy in a room that contains only a table and three chairs!

Then, yet again, Jean Elspeth, before the gentlemen in Armenia and Madagascar had been disappointed in their water-works and caoutchouc, had had very little to do. She was scarcely even allowed to read. For Tabitha was convinced that most reading was a waste of time, and trash at that; while improving books had never the least bit improved Jean Elspeth. But now she had so many things to do that it was perfect joy to fit them all in (like the pieces of a puzzle). And the perfectest joy of all was to scramble into her truckle bed, which had formerly been Sally McGullie's bed, and, with a tallow candle stuck by its own grease to the lefthand knob, to read and read and read.

The hours she spent like this, with no living company but roving mice and flitting moths and, in autumn, perhaps a queen wasp. When her upper parts grew cold in winter weather, she spread her skirt over the quilt. One thin blanket, indeed, is not much comfort on cold nights when one is lying up North there, almost in positive view of the Grumpy Ones. As for her feet, she used to boil some water in the great solitary kitchen in a kettle and fill a wine-bottle.

This, of course, broke a good many bottles; and it was an odd thing that until there was only one left, Tabitha

194

(whose feet were like slabs of ice) refused to hear of anything so vulgar. And *then* she changed her mind. And medicine-bottles are too small.

Apart from all this, queer things now happened in Stoneyhouse. Little things, but entrancing. The pantechnicon men, for example, had broken a window on a lower staircase as they were heaving down old Mr MacKnackery's best wardrobe. A sweetheart pair of robins in the springtime noticed this hole, and decided to build their nest in a nook of the cornice. Jean Elspeth (with her tiny whistling) was accepted as the bosom friend of the whole family.

There was, too, a boot cupboard, one too far from the kitchen for Mrs O'Phrump to range. Its window had been left open. And when, by chance, Jean Elspeth looked in one sunny afternoon, there hung within it a marvellous bush of Traveller's Joy, rather pale in leaf, but actually flowering there; and even a butterfly sipping of its nectar. After that, not a day passed now but she would peep in at this delicate green visitor, and kiss her hand. It was, too, an immense relief to Jean Elspeth to have said goodbye for ever to lots of things in the house that seemed to her to have been her enemies ever since she was five years old.

She wandered up into rooms she had never seen before, and looked out of windows whose views had never before lain under her eyes. Nor did she cease to day-dream, but indulged in only tiny ones that may come and go, like swifts, between two ticks of a clock. And although, of course, Tabitha strongly disapproved of much that delighted Jean Elspeth now, there was not nearly so much time in which to tell her so.

Besides, Jean Elspeth was more useful in that great barracks of a place than ten superior parlour-maids would have been. She was much more like a steam-engine than a maiden lady. And, like a steam-engine, she refused to be angry; she refused to sulk; and she usually refused to answer back. When nowadays, however, she *did* answer back, her tongue had a sting to it at least as sharp (though never so venomous) as that of the busy bee.

And last, but no less, there was the *outside* of the house. As soon as ever Mr McPhizz and his under-gardeners had departed with their shears and knives and edging-irons and mowing machines, wildness had begun to creep into the garden. Wind and bird carried in seeds from the wilderness, and after but two summers, the trim barbered lawns sprang up into a marvellous meadow of daisies and buttercups, plantains, dandelions, and fools' parsley, and then dock, thistle, groundsel and feathery grasses. Ivy, hop, briony, convolvulus roved across the terrace; Hosts of the Tiny blossomed between the stones. Moss, too, in mats and cushions of a green livelier than the emerald, or even than a one-night-old beech-leaf. Rain-stains now softly coloured the white walls, as if a stranger had come in the night and begun to paint pictures there. And the roses, in their now hidden beds, rushed back as fast as ever they could to bloom like their wild-briar sisters again.

And not only green things growing. Jean Elspeth would tiptoe out to see complete little immense families of rabbits nibbling their breakfast or supper of dandelion leaves on the very flagstones under the windows. Squirrels nutted; moles burrowed; hedgehogs came beetle-hunting; mice of every tiny size scampered and twinkled and danced and made merry.

As for the birds – birds numberless! And of so many kinds and colours and notes that she had to sit up half the night looking out their names in the huge birdbook her father had given her on her eleventh Christmas. This was the one treasure she had saved from the pantechnicon men. She had wrapped it up in two copies of the *Scotsman*, and hidden it in the chimney. She felt a little guilty over it at times, but none the less determined that the Four Lawyers should never hear of *that*.

It was strange, exceedingly strange, to be so happy; and Jean Elspeth sometimes could hardly contain herself, she was so much ashamed of it in the presence of her sisters. Still, she now drew the line, as they say, at Lucy.

And that was the strangest and oddest thing of all. After the dreadful shock of the Four Lawyers' letter, after the torment and anxiety and horror, the pantechnicons and the trades-people, poor Tabitha and Euphemia – however brave their faces and stiff their backs – had drooped within like flowers in autumn nipped by frost. In their pride, too, they had renounced even the friends who would have been faithful to them in their trouble.

They shut themselves up in themselves more than ever, like birds in cages. They scarcely ever even looked from the windows. It was only on Sundays they went out of doors. Euphemia, too, had sometimes to keep her bed. And Jean Elspeth would cry to herself, 'Oh, my dear! oh, my dear!' at the sight of Tabitha trailing about the house with a large duster and so little to dust. To see her sipping at her water-porridge as if she were not in the least hungry, as if it was the daintiest dish in Christendom, was like having a knife stuck in one's very breast.

Yet, such was Tabitha's 'strength of mind' and hardihood, Jean Elspeth never dared to comfort her, to cheer her up, to wave her spoon by so much as a quarter of an inch in *her* direction.

In these circumstances it had seemed to Jean Elspeth it would be utterly unfair to share Lucy's company, even in her hidden mind. It would be like stealing a march, as they say. It would be cheating. At any rate, it might hurt their feelings. They would see, more stark than ever before, how desolate they were. They would look up and realize by the very light in her eyes that her old playmate had not deserted her. No. She would wait. There was plenty of time. She would keep her wishes down. And the little secret door of her mind should be left, not, as it once was, wide open, but just ajar.

How, she could not exactly say. And yet, in spite of all this, Lucy herself, just as if she were a real live ghost, seemed to be everywhere. If in her scrubbing Jean Elspeth happened to glance up suddenly out of the window – whether mere fancy or not – that fair gentle face might be stealthily smiling in. If some moonlight night she leaned for a few precious sweet cold moments over her bedroom sill, as likely as not her phantom would be seen wandering, shadowless, among the tall whispering weeds and grasses of the lawn.

Phantoms and ghosts are usually very far from welcome company. Lucy was nothing but gentleness and grace. The least little glimpse of her was like hearing a wild bird singing – black-bird or black-cap, not in the least like the solitary hoot-owl whose long, bubbling, grievous notes seem to darken the darkness. Having this ghost, then, for company, however much she tried not to heed it, all that Jean Elspeth had to do in order just to play fair – and she did it with all her might – was not to *look* for Lucy, and not to *show* that she saw her, when there she was, plain to be seen, before her very eyes. And when at last she realized her plan was succeeding, that Lucy was gone from her, her very heart seemed to come into her mouth.

And so the years went by. And the sisters became older and older, and Stoneyhouse older and older too. Walls, fences, stables, coach-house, hen-house, and the square lodge crept on steadily to rack and ruin. Tabitha kept more and more to herself, and the sisters scarcely spoke at meal-times.

Then at last Euphemia fell really ill; and everything else for a while went completely out of Jean Elspeth's life and remembrance. She hadn't a moment even to lean from her window or to read in her bed. It was unfortunate, of course, that Euphemia's bedroom was three stair-flights up. Jean Elspeth's legs grew very tired of climbing those long ladders, and Tabitha could do little else but sit at the window and knit – knit the wool of worn-out shawls and stockings into new ones. So she would stay for hours together, never raising her eyes to glance over the pair of horn-rimmed spectacles that had belonged to her grandfather, and now straddled her own lean nose. Dr Menzies, too, was an old man now, and could visit them very seldom.

Jean Elspeth herself seldom even went to bed. She sat on a chair in Euphemia's room and snatched morsels of sleep, as a hungry dog snatches at bits of meat on a butcher's tray. It was on such a night as this, nodding there in her chair, that, after having seemed to fall into a long narrow nightmare hole of utter cold and darkness, and to have stayed there for centuries without light or sound, she was suddenly roused by Euphemia's voice.

It was not Euphemia's usual voice, and the words were following one another much more rapidly than usual, like sheep and lambs running through a gate. Daybreak was at the window. And in this first chill eastern light Euphemia was sitting up in bed – a thing she had been unable to do for weeks. And she was asking Jean Elspeth to tell her who the child was that was now standing at the end of her bed.

Euphemia described her, too – 'A fair child with straight hair. And she is carrying a bundle of gorse, with its prickles, and flowers wide open. I can smell the almond smell.

And she keeps on looking and smiling first at me, and then at you. Don't you *see*, Elspeth? Tell her, please, to go away. Tell her I don't want to be happy like that. She is making me afraid. Tell her to go away at once, please.'

Jean Elspeth sat shivering, colder than a snail in its winter shell. The awful thing was to know that this visitor must be Lucy, and yet not to be able to see her – not a vestige, nothing but the iron bed and the bedpost, and Euphemia sitting there, just gazing. How, then, could she tell Lucy to go away?

She scurried across the room, and took Euphemia's cold hands in hers. 'You are dreaming, Euphemia. *I* see nothing. And if it is a pleasant dream, why drive it away?'

'No,' said Euphemia, in the same strange, low, clear voice. 'It is not a dream. You are deceiving me, Elspeth. She has come only to mock at me. Send her away!'

And Jean Elspeth, gazing into her sister's wide light eyes, that now seemed deeper than the deepest well that ever was on earth, was compelled to answer her.

'Please, please, Euphemia, do not think of it any more. There is nothing to fear – nothing at all. Why, it sounds like Lucy – that old silly story; do you remember? But I have not seen her myself for ever so long. I *couldn't* while you are ill.'

The lids closed gently down over the wide eyes, but Euphemia still held tight to Jean Elspeth's work-roughened hand. 'Never mind, then,' she whispered, 'if that is all. I had no wish to take her away from you, Elspeth. Keep close to me. One thing, we are happier now, you and I.'

'Oh, Euphemia, do you mean that?' said Jean Elspeth, peering closer.

'Well,' Euphemia replied; and it was as if there were now two voices speaking: the old Euphemia's and this low, even, dream-like voice. 'I mean it. There is plenty of air now – a different place. And I hope your friend will come as often as she pleases. There's room for us all.'

And with that word 'room', and the grim smile that accompanied it, all the old Euphemia seemed to have come back again, though a moment after she dropped back upon her pillow and appeared to be asleep.

Seeing her thus quiet once more, Jean Elspeth very, very cautiously turned her head. The first rays of the sun were on the window. Not the faintest scent of almond was borne to her nostrils on the air. There was no sign at all of any company. A crooked frown had settled on her forehead. She was cold through and through, and her body ached; but she tried to smile, and almost imperceptibly lifted a finger just as if it held a teaspoon and she was waving it in her own old secret childish way to her father's portrait on the wall.

Now and again after that Jean Elspeth watched the same absent far-away look steal over Euphemia's face, and the same fixed smile, dour and grim, and yet happy – like still deep water under waves. It was almost as if Euphemia were amused at having stolen Lucy away.

'You see, my dear,' she said suddenly one morning, as if after a long talk, 'it only proves that we all go the same way home.'

'Euphemia, please don't say that,' whispered Jean Elspeth.

'But why not?' said Euphemia. 'So it is. And *she* almost laughing out loud at me. The hussy! ...'

None of their old friends knew when Euphemia died, so it was only Dr Menzies and his sister who came to Stoneyhouse for the funeral. And though Jean Elspeth would now have been contented to do *all* the work in the house and to take care of Tabitha and her knitting into the bargain, they persuaded her at last that this would be impossible.

And so, one blazing hot morning, having given a little parting gift to Tom Piper and wept a moment or two on Mrs O'Phrump's ample shoulder, Jean Elspeth climbed with Tabitha into a cab, and that evening found herself hundreds of miles away from Stoneyhouse, in the two upper rooms set apart for the two ladies by Sally McGullie, who had married a fisherman and was now Mrs John Jones.

Jean Elspeth could not have imagined a life so different. It was as if she had simply been pulled up by the roots. Whenever Tabitha could spare her – and that was seldom now – she would sit at her window looking on the square stone harbour and the sea, or in a glass shelter on its narrow front. But now that time stretched vacantly before her, and she was at liberty if she pleased to 'pretend' whenever she wished, and to fall into day-dreams one after another just as they might happen to come, it was life's queer way that she could scarcely picture Lucy now, even with her inward eye, and never with her naked one.

It was, too, just the way of this odd world that she should pine and long for Stoneyhouse beyond words to tell. She felt sometimes she must die – suffocate – of home-sickness, and would frown at the grey moving sea, as if that alone were the enemy who was keeping her away from it. Not only this, but she saved up in a tin money-box every bawbee which she could spare of the little money the Four Lawyers had managed to save from the caout-chouc. And all for one distant purpose.

And at length, years and years afterwards, she told Mrs Jones that she could bear herself no longer, that – like the cat in the fairy-tale – she must pay a visit, and must go alone ...

It was on an autumn afternoon, about five o'clock, and long shadows were creeping across the grasses of the for-saken garden when Jean Elspeth came into sight of Stoneyhouse again, and found herself standing some little distance from the gaunt walls beside a shallow pool of water that now lay in a hollow of the garden. Her father had delighted in water; and, putting to use a tiny stream that coursed near by, had made a jetting fountain and a fishpond. The fountain having long ceased to flow and the pond having become choked with water-weeds, the stream had pushed its way out across the hollows, and had made itself this last dark resting-place. You might almost have thought it was trying to copy Jean Elspeth's life in Sallie Jones's seaside cottage. On the other hand, the windows of the great house did not stare so fiercely now; they were blurred and empty like the eyes of a man walking in his sleep. One of the chimney-stacks had toppled down, and creepers had rambled all over the wide expanse of the walls.

Jean Elspeth, bent-up old woman that she now was, in her dingy black bonnet and a beaded mantle that had belonged to Euphemia, stood there drinking the great still scene in, as a dry sponge drinks in salt water.

And after hesitating for some little time, she decided to venture nearer. She pushed her way through the matted wilderness of the garden, crossed the terrace, and presently peered in through one of the dingy dining-room windows. Half a shutter had by chance been left unhasped. When her eyes were grown accustomed to the gloom within, she discovered that the opposite wall was now quite empty. The portrait of her grandfather must have slowly ravelled through its cord. It had fallen face upwards on to the boards beneath.

It saddened her to see this. She had left the picture hanging there simply because she felt sure that Euphemia would so have wished it to hang. But though she wearied herself out seeking to find entry into the house, in order, at least, to lean her grandfather up again against the wall, it was in vain. The doors were rustily bolted; the lower windows tight-shut. And it was beginning to be twilight when she found herself once more beside the cold stagnant pool.

All this while she had been utterly alone. It had been a dreadful and sorrowful sight to see the great house thus decaying, and all this neglect. Yet she was not unhappy, for it seemed with its trees and greenery in this solitude to be uncomplaining and at rest. And so, too, was she. It was as if her whole life had just vanished and flitted away like a dream, leaving merely her body standing there in the evening light under the boughs of the great green chestnut-tree overhead.

And then by chance, in that deep hush, her eyes wandered to the surface of the water at her feet, and there fixed themselves, her whole mind in a sudden confusion. For by some curious freak of the cheating dusk, she saw gazing back at her from under a squat old crape bonnet, with Euphemia's cast-off beaded mantle on the shoulders beneath it, a face not in the least like that of the little old woman inside them, but a face, fair and smiling, as of one eternally young and happy and blessed – Lucy's. She gazed and gazed, in the darkening evening. A peace beyond understanding comforted her spirit. It was by far the oddest thing that had ever happened to Jean Elspeth in all the eighty years of her odd long life on earth.

Miss Jemima

It was a hot, still evening; the trees stood motionless; and not a bird was singing under the sky when a little old lady and a child appeared together over the crest of the hill. They paused side by side on the long, green, mounded ridge, behind which the sun was now descending. And spread out flat beneath them were the fields and farms and the wandering stream of the wide countryside. It was quite flat, and a faint thin mist was over it all, stretching out as if to the rim of the world. The stooping old lady and the child presently ventured a few further paces down the hillside, then again came to a standstill, and gazed once more, from under the umbrella that shaded them against the hot sun, on the scene spread out beneath them.

'Is *that* the house, Grannie,' said the child, 'that one near the meadow with the horses in it, and the trees? And is that *queer* little grey building right in the middle of that green square field the church?'

The old lady pressed her lips together, and continued to gaze through her thick glasses at the great solitary country scene. Then she drew her umbrella down with a click, placed it on the turf beside her, and sat down on it.

'I don't suppose the grass *is* damp, my dear, after this long hot day; but you never know,' she said.

'It's perfectly dry, Grannie dear, and *very* beautiful,' said the child, as if she could hardly spare the breath for the words. Then she too sat down. She had rather long fair hair, and a straight small nose under her round hat with its wreath of buttercups. Her name was Susan.

'And *is* that the house, Grannie?' she whispered once
more. 'And *is* that the church where you did really and
truly see it?'

The old lady never turned her eyes, but continued to
overlook the scene as if she had not heard the small voice
questioning; as if she were alone with her thoughts. And at
that moment, one after another, a troop of gentle-stepping,
half-wild horses appeared on a path round the bluff of the
hill. Shyly eyeing these two strange human figures in their
haunts, one and another of them lifted a narrow lovely
head to snort; and a slim young bay, his mane like rough
silk in the light, paused to whinny. Then one by one they
trotted along the path, and presently were gone. Susan
watched them out of sight, then sighed.

'This is a lovely place to be in, Grannie,' she said, and
sighed again. 'I wish I had been here too when I was little.
Please do tell me again about the – *you* know.'

Her voice trailed off faintly in the still golden air up there
on the hill, as if she were now a little timid of repeating the
question. She drew in closer beside her grannie, and pushing her small fingers between those of the bent-up, black-
gloved hand in the old lady's lap, she stooped forward after
yet another pause, looked up into the still grey face with
its spectacles, and said very softly, '*How* many years ago
did you say?'

There was a mild far-away expression in the slate-grey
eyes into which Susan was looking, as if memory were
retracing one by one the years that had gone. Never had
Susan sat like this upon a green hill above so immense a
world, or in so hushed an evening quiet. Her busy eyes
turned once more to look first in the direction in which
the trotting comely horses had vanished, then down again
to the farmhouse with its barns and byres and orchard.

They then rested once more on the grey stone church –
which from this height looked almost as small as an old
cottage – in the midst of its green field.

'*How* many years ago, Grannie?' repeated Susan.

'More than I scarcely dare think of,' said the old woman
at last, gently pressing her fingers. 'Seventy-five, my dear.'

'Seventy-five!' breathed Susan. 'But that's not so very
many, Grannie dear,' she added quickly, pushing her head
against her grannie's black-caped shoulder. 'And now, before it is too late, please will you tell me the story. You
see, Grannie, soon we shall have to be going back to the
cab, or the man will suppose we are not coming back at all.
Please.'

'But you know most of it already.'

'Only in pieces, Grannie; and besides, to think that here
we are – here, in the very place!'

'Well,' began the old voice at last, 'I will tell it you all
again, if you persist, my dear; but it's a little *more* than
seventy-five years ago, for – though you would not believe
it of such an old person – I was born in May. My mother,
your great-grandmother, was young then, and in very
delicate health after my father's death. Her doctor had said
she must go on a long sea voyage. And since she was not
able to take me with her, I was sent to that little farmhouse down there – Green's Farm, as it was called – to
spend the months of her absence with my Uncle James and
his housekeeper, who was called Miss Jemima.'

'Miss Jemima!' cried the little girl, stooping over suddenly with a burst of laughter. 'It *is* a queer name, you
know, Grannie.'

'It is,' said the old lady. 'And it belonged to one to
whom it was my duty to show affection, but who never
cared much for the little girl she had in her charge. And
when people don't care for you, it is sometimes a little

207

difficult, Susan, to care for them. At least *I* found it so. I don't mean that Miss Jemima was unkind to me, only that when she was kind, she seemed to be kind on purpose. And when I had a slice of plum cake, her face always seemed to tell me it was *plum* cake, and that I deserved only plain. My Uncle James knew that his housekeeper did not think me a pleasant little girl. I was a shrimp in size, with straight black hair which she made me tie tightly back with a piece of velvet ribbon. I had small dark eyes and very skimpy legs. And though he himself was kind, and fond of me, he showed his affection only when we were alone together, and not when she was present. He was ill, too, then, though I did not know *how* ill. And he lay all day in a long chair with a check rug over his legs, and Miss Jemima had charge not only of me, but of the farm.'

'*All* the milking, and the ploughing, and the chickens, and the pigs, Grannie?' asked Susan.

The old lady shut her eyes an instant, pressed her lips together and said, 'All.'

'The consequence was,' she went on, 'I was rather a solitary child. Whenever I could, I used to hide myself away in some corner of the house – and a beautiful house it is. It's a pity, my dear, I am so old and you so young and this hill so steep. Otherwise we could go down and – well, never mind. That row of small lattice windows which you can see belong to a narrow corridor; and the rooms out of it, rambling one into the other, were walled in just as the builders fancied, when they made the house three hundred years or more ago. And that was in the reign of Edward VI.'

'Like the Bluecoat boys,' said Susan, 'though I can't say I like the yellow stockings, Grannie, not that *mustard* yellow, you know.'

'Like the Bluecoat boys,' repeated her grandmother. 'Well, as I say, the house was a nest of hiding-places; and as a child I was small – smaller even than you, Susan. I would sit with my book; or kneel up on a chair and watch from a window, lean *out* too sometimes – as if by doing so I might be able to see my mother in India. And whenever the weather was fine, and sometimes when it was not, I would creep out of the house and run away down that shaggy lane to the little wood down there. There is a brook in it (though you can't see that) which brawls continuously all day long and all the night too. And sometimes I would climb up this very hill. And sometimes I would creep across the field to that little church.

'It was there I most easily forgot myself and even my little scrapes and troubles – with the leaves and the birds, and the blue sky and the clouds overhead; or watching a snail, or picking kingcups and cowslips, or staring into the stream at the fish. You see I was rather a doleful little creature: first because I was usually alone; next because my Uncle James was ill and so could not be happy; and last because I was made to feel more homesick than ever by the cold glances and cold tongue of Miss Jemima.'

'Miss Jemima!' echoed Susan, burying her face in her amusement an instant in her hands.

'Miss Jemima,' repeated the old voice solemnly. 'But I was not only dismal and doleful. Far worse: I made little attempt to be anything else, and began to be fretful too. There was no company of my own age, for, as you see, the village is a mile or two off – over there where the sun is lighting the trees up. And I was not allowed to play with the village children. The only company I had was a fat little boy of two, belonging to one of the farm-hands. And he was so backward a baby that even at that age he could scarcely say as many words.'

'I began to talk at one,' said Susan.

'Yes, my dear,' said her grannie, 'and you are likely, it seems, to go on talking the clock round.'

'Grannie, dear,' said Susan, 'I simply *love* this story – until – *you* know.'

'Well, of all the places strictly forbidden me to play in,' continued the old lady, 'that peaceful little churchyard came first. My "aunt", as I say, thought me a fantastic silly-notioned little girl, and she didn't approve of my picking flowers that grow among tombstones. Indeed, I am not now quite sure myself if such flowers belong to the living at all. Still, once or twice in the summer the old sexton – Mr Fletcher he was called, and a very grumpy old man he was – used to come with his scythe and mow the lush grasses down. And you could scarcely breathe for the sweet smell of them. It seemed a waste to see them lying in swathes, butterflies hovering above them, fading in the sun. There never were such buttercups and dandelion-clocks and meadow-sweet as grew beneath those old grey walls. I was happy there; and coming and going, I would say a prayer for my mother. But you will please understand, Susan, that I was being disobedient; that I had no business to be there at all at any time. And perhaps if I had never gone, I should never have known that there was somebody else in the churchyard.'

'Ah! somebody else,' sighed Susan, sitting straight up, her eyes far away.

'It was one evening, rather like this one, but with a mackerel sky. The day before I had been stood in the corner for wearing an orange ribbon in my hair; and then sent to bed for talking to the grandfather's clock. I did it on purpose. And now – *this* evening, I was being scolded because I would not eat blackberry jam with my bread for tea. I was told it was because I had been spoilt, and was

a little town child who did not know that God had made
the wild fruits for human use, and who thought that the
only things fit to eat grew in gardens.

'Really and truly I disliked the blackberry jam because
of the pips, and I had a hollow tooth. But I told my "aunt"
that my mother didn't like blackberry jam either, which
made her still more angry.

' "Do you really think, James," she said to my uncle,
"we should allow the child to grow up a dainty little minx
like that? Now, see here, Miss, you will just stay there until
you have eaten up the whole of that slice on your plate."

' "Well, then, Miss Jemima," I said pertly, "I shall stay
here till I am eighty."

' "Hold your tongue," she cried out at me, her eyes
blazing.

' "I can't bear the horrid —" I began again, and at
that she gave me such a slap on my cheek that I over-
balanced, and fell out of my chair. She lifted me up from
the floor, with a shake set me in my chair again, and pushed
it against the table till the edge was cutting into my legs.
"And now," she said, "sit there till you are eighty!"

'A look I had never seen before came into my uncle's
face; his hands were trembling. Without another word to
me, Miss Jemima helped him rise from his chair, and I
was left alone.

'Never before had I been beaten like that. And I was at
least as much frightened as I was hurt. I listened to the tall
clock ticking. "Wick-ed child, stubborn child", and my tears
splashed slowly down on the odious slice of bread-and-
jam on my plate. Then all of a sudden I clenched and
shook my ridiculous little fist at the door by which she had
gone out, wriggled back my chair, jumped out of it, rushed
out of the house, and never stopped to breathe or to look
back, until I found myself sitting huddled up under the

biggest tomb in the churchyard; crying there, if not my
heart out, at least a good deal of my sour little temper.'

'Poor Grannie!' said Susan, squeezing her hand.

'There was not much "poor" about that,' was the reply.
'A pretty sight I must have looked, with my smeared face,
green-stained frock and hair dangling. At last my silly
sobbing ceased. The sky was flaming with the sunset. It
was in June, and the air was cool and mild and sweet. But
instead of being penitent and realizing what a bad and
foolish child I was, I began to be coldly rebellious. I stared
at the rosy clouds and vowed to myself I'd give Miss
Jemima a fright. I'd rather die than go back to the house
that night. And when the thought of my mother came into
my mind, I shut it out, saying to myself that she could
not have cared how much I loved her, to leave me like
this. And yet only a fortnight before a long letter had come
to me from India!

'Well, there I sat. A snail came out of his day's hiding-
place; little moths were flitting among the grasses; the
afternoon's butterflies had all gone to rest. Far away I
heard a hooting – and then a step. Cautiously peering up
above my tombstone, I saw Maggie, one of the girls that
helped on the farm. Her face was burning hot, and she was
staring about her round the corner of the little church
tower with her saucer-blue eyes. She called to me, but
couldn't see me, and at that my mouth opened and I let
out, as they say, a shrill yelping squeal. It alarmed even
me a little to hear it. She screeched; her steel-tipped boot
slipped on the flagstones; in an instant she was gone. And
once more I was alone.'

'Ah, but you weren't *really* alone, Granny,' whispered
Susan, '*were* you?'

'That is just what I was going to tell you, my dear.
Immediately in front of my face stood a few late dandelion

stalks, with their beautiful clocks, grey in the still evening light. And there were a few other gently nodding flowers. As I stared across them, on the other side of the flat gravestone a face appeared. I mean it didn't rise up. It simply came into the air. A very small face, more oval than round, its gold-coloured hair over its wild greenish eyes falling on either side its head in a curious zigzag way – like this, I mean.' The old lady took the hem of her skirt, and three or four times folded it together, then loosened it out.

'You mean, Grannie, as if it had been pleated,' said Susan.

'Yes,' said her grannie. 'And strange and lovely it looked in the reddish light. The face was not smiling, and she did not appear to see me. And yet I knew *she* knew that I was there. And though I did not think she minded my being there, I felt more frightened than I had ever been in my life. My mouth opened; I was clutching tight the grass on either side. And I saw nothing else as I stared into that face.'

'That was the Fairy, Grannie,' said Susan, stooping forward again as if to make her words more impressive. The old lady glanced fixedly at the two blue eyes bent on her from under the brim of the round straw hat.

'At that moment, my dear, I did not know *what* it was. I was far too frightened to think. Time must have been passing, too, very quickly, for as I stared on, it was already beginning to be gloaming between us, and silent. Yes, much more silent even than this. Then, suddenly, behind me a low, sweet, yet sorrowful voice began to sing from out of the may-bushes, the notes falling like dewdrops in the air. I knew it was a nightingale. And at the very moment that the thought came to me – "That is a nightingale" – the face on the other side of the rough grey stone vanished.

213

'For a few minutes I sat without moving – not daring to move. And then I ran, straight out of the churchyard by the way I had come as fast as my legs could carry me. I hardly know what I thought, but as soon as I saw the lights in the upper windows of the farm, I ran even faster. Up under the ilexes and round through the farmyard to the back door. It was unlatched. I slipped through, quiet as a mouse, into the kitchen, climbed into the chair, and at once devoured every scrap of that horrid bread-and-jam!

'And still, my dear, I don't believe I was really thinking, only dreadfully afraid, and yet with a kind of triumph in my heart that Miss Jemima should never know anything at all about the face in the churchyard. It was all but dark in the kitchen now, but I still sat on in my chair, even at last lifted the plate, and insolently licked up with my tongue every jammy crumb that was left.

'And then the door opened, and Miss Jemima stood there in the entry with a lighted brass candlestick in her hand. She looked at me, and I at her. "Ah, I see you have thought better of it," she said. "And high time too. You are to go straight to bed."

'If you can imagine, Susan, a cake made almost entirely of plums, and every plum a black thought of hatred, I was like that. But I said never a word. I got down from my chair, marched past her down the flagstone passage, and she followed after. When I came to my uncle's door, I lifted my hand towards the handle. "Straight on, Miss," said the voice behind me. "You have made him too ill and too unhappy to wish you good night." Straight on I went, got into bed with all my clothes on, even my dew-wet shoes, and stared at the ceiling till I fell asleep.'

'You know, Grannie,' said Susan, 'it was very curious of you not even to undress at all. Why do you think you did that?'

'My dear,' said her grannie, 'at that moment I had such a hard, hot heart in me, that there was not any room for a why. But you see that little jutting attic window above the trees – it was in the room beyond that and on the other side of the house that I lay. And it's now seventy-five years ago. It may be there was even then a far-away notion in my mind of getting up in the middle of the night and running away. But whether or not, I was awakened by the sun streaming through my lattice window, for my bedroom lay full in the light of the morning.

'I could think of but one thing – my disgrace of the night before, and what I had seen in the churchyard. It was a dream, I thought to myself, shutting my eyes, yet knowing all the time that I did not believe what I was saying. Even when I was told at breakfast that my uncle was no better, I thought little of him, and gobbled down my porridge, with the one wish to be out of the house before I could be forbidden to go. But the only sign of Miss Jemima was my dirty jam-stained plate of the night before, upon which she had put my hunch of breakfast bread. Yet although I was so anxious to get out, for some reason I chose very carefully what I should wear, and changed the piece of ribbon in my hat from blue to green. A rare minx I was.'

'You were, Grannie,' said Susan, clasping her knees. 'And then you went out to the churchyard again?'

'Yes. But all seemed as usual there; except only that a tiny bunch of coral-coloured berries lay on a flat leaf, on the very tombstone where I had hid. Now though I was a minx, my dear, I was also fairly sharp for my age, and after the first gulp of surprise, as I stood there among the nodding buttercups, the sun already having stolen over the grey roof and shining upon the hot tombstones, I noticed a beady dewdrop resting on the leaf, and the leaf of as fresh a green as lettuce in a salad. Looking at the dewdrop I realized at once that the leaf could not have been there very long. Indeed, in a few minutes the sun had drunk up that one round drop of water, for it was some little time before I ventured to touch the berries.

'Then I knew in my heart I was not alone there, and that the green dish had been put there on purpose, just before I had come. The berries were strange yet beautiful to look at, too; of a coral colour edging into rose; I could not guess from what tree they had come. And I don't think it was because I had long ago been warned not to taste any wild fruit – except blackberries! – but because I was uneasy in conscience already, that I did not nibble one then and there.

'It was very quiet in that green place, and on and on I watched, as still as a cat over a mouse's hole, though I myself really and truly was the mouse. And then, all of a sudden, flinging back my green dangling hat-ribbon, I remember, over my shoulder, I said half aloud, in an affected little voice, "Well, it's very kind of you, I am sure," stretched my hand across, plucked one of the berries, and put it into my mouth.

'Hardly had its juice tartened my tongue when a strange thing happened. It was as if a grasshopper was actually sitting in my hair, the noise of that laughter was so close. Besides this, a kind of heat began to creep into my cheek, and it seemed all the colours around me grew so bright that they dazzled my eyes. I closed them. I must have sat there for a while quite unconscious of time, for when I opened them again, the shadow had gone perceptibly back from the stone, and it was getting towards the middle of the morning.

'But there was still that dazzle in my eyes, and everything I looked at – the flowers and the birds, even the moss

217

and lichen on the old stones – seemed as if they were showing me secrets about themselves that I had not known
before. It seemed that I could share the very being of the
butterfly that was hovering near; and could almost hear
not only what the birds were singing but what they were
saying.'

'Just like the fairy-tales, Grannie.'

'Yes,' said the little old woman, 'but the difference is that
I was not happy about it. The flush was still in my cheek,
and I could hear my heart beating under my frock, and I
was all of an excitement. But I knew in my inmost self
that I ought not to feel like that at all; that I had crept into
danger through my wicked temper; that these little unknown coral fruits on the tombstone had been put there for
a trap. It was a bait, Susan; and I was the silly fish.'

'Oh, Grannie, a "silly fish"!' said Susan. 'I can see you
might feel wicked,' she added, with a sage little nod, 'but
I don't *exactly* see why.'

'That is just when it's most dangerous, my child,' said
her grandmother, sharply closing her mouth, very much
indeed like a fish. 'But I must get on with my story, or we
shall never get home.

'I sat on, keeping my eyes as far as I could fixed on the
invisible place in the air where I had seen the face appear,
but nothing came, and gradually the scene lost its radiance,
and the birds were chirping as usual again, and the buttercups were the same as ever. No, not the same as ever,
because, although it was a burning, sunny day, it seemed
now that everything was darker and gloomier than usual
on so bright a morning, and I skulked away home, feeling
not only a little cold, but dejected and ashamed.

'As I went in through the gate between those two stone
pillars you can just see by the round green tree down
there, I looked up at the windows. And a dreadful pang

seized me to see that their curtains were all drawn over
the glass. And though I didn't know then what that meant,
I knew it meant something sorrowful and tragic. Besides,
they seemed like shut eyes, refusing to look at me. And
when I went in, Miss Jemima told me that my uncle was
dead. She told me, too, that he had asked to see me an
hour or two before he died. "He said, 'Where is my little
Susan?' And where you have been," added Miss Jemima,
"is known only to your wicked wilful self." I stared at her,
and seemed to shrink until she appeared to be twice as large
as usual. I could not speak, because my tongue would not
move. And then I rushed past her and up the stairs into a
corner between two cupboards, where I used sometimes to
hide, and I don't know what I did or thought there; I simply
sat on and on, with my hands clenched in my lap, everything I looked at all blurred, and my lips trying to say a
prayer that would not come.

'From that day on I became a more and more wretched
and miserable little girl, and, as I think now, a wickeder
one. It all came of three things. First, because I hated
Miss Jemima, and that is just like leaving a steel knife in
vinegar, it so frets and wastes the heart. Next, because of
the thought of my poor uncle speaking of me so gently
and kindly when he was at death's door; and my remorse
that I could never now ask him to forgive me. And last,
because I longed to see again that magical face in the
churchyard, and yet knew that it was forbidden.'

'But, Grannie dear, you know,' said Susan, 'I never can
see why you should have thought that then.'

'No,' replied the old lady. 'But the point was, you see,
that I *did* think it, and I knew in my heart that it would
lead to no good. Miss Jemima made me go next day into
the room where my uncle lay in his coffin. But try as she
might to persuade and compel me, she could not make me

open my eyes and look at him. For that disobedience she sent me to my bedroom for the rest of the day.

'When all was still, I crept out across the corridor into another room, and looked out over the trees towards the little church. And I said to myself, as if I were speaking to someone who would hear, "I am coming to you soon, and nobody, *nobody* here shall ever see me again."

'Think of it; a little girl not yet nine, angry with the whole world, and hardly giving a thought to the mother who was longing to see her, and – though I didn't know it then – was very soon to be in England again.

'Well, then came the funeral. I was dressed – I can see myself now, as I stood looking into the looking-glass – in a black frock trimmed with crape, with a tucker of white frilling round the neck, and an edging of it at the sleeves; my peaked white face and coal-black eyes.

'It was, as you see, but a very little distance to my poor uncle's last resting-place, and in those days they used a long hand-cart on wheels, which the men pushed in front of us, with its flowers. And Miss Jemima and I followed after it across the field. I listened to the prayers as closely as I could. But at last my attention began to wander, and, kneeling there beside Miss Jemima in the church, my hands pressed close to my eyes, for an instant I glanced out and up between my fingers.

'The great eastern window, though you cannot see it from here, is of centuries-old stained glass, crimson, blue, green. But in one corner, just above the narrow ledge of masonry outside, it had been broken many, many years ago by the falling of a branch of a tree, and had been mended with clear *white* glass. And there, looking steadily in and straight across and down at me, was the face and form of the being I had seen beside the tombstone.

'I cannot tell you, Susan, how beautiful that face looked

then. Those rich colours of the saints and martyrs sur-
rounding that gold hair – living gold – and the face as pale
and beautiful – far more beautiful than anything else I
had ever seen in my life before. But even then I saw, too,
that into the morning church a cold and shadowy darkness
had come, and the stone faces on either side the window,
with their set stare, looked actually to be alive. I peeped
out between my fingers, hearing not a single word of what
the old clergyman was saying, wondering when anyone else
would see what I saw, and knowing that the coldly smiling
lips were breathing across at me, "Come away, come
away!"

'My bones were all cramped, and at last I managed to
twist my head a little and glance up at Miss Jemima. The
broad face beneath her veil had its eyes shut, and the lips
were muttering. She had noticed nothing amiss. And when
I looked again, the face at the window had vanished.

'It was a burning hot day – so hot that the flowers beside the grave were already withering before Miss Jemima
took me home. We reached the stone porch together, and
in its cold shadow she paused, staring down on me through
her veil. "You will be staying on here for a while, because
I don't know what else to do with you," she said to me.
"But you will understand that this is my house now. I am
telling your mother how bad a child you are making yourself, and perhaps she will ask me to send you away to a
school where they will know how to deal with stubborn
and ungrateful beings like yourself. But she will be sorry,
I think, to hear that it was your wickedness that brought
that poor kind body to its grave over there. And now, miss,
as the best part of the day is over, you shall have your
bread-and-butter and milk in your bedroom, and think
over what I have said." '

'I think, Grannie,' cried Susan, suddenly bending herself

over her knees, 'that that Miss Jemima was the most dreadful person I have ever heard of.'

'Well, my dear,' said her grandmother, 'I have lived a
good many years, and believe it is wiser to try and explain
to oneself people as well as things. Do you suppose she
would have been as harsh to me if I hadn't hated her?
And now she lies there too, and I never had her forgiveness either.'

Susan turned her head away and looked out over the
countryside to the north, to where the roving horses had
vanished, and where evening was already beginning
gradually to settle itself towards night.

'And *did* you think over what Miss Jemima had said,
Grannie?' she asked in a low voice.

'The first thing I did was to throw the bread-and-butter
out of the window, and while I watched the birds wrangling
over it and gobbling it up, I thought of nothing at all. It
was cooler in the shade on that side of the house. My head
ached after the hot sorrowful walk to the church and back.
I came away from the window, took off my black frock,
and sat there on the edge of my bed, I remember, in my
petticoat, not knowing what to do next. And then, Susan,
I made up my mind that I could not bear to be in Miss
Jemima's house for a day longer than I needed.

'I was just clever enough to realize that if I wanted to
run away I must take care not to be brought back. I grew
hot all over, remembering what she had said to me, never
thinking how weak and silly I was not to be able to endure
patiently what could only be a few more days or weeks
before another letter came from my mother. Then I tore
a leaf from a book that was in my room – a Prayer Book
– and scrawled a few words to my mother, saying how
miserable *and* wicked I had been, and how I longed to see
her again. It's a curious thing, Susan, but I was pitying

myself while I wrote those words, and thinking how grieved my mother would be when she read them, and how well Miss Jemima would deserve whatever my mother said to her. But I didn't utter a word in the letter about where I was going.'

'You didn't really *know* where you were going, Grannie,' whispered Susan, edging a little nearer. 'Did you? Not *then*, I mean?'

'No, but I had a faint notion whom I was going *to*; for somehow, from old fairy tales I had got to believe that human children could be taken away to quite a different world from this – a country of enchantment. And I remembered having read, too, about two children that had come back from there, and had forgotten their own English.'

'I know two poems about it,' said Susan. 'One about "True Thomas" – "Thomas the Rhymer", you know, Grannie, who stayed with the Queen of Elfland for seven whole years, and another about ... I do wonder – But please, *please*, go on.'

'Well, I hid my little letter in a cranny in the wainscot, after sewing a piece of cotton to it so that I might pull it out again when I wanted it. The next morning, I got up early, and slipping on my clothes, tiptoed out of the house before breakfast, and made my way to the church. I thought deceitfully that Miss Jemima would be sure to find out that I had gone, and that if for a morning or two she discovered me quietly sitting in the churchyard she would not suppose at another time, perhaps, that I was not safely there again. Plots, Susan, are tangled things, and are likely to entangle the maker of them too.

'The old man who took care of the church, Mr Fletcher, to save himself the trouble of carrying the key to the door, used to hide it under a large stone beneath the belfry tower. I had watched him put it there. It was a fresh sparkling day, I remember, with one or two thin silver clouds high in the sky – angels, I used to call them – and I forgot for the moment in the brightness of it all my troubles, as I frisked along past the dewy hedges.

'My first thought was to make quite, quite sure about the strange being in the churchyard, my next to plan a way of escape. I gathered a bunch of daisies, and having come to the belfry door, I somehow managed to open it with the key which I fetched out from beneath its stone, and crept into the still, empty coolness. I had come to the conclusion, too, Susan, young though I was, that if the elf or fairy or whatever she might be actually came into the church to me, it would be a proof there was no harm in her company, though I knew in my heart that I was in some mysterious danger.

'There are a few old oak pews in the little church, with heads carved upon them, and one or two have side seats that draw out from beneath into the aisle. On one of these I sat down, so that while I could be intent on my daisy-chain – just to show I had something to do there – I could see out of the corner of my eye the open door by which I had come in. And I hadn't very long to wait.

'In the midst of the faint singing of the wild birds, out of the light that lay beyond the stone church wall I spied her come stealing. My heart almost stopped beating, nor did I turn my head one inch, so that my eyes soon ached because they were almost asquint with watching. If you can imagine a figure – even now I cannot tell you how tall she was – that seems to be made of the light of rainbows, and yet with every feature in its flaxen-framed face as clearly marked as a cherub's cut in stone; and if you can imagine a voice coming to you, close into your ear, without your being able to say exactly where it is coming *from* – *that* was what I saw and heard beneath that grey roof down there on that distant morning, seventy-five years ago. The longer I watched her out of the corner of my eye, the more certain I became that she was using every device she knew to attract my attention, even that she was impatient at my stupidity, and yet that she could not or that she dared not cross the threshold. And so I sat and watched her, fumbling on the while with my limpening daisy-stalks. Many strange minutes must have passed like this.

'At last, however, having fancied I heard a footfall, I was surprised out of myself, and suddenly twisted my head. She too had heard, and was standing stiller than a shadow on snow, gazing in at me. I suppose thoughts reveal themselves in the face more swiftly than one imagines. I was partly afraid, partly longing to approach closer. I wished her to realize that I longed for her company, but that danger was near, for I was well aware whose step it was I had heard. And, as I looked at her, there came a sharpness into her face, a cold inhuman look – not of fear, but almost of hatred – and she was gone. More intent than ever, I stooped over my daisies. And in the hush there was a faint sound as of an intensely distant whistle.

'Then a shadow fell across the porch, and there was Miss Jemima. It's a strange thing, Susan, but Miss Jemima also did not enter the church. She called to me from where she stood, in almost a honeyed voice: "Breakfast is ready, Susan."'

'I can imagine *exactly* how she said that, Grannie,' said the little girl, 'because my name's Susan, too.'

'Yes, my dear,' said the old lady, squeezing her hand. 'It was passed on to you from me by your dear mother just because it was mine. And I hope you will always be the Susan I have *now*.' ... From near at hand upon the hill a skylark suddenly took its flight into the evening blue.

The old lady listened a moment before going on with her story.

'Well,' she began again, 'I gathered up my apron and walked towards Miss Jemima down the aisle. Suddenly there came a slight rumbling noise, which I could not understand. Then instantly there followed a crash. And at Miss Jemima's very feet, in the sunlight, I saw lying a piece of stone about the size of a small plum pudding. Miss Jemima gave a faint scream. Her cheek, already pale, went white; and she stared from me to the stone and back again, as I approached her.

' "You were talking in there to someone – in God's church," she whispered harshly, stooping towards me. "To whom?"

'I shook my head, and stood trembling and gazing at the stone.

' "Look into my face, you wicked child," she whispered. "Who were you talking to in there?"

'I looked up at last. "It's empty," I said.

' "There's a lying look in your eyes!" cried Miss Jemima. "And *you* are the child that goes into a sacred place to weave daisy-chains! Turn your face away from me. Do you hear me, miss? Miserable little *sorceress* that you are!"

'The word seemed to flame up in my mind as if it had been written in fire on smoke; and still I stared at the stone. I felt but did not see Miss Jemima steadily turn her head and look around her.

' "A few inches," she added in a low voice, "and you would have killed me."

' "Me!" I cried angrily. "What has it to do with *me*, Miss Jemima?"

' "Ah!" said she. "We shall know a little more about that when you have told me what company you find here where your poor uncle might hope to be at rest."

'It's a dreadful thing to confess, Susan, but up to that moment, though I had again and again cried by myself at memory of him, though tears were always in my heart for him, I hadn't thought of my uncle that morning.

' "And perhaps," added Miss Jemima, "bread and water and solitude for a day or two will help to loosen your tongue."

'I followed her without another word across the fields, and in a few minutes was alone once more in my bedroom with a stale crust and a glass of water to keep me company.

'I should think that if my angry tears had run into the water that morning they would have actually made it taste salt. But I cried so that not even a mouse could have heard me. Every other thought was now out of my mind – for I dared not even talk to myself about the stone – but that of getting away from the house for ever. One thing I could not forget, however. And that was the word "sorceress". It terrified me far more than I can tell you. I knew in my mind that Miss Jemima was treating me wickedly, however wicked *I* had been, and I knew too, in fear and horror, that the stone might not have fallen by accident. I had seen the look on the Fairy's face and ...' The old lady suddenly broke off her story at this point, and looked about her in alarm. 'My dear, we must go at once; the dew is beginning to fall, and the air is already colder.'

'Oh, Grannie,' said the child, 'how I wish we might stay – a little, *little* longer!'

'Well, my dear, so do I. For I am old, and I shall never see this place again. It brings many memories back. Who knows what might have happened if –'

'But, Grannie,' interrupted the child hastily, picking up the umbrella from the grass. 'Please tell me the rest of the story straight, straight, straight on as we go back.' It seemed to Susan, so rapt was her grandmother's face at that moment, and so absent her eyes – that she could not have heard her. Those small aged eyes were once more looking carefully down on the scene below. For an instant they shut as if the old lady had thought so to remember it more completely. And then the two of them began slowly to climb the hill, and the story proceeded.

'No one disturbed me during that long morning,' continued the quiet voice, 'but in the afternoon the door was unlocked, and Miss Jemima opened it to show in a clergyman, Mr Wilmot, who conducted the service in the church every other Sunday. I won't tell you all he said to me. He was a kind and gentle old man, but he didn't so much as think it possible there was any being or thing in the churchyard but its birds, its tombstones, and now and then a straying animal. He only smiled about all that, nor did he ask me Miss Jemima's question.

'He took my hand in his great bony one and begged me to be a good little girl. And I see his smiling face as he asked it. "Not only for your mother's sake," he said, "but *for 'goodness' sake'*."

' "I am sure, my dear," he went on, "Miss Jemima *means* to be kind, and all that *we* have to do is to mean to be good."

'I gulped down the lump in my throat and said, "But don't you think *sorceress* is a very wicked word?"

'He stood up, holding both my hands in his. "But my poor little lamb," he cried, "Miss Jemima is no more a sorceress than I am a Double Dutchman!" And with that he stooped, kissed the top of my head, and went out of the room.

'In a minute or two his footsteps returned. He opened the door an inch and peeped in. "Why, we are better already!" He smiled at me over his spectacles. Then he came in, carrying a plate with a slice of bread-and-jam upon it, and a mug of milk. "There," he said, "there's no sorcery in that, is there? And now you will be an obedient and gentle child, and think how happy your mother will be to see you?" '

'I think,' said Susan stoutly, 'that that Mr Wilmot is one of the kindest men I ever knew.'

Her grandmother looked down on her with a peculiar smile on her face. 'He was so kind, Susan, that I never mentioned to him that the blackberry-jam on the bread was not a great favourite of mine! A moment after the sound of his footsteps had died away I heard the key once more in the lock. And what did I say to myself when he was gone? I looked forlornly at the plate, then out of the window, and I believe, Susan, that I did what they sometimes describe in the story-books – I wrung my hands a little, repeating to myself, *"He doesn't understand. No! No! He doesn't understand."*

'In an hour or two, Miss Jemima herself opened the door and looked in. She surveyed me where I sat, and then her glance fell on the untouched slice of bread-and-jam.

' "Ah," said she, "a good man like Mr Wilmot cannot realize the hardness of a stubborn heart. I don't want to be unkind to you, Susan, but I have a duty to perform to your mother and to your poor dead uncle. You shall not leave this room until you apologize to me for your insolence of this morning, and until you tell me whom you were speaking to in the church."

'The lie that came into my mind – "But I was not speaking to anyone, Miss Jemima" – faded away on my tongue. And I simply looked at her in silence.

' "You have a brazen face, Susan," said she, "and if you grow up as you are now, you will be a very wicked woman." '

'I think,' said Susan, 'that was a perfectly *dreadful* thing to say, Grannie.'

'Times change, my dear,' said the old lady. 'And now – well, it is fortunate there is very little more to tell. For this hill has taken nearly all the breath out of my body!'

The two of them stood now on the crest of the hill. The light was beginning to die away in the sky, and the mists to grow milkier in the hollows of the flat country that lay around and beneath them. Far, far away, facing them across the world, a reddish-coloured moon was rising. From far beneath them a dog barked – it might be from dead Miss Jemima's farmyard. The little church surrounded by its low wall seemed to have gathered in closer to its scattered stones.

'Yes, Grannie, dear?' breathed Susan, slipping her hand into the cotton-gloved one that hung near. 'What then?'

'Then,' replied her grandmother, 'the door was locked again. Anger and hatred filled that silly little body sitting in the bedroom, and towards evening I fell asleep. And I must have dreamed a terrifying dream, though when I awoke I could not remember my dream – only its horror. I was terrified at it in that solitude, and I knew by the darkening at the window that it must be at least nine or ten o'clock. Night was coming, then. I could scarcely breathe at the thought. Another mug of milk had been put beside the plate; but I could not even persuade myself to drink any of it.

'Then in a while I heard Miss Jemima's footsteps pass my room. She made no pause there, and presently after I knew that she had gone to bed, having not even troubled to look in on her wretched little prisoner. The hardness of that decided me.

'I waited until it seemed certain she was asleep. Then I

tiptoed over to the door, and with both hands softly twisted the handle. It was still locked. Then I went to the window and discovered, as if the fairy creature herself had magicked it there, that a large hay-wain half full of hay, its shafts high in the air, had been left drawn up within a few feet of my window. It looked dangerous, but it was not actually a very difficult jump even for a child of my age; and I believe I should have attempted it if there had been no cart at all. My one wild thought was to run away. *Any*where – so long as there was no chance of Miss Jemima's ever finding me again. Could you ever have dreamed of such a little silly, Susan?

'But even in that excited foolish moment I had sense enough left – before I jumped out of the window – to take a warm woollen jacket out of my chest-of-drawers, and to wrap my money-box up in a scarf so that it should not jangle too much. I pulled my letter up from its cranny in the wainscot by its thread, and put it on the pink dressing-table. And at that moment, in the half dark I saw my face in the looking-glass. I should hardly have recognized it. It looked nearly as old, Susan, as I do now.'

'Yes, dear Grannie,' said Susan.

'Then I jumped – without the slightest harm to myself. I scrambled down into the yard and, keeping close to the house, crept past the kennel, the old sheep-dog merely shaking his chain with his thumping tail a little as I passed. And then, as soon as I was beyond the tall stone gate-posts, I ran off through the farm-yard, past the barns, and along the cart-track as fast as I could.'

'But *not*,' cried Susan almost with a shout in the still air, '*not* to the churchyard, Grannie. I think that was the most wonderful thing of all.'

'Not so very wonderful, my dear, if you remember that I was now intensely afraid of the fairy, after seeing that look of evil and hatred in her face when Miss Jemima was approaching the church. Something in me, as you know, had never ceased to counsel me, *Don't be deceived by her. She means you no good.* I cannot explain that; but so it was. Yet all the time I had been longing to follow wherever she might lead. Why she should wish to carry off a human child I don't know, but that she really wanted me I soon discovered for certain.

'If you follow the tip of my umbrella, you will now just be able to see, Susan, that great meadow sloping upwards beyond the farm. But I don't think even your sharp eyes will detect the circle of old grey stones there. They are called the Dancers, and though I was dreadfully frightened of passing them in the darkness, this was the only way to take. Gradually I approached them, my heart beating beneath my ribs like a drum, until I had come near.

'And there, lovelier than ever, shining in that dark as if with a light of her own, and sitting beneath the largest of the Dancers directly in my path, was She. But this time I knew she was not alone. I cannot describe what passed in my heart. I longed to go on, and yet was in anguish at the thought of it. I didn't dare to look at her, and all I could think to do was to pretend not to have seen her at all. How I found the courage I cannot think. Perhaps it was the courage that comes when fear and terror are almost beyond bearing.

'I put my money-box on to the grass; the scarf was already wet with dew. Then, very slowly, I put my black jacket on and buttoned it up. And then, with my eyes turned away, I walked slowly on down the path, between the Dancers, towards the one that is called the Fiddler, in their midst. The night air here was cold and still. But as I approached the stone, it seemed as if the air was full of voices and patterings and sounds of wings and instruments. It terrified and bewildered me; I could think of nothing.

'I just kept saying, "Oh, please, God; oh, please, God!" and walked on. And when at last I came to the stone, the whole world suddenly seemed to turn dark and cold and dead. And then! Apart from the ancient stone, jutting up out of the green turf as it had done for centuries, there was not a sign, not a vestige, Susan, of anything or anybody there!'

'I think I can *just* see the stone, Grannie, but I don't think I could dare to be alone there in the dark, not for anything – anything in the world ... I expect it was what you *said* made the Fairy go. And then, Grannie?'

'Then, Susan, my heart seemed to go out of me. I ran on, stumbling blindly for a little way, then lost my balance completely over a tussock of grass or a mole-heap and fell flat on my face. Nettles too! Without any words that I can remember, I lay praying in the grass.

'But even that did not turn me back. I got up at last and ran on more slowly, and without looking behind me, across the field. Its gate leads into a by-road. It was padlocked, and as I mounted to the top my eyes could see just above a slight rise in the ground, for the lane lies beneath a little hill there.

'And coming along the road towards me there were shining the lamps of a carriage. I clambered down and crouched in the hedge-side, and in a few moments the lamps reappeared at the top of the incline and the horse came plod-plodding along down the hill. It was a wonderful summer night, the sky all faint with stars. What would have happened if it had been cold or pouring with rain, I cannot think. But because it was so warm, the air almost like milk, the hood of the carriage was down.

'And as it came wheeling round by the hedge-side, I saw in the filmy starlight who it was who was sitting there. Neither horse nor coachman had seen me. I jumped to my feet and ran after the carriage as fast as my legs could carry me, screaming at the top of my voice, "Mother, Mother!"

'Perhaps the grinding of the wheels in the flinty dust and the thump of the hoofs drowned my calling. But I still held tight to my money-box, and though it was muffled by the scarf in which it was wrapped, at each step it made a dull noise like a bird-scare, and this must at last have attracted my mother's attention. She turned her head, opened her mouth wide at sight of me – I see her now – then instantly jumped up and tugged at the coachman's buttoned coat tails. The carriage came to a standstill ...

'And that,' said the old lady, turning away her head for one last glance of the countryside around her, 'that is all, Susan.'

Susan gave a last great sigh. 'I can't think what you must have felt, Grannie,' she said, 'when you were safe in the carriage. And I can't –' But at this point she began to laugh very softly to herself, and suddenly stood still. 'And I can't think either,' she went on, 'what Miss Jemima must have thought when you and *Great*-Grannie knocked at the door. You did tell me once that she opened her bedroom window at the sound of the knocking, and looked out in her nightdress. I expect she was almost as frightened as you had been, amongst those Dancers.'

The two of them were now descending the hill on the side away from the farm and the church. And they could see not only their carriage standing beneath them, but the evening star had also come into view. There could not be a more peaceful scene – the silver birches around them standing motionless under the deep, pale sky, clothed with their little leaves, and the rabbits at play among the gorse and juniper.

'Bless me, Mum,' said the old cabman as he opened the carriage door, 'I was just beginning to think them *fairises* must have runned away with you and the young lady.'

Susan burst completely out laughing. 'Now don't you think, Grannie,' she said, 'that is a very, very, very curious quincidence?'

The Magic Jacket

When, that May Day morning, Admiral Rumbold stepped out of his four-wheeled cab at the corner of Pall Mall, he was carrying a small brown-paper parcel. Why he had not told his cabman who – hunched up on his box – looked older even than his horse, to take him on to exactly where he wanted to go, he hardly knew. He paid the old man his fare; and he added an extra sixpence.

'Thank'ee,' he said with a curt nod, then turned to continue on his way. Admiral Rumbold was not exactly a stout man, but in his navy-blue clothes, his neat boots, and brown billycock hat, he looked rather tightly packed. His broad face shone almost as red as a tomato above his white linen collar and blue-and-white spotted silk sailor's knot. He clasped his neat little brown-paper parcel closely under his elbow, and at a good round pace proceeded along Pall Mall.

He glanced neither to right nor left of him, but kept his sea-bleached blue eyes fixed steadily ahead. Nor did he show the least sign of recognition when he caught sight of an old friend brandishing a silver-headed cane in his direction from under the hood of a hansom-cab. On this particular morning – and the houses and shops looked sparklingly gay in the spring sunshine – Admiral Rumbold wished to be alone. He marched straight on, his eyes fixed, his mouth tight-shut, almost as if he were walking in his sleep.

He turned sharply up St James's Street, past the saddler's

with the jockey caps and jackets behind the glass, past the little bow-windowed snuff-and-tobacco shop, and so into King Street. From King Street he turned off into Duke Street, and then on into Great St Ann's. After the bustle and traffic now behind him, the quiet sunshine and shadow of Little St Ann's beyond it was like port after stormy seas.

Now a few paces past the hatter's shop that stood at the corner of Little St Ann's lay a wide smooth stretch of flat paving-stones under a high old brick wall. It was here that a screever or pavement artist had made his pitch; and here in the sunshine Admiral Rumbold came to a halt and looked about him.

The street was still, and, at this early hour of the morning, almost deserted. For a while, firm as a rock, he continued so to stand. But having failed to catch a glimpse of what he was after, he began to survey a little vacantly the pictures chalked on the stones at his feet.

The first of them was of a ship with bare masts and lanky spars, tossing on an indigo sea, its waves yeastily crested with spray. Next to this there was a windmill in a gaudy country green, the miller himself standing up like Shem, Ham, and Japhet at the little rounded door above the wide wooden ladder. Next, there was a gaping brace of rainbow-coloured, rather flabby-looking mackerel. Next, a loaf of bread, a cut cheese, and a neat little long-tailed mouse at her supper. And last – and best of all to some tastes – there stood a lonely country mansion among its wintry trees, a wild moon gleaming down on its walls. Scrawled beneath this picture, in a flowery lettering, was the one word, 'H O R N T E D'.

Admiral Rumbold had taken a good long look at these pictures only the evening before. They showed a little livelier in the morning sunshine. Still, he had come back not to have another look at them, but to have a word with the young artist. Few street chalkers, the Admiral had noticed in his walks abroad, are much less than forty. The one he now had in mind could not be more than fourteen. The Admiral had taken a liking to him at first sight, had often watched him at his work, and had dropped many a tuppence into the old cloth cap that usually lay (as if with its mouth wide open) beside the pictures. Now he wished to speak to him.

To an old gentleman with a temper as peppery as the Admiral's it was therefore an unpleasant jar to find that when he wanted the boy he was nowhere to be seen. Besides, he was anxious to get rid of the brown-paper parcel under his arm. He had a dislike to carrying anything at all – even an umbrella so massive that it looked more like a war-club. On the other hand he was a man who, having once made up his mind, kept it made up.

He crossed the street, and spent the next few minutes pacing solemnly up and down, glancing ever and again as he did so down the area railings or up at the upper windows of the houses on that side of it, in order to pretend to himself that he was not being kept waiting. And every time he turned smartly on his heel, he glared first up the street, then down the street, and then into the deep-blue empty sky.

At last he had his reward. Shuffling along close to the railings from out of a neighbouring alley, in shoes that even at this distance looked a good deal more roomy than comfortable, appeared the boy the Admiral was in wait for. A coat that was at least two sizes too large for its present wearer hung down from his bony shoulders. But he had turned the cuffs up over the sleeves, so that his claw-like hands came out free from beneath them.

His odd, almost ugly face was pale and not too clean. His brown hair was lank and tousled. But as the Admiral had noticed before, the skull beneath the hair was nut-shaped and compact, clear over the forehead and wide towards the back. It looked as if it closely fitted something valuable inside it. Besides which, the boy had a pair of eyes in the pinched face looking out from under that skull, which once seen were not easily forgotten.

Admiral Rumbold, at sight of him, had slipped in under the carved shell-shaped porch of one of the neighbouring houses. From here he could see without being seen.

First, the boy glanced into his cap, then took it up, turned it upside down, shook it, and replaced it on the pavement. He then drew a large dingy rag out of his pocket, that might once have been the flap of a man's shirt or a woman's petticoat. With both hands he waved this to and fro above his pictures to waft away the dust and straw and soot-smuts. He then pushed the rag into his pocket again, and had a steady look at the pictures, as if he had never seen them before and could not make up his mind whether or not to give himself a penny. He then sighed – a sigh that in the morning quietness was clearly audible. At this Admiral Rumbold stepped out of his hiding-place, crossed the road, and accosted him.

'Good morning, my boy,' was his greeting. 'How's business?'

The boy looked up into the round red face of the old gentleman, with its small beak-like nose and sky-blue eyes, and a timid smile passed over his own as he shook his head.

'So, so!' said Admiral Rumbold bluffly. 'Nothing much, eh? There's a bit of east in the wind this morning and perhaps that keeps folk moving. Or perhaps ... Well, there we are! Had any breakfast! No? Good! I want a word with 'ee. Is there a place handy where we can sit and talk?'

The boy coloured, glanced swiftly from right to left, and told the Admiral of a coffee-shop near at hand where he sometimes went himself. Then he looked up at the old Admiral again, became redder than ever, and broke off.

'Full steam ahead, then,' said his friend. 'And do you lead the way.'

The boy buttoned his coat: away they went together; and in a minute or two the pair of them were sitting face to face on two benches between wooden partitions – like the high pews in old churches – and on either side of a table in an eating-house halfway up the neighbouring alley. The Admiral asked the boy what he would take. He said a mug of thick.

At this the Admiral cocked one of his bright blue eyes, and enquired if he would like anything to eat with it. The boy hesitated, and suggested a doorstep.

'H'm!' said the Admiral, 'and anything for a sweet tooth to follow?'

The boy said he would like a cat's eye. Whereupon Admiral Rumbold rapped smartly on the table. A man with greasy black hair, of a dark face, wearing a rather dingy apron, appeared from his den behind the shop.

'Good morning,' said the Admiral. 'Two mugs of thick, a door-step, and a cat's-eye.' And he said the words as if he had been used to them all his life and knew exactly what they meant.

The mugs of thick proved to be cocoa; the door-step a slab of bread with a scrimp of butter; and the cat's-eye was a large yellow bun with a burnt raisin stuck in its crown. And while the two of them sipped their thick, and the boy from nibbling went on to munching at his door-step, Admiral Rumbold explained what he was after.

But first he asked him a little about himself and his work. He learned that the boy was pretty well alone in the world. His father, who had been a carriage painter, had died when he was six. His own business was fair in fine weather, but it was hard to find a pitch where there were neither too many passers-by nor too few. 'And then there's the bobbies,' said the boy. Summer was better than winter, but up to the last week or two there had been too much rain for any business at all.

'Ay, ay,' said the Admiral, looking at him over the thick brim of his mug as he took another sip of cocoa, 'a fine-weather trade, I take it.' And he asked him what his name was. It was Mike.

'Well now, Mike,' said Admiral Rumbold at last, 'I've been keeping an eye on you for some little time. I've been *wanting* to keep an eye on someone of your age and looks for a good deal longer. I like your pictures; in fact, I *admire* them. If *I* were to sit down under that wall with every scrap of chalk you've got and do my level best with them, rain or no rain, I warrant my takings wouldn't be fourpence a month. It's the knack you want. And it's the knack, my lad, you have.

'Not, mind you,' he went on, 'that I know any more about pictures than what I *like*. I leave the rest to them that do. But I've lived a good many years in the world now, and my belief is that every walk in life begins with a steepish bit of hill. When I was a boy – and we're not concerned just now with where *my* walk's led *me* – I had to face mine. And in this parcel here is – well, what helped me in the climbing of it.

'*Here*,' repeated the Admiral and said no more for the moment. For he had brought his square solid hand down on the parcel beside his mug with such a thump that the man in the apron came hurrying up to see what more was wanted.

'I'll have,' said the Admiral promptly, 'another mug of thick and another couple of door-steps. And this time put in a slice or two or more of beef and bacon by way of cement.'

The sandwiches that followed were almost as much meat as bread, and Mike's eyes fairly watered as they were handed over to him.

'In this parcel, as I was saying,' continued the Admiral, 'is the *story* of what I've been telling you. A yarn, you'll understand. Tell me, can you *read*?' Mike nodded violently; his mouth was full.

'Good!' said the Admiral. 'All I want you to do is to read it – it's about a *jacket* – what might be called a slice out of my early days, just as that bacon there maybe a slice out of the early days of the pig it came from. There's no hurry –' he glanced at the clock and then at his gold repeater – 'it's seventeen and a half minutes past ten. Sit here quietly and read as much of it as you can. When you have finished, come along to me. At eleven sharp I'll be waiting near the pitch.

'Mind ye,' he ended as he rose to his feet, 'there's no shadow of *must* in that package whatsoever. Nor do I vouch for anything beyond what's written – and I've had it printed out on one of those new-fangled machines so that it can be read plain and easy. Take it quietly; ask for anything you want while I'm away; and in half an hour we meet again.'

He put down half-a-crown on the table for the doorsteps, etc., laid his hand an instant on Mike's shoulder, and looked him hard but friendly in the eye. Then he instantly flung open the swing-door of the coffee-shop and went out into the street.

To judge from his face, the old gentleman was very well pleased with himself at this moment. He returned to the pictures, and spent the next half-hour, as cautiously as before, in pacing to and fro along the street. Whenever he passed them he paused to look at them, dropped a copper or two into the cap, and went on. At this, some curious passer-by would also stop and glance over Mike's gallery. And, maybe, he too would fling in a penny to join the Admiral's – and, maybe, not.

Meanwhile, Mike, left to himself and now the only customer in the coffee-shop, took a good long swig of his mug of cocoa and a munch at his sandwich before setting to work on the Admiral's story. And this was what he read :

'Coming down to facts at once, I was born all but seventy years ago, in a town in Shropshire of the name of P—. My father was a grocer – retail. His shop wasn't much to look at from outside, but there was little that his customers wanted in the way of groceries that couldn't be found even then on his shelves.

'My father was a man of about forty when I came into the world. My mother was a good deal younger; and mightily pleased they were to have me. No doubt about that. They christened me Andrew and called me Sandy, there being Scotch blood on my father's side. And if hard work and steady is a short cut to success, that was my father's way.

'At first, my father and mother were content to live over the shop – three rooms in all, not including one not much bigger than a bandbox, which was called the nursery. When I was six, things were going so well with the business that they decided to let the rooms above the shop, and to move into a small but comfortable, high and (what they call) semi-detached house, half a mile or so out of the town. We had a good strip of garden there – a few apple and plum trees, some currant and gooseberry bushes, and old country flowers.

'My mother loved that garden, and spent all the time she

243

could spare from the house in it, with me beside her, or digging away at a patch of soil, three yards by one, with scallop shells round the border, which she let me have to do what I pleased with. That was *my* garden. *Sandy-land*, she called it. Candytuft, Virginia stock, and Sweet Williams were my own particular crops.

'My mother, I remember, bless her soul, was a great talker. I don't mean by this that she talked too much, or talked to everybody, or never listened. I mean she was a great talker to me, though not so much to my father. What she and I chattered about when we went out shopping in the morning together, or when I used to help her make the beds, would fill a book. Everything under the sun, not to mention the other side of it.

'I don't know what there was about my mother – brown eyes, brown hair, and so on. But hanging up over the pianoforte in what was called our drawing-room was a portrait of her as a girl of eighteen or thereabouts which if I had been any kind of young man with an eye in his head I should have fallen in love with at first sight. But it wasn't her looks; it was her ways. How to put it I don't know, but she always seemed to be talking as if to somebody over her shoulder as well as to me myself.

'Never – and mine's a pretty long life now – never have I come across anyone with such a loving delight in birds, flowers, trees, clouds, stars, moss, butterflies, and all that. She knew them by heart. You might have thought she'd had a hand in their making. Words aren't my tools, and I must just get things down as straight as I *can*. But that was the way of it. To see her look at a toadstool, with some bright colour to its gills, or peep into a wren's or chaffinch's nest, or stand watching a bevy of long-tailed tits gossiping together for a minute or two in one of our tufted old apple-trees on their way to somebody else's, was like – well, I don't know what it wasn't like, except that it was like nothing on earth but my mother. She wasn't any *age* at all. We might have been a couple of brothers or sisters – old cronies, as you might say. We could hardly tell each other apart – except when my father was by.

'Now, I'm not going to say anything against *him*. He died when I was not much more than a quarter of the way up the ladder I was afterwards to set myself to climb. He did his best by me; and if it hadn't been for my own stubborn interference, he might have done better for me than I've done for myself. Can't say; don't *know*. What I wanted was to go my own way, as at last I went. And your own way is nobody else's way. It's a man's self – his *innards*, to speak abruptly – that counts. Not the stripes on his arm, or the cut of his jib, or the cash in his bank, or even what he's *done*.

'But enough of that. The truth is perhaps that being so much alone with my mother, and as contented in her company, at least in those first few years, as a butterfly with a flower, I became a bit of an apron-string child. She did not much care for going out, and she had a mighty small opinion of any young Two-Legs in the street except the one she herself had brought into the world, so I was only allowed to play with any small Tom, Dick, or Harry belonging to our neighbours provided I never went beyond view of her bedroom window. And that's not much of a playground for a healthy young sprat that ought to be learning what the sea looks like.

'Alone with her, and at peace, I wanted nothing else and could chatter away like a grasshopper. Away from her, I was usually little better than a tongue-tied numskull, flushing up to the eyebrows at a word from a stranger, and looked too shy and timid to say Boh to a goose – even to the goose in my own looking-glass! Well, numskull is as numskull does; and as the old wooden-legged sailor said,

When all you've got is a couple of stump,
There's nowt to do but go *clump – clump –clump*!

'My father could not see it that way. He began to think
I was stupid on purpose. There was not a sharper tradesman in the county, nor a more honest tradesman either, in
spite of the "sharp". All his wits were at his finger-tips.
He had a memory like a dictionary. He knew where everything was or ought to be. He could tell a bargain at
first wag of its tail and a good customer before he opened
his mouth. He lived long enough to make three fine shops
of his poky first one – plate-glass windows, plenty of gold
paint, three smart vans and about a dozen glossy-haired
assistants in clean white aprons. And he stowed a hand-
somer show of tea-chests, sugar loaves, jam-jars and
piccalilli pots behind those windows than any other grocer
in the town. I owe him unspeakably more than the little
fortune he left me.

'But being what he was, he was impatient with anything
else, and particularly with me, his own son. *Now*, I understand it. *Then*, the moment I saw his black hat above the
hedge, or heard his key in the lock, I would scuttle away
like a frightened rabbit. If we were left alone together, I
would sit as glum as a cold plum-duff pudding – without
any plums in it! If he asked me a question, every word
would fly out of my head, like rooks at a rattle. The mere
look of me at such times – fumbling and stammering –
made him angry. The more angry he grew the more tongue-
tied and lumpish grew I, and that would set my poor
mother weeping. And I have never yet met a father who
enjoyed being told that he could not understand his own
son. Not that he loved me a penny the less; far from it.
But love, my boy, is like coal. You can burn it, and warm

and comfort yourself with its light and heat. Or you can keep it in a cellar. My father kept his in a cellar – and it was I who helped him stack it up!

'With my mother, as I have said already, everything was different. We would gossip away together for hours. And when she wasn't with me I would talk to myself. I had plenty of books in my bedroom under the roof – books that had belonged to my mother's younger brother who died at sea. And I read like a limpet. When in those days I opened a book that seemed meant for me – travels, voyages, that kind of thing – it was like exploring another world. Fancy tales I never took to – except journeys to the moon, or the middle of the earth, and such-like – nor could even my mother win me to rhymes.

'Maybe it was all this book-stuff and solitude and having nobody to play with that began this odd habit in me of talking to myself when I was alone. And it was this talking to myself that led on to the great discovery. One evening, I remember, I was reading about the supper to which Sir Francis Drake invited the officer on his ship who had been stirring up mutiny against him, and whom he hanged next morning. And as I was listening to myself talking like the officer and putting up as stiff a lip as I could at the prospect of so harsh a breakfast, I suddenly discovered that there was not *one* of me, so to say, but two. I discovered what's called a second self – though of course he must have been there all the time. To make things plain and ship-shape, let us call the first of these two selves, Sandy One; and the second of these two selves, Sandy Two.

'There was first the Sandy One that was my father's son, and stayed at home with his mother in the high, oblong box of a house, standing up high on the hill with its neighbours, all in a row. This was the nervous, timid, stuttering

Sandy, the Sandy who did not know where he kept his own tongue, the skulker, the dunderhead whom my father could not make head or tail of. There was next the Sandy who when alone did more or less what he liked and went where he pleased – desert islands, Red Indians, lions and tigers, castaways, cannibals, *bonum omens* – all that kind of thing. Ay, and the whole world over. *He* pined for freedom. He wanted to do and dare things. He wanted to eat his cake and chance the stale crusts afterwards. This happy-go-lucky, scatter-brained, dare-devil creature boxed up inside me was Sandy Two. We'll call him, as I say, Sandy Two: and, Here's good luck to him! – for he needed it!

'Now, do you see, my mother knew something of both Sandies, though more of One than Two. My father never so much as dreamt of Two and saw not much more of One than his worst. And Sandy Two, at his darndest and daringest, was at present inside my head and kept for myself and my books alone.

'Now Schooling...'

Mike took a long slow look at this word before going any further. He was already a little tired of reading. He wanted to get to the jacket. Still, he had promised the old gentleman, who seemed to be an old gentleman who expected his promises to be kept, that he would do his best, and he had had an *uncommonly* good breakfast. So he swallowed another gulp of his tepid cocoa, took another huge bite of his door-step, and plodded on.

'Now Schooling. Well, I went to school like most boys of my age. It was what is called a Private School, and the headmaster's name was Smiles; and his name was not only where his smiles began but also ended. From the instant my father led me into his stuffy back-room, this Mr Smiles took me for a Dunce. One glance at my sheepish mottled face – Sandy One's – was enough for that. And as dunce he treated me almost until we parted. Dunce was his chief dish with me, from beginning to end – and plenty of cane sauce.

'I hated school. I hated learning. And as I was told to go straight home the moment my lessons were over, I was never much of a favourite with the other boys. They took me for a molly-coddle, and called me Tallow-candy. Which was true of course of Sandy One. And for some little time they never caught sight of Sandy Two. That came later. Still, whenever Sandy One warmed up so much in a scrap as to bring Sandy Two into it, it wasn't the other fellow that left off last!

'Well now, to make a long story short, my father's heart, as I have been saying, was in groceries. And you can take my word for it that there is one thing at least worse than a quick profit on pickles, and that is a dead loss on 'em. His business was growing; he pulled his weight wherever he went; he was soon to be Mayor; and having only one son, he hoped and meant that that son should go into groceries too, and perhaps some day *double* his fortune, keep a carriage, and become *Lord* Mayor. He wanted his son to "get on", and what father doesn't?

'So in the old days, just to polish my wits, he would ask me such questions as what raisins are, or where currants come from, or why peel is called candied; and then – with a flicker of his eyelids – who discovered the Macaroni Tree, or how much fresh there is to a pound of salt butter, or where the natives dig up nutmegs, or what is the temperature of Cayenne pepper, or what is the cost of a hogs-head of treacle at $2\frac{3}{4}$d. an ounce. The point is, I never even *wanted* to know such things. And worse, I couldn't even laugh at them!

'If my father had asked me what kind of birds you'd be likely to see flitting about in the craters of the moon; or what the war-whoop and scalping habits of the Objibwas or the Cherokees were; or how many brothers riding on white asses Abimelech had; I believe Sandy Two would have consented to answer. But Sandy Two (apart from toffee) had no interest whatever in Demerara or Barbados sugar; and Sandy One was no better than a blockhead at any questions whatsover, except when his mother asked them, or when he was alone.

'One Sunday morning, after I had first said I couldn't answer, and then refused to try to answer, some such questions as these, I looked up and told my father that I hated grocery shops. I said of all shops I hated grocery shops the most. I said I detested school, and that the only thing in the world I wanted was to run away to sea. Then I burst out crying. At this moment my mother came in, so I never got the thrashing I richly deserved.

'But my father must have thought things over; for after that, Dr Smiles paid very particular attention to the *grocery* side of history, geography, arithmetic and dictation. Even of French: "Has your neighbour's gardener the oranges from Jaffa, the tapioca from Brazil, and the chicory for the coffee of his aunt?" – that kind of thing.

'Then one night I overheard my mother and father talking. Sandy Two had come stealing downstairs about half-past nine to see what he could find in the larder. The door of the drawing-room was ajar, and I heard my father say: "He is not only half-witted, but as limp and flabby as a rag doll – and what's more, here's that bladder-of-lard, schoolmaster Smiles, saying exactly the same thing. And yet *you* ..." At these words Sandy One at once fled back to bed – taking Sandy Two with him. And I awoke next morning remembering what my father had said as distinctly as if it had been tattooed into my skin. For days together after that Sandy Two never so much as showed the tip of his nose in the house.

'Then, one afternoon, on my way home from school, I ventured down a shabby side-street, because at the far end of it I had caught the noise of a Punch-and-Judy Show. I could hear the children roaring with laughter, and the squeaking and the thumping and cockadoodle-ing of Mr Punch. Sandy Two told Sandy One he would like to go and see it. So he went.

'Coming back, we passed a dingy little shop I had never noticed there before, and we stopped to look in at the window. *Marine Store* was printed up in white letters over the green front. There was some queer junk behind that window: old shoes and shawls and old hats, a ship in a bottle, a green glass rolling-pin, a telescope that must have belonged to Noah, a ship's compass, a brass cannon, a bed-warmer, a picture made of humming-birds' feathers – such old curios as they call 'em as that. They looked as if they had been there for centuries – verdigris, mould, fluff, dust. Most of these articles had their prices marked on scraps of paper: *"Grate Bargin, 3s. 6d."* and so on.

'And hanging up on a nail in a corner of the window and almost out of sight, was a kind of garment I couldn't quite put name to. But a piece of paper was pinned to it, and on that was scrawled the words: *Majick Jacket*. Just that and nothing more. But it was enough. I had already gloated on the telescope and the ship and the brass cannon. But those two words, *Majick Jacket*, fairly took my breath away. They stirred me up as if with a ladle – me myself, Sandy Two, and even Sandy One. At last I could bear the strain no longer.

'I pushed open the crack-paint little door – I can hear even now the jingle of its rusty bell – and in I went. The place smelt like an old cellar. It was as soundless as a vault. For what seemed hours nothing happened, except that I heard a far-away canary singing; then Sandy One began to be alarmed, and I tiptoed off towards the door.

'Just as I was about to whip it open and bolt out into the street again, an old man, with thick magnifying spectacles on his nose and a beard like a goat, came shuffling out of the back parts of the shop, and asked me what I wanted.

'I said would he please tell me the price of the brass cannon – though I knew it already. Then I asked to see the ship in the bottle. And then, at last, with hardly any breath left in my body, I managed to point to the jacket.

' "That," he said, looking at it and then at me, "that's ten shillin'." '

'I got as red as a turkey-cock, coughed, turned about, and opened the door.

' "I say! I say, Mister!" he called after me. "What are you running away for? Come back and *see* it. Come back and look at it – *feel* it. No harm in that!" He was already climbing up on to a stool. Then he thrust his head in among the rags and drabs in the window, brought down the jacket, and laid it on the counter. And close-to, like this, it was nothing much, I must say, to look at.

'It was made of some kind of foreign dark Chinese-looking stuff, with a faint wavy pattern on it, and it had flat stone buttons with green crocodiles curled round on them. The braid was frayed at the neck and cuffs. I looked hard at it on the counter, but didn't touch it. Then I blurted out: "Who made it?"

' "Made it?" snapped the old man, "that's a *magic* jacket. That's come from Pekin and Madagascar and Seringapatam and I don't know what, and if once you get inside of it you'll never want to get out again."

'I swallowed. "Have *you* ever put it on?" I inquired.

'"Me?" he almost bellowed at me. "Me! with all these old slops hanging round! Where should I be if I put 'em all on? Where's the *sale*?"

'Now I wanted that jacket with the crocodiles on the buttons more than anything else past, present or future in the whole wide world. But I had only two-and-ninepence in my pocket – and that was riches for *me*. To be on the safe side, I told the old man this. He stared at me through his rusting spectacles.

'"See here!" he said, as if in a violent temper, and whisking out a piece of newspaper from under the counter: "See here now, snap it!" And he wrapped up the jacket in a flash. "Give me all you've got, and come back with the rest. There's a summat in your eye, young man, that never went with a cheat."

'Then I knew that the old man was charging me at least double what he had meant to ask for the jacket. But I gave him my two-and-ninepence all the same, and went out of the shop. Before his door bell had stopped clanging I had pushed the parcel up under my waistcoat, and walked off, keeping my stomach in, because I didn't want anybody to ask questions.

'Once safely home, I crept upstairs and slipped the parcel in at the back of a drawer, and for that night there it stayed. I didn't dare to meddle with it, partly for fear of what might happen, but mostly of what might *not*!

'All the next morning I was in torture. I was afraid my mother might find the jacket – and give it away to some tramp for a fern or a pot of geraniums. Every time I thought of it I could scarcely breathe, and that didn't help much in my school-work. I was kept in. And when I came home I told my mother I had a headache – which was true – but persuaded her at last to go out and leave me to myself. Then I stole up to my bedroom, shut the door, opened the drawer, and with my heart in my mouth, felt for the parcel. All safe! All *safe*! I took it out, undid the string, opened the paper, and there was the jacket – wavy pattern, crocodile buttons, frayed braid and all.

'With a last wild look towards the window I took off my own coat and put it on. I put it on. And nothing happened. Nothing whatever. At first blush, I mean. Except that I suddenly noticed that the room was full of sunshine and that a thrush was singing in a pear tree at the bottom of the garden. I noticed it because he sang so clear and shrill, and as though straight at *me*. If you could put sound for sight, it was as if I were listening to him through a telescope. I could see him, too, the speckles on his breast, and his bill opening and shutting – singing like an angel.

'And as I listened I noticed in the sunlight through the window the colours of my faded rose-patterned carpet and an old boot. It sounds silly, but I had never before seen an old boot look like that. I don't want to mince words, and maybe I didn't realize it then, but the fact of the matter is that the old boot on the carpet looked astonishingly *beautiful* – the light on the old leather, the tongue coming out, and the gleam of the metal eyelets. A landshark's word that – *beautiful* – but there you are.

'Well, I was soon a little impatient with all this – a new life seemed to have edged into things, or at least into me. Very peculiar. So, to get back to common sense again, I began Sandy One's *Physical Exercises*. Exercises! Why, it was as though all of a sudden I had become nothing but a twist of wire and catgut. I skipped through those jimmin-asticals as if I were half out of my senses. Then I tried tricks never so much as dreamt of before – hopping along my bedrail; standing on my head, first on the bedpost, then on my water-jug; balancing myself – two hands, then one hand – on the back of a chair. Whatever, within the bounds of reason or thereabouts, I gave myself to do, I *did* – and with ease. Like the thrush singing. Nothing very much perhaps, but new to *me*! Mind you, I had never been quite the mollie my father thought me. And Sandy Two hadn't been idle, body or wits. But a little confidence, though not too much, is what you want. After a while I began to be a little alarmed at the effects of the jacket. I began, so to speak, to suspect my own company!

'So, hot and breathless, I sat down at the table where I always did (or didn't do) my homework, and began my "composition". The subject was the Battle of Trafalgar. Before I had finished I had written about fourteen pages on the Battle of Trafalgar! I had described how the *Victory* went to sea, and what Lord Nelson felt like – that last day coming, and why he kept his medals on, and all about Captain Hardy. And I put the weather in, and didn't forget old Froggy Villeneuve either – a gallant sailor and a bad end. When I looked up from page fourteen I could hardly see. It was as if I had come out of the heavenly Jerusalem! And then, almost at that moment, I heard my mother come in down below, and the front door shut.

'I felt like a keg of quicksilver, and yet dead beat. I undressed in less time than a lizard takes to slough its tail, and tumbled into bed, slipping my Chinese jacket in under the bedclothes.

'And no doubt I looked headachy enough when my mother came up to say good night. She felt my forehead; it was burning hot. And she murmured faintly in a very small voice something about castor oil. Even Sandy One could put his foot down when it came to castor oil! But this time I didn't make the least fuss about it. I said, "Right you are. Warm the glass, mother, and put plenty of lemon juice in." I swigged it down, and even smacked my lips over it. Then I began to talk – so fast, and with such nonsense mixed up with the sense, that my mother was on the point of calling in the doctor. At that I sobered down again.

'The next day all was well, but I didn't go to school. The next day after that saw me back in my place again, though not in the magic jacket! But I had cut off one of the pale-green crocodile buttons to carry about in my waistcoat pocket for a kind of charm or amulet. I got a caning for the French I hadn't done, and another caning for the arithmetic which I had. Mr Schoolmaster Smiles himself read my *Essay on the Battel of Trafalger* then and there. He hauled me out again before the class, and asked me what help I had had. I said none. He glared at me: "Are you positively sure, sir? Not even in the spelling?"

'I said, "No, sir; none sir." What was queer, he believed me.

'Still, he had talked to me once or twice about the sea and the Navy. And I too had asked him questions, because while I was wrapped up in the thought of them, I wasn't so frightened of him. Besides, on looking back, I don't believe he really cottoned to groceries much more than I did. Anyhow, he gave me full marks and a bit over for my Trafalgar, but warned me another time I mustn't "spread" myself out like that.

'I went home feeling like a turkey-cock, marched straight upstairs, sat down at my open window, and – put on the jacket again. But I had hardly got my arms into the sleeves when I heard my mother calling me. I hustled on my own jacket over the top of the other – which was not difficult, because my Chinese one was a very tight fit, especially at the armpits – and met her on the landing. She was as white as a sheet and could scarcely speak. She said my father wanted to see me at once, and that he had a friend with him, a Mr Turner.

'"And, oh, my dear," she implored me, "do try and answer your father's questions. Just *listen*, Sandy. Then perhaps you'll hear. And speak up to Mr Turner, too, if he speaks to you. Think it's *me*. Don't be frightened; don't be *sulky*. Nobody can eat you. Fancy it's only just you and me talking. For my sake, Sandy."

'I said, "Right, mother!" and slid from top to bottom down the banisters of the three flights of stairs almost before she had stirred foot to follow me. At the dining-room door I pulled myself together, and went in.

'My father was sitting on the other side of the fireless hearth, talking to a stranger. I liked the look of this stranger. He was short and broad; his face was burnt with the sun; he had a fringe of reddish hair round his head, and wore thick-soled shoes. "Here he is," said my father to the stranger, then turned to me. "This gentleman is Mr Turner, Andrew. If you want to know anything about the sea, he'll tell you." I put out my hand.

'"I hear you've no stomach for dry goods," said Mr Turner, staring at me, but in a friendly fashion. "Have a hankering after salt water, eh?"

'"Yes," I said, "the Navy." Out of the corner of my eye I saw my father start at this. He had never before heard me answer so direct a question without stammering or flushing or just goggling like a red herring with its mouth open.

'"And what do you know about the sea?" said Mr Turner, looking at me steadily. "It's pretty deep!"

'I looked back at him no less steadily. I liked him more and more, and thought I would try him with a few tit-bits out of my fourteen pages on the Battle of Trafalgar. There was a queer silence when I had finished. And I realized that my mother had at that moment stolen away after listening at the door. As for my father, he sat in his chair dumb with amazement. He shut his eyes for an instant and then began to explain that I was not perhaps so backward in some things as in others. But, apart from mere book-learning, did Mr Turner think that I had the framework, the grit, the *health* for a life in the open? "You see, his mother . . ."

' "He looks a bit pasty," said Mr Turner, still quietly grinning at me. "But you can't always tell by the skin. What about those biceps, young man?"

'I put out my arm, and he gripped it hard above the elbow, not noticing, perhaps, that I had two jackets on. And he said, "Pretty good. Do they drill you much at school? Or is it nothing but book-learning?" I nodded, and said, "Yes; and things at home, too."

' "What do you do at home?" says he.

'Now all this time I had been feeling like a bottle of ginger-beer before the cork pops out. So when he gave the word, so to speak, I upped with my heels and pretty nearly *trotted* across the room on the palms of my hands.

' "Bravo," said Mr Turner. "Try that on the table."

'It was a circular solid old-fashioned mahogany table, made when Queen Victoria was a girl, and I circumnavigated it on my fingers and thumbs as nimbly as a cat. But now my blood was up. To give me room, a couple of tumblers, a bottle of water, and a decanter of whisky had been pushed into the middle of the table. Balancing myself on one hand, I poured out with the other a noggin of the water – for I couldn't quite venture on the whisky – into one of the tumblers, and singing out, *"Nelson, for ever!"* drank it off. Then, spluttering and half-choking, I got down from the table, and at last looked at my father.

'He was so pale as to be all but green. He looked as if

he was sea-sick. He said, "Has your mother ever seen you do such things as that?" I shook my head. But Mr Turner was laughing. What's more, he hadn't finished with me yet.

' "Have you got such a thing as a stout piece of rope, William – say a dozen fathom?" he asked my father. There were few things my father was *not* possessor of. We went out into the garden, and as neat as ninepence Mr Turner flung a bight of the rope over one of the upper branches of a fine shady sycamore that grew so close to the house that its leaves in summer actually brushed against its windows.

' "Try that, young man," said my father's friend, Mr Turner, when he had made it fast.

'Well, whether it was due to the devil in Sandy Two or only to the workings of the magic jacket, I don't know, but I shinned up that unknotted rope like a monkey up a palm tree. And when I reached the top, I edged along on my stomach till I was almost at the end of the bough. Then at arms' length I began to dandle on it – up and down, up and down, like a monkey on elastic. When it had given me enough swing and impetus – what's called *momentum* – I let go – and landed as pat as a pea-shooter through the open window on to the landing, the sill of which was some twelve feet from the ground.

'When I came down into the garden again, my father and Mr Turner were having a close, earnest talk together, under the sycamore. My father looked at me as if I had just come back from the Andaman Islands.

'I said, "Was that all right, daddy?"

'But he made no answer; only patted me on the shoulder, turning his head away. And from that moment, and for ever after, we were the best of friends, my father and I; though he never had the ghost of a notion of what caused

259

Sandy Two – whom, mind you, he had never noticed before – to sprout like that!

'But then, that's how things go. And – to cut a long story short – by hook and by crook, by twisting and turning – chiefly my father's – which would take too long to put down in black and white, I won free of groceries at last for good and all. And the next spring I went to sea for a trial voyage. And after *that*, though it was pretty hard going – well, I got into the Navy.

'And now, here I am, for good and all on land again. Not much short of being an old man, but still, thank God, hale and hearty, and able and willing, I hope, to do a fellow creature a good turn at need. And this, my lad, is where *you* come in.

'The fact of the matter is, I had watched you scrabbling away with your chalks at your pitch in Little St Ann's a good many days before you knew it. And I came to two conclusions. First, that your pictures are proof that you can do good work. And second, that you could do much better. What I feel is you keep *yourself* back, do you see? It's the old story of Sandy One and Sandy Two. You haven't the confidence, the go, the guts (in a word), to forge clean ahead, *your* way.

'That's what I say. I see you setting to work in the morning like a young cockatrice, but presently you begin to waver, you become slack and dispirited. The least little mishap – a broken chalk, some oaf *walking* over the pictures, even a cloud floating up over the sun – shakes your nerve. At such times you don't seem to be sure even of what you want to do, let alone how to do it. You niggle at a picture first one way, then another, and at the end give it up in despair, the zest gone, and the fancy gone, and the spirit – what I call the innards – gone too. And when any stranger speaks to you, or drops a copper in your cap, you flush up, droop, go limp and dumb, and look as if butter wouldn't melt in your mouth.

'Now first, my boy, don't mind what I am saying. It is for your *sake*. I wouldn't be taking the trouble except only and solely in the hope and wish of doing you a small service. And remember this, I've been through it all before you – and may, when the end comes, again. I've known what it is to feel my bones melt in my body, to tremble like a jelly, my face like a plaster mask and my skull as empty as a hulk on a sandbank. In two words, I know of old what it's like to be *Sandy One*. So, you see, it's because I'm morally certain there's a Sandy *Two* in *you* – and maybe one beyond anything I can conjecture – that I'm writing this now.

'I like the cut of your jib, and the way you stick to things in spite of all dispiritment and the dumps. I had my eye on him when you marked the mug (for good, I hope) of that suety butcher's boy the other day who spat on your Old Boney. I want to give you a hand *in your own line*, and see no better way of doing it than by just lending you my old Pekin jacket for a bit. Now what do you think about that?

'Maybe it won't work. Maybe its magic's gone. Maybe I imagine as much as I remember about it. But I can say *this* – the last time I squeezed into it before the toughest engagement I ever came out of alive I reckon it blew up the enemy's ship at least two hours before she'd have gone to the bottom in the usual way. Mind you, I haven't *often* used it. When I was your age, an hour or two of it tired me out for half the next week. A day or two of it might take a complete month to recover from. Besides, if you look at the matter by and large, and fair and square, you can see it wouldn't do. In the long run we have to trust to what we have in us that's constant and natural, so to speak, and work like a nigger at that. It's only in tight corners we need a little extra fire and frenzy. *Then* maybe Dame Fortune will see fit to lend a helping hand.

'So all I say is, give the jacket a trial. There is almost room for two of you in it – so if you don't want it to be noticeable, put it on under your own coat, and see how things go. And last, remember this, my boy; whatever happens, I shall still be keeping an eye on you. As my dear mother used to say, "There may be more than one way home, Sandy – but it's trudging does it." And here's good luck; God bless you; and *Finis*.'

It was the last page of Admiral Rumbold's 'yarn'. Mike turned it over, looked at the back, coughed, and drank down what was left of his cold cocoa. He wiped his mouth with the back of his hand, and looked up as he did so at the round yellow face of the clock that hung on the wall at the further end of the shop. At that very moment, it seemed, it had begun to tick. The long hand stood at two minutes before the hour. The old gentleman must be expecting him now – this very minute! Had he meant him to open the parcel and put on the jacket inside it there and then? His face flushed, then paled – he couldn't make up his mind. His head was in a whirl; his heart thumping under his ribs; he broke out hot and damp all over.

While he was still debating what he should do, he noticed that the man who had brought him the food – with his long tallow-coloured face and pale grey eyes – was steadily though vacantly watching him. Mike got up in haste, pushed the remnants of his last door-step of beef and bacon into his pocket, hastily snatched up the Admiral's manuscript and brown-paper parcel, and left the eating-house.

Before actually turning the corner which would bring him in sight of his pitch, he peeped round to see if the old gentleman was anywhere to be seen. He certainly was. At this actual moment he was walking away from Mike – square compact shoulders, brown billycock hat, and firm rolling tread. When once more he returned to the pictures he paused, looked them over one by one, dropped something into the cap, and continued on his way. In less than a minute or so he was back again, had taken another look, and once more paid his fee.

It appeared as if Admiral Rumbold had been so engaged ever since he had left Mike in the coffee-shop; and there could be no doubt he had by this means attracted passers-by to follow his example and look at the pictures. Many, it is true, just glanced and passed on; but a few paid their coppers. The old gentleman was now approaching the street corner where Mike was in hiding, so Mike stepped out a little shamefacedly, and met him there and then.

'Aha!' cried Admiral Rumbold. 'So there you are! Good! And sharp to time. Did you finish it? Good! Have you got it on?'

Mike went red, then white. He said: 'I have read it, every page, sir, but the jacket's still in the paper, because –'

'Be dashed to "Because"!' cried the Admiral. 'Come a pace or two down that alley yonder. We'll soon put that right.'

So they went off together into the shelter of an alley near by, above which the green leaves of a plane tree showed over the glass-bottled wall; and Mike, having taken off his own old loose long coat, slipped into the Chinese jacket as easily as an eel, and then back into his own again on top of it. Admiral Rumbold, having crushed up the brown paper into a ball, tied the string round it, and lightly flung it over the wall. 'Good luck to it!' said he.

'Now,' he added, and looked at Mike – then paused. The boy stood motionless, as though he were frozen, yet he was trembling. His lips were moving. He seemed to be trying to say something for which he could not find the words. When at last he lifted his face and looked up, the old Admiral was astonished at the black-blue of his eyes in his pale face. It was the dark dazzling blue of deep seas. The Admiral could not for the life of him remember where he had seen eyes resembling them. They were unlike the eyes of boy or man or child or woman, and yet *somewhere* he had seen their like. Mike was smiling.

'The green crocodiles, sir,' he said, fingering one of the buttons. 'Most of them are not much bigger than ha'pennies, but you can feel all the horny parts, and even the eyes stickin' out of their heads.'

'Ay, ay,' said the Admiral. 'That's Chinese work. That's how *they* work – at least in times gone by. But how do you feel, how do you *feel,* my lad?'

Mike gazed up an instant at his old friend; then his glance roved on and upward towards the pale-green pentagonal plane leaves above his head and the patch of blue and sunny sky beyond. A smart north-west breeze was blowing, and a mountainous cloud was moving up into the heights of noonday.

'I'd like,' he answered huskily, 'to get back to the pitchers, sir.'

'Ay, ay!' cried the Admiral. And again, 'Ay, ay! Back we go.' So the two of them set off together.

And though to all outward appearance the old gentleman, whose face was all but as red as a pimento, was as cool as a cucumber when he came stumping along beside his young acquaintance, his excitement was intense. It was Mike who had now taken the lead. The Admiral was merely following in his wake. The boy seemed utterly changed, made over again. There was a look to him even as he walked that was as lively as a peal of bells. It was as

if *his* bright and burning sun had suddenly shone out
between clouds as cold as granite, lighting up the heavens.
What was to happen next?

First, Mike took up his cap, and with not even a glance
at what was inside it, emptied its contents into his coat
pocket. He then paced slowly on from one picture to the
next, until he had scrutinized the complete seven. From
the pocket with the remains of the 'door-step' in it he then
drew out his capacious strip of rag and hurried off to a
dribbling water standard with a leopard's head on the
spout about twenty-five yards away. There he wetted his
rag through and through. He came back to his pictures and
in a few moments had completely rubbed every one of
them out. No more than the faintest blur of pink and
yellow was left to show that the paving-stones had ever
lost their usual grey and in three minutes that was dowsed
out too.

When he had finished this destruction, and the warm
morning air had dried the stones again, he knelt down and
set to work. He seemed to have forgotten the old Admiral,
the Chinese jacket, everything that had happened that
morning. He seemed to be wholly unaware of the passers-
by, the dappling sunbeams, the clatter and stir of the street,
and even who and where and what he was. Skinny and
engrossed, he squatted on his hams there, huddled up
under the wall, and *worked*.

Admiral Rumbold, as he watched him, became almost
alarmed at the rapidity with which things were taking
shape on the blank paving-stones. As if by magic and before his very eyes there had loomed into view a full-rigged
ship, swimming buoyant as a swan on the blue of its
waters; its masts tapering up into the heavens, its sails
bellying like drifts of snow; while from its port-holes
pushed the metal mouths of such dogs as he himself had

often heard bark, and seldom to no purpose.

It was not so much the resemblance of this picture to a real ship on a real sea under a real sky that drew out of his mouth a grunted, 'Begad, begad!' but something in the look of the thing, some spirit living and lovely and everlasting behind it all, to which he could not have given name, but which reminded him of the eyes that had looked up at him a few minutes before under the plane leaves in the alley after their first intense glance at the crocodile buttons. Yes, and reminded him too of an evening long ago when he had made the circuit of his mother's mahogany dining-table on little more of his anatomy than his thumbs.

By this time a few other wayfarers had begun to collect and to watch the young street artist at his work. It did not seem to matter that he had forgotten to put back his cap in its customary place, that in fact it was on his head, for, oddly enough, when these idlers turned away, though every single one of them seemed to marvel at the quickness and skill of the boy, yet they all seemed *anxious* to be gone, and nobody gave him a ha'penny.

Admiral Rumbold could stand the strain no longer. He firmly placed a half-crown beside the little heap of coloured chalks, coughed loudly, paused an instant, and then, seeing that Mike had not noticed him, stole off and left him to his work.

The worst of the Admiral's anxieties were over. There could be no doubt in the world that the magic jacket had lost not one whit of its powers since first he had slipped into it himself all but sixty years ago. The only thing that troubled him was that not a single farthing had been bestowed on the young artist in the last quarter of an hour. Nevertheless, he thought he knew why.

'They're scared!' he muttered to himself. 'They don't know what to make of it. They see it's a marvel and a

miracle – and beyond 'em. They don't like the smell of it.
They think it's dangerous. They just watch and wonder and
sneak away. Well, my dear Rumbold, why *not*? Have
patience. Never mind that. Wait and see!'

He loaded himself up with coppers the next morning,
and returned very early to the narrow terrace behind Great
St Ann's. The night before had been rainless; only the
lightest of dews had fallen. It had been windless, too, and
there was a moon; so that the row of pictures which Mike
had left unfinished on the pavement must have faintly
bloomed under her beams that whole night long, and now
were as fresh as they were at the first making of them.
Admiral Rumbold had sallied out at this unusual hour to
steal a glance at them alone; but Mike had been up before
him.

There he was – on his knees once more – deaf and blind
it seemed to everything in the world outside him, and intent
only on his pictures. His old friend didn't interrupt him,
but left him to himself, and went off to get some breakfast
at his club. When he returned the boy had vanished for the
time being. Five pictures out of the customary seven were
now complete.

The Admiral stared and stared at them, part in astonishment, part in inexpressible delight, and part in the utmost
dismay. Two of them – the ship, 'The Old Victery' and the
new 'Hornted' – were more vivid and astonishing things
than (with French chalks and paving-stones) he had thought
even possible. The rest he felt uneasily were beyond his
comprehension. He could hardly make head or tail of them.

One was called 'Peepul at Sunset'. It reminded him of
Shadrach, Meshech, and Abed-nego walking in the midst
of the burning fiery furnace. Another was called 'The Blind
Man'; it showed a chair, a table with a bowl of flowers, and
a dish of fruit on it. There was an open window, too. It

seemed to shimmer and glow and blaze like precious stones. But to the Admiral's eye the chair was all clumped and crooked, and the flowers looked queer – half human. He had never in all his born days seen a picture of a chair like that. Besides, there was not even a sign of a human being, let alone a blind man, to be seen! He stirred, coughed softly. He sighed; and glanced into the ragged cap. It was now a quarter to ten; the cap contained a French penny, a British ha'penny, and a three-penny bit with a hole in it. The Admiral lugged out of his pocket a handful of coppers, and added them to what was there. Off and on throughout the day he kept an eye on the young street artist. Of two things he was at last certain: first that Mike was still wearing the jacket; and next, that he had made (apart from his own donations) practically no profit. For you cannot pick up coloured chalks in the gutter, or patch the knees of your old breeches with the empty air! The boy could hardly have taken an independent sixpence.

Admiral Rumbold began to be a little anxious as he thought this dark fact over, but decided not to interfere. Next day he knocked fairly early at the door of a lodging-house nearly opposite Mike's pitch.

'Good morning,' he said, as soon as it was opened. 'I'd like, if you please, to have the window again. Is it free?'

'Certainly, sir,' said the woman who had answered his knock. 'I'm glad you enjoy the view, sir. It's a pity there's so much wall.'

'It's not the bricks, ma'am, but the people,' replied the Admiral, as he followed her up a flight of stairs into a room which immediately overlooked the street.

There – behind the Brussels curtains at the window, and seated on a rather lumpy armchair – the Admiral spent most of his morning, watching all that went on in the street below, but especially the boy. And once more he came to two conclusions: first, that Mike was *not* now wearing the jacket, and next that he was making less money even than the day before. *Life* seemed to be gone out of him. He sat hunched up beside his chalks and his empty cap – his bony face as grey as ashes. He hardly dared even raise his eyes when anybody paused to examine his pictures. Now and again, however, he would glance up and down the street as if in search of somebody.

'He's looking for me,' muttered the Admiral to himself. 'He wants to return the jacket. God bless *me*! Still, steady does it; steady does it.'

He returned to his window in the early afternoon. The boy looked even more miserable and dejected than ever, but none the less he had begun to tinker at his picture, 'The Old Victory'. On this occasion the Admiral had brought field-glasses with him. With these he could now watch his young friend at work so closely as almost to fancy he could hear him breathe. Indeed, he could see even a round-headed ant making its way along the crack between two paving-stones; and the tiny bits of chalk resembled coloured rocks.

Mike laboured on, now rubbing out, now chalking in, and the Admiral could follow every tint and line and stroke. At last – though by no means as if he were satisfied – the boy stood up and examined what he had done. At sight of it he seemed to droop and shrink. And no wonder. The Admiral almost wept aloud. The thing was ruined. There was the ship, there the sea, and there the sky; but where the lovely light and airiness, the romance, the wonder? Where the *picture*?

Admiral Rumbold was at his wits' end. The day was drawing on. He began to think that his intended kindness had ruined the boy for good and all. He sat back in his chair absolutely at a loss what to do next. One thing was

269

certain. He must go soon and have a word with the boy –
hearten and liven him up. He must give him a good square
meal, put some 'beef' into him, and – perhaps – take the
jacket back. It had been little but a deceit and a failure.
He must take the jacket back, then think things over.

He leant forward to rise from his chair, and as he did so
cast a last desperate glance at the opposite side of the
street. Then he paused. Fine weather was still in the
heavens. The first colours of evening were beginning to
stretch across London's skies – shafts of primrose, melted
gold, and faint crimson lighting up the walls of the houses,
flooding the streets with light. And Mike was no longer
alone. He was still squatting tailor-fashion under his wall
and as motionless as if he had been carved out of ebony,
but a pace or so away stood an odd-looking old gentleman
in a sort of long curry-coloured ulster. This old gentleman
had a beard and wore a high conical black felt hat with a
wide rim to it. An umbrella, less neat but more formidable
in appearance even than the Admiral's, was tucked under
his arm.

He was not merely looking at, he was intent on, 'lost' in
the pictures. He stooped over them each in turn, spending
at least two or three minutes over every one, except 'The
Old Victery', at which he just glanced and went on.

When he found himself at the end of the row, he turned
back and examined them all over again. Admiral Rumbold
watched these proceedings with bated breath. The old man
in the ulster had now turned to Mike, who at once
scrambled to his feet, leaving his chalks, his cap, and a
small newspaper parcel on the pavement. The two of them
in the clear-coloured evening light were soon talking together almost as if they were father and son. They were
talking about the pictures, too; for every now and again
Mike's new acquaintance, bent almost double, would point

with the stump of his umbrella at one of them, tracing out a line, or hovering over a patch of colour. At the same time, his beard turned over his shoulder towards Mike, he would seem to be praising, or criticizing, or explaining, or asking questions. Once, indeed, he stooped, caught up a piece of chalk, and himself drew a few lines on the pavement as if to show the boy exactly what he meant. 'So!' the Admiral heard him end, brushing his fingers.

There could be no doubt this eccentric old gentleman in the wide black hat was interested not only in the pictures but also in Mike. He looked as if in his excitement he might go on talking till midnight. But no; at this very moment he seemed to be making some kind of proposal to the boy. He had put his hand on his shoulder as if in encouragement. Mike hesitated; then cast a long look into the sky, as if to consult the weather. After that his mind seemed to be made up. He hastily took up his cap, his chalks, and his parcel, and the two of them set off down Little St Ann's together.

At this Admiral Rumbold paused no longer. He seized his hard billycock hat, his field-glasses and his malacca cane, and clattered down the stairs out into the street. Keeping well behind them, he followed Mike and the old gentleman out of Little St Ann's into Ashley Court, and so across into Jermyn Street. At this corner, so intent was he in his pursuit, that he barely escaped being run over by a two-horse grocery van.

Mike and the old gentleman were now so clearly in sight that the Admiral had time to pause and address a policeman.

'Good evening, constable,' he said. 'I want you to tell me if by any chance you happen to know the *name* of that old gentleman in the hat yonder, walking with that lad there?'

The policeman fixed his eyes on the pair.

'Well, sir, to tell you the truth, sir,' he said at last, 'I've *seen* him somewhere though I couldn't say rightly just where. I've even been told who he *is*. But bless me, if I can lay tongue to the name of him. I wish I could, sir. He looks as if it might be worth while.' Admiral Rumbold thanked the policeman and hastened on.

At the moment when he once more came within sight of the two of them a long-haired youngish man in a dark, loose cape or cloak had but just met and passed them by. This young man was also wearing a black wide-brimmed hat. As soon as politeness permitted, he not only stopped dead, but stood intently watching the pair until Admiral Rumbold himself had come up with him. The Admiral glanced him over.

'You will excuse me, sir,' he said, 'but if I am not mistaken, you are as much interested in that old gentleman yonder as I am myself. A most impressive figure! Could you oblige me with his *name*?'

'His *name*, sir!' exclaimed the young man. 'Gracious heavens! why, that's old B—. That's "old B. in a Bonnet"! – the crankiest, craziest old creature in the British Isles. But make no mistake, sir. What that old boy doesn't know about pictures and painting isn't worth a tallow candle. He's a Master. Wait till he's dead, that's all. Then the whole world will be wagging with him.'

'You don't say *so*!' shouted the Admiral. 'A *Master*! *Painting*! – eh? I am very greatly obliged to 'ee – very greatly obliged. And you think if he's taken a fancy to that lad there – *sees* promise in him, I mean – well – that the lad's in luck's way?'

'"Think?"' replied the young man. 'Bless your heart, sir, I *know*.'

The Admiral detained him no longer. He saluted him

and passed on. He could say no more. He was satisfied. All was well. The magic jacket, then, had *not* played him false; Mike's 'steepish bit of hill' was well begun. He found himself at the further end of Jermyn Street, and in the traffic of Haymarket. The old man in the ulster had disappeared. But no, there he was – old B. – some little distance down on the opposite side of the street, and at the window of a print-seller's shop. He was talking to the boy at his side – pointing, gesticulating, his bushy beard wagging. And Mike was listening, gazing in, entranced. Admiral Rumbold turned on his heel. He had never professed to know much about pictures. Then why should he now suddenly feel downcast and depressed? He was tired, too, and extremely thirsty. It was almost as if he missed his jacket.

The Lord Fish

Once upon a time there lived in the village of Tussock in Wiltshire a young man called John Cobbler. Cobbler being his name, there must have been shoemaking in his family. But there had been none in John's lifetime; nor within living memory either. And John cobbled nothing but his own old shoes and his mother's. Still, he was a handy young man. He could have kept them both with ease, and with plenty of butter to their bread, if only he had been a little different from what he was. He was lazy.

Lazy or not, his mother loved him dearly. She had loved him ever since he was a baby, when his chief joy was to suck his thumb and stare out of his saucer-blue eyes at nothing in particular except what he had no words to tell about. Nor had John lost this habit, even when he was being a handy young man. He could make baskets – of sorts; he was a wonder with bees; he could mend pots and pans, if he were given the solder and could find his iron; he could grow cabbages, hoe potatoes, patch up a hen-house or lime-wash a sty. But he was only a jack of such trades and master of none. He could seldom finish off anything; not at any rate as his namesake the Giant Killer could finish off his giants. He began well; he went on worse; and he ended, yawning. And unless his mother had managed to get a little washing and ironing and mending and sweeping and cooking and stitching from the gentry in the village, there would often have been less in the pot for them both than would keep their bodies and souls – and the two of them – together.

Yet even though John was by nature idle and a day-dreamer, he might have made his mother far easier about his future if only he could have given up but one small pleasure and pastime; he might have made not only good wages, but also his fortune – even though he would have had to leave Tussock to do it quick. It was his love of water that might some day be his ruin. Or rather, not so much his love of water as his passion for fishing in it. Let him catch sight of a puddle, or of rain gushing from a waterspout, or hear in the middle of the night a leaky tap singing its queer *ding-dong-bell* as drop followed drop into a basin in the sink, let the wind but creep an inch or two out of the east and into the south; and every other thought would instantly vanish out of his head. All he wanted then was a rod and a line and a hook and a worm and a cork; a pond or a stream or a river – or the deep blue sea. And it wasn't even fish he pined for, merely fishing.

There would have been little harm in this craving of his if only he had been able to keep it within bounds. But he couldn't. He fished morning, noon, and even night. Through continually staring at a float, his eyes had come to be almost as round as one, and his elbows stood out like fins when he walked. The wonder was his blood had not turned to water. And though there are many kinds of tasty English fish, his mother at last grew tired of having *any* kind at every meal. As the old rhyme goes:

> A Friday of fish
> Is all man could wish.
> Of vittles the chief
> Is mustard and beef.
> It's only a glutton
> Could live on cold mutton;
> And bacon when green
> Is too fat or too lean.

But all three are sweeter
To see in a dish
By any wise eater
Than nothing but FISH!

Quite a little fish, too, even a roach, may take as
many hours to catch and almost as many minutes to cook
as a full-sized one; and they both have the same number
of bones. Still in spite of his fish *and* his fishing, his
mother went on loving her son John. She hoped in time
he might weary of them himself. Or was there some secret
in his passion for water of which she knew nothing? Might
he some day fish up something really worth having –
something to keep? a keg perhaps of rubies and diamonds,
or a coffer full of amber and gold? Then all their troubles
would be over.

Meanwhile John showed no sign at all of becoming less
lazy or of growing tired of fishing, though he was no longer
content to fish in the same places. He would walk miles
and miles in hope to find pond, pool or lake that he had
never seen before, or a stream strange to him. Wherever
he heard there was water within reach between dawn and
dark, off he would go to look for it. Sometimes in his
journeyings he would do a job of work, and bring home
to his mother not only a few pence but a little present for
herself – a ribbon, or a needle-case, a bag of jumbles or
bull's-eyes, or a duck's egg for her tea; any little thing that
might take her fancy. Sometimes the fish he caught in far-
off waters tasted fresher, sweeter, richer, juicier than those
from nearer home; sometimes they tasted worse – dry,
poor, rank and muddy. It depended partly on the sort of
fish, partly on how long he had taken to carry them home,
and partly on how his mother felt at the moment.

Now there was a stream John Cobbler came to hear
about which for a long time he could never find. For

whenever he went to look for it – and he knew that it lay a good fourteen miles and more from Tussock – he was always baulked by a high flintstone wall. It was the highest wall he had ever seen. And, like the Great Wall of China, it went on for miles. What was more curious, although he had followed the wall on and on for hours at a stretch, he had never yet been able to find a gate or door to it, or any way in.

When he asked any stranger whom he happened to meet at such times if he knew what lay on the other side of this mysterious wall, and whether there were any good fish in the stream which he had been told ran there, and if so, of what kind, shape, size and flavour they might be – every single one of them told him a different tale. Some said there was a castle inside the wall, a good league or so away from it, and that a sorcerer lived in it who had mirrors on a tower in which he could detect any stranger that neared his walls. Others said an old, old Man of the Sea had built himself a great land mansion there in the middle of a Maze – of water and yew trees; an old Man of the Sea who had turned cannibal, and always drowned anybody who trespassed over his wall before devouring him. Others said water-witches dwelt there, in a wide lake made by the stream beside the ruinous walls of a palace which had been the abode of princes in old times. All agreed that it was a dangerous place, and that they would not venture over the wall, dark or daylight, for a pocketful of guineas. On summer nights, they said, you could hear voices coming from away over it, very strange voices, too; and would see lights in the sky. And some avowed they had heard hunting-horns at the rise of the moon. As for the fish, all agreed they must be monsters.

There was no end to the tales told John of what lay beyond the wall. And he, being a simple young man, believed each one of them in turn. But none made any difference to the longing that had come over him to get to the other side of this wall and to fish in the stream there. Walls that kept out so much, he thought, must keep something well worth having *in*. All other fishing now seemed tame and dull. His only hope was to find out the secret of what lay beyond this high, grey, massive, mossy, weed-tufted, endless wall. And he stopped setting out in its direction only for the sake of his mother.

But though for this reason he might stay at home two or three days together, the next would see him off again, hungering for the unknown waters.

John not only thought of the wall all day, he dreamed of it and of what might be beyond it by night. If the wind sighed at his window he saw moonlit lakes and waters in his sleep; if a wild duck cried overhead under the stars, there would be thousands of wild duck and wild swans too and many another water-bird haunting his mind, his head on his pillow. Sometimes great whales would come swimming into his dreams. And he would hear mermaids blowing in their hollow shells and singing as they combed their hair.

With all this longing he began to pine away a little. His eye grew less clear and lively. His rib-bones began to show. And though his mother saw a good deal more of her son John since he had given up his fishing, at last she began to miss more and more and more what she had become accustomed to. Fish, that is – boiled, broiled, baked, fried or Dutch-ovened. And her longing came to such a pass at last that she laid down her knife and fork one supper-time beside a half-eaten slice of salt pork and said, 'My! John, how I would enjoy a morsel of tench again! Do you remember those tench you used to catch up at Abbot's Pool? Or a small juicy trout, John! Or some stewed eels!

Or even a few roach out of the moat of the old Grange, even though they *are* mostly mud! It's funny, John, but sea-fish never did satisfy me even when we could get it; and I haven't scarcely any fancy left for meat. What's more, I notice cheese now gives you nightmares. But fish? – never!'

This was enough for John. For weeks past he had been sitting on the see-saw of his mind, so that just the least little tilt like that bumped him clean into a decision. It was not fear or dread indeed, all this talk of giants and wizardry and old bygone princes that had kept him from scaling the great wall long ago, and daring the dangers beyond it. It was not this at all. But only a half-hidden feeling in his mind that if once he found himself on the other side of it he might never be quite the same creature again. You may get out of your bed in the morning, the day's usual sunshine at the window and the birds singing as they always sing, and yet know for certain that in the hours to come something is going to happen – something that hasn't happened before. So it was with John Cobbler. At the very moment his mother put down her knife and fork on either side of her half-eaten slice of pork and said, 'My! John, how I would enjoy a morsel of tench again! ... Or a small juicy trout, John!' his mind was made up.

'Why, of course, Mother dear,' he said to her, in a voice that he tried in vain to keep from trembling. 'I'll see what I can do for you tomorrow.' He lit his candle there and then, and scarcely able to breathe for joy at thought of it, clumped up the wooden stairs to his attic to look out his best rod and get ready his tackle.

While yet next morning the eastern sky was pale blue with the early light of dawn, wherein tiny clouds like a shoal of silver fishes were quietly drifting on – before, that is, the flaming sun had risen, John was posting along out of

Tussock with his rod and tackle and battered old creel, and a hunk of bread and cheese tied up in a red spotted handkerchief. There was not a soul to be seen. Every blind was down; the chimneys were empty of smoke; the whole village was still snoring. He whistled as he walked, and every now and again took a look at the sky. That vanishing fleecy drift of silver fishes might mean wind, and from the south, he thought. He plodded along to such good purpose, and without meeting a soul except a shepherd with his sheep and dog and an urchin driving a handful of cows – for these were solitary parts – that he came to the wall while it was still morning, and a morning as fresh and green as even England can show.

Now John wasn't making merely for the wall, but for a certain place in it. It was where, one darkening evening some little time before, he had noticed the still-sprouting upper branches of a tree that had been blown down in a great wind over the edge of the wall and into the narrow grassy lane that skirted it. Few humans seemed ever to come this way, but there were hosts of rabbits, whose burrows were in the sandy hedgerow, and, at evening, nightjars, croodling in the dusk. It was too, John had noticed, a favourite resort of bats.

After a quick look up and down the lane to see that the coast was clear, John stood himself under the dangling branches – like the fox in the fable that was after the grapes – and he jumped, and jumped. But no matter how high he jumped, the lowermost twigs remained out of his reach. He rested awhile looking about him, and spied a large stone half-buried in the sandy hedgerow. He trundled it over until it was under the tree, and after a third attempt succeeded in swinging himself up into its branches, and had scrambled along and dropped quietly in on the other side almost before news of his coming had spread among the wild things that lived on the other side of it. Then blackbird to blackbird sounded the alarm. There was a scurry and scamper among the leaves and bracken. A host of rooks rose cawing into the sky. Then all was still. John peered about him; he had never felt so lonely in his life. Never even in his dreams had he been in a place so strange to him as this. The foxgloves and bracken of its low hills and hollows showed bright green where the sunshine struck through the great forest trees. Else, so dense with leaves were their branches that for the most part there was only an emerald twilight beneath their boughs. And a deep silence dwelt there.

For some little time John walked steadily on, keeping his eyes open as he went. Near and far he heard jays screaming one to the other, and wood-pigeons went clattering up out of the leaves into the sun. Ever and again, too, the hollow tapping of a woodpecker sounded out in the silence, or its wild echoing laughter, and once he edged along a glade just in time to see a herd of deer fleeting in a multitude before him at sight and scent of man. They sped soundlessly out of view across the open glade into covert. And still John kept steadily on, lifting his nose every now and again to snuff the air; for his fisherman's wits had hinted that water was near.

And he came at length to a gentle slope waist-high with spicy bracken, and at its crest found himself looking down on the waters of a deep and gentle stream flowing between its hollow mossy banks in the dingle below him. 'Aha!' cried John out loud to himself; and the sound of his voice rang so oddly in the air that he whipped round and stared about him as if someone else had spoken. But there was sign neither of man nor bird nor beast. All was still again. So he cautiously made his way down to the bank of the stream and began to fish.

For an hour or more he fished in vain. The trees grew thicker on the further bank, and the water was deep and dark and slow. None the less, though he could see none, he knew in his bones that it was fairly alive with fish. Yet not a single one of them had as yet cheated him even with a nibble. Still, John had often fished half a day through without getting so much as a bite, and so long as the water stole soundlessly on beneath him and he could watch the reflection of the tree boughs and of the drifts of blue sky between them in this dark looking-glass, he was happy and at ease. And then suddenly, as if to mock him, a fish with a dappled green back and silver belly and of a kind he never remembered to have seen before, leapt clean out of the water about three yards from his green and white float, seemed to stare at him a moment with fishy lidless eyes, and at once plunged back into the water again. Whether it was the mere noise of its water-splash, or whether the words had actually sounded from out of its gaping jaws he could not say, but it certainly seemed as if before it vanished he had heard a strange voice cry, 'Ho, there! John! ... Try lower down!'

He laughed to himself; then listened. Biding a bit, he clutched his rod a little tighter, and keeping a more cautious look-out than ever on all sides of him, he followed the flow of the water, pausing every now and again to make a cast. And still not a single fish seemed so much as to have sniffed (or even sneered) at his bait, while yet the gaping mouths of those leaping up out of the water beyond his reach seemed to utter the same hollow and watery-sounding summons he had heard before: 'Ho, John! Ho! Ho, you, John Cobbler, there! Try lower down!' So much indeed were these fish like fish enchanted that John began to wish he had kept to his old haunts and had not ventured over the wall; or that he had at least told his mother where he meant to go. Supposing he never came back? Where would she be looking for him? Where? Where? And all she had asked for, and perhaps for his own sake only, was a fish supper!

The water was now flowing more rapidly in a glass-green heavy flood, and before he was ready for it John suddenly found himself staring up at the walls of a high dark house with but two narrow windows in the stone surface that steeped up into the sky above. And the very sight of the house set his heart beating faster. He was afraid. Beyond this wall to the right showed the stony roofs of lesser buildings, and moss-clotted fruit trees gone to leaf. Busying to and fro above the roof were scores of rooks and jackdaws, their jangled cries sounding out even above the roaring of the water, for now close beneath him the stream narrowed to gush in beneath a low-rounded arch in the wall, and so into the silence and darkness beyond it.

Two thoughts had instantly sprung up in John's mind as he stared up at this strange solitary house. One that it must be bewitched, and the other that except for its birds and the fish in its stream it was forsaken and empty. He laid his rod down on the green bank and stole from one tree-trunk to another to get a better view, making up his mind that if he had time he would skirt his way round the walled garden he could see, but would not yet venture to walk out into the open on the other side of the house.

It was marvellously quiet in this dappled sunshine, and John decided to rest awhile before venturing further. Seating himself under a tree he opened his handkerchief, and found not only the hunk of bread and cheese he had packed in it, but a fat sausage and some cockled apples which his mother must have put in afterwards. He was uncommonly hungry, and keeping a wary eye on the two dark windows from under the leaves over his head, he continued to munch. And as he munched, the jackdaws, their black wings silvered by the sun, continued to jangle, and the fish silently to leap up out of their watery haunts and back again, their eyes glassily fixed on him as they did so, and the gathering water continued to gush steadily in under the dark rounded tunnel beneath the walls of the house.

But now as John listened and watched he fancied that above all these sounds interweaving themselves into a gentle chorus of the morning, he caught the faint strains as of a voice singing in the distance – and a sweet voice too. But water, as he knew of old, is a curious deceiver of the ear. At times, as one listens to it, it will sound as if drums and dulcimers are ringing in its depths; at times as if fingers are plucking on the strings of a harp, or invisible mouths calling. John stopped eating to listen more intently.

And soon there was no doubt left in his mind that this was no mere water-noise, but the singing of a human voice, and that not far away. It came as if from within the walls of the house itself, but he could not detect any words to the song. It glided on from note to note as though it were an unknown bird piping in the first cold winds of April after its sea-journey from Africa to English shores; and though he did not know it, his face as he listened puckered up almost as if he were a child again and was going to cry.

He had heard tell of the pitiless sirens, and of sea-wandering nereids, and of how they sing among their island rocks, or couched on the oceanic strands of their sunny islands, where huge sea-fish disport themselves in the salt water; porpoise and dolphin, through billows clear as glass, and green and blue as precious stones. His mother too had told him as a child – and like Simple Simon himself he had started fishing in her pail! – what dangers there may be in listening to such voices; how even sailors

285

have stopped up their ears with wax lest they should be enticed by this music to the isles of the sirens and never sail home again. But though John remembered this warning, he continued to listen, and an intense desire came over him to discover who this secret singer was, and where she lay hid. He might peep perhaps, he thought to himself, through some lattice or cranny in the dark walls and not be seen.

But though he stole on, now in shadow, now in sun, pushing his way through the tangled brambles and briars, the bracken and bryony that grew close in even under the walls of the house, he found – at least on this side of it – no doorway or window or even slit in the masonry through which to look in. And he came back at last, hot, tired and thirsty, to the bank of the stream where he had left his rod.

And even as he knelt down to drink by the waterside, the voice which had been silent awhile began to sing again, as sad as it was sweet; and not more than an arm's length from his stooping face a great fish leapt out of the water, its tail bent almost double, its goggling eyes fixed on him, and out of its hook-toothed mouth it cried, '*A-whoof! Oo-ougoolkawott!*' That at least to John was what it seemed to say. And having delivered its message, it fell back again into the dark water and in a wild eddy was gone. Startled by this sudden noise John drew quickly back, and in so doing dislodged a large moss-greened stone on the bank, which rolled clattering down to its plunge into the stream; and the singing again instantly ceased. He glanced back over his shoulder at the high wall and vacant windows, and out of the silence that had again descended he heard in mid-day the mournful hooting as of an owl, and a cold terror swept over him. He leapt to his feet, seized his rod and creel, hastily tied up what was left of his lunch in his red-spotted handkerchief, and instantly set out for home. Nor did he once look back until the house was hidden from view. Then his fear vanished, and he began to be heartily ashamed of himself.

And since he had by now come into sight of another loop of the stream, he decided, however long it took him, to fish there until he had at least caught *something* – if only a stickleback – so that he should not disappoint his mother of the supper she longed for. The minnow smeared with pork marrow which he had been using for bait on his hook was already dry. None the less he flung it into the stream, and almost before the float touched the water a swirl of ripples came sweeping from the further bank, and a greedy pike, grey and silver, at least two feet long if he was an inch, had instantly gobbled down bait and hook. John could hardly believe his own eyes. It was as if it had been actually lying in wait to be caught. He stooped to look into its strange motionless eye as it lay on the grass at his feet. Sullenly it stared back at him as though, even if it had only a minute or two left to live in, it were trying heroically to give him a message, yet one that he could not understand.

Happy at heart, he stayed no longer. Yet with every mile of his journey home the desire grew in him to return to the house, if only to hear again that dolorous voice singing from out of the darkness within its walls. But he told his mother nothing about his adventures, and the two of them sat down to as handsome a dish of fish for supper as they had ever tasted.

'What's strange to me, John,' said his mother at last, for they had talked very little, being so hungry, 'is that though this fish here is a pike, and cooked as usual, with a picking of thyme and marjoram, a bit of butter, a squeeze of lemon and some chopped shallots, there's a good deal more to him than just that. There's a sort of savour and sweetness to him, as if he had been daintily fed. Where did you catch him, John?'

But at this question John was seized by such a fit of coughing – as if a bone had stuck in his throat – that it seemed at any moment he might choke. And when his mother had stopped thumping him on his back she had forgotten what she had asked him. With her next mouthful, too, she had something else to think about; and it was fortunate that she had such a neat strong row of teeth, else the crunch she gave to it would certainly have broken two or three of them in half.

'Excuse me, John,' she said, and drew out of her mouth not a bone, but something tiny, hard and shiny, which after being washed under the kitchen tap proved to be a key. It was etched over with figures of birds and beasts and fishes, that might be all ornament or might, thought John, his cheeks red as beetroot, be a secret writing.

'Well I never! Brass!' said his mother, staring at the key in the palm of her hand.

'Nor didn't I,' said John. 'I'll take it off to the blacksmith's at once, Mother, and see what he makes of it.'

Before she could say Yes or No to this, John was gone. In half an hour he was back again.

'He says, Mother,' said he, 'it's a key, Mother; and not brass but solid gold. A gold key! Whoever? And in a fish!'

'Well, John,' said his mother, who was a little sleepy after so hearty a supper, 'I never – mind you – did see much good in fishing except the fish, but if there are any more gold keys from where that pike came from, let's both get up early, and we'll soon be as rich as Old Creatures.'

John needed no telling. He was off next morning long before the sun had begun to gild the dewdrops in the meadows, and he found himself, rod, creel and bait, under the magician's wall a good three hours before noon. There was not a cloud in the sky. The stream flowed quiet as molten glass, reflecting the towering forest trees, the dark stone walls, and the motionless flowers and grass-blades at its brim. John stood there gazing awhile into the water, just as if today were yesterday over again, then sat himself down on the bank and fell into a kind of daydream, his rod idle at his side. Neither fish nor key nor the freshness of the morning nor any wish or thought was in his mind but only a longing to hear again the voice of the secret one. And the shadows around him had crept less even than an inch on their daily round, and a cuckoo under the hollow sky had but thrice cuckoo'd in some green dell of the forest, when there slid up into the air the very notes that had haunted him, waking and sleeping, ever since they had first fallen on his ear. They rang gently on and on, in the bush, clear as a cherub in some quiet gallery of paradise, and John knew in his heart that she who sang was no longer timid in his company, but out of her solitude was beseeching his aid.

He rose to his feet, and once more searched the vast frowning walls above his head. Nothing there but the croaking choughs and jackdaws among the chimneys, and a sulphur-coloured butterfly wavering in flight along the darkness of their stones. They filled him with dread, these echoing walls; and still the voice pined on. And at last he fixed his eyes on the dark arch beneath which coursed in heavy leaden flow the heaped-up volume of the stream. No way in, indeed! Surely, where water could go, mightn't *he*?

Without waiting a moment to consider the dangers that might lie in wait for him in the dark water beneath the walls, he had slipped out of his coat and shoes and had plunged in. He swam on with the stream until he was within a little way of the yawning arch; then took a deep breath and dived down and down. When he could hold it no longer he slipped up out of the water – and in the nick of time. He had clutched something as he came to the surface, and found himself in a dusky twilight looking up from the foot of a narrow flight of stone steps – with a rusty chain dangling down the middle of it. He hauled himself up out of the water and sat down a moment to recover his breath, then made his way up the steps. At the top he came to a low stone corridor. There he stayed again.

But here the voice was more clearly to be heard. He hastened down the corridor and came at last to a high narrow room full of sunlight from the window in its walls looking out over the forest. And, reclining there by the window, the wan green light shining in on her pale face and plaited copper-coloured hair, was what John took at first to be a mermaid; and for the very good reason that she had a human head and body, but a fish's tail. He stayed quite still, gazing at her, and she at him, but he could think of nothing to say. He merely kept his mouth open in case any words should come, while the water-drops dripped from his clothes and hair on to the stone flags around him. And when the lips in the odd small face of this strange creature began to speak to him, he could hardly make head or tail of the words. Indeed she had been long shut up alone in this old mansion from which the magician who had given her her fish's tail, so that she should not be able to stray from the house, had some years gone his way, never to come back. She had now almost forgotten her natural language. But there is a music in the voice that tells more to those who understand it than can any words in a dictionary. And it didn't take John very long to discover that this poor fish-tailed creature, with nothing but the sound of her own sad voice to comfort her, was mortally unhappy; that all she longed for was to rid herself of her cold fish's tail, and so win out into the light and sunshine again, freed from the spell of the wizard who had shut her up in these stone walls.

John sat down on an old wooden stool that stood beside the table, and listened. And now and then he himself sighed deep or nodded. He learned – though he learned it very slowly – that the only company she had was a deaf old steward who twice every day, morning and evening, brought her food and water, and for the rest of the time shut himself up in a tower on the further side of the house looking out over the deserted gardens and orchards that once had flourished with peach and quince and apricot, and all the roses of Damascus. Else, she said, sighing, she was always alone. And John, as best he could, told her in turn about himself and about his mother. 'She'd help you all she could to escape away from here – I know *that*, if so be she *could*. The only question is, How? Since, you see, first it's a good long step for Mother to come and there's no proper way over the wall, and next if she managed it, it wouldn't be easy with nothing but a tail to walk on. I mean, lady, for you to walk on.' At this he left his mouth open, and looked away, afraid that he might have hurt her feelings. And in the same moment he bethought himself of the key, which, if he had not been on the verge of choking, his mother might have swallowed in mistake for a mouthful of fish. He took it out of his breeches' pocket and held it up towards the window, so that the light should shine on it. And at sight of it it seemed that something between grief and gladness had suddenly overcome the poor creature with the fish's tail, for she hid her face in her fingers and wept aloud.

The Lord Fish

This was not much help to poor John. With his idle ways and love of fishing, he had been a sad trial at times to his mother. But she, though little to look at, was as brave as a lion, and if ever she shed tears at all, it was in secret. This perhaps was a pity, for if John had but once seen her cry he might have known what to do now. All that he actually did do was to look very glum himself and turn his eyes away. And as they roved slowly round the bare walls he perceived what looked like the crack of a little door in the stones and beside it a tiny keyhole. The one thing in the world he craved was to comfort this poor damsel with the fish's tail, to persuade her to dry her eyes and smile at him. But as nothing he could think to say could be of any help, he tiptoed across and examined the wall more closely. And cut into the stone above the keyhole he read the four letters – *C.A.V.E.!* What they meant John had no notion, except that a cave is something hollow – and usually empty. Still, since here was a lock and John had a key, he naturally put the key into the lock with his clumsy fingers to see if it would fit. He gave the key a gentle twist. And lo and behold, there came a faint click. He tugged, drew the stone out upon its iron hinges, and looked inside.

What he had expected to see he did not know. All that was actually within this narrow stone cupboard was a little green pot, and beside it a scrap of what looked like parchment, but was actually monkey skin. John had never been much of a scholar at his books. He was a dunce. When he was small he had liked watching the clouds and butterflies and birds flitting to and fro and the green leaves twinkling in the sun, and found frogs and newts and sticklebacks and minnows better company than anything he could read in print on paper. Still he had managed at last to learn all his letters and even to read, though he read so slowly that he sometimes forgot the first letters of a long word before he had spelled out the last. He took the piece of parchment into the light, held it tight between his fingers, and, syllable by syllable, muttered over to himself what it said – leaving the longer words until he had more time.

And now the pale-cheeked creature reclining by the window had stopped weeping, and between the long strands of her copper hair was watching him through her tears. And this is what John read:

> Thou who wouldst dare
> To free this Fair
> From fish's shape,
> And yet escape
> O'er sea and land
> My vengeful hand: –
> Smear this fish-fat on thy heart,
> And prove thyself the jack thou art!

> With tail and fin
> Then plunge thou in!
> And thou shalt surely have thy wish
> To see the great, the good Lord Fish!

> Swallow his bait in haste, for he
> Is master of all wizardry.
> And if he gentle be inclined,
> He'll show thee where to seek and find
> The Magic Unguent that did make
> This human maid a fish-tail take.

> But have a care
> To make short stay
> Where wields his sway,
> The Great Lord Fish;
> 'Twill be too late
> To moan your fate
> When served with sauce
> Upon his dish!

John read this doggerel once, he read it twice, and though he couldn't understand it all even when he read it a third time, he understood a good deal of it. The one thing he could not discover, though it seemed the most important, was what would happen to him if he did as the rhyme itself bade him do – smeared the fish-fat over his heart. But this he meant to find out.

And why not at once, thought John, though except when he hooked a fish, he was seldom as prompt as that. He folded up the parchment very small, and slipped it into his breeches' pocket. Then imitating as best he could the motion of descending the steps and diving into the water, he promised the maid he would return to her the first moment he could, and entreated her not to sing again until he came back. 'Because ...' he began, but could get no further. At which, poor mortal, she began to weep again, making John, for very sadness to see her, only the more anxious to be gone. So he took the little pot out of the stone cupboard, and giving her for farewell as smiling and consoling a bob of his head as he knew how, hurried off along the long narrow corridor, and so down the steep stone steps to the water.

There, having first very carefully felt with his finger-tips exactly where his heart lay beating, he dipped his finger into the green ointment and rubbed it over his ribs. And with that, at once, a dreadful darkness and giddiness swept over him. He felt his body narrowing and shortening and shrinking and dwindling. His bones were drawing themselves together inside his skin; his arms and legs ceased at last to wave and scuffle, his eyes seemed to be settling into his head. The next moment, with one convulsive twist of his whole body, he had fallen plump into the water. There he lay a while in a motionless horror. Then he began to stir again, and after a few black dreadful moments found himself coursing along so swiftly that in a trice he was out from under the arch and into the green gloaming of the stream beyond it. Never before had he slipped through the water with such ease. And no wonder!

For when he twisted himself about to see what had happened to him, a sight indeed met his eye. Where once had been arms were now small blunt fins. A gristly little beard or barbel hung on either side of his mouth. His short dumpy body was of a greeny brown, and for human legs he could boast of nothing now but a fluted wavering tail. If he had been less idle in his young days he might have found himself a fine mottled trout, a barbel, a mullet, or a lively eel, or being a John he might well have become a jack. But no, he was fisherman enough to recognize himself at first sight – a common tench, and not a very handsome one either! A mere middling fish, John judged. At this horrifying discovery, though the rhyme should have warned him of it, shudder after shudder ran along his backbone and he dashed blindly through the water as if he were out of his senses. Where could he hide himself? How flee away? What would his mother say to him? And alackaday, what had become of the pot of ointment? 'Oh mercy me, oh misery me!' he moaned within himself, though not the faintest whisper sounded from his bony jaws. A pretty bargain this!

He plunged on deeper and deeper, and at length, nuzzling softly the sandy bed of the stream with his blunt fish's snout, he hid his head between two boulders at the bottom. There, under a net of bright green water-weed, he lay for a while utterly still, brooding again on his mother and on what her feelings would be if she should see him no more – or in the shape he was? Would that he had listened to her counsel, and had never so much as set eyes on rod or hook or line or float or water. He had wasted his young days in fishing, and now was fish for evermore.

But as the watery moments sped by, this grief and despondency began to thin away and remembrance of the crafty and cruel magician came back to mind. Whatever he might look like from outside, John began to be himself again within. Courage, even a faint gleam of hope, welled back into his dull fish's brains. With a flick of his tail he had drawn back out of the gloomy cranny between the boulders, and was soon disporting himself but a few inches below the surface of the stream, the sunlight gleaming golden on his scales, the cold blood coursing through his body, and but one desire in his heart.

These high spirits indeed almost proved the end of him. For at this moment a prowling and hungry pike having from its hiding-place spied this plump young tench, came flashing through the water like an arrow from a bow, and John escaped the snap of its sharp-toothed jaws by less than half an inch. And when on land he had always supposed that the tench who is the fishes' doctor was safe from any glutton! After this dizzying experience he swam on more heedfully, playing a kind of hide-and-seek among the stones and weeds, and nibbling every now and again at anything he found to his taste. And the world of trees and sky in which but a few hours before he had walked about on his two human legs was a very strange thing to see from out of the rippling and distorting wavelets of the water.

When evening began to darken overhead he sought out what seemed to be a safe lair for the night, and must soon have fallen into a long and peaceful fish's sleep – a queer sleep too, for having no lids to his eyes they both remained open, whereas even a hare when he is asleep shuts only one!

Next morning very early John was about again. A south

wind must be blowing, he fancied, for there was a peculiar mildness and liveliness in the water, and he snapped at every passing tit-bit carried along by the stream with a zest and hunger that nothing could satisfy. Poor John, he had never dreamed a drowned fly or bee or a grub or caterpillar, or even water-weed, could taste so sweet. But then he had never tried to find out. And presently, dangling only a foot or two above his head, he espied a particularly juicy-looking and wriggling red worm.

Now though, as has been said already, John as a child or even as a small boy, had refrained from tasting caterpillars or beetles or snails or woodlice, he had once – when making mud pies in his mother's garden – nibbled at a little earth-worm. But he had not nibbled much. For this reason only perhaps, he stayed eyeing this wriggling coral-coloured morsel above his head. Memory too had told him that it is not a habit of worms to float wriggling in the water like this. And though at sight of it he grew hungrier and hungrier as he finned softly on, he had the good sense to cast a glance up out of the water. And there – lank and lean upon the bank above – he perceived the strangest shape in human kind he had ever set eyes on. This bony old being had scarcely any shoulders. His grey glassy eyes bulged out of his head above his flat nose. A tuft of beard hung from his cod-like chin, and the hand that clutched his fishing-rod was little else but skin and bone.

'Now,' thought John to himself, as he watched him steadily from out of the water, 'if that old rascal there ain't the Lord Fish in the rhyme, I'll eat my buttons.' Which was an easy thing to promise, since at this moment John hadn't any buttons to eat. It was by no means so easy to make up his hungry fishy mind to snap at the worm and chance what might come after. He longed beyond words to get back into his own body again – but only

(and John seemed to be even stubborner as a fish than he had been as a human), *only* if the beautiful lady could be relieved of her tail. And how could there be hope of any of these things if he gave up this chance of meeting the Lord Fish and of finding the pot of 'unguent' he had read of in the rhyme? The other had done its work with him quick enough!

If nothing had come to interrupt these cogitations, John might have cogitated too long. But a quick-eyed perch had at this moment finned into John's pool and had caught sight of the savoury morsel wriggling and waggling in the glass-clear water. At very first glimpse of him John paused no longer. With gaping jaws and one mad swirl of his fish-tail he sprang at the worm. A dart of pain flashed through his body. He was whirled out of the water and into the air. He seemed on the point of suffocation. And the next instant found him gasping and floundering in the lush green grass that grew beside the water's brink. But the old angler who had caught him was even more skilful in the craft of fishing than John Cobbler was himself. Almost before John could sob twice, the hook had been extracted from his mouth, he had been swathed up from head to tail in cool green moss, a noose had been slipped around that tail, and poor John, dangling head downwards from the fisherman's long skinny fingers, was being lugged away he knew not where. Few, fogged and solemn were the thoughts that passed through his gaping, gasping head on this dismal journey.

Now the Lord Fish who had caught him lived in a low stone house which was surrounded on three sides by a lake of water, and was not far distant from his master's – the Sorcerer. Fountains jetted in its hollow echoing chambers, and water lapped its walls on every side. Not even the barking of a fox or the scream of a peacock or any sound of birds could be heard in it; it was so full of the suffling and sighing, the music and murmuration of water, all day, all night long. But poor John being upside down had little opportunity to view or heed its marvels. And still muffled up in his thick green overcoat of moss he presently found himself suspended by his tail from a hook in the Lord Fish's larder, a long cool dusky room or vault with but one window to it, and that only a hole in the upper part of the wall. This larder too was of stone, and apart from other fish as luckless as John who hung there gaping from their hooks, many more, plumper and heavier than he, lay still and cold on the slate slab shelves around him. Indeed, if he could have done so, he might have hung his head a little lower at being so poor a fish by comparison.

Now there was a little maid who was in the service of this Lord Fish. She was the guardian of his larder. And early next morning she came in and set about her day's work. John watched her without ceasing. So fish-like was the narrow face that looked out from between the grey-green plaits of her hair that he could not even guess how old she was. She might, he thought, be twelve; she *might*, if age had not changed her much, be sixty. But he guessed she must be about seventeen. She was not of much beauty to human eyes – so abrupt was the slope of her narrow shoulders, so skinny were her hands and feet.

First she swept out the larder with a besom and flushed it out with buckets of water. Then with an earthenware watering pot, and each in turn, she sprinkled the moss and weed and grasses in which John and his fellows were enwrapped. For the Lord Fish, John soon discovered, devoured his fish raw, and liked them fresh. When one of them, especially of those on the shelves, looked more solemn and motionless than was good for him, she dipped him into a shallow trough of running water that lay outside the door of the larder. John indeed heard running water all day long – while he himself could scarcely flick a fin. And when all this was done, and it was done twice a day, the larder-maid each morning chose out one or two or even three of her handsomest fish and carried them off with her. John knew – to his horror – to what end.

But there were two things that gave him heart and courage in this gruesome abode. The first was that after her second visit the larder-maid treated him with uncommon kindness. Perhaps there was a look on his face not quite like that of her other charges. For John with his goggling ogling eyes would try to twist up his poor fish face into something of a smile when she came near him, and – though very faintly – to waggle his tail tips, as if in greeting. However that might be, there was no doubt she had taken a liking to him. She not only gave him more of her fish-pap than she gave the rest, to fatten him up, but picked him out special dainties. She sprinkled him more slowly than the others with her water-pot so that he could enjoy the refreshment the more. And, after a quick, sly glance over her shoulder one morning she changed his place in the larder, and hung him up in a darker corner all to himself. Surely, surely, this must mean, John thought, that she wished to keep him as long as she could from sharing her master's table. John did his best to croak his thanks, but was uncertain if the larder-maid had heard.

This was one happy thing. His other joy was this. Almost as soon as he found himself safe in his corner, he had discovered that on a level with his head there stood on a shelf a number of jars and gallipots and jorams of glass and earthenware. In some were dried roots, in some what seemed to be hanks of grass, in others black-veined lily bulbs, or scraps of twig, or dried-up buds and leaves, like

301

tea. John guessed they must be savourings his cook-maid kept for the Fish Lord to soak his fish in, and wondered sadly which, when his own turn came, would be his. But a little apart from the rest and not above eighteen inches from his nose, there stood yet another small glass jar, with greenish stuff inside it. And after many attempts and often with eyes too dry to read, John spelled out at last from the label of this jar these outlandish words: UNGUENTUM AD PISCES HOMINIBUS TRANSMOGRIFICANDOS. And he went over them again and again until he knew them by heart.

Now John had left school very early. He had taken up crow-scaring at seven, pig-keeping at nine, turnip-hoeing at twelve – though he had kept up none of them for very long. But even if John had stayed at school until he was grown-up, he would never have learned any Latin – none at all, not even dog Latin – since the old dame who kept the village school at Tussock didn't know any herself. She could cut and come again as easily as you please with the cane she kept in her cupboard, but this had never done John much good, and she didn't know any Latin.

John's only certainty then, even when he had learned these words by heart, was that they were not good honest English words. Still, he had his wits about him. He remembered that there had been words like these written in red on the parchment over the top of the rhyme that now must be where his breeches were, since he had tucked it into his pocket – though where *that* was he hadn't the least notion. But *unguent* was a word he now knew as well as his own name; and it meant ointment. Not many months before this, too, he had mended a chair for a great lady that lived in a high house on the village green – a queer lady too though she was the youngest daughter of a marquis of those parts. It was a job that had not taken

John very long, and she was mightily pleased with it. 'Sakes, John,' she had said, when he had taken the chair back and put it down in the light of a window, 'sakes, John, what a *transmogrification*!' And John had blushed all over as he grinned back at the lady, guessing that she meant that the chair showed a change for the better.

Then, too, when he was a little boy, his mother had often told him tales of the *piskies*. 'Piskies, P I S C E S,' muttered John to himself on his hook. It sounded even to *his* ear poor spelling, but it would do. Then, too, H O M I N I B U S. If you make a full round O of the first syllable it sounds uncommonly like *home*. So what the Lord Fish, John thought at last, had meant by this lingo on his glass pot must be that it contained an U N G U E N T to which some secret P I S K Y stuff or what is known as wizardry had been added, and that it was useful for 'changing' for the better anything or anybody on which it was rubbed when away from H O M E. Nobody could call the stony cell in which the enchanted maid with the fish-tail was kept shut up a *home*; and John himself at this moment was a good many miles from his mother!

Besides, the stuff in the glass pot was uncommonly like the ointment which he had taken from the other pot and had smeared on his ribs. After all this thinking John was just clever enough to come to the conclusion that the one unguent had been meant for turning humans into fish, and that this in the pot beside him was for turning fish into humans again. At this his flat eyes bulged indeed in his head, and in spite of the moss around them his fins stood out stiff as knitting needles. He gasped to himself – like a tench out of water. And while he was still brooding on his discovery, the larder-maid opened the door of the larder with her iron key to set about her morning duties.

'*Ackh*,' she called softly, hastening towards him, for

now she never failed to visit him first of all her charges, '*ackh*, what's wrong with 'ee? What's amiss with 'ee?' and with her lean finger she gently stroked the top of his head, her narrow bony face crooked up with care at seeing this sudden change in his looks. She did not realize that it was not merely a change but a transmogrification! She sprinkled him twice, and yet a third time, with her ice-cold water, and with the tips of her small fingers pushed tiny gobbet after gobbet of milk-pap out of her basin into his mouth until John could swallow no more. Then with gaspings and gapings he fixed his nearer eye on the jar of unguent or ointment, gazed back rapidly at the little larder-maid, then once again upon the jar.

Now this larder-maid was a great-grandniece of the Lord Fish, and had learned a little magic. 'Aha,' she whispered, smiling softly and wagging her finger at him. 'So that's what you are after, Master Tench? That's what you are after, you crafty Master Sobersides. Oh, what a scare you gave me!'

Her words rang out shrill as a whistle, and John's fellow fish, trussed up around him in their moss and grass and rushes on their dishes, or dangling from their hooks, trembled at sound of it. A faint chuffling, a lisping and quiet gaggling, tiny squeaks and groans filled the larder. John had heard these small noises before, and had supposed them to be fish talk, but though he had tried to imitate them he had never been sure of an answer. All he could do, then, was what he had done before – he fixed again his round glassy eye first on the jar and then on the little larder-maid, and this with as much gentle flattery and affection as he could manage. Just as when he was a child at his mother's knee he would coax her to give him a slice of bread pudding or a spoonful of jam.

'Now I wonder,' muttered the larder-maid as if to herself, 'if you, my dear, are the one kind or the other. And if you are the *other*, shall I, my gold-green Tinker, take the top off the jar?'

At this John wriggled might and main, chapping with his jaws as wide and loud as he could, looking indeed as if at any moment he might burst into song.

'Ah,' cried the maid, watching with delight, 'he understands! That he does! But if I did, precious, what would my lord the Lord Fish say to me? What would happen to *me*, eh? You, Master Tench, I am afraid, are thinking only of your own comfort.'

At this John sighed and hung limp as if in sadness and dudgeon and remorse. The larder-maid eyed him a few moments longer, then set about her morning work so quickly and with so intense a look on her lean narrow face, with its lank dangling tresses of green-grey hair, that between hope and fear John hardly knew how to contain himself. And while she worked on, sprinkling, feeding, scouring, dipping, she spoke to her charges in much the same way that a groom talks to his horses, a nurse to a baby, or a man to his dogs. At last, her work over, she hastened out of the larder and shut the door.

Now it was the habit of the Lord Fish on the Tuesdays, Thursdays and Saturdays of every week, to make the round of his larder, eyeing all it held, plump fish or puny, old or new, ailing or active; sometimes gently pushing his finger in under the moss to see how they were prospering for his table. This was a Thursday. And sure enough the larder-maid presently hastened back, and coming close whispered up at John, 'Hst, he comes! The Lord Fish! Angry and hungry. Beware! Stay mum as mum can be, you precious thing. Flat and limp and sulky, look 'ee, for if the Lord Fish makes his choice of 'ee now, it is too late and all is over. And above all things, don't so much as goggle for a moment at that jar!'

She was out again like a swallow at nesting-time, and

presently there came the sound of slow scraping footsteps on the flagstones and there entered the Lord Fish into the larder, the maid at his heels. He was no lord to look at, thought John; no marquis, anyhow. He looked as glum and sullen as some old Lenten cod in a fishmonger's, in his stiff drab-coloured overclothes. And John hardly dared to breathe, but hung – mouth open and eyes fixed – as limp and lifeless from his hook in the ceiling as he knew how.

'Hoy, hoy, hoy,' grumbled the Lord Fish, when at last he came into John's corner. 'Here's a dullard. Here's a rack of bones. Here's a sandy gristle-trap. Here's a good-as-dead-and-gone-and-useless! Ay, now my dear, you can't have seen him. Not this one. You must have let him go by, up there in the shadows. A quick eye, my dear, a quick watchful eye! He's naught but muddy sluggard tench 'tis true. But, oh yes, we can better him! He wants life, he wants exercise, he wants cosseting and feeding and *fattening*. And then – why then, there's the makings in him of as comely a platter of fish as would satisfy my Lord Bishop of the Seven Sturgeons himself.' And the little larder-maid, her one hand clutching a swab of moss and the other demurely knuckled over her mouth, sedately nodded.

'Ay, master,' said she, 'he's hung up there in the shadows, he is. In the dark. He's a mumper, that one, he's a moper. He takes his pap but poorly. He shall have a washabout and a dose of sunshine in the trough. Trust me, master, I'll soon put a little life into him. Come next Saturday, now!'

'So, so, so,' said the Lord Fish. And having made the round of John's companions he retired at last from out of his larder, well content with his morning's visit. And with but one quick reassuring nod at John over her narrow shoulder, his nimble larder-maid followed after him. John was safe until Saturday.

Hardly had the Lord Fish's scuffling footsteps died away when back came the little maid, wringing her hands in glee, and scarcely able to speak for laughing. 'Ay, Master Tench, did you hear that? "Up there in the shadows. Here's a dullard; here's a rack of bones; here's a gristle-trap. He wants cosseting and feeding and fattening." — Did he not now? Was I sly? Was I cunning? Did the old Lord nibble my bait, Master Tench? Did he *not* now? Oho, my poor beautiful; "fatten", indeed!' And she lightly stroked John's snout again. 'What's wrong with the old Lord Fish is that he eats too much and sleeps too long. Come 'ee now, let's make no more ado about it.'

She dragged up a wooden stool that stood close by, and, holding her breath, with both hands she carefully lifted down the jar of green fat or grease or unguent. Then she unlatched John from his hook, and laid him gently on the stone slab beside her, bidding him meanwhile have no fear at all of what might happen. She stripped off his verdant coat of moss, and, dipping her finger in the ointment, smeared it on him, from the nape of his neck clean down his spine to the very tip of his tail.

For a few moments John felt like a cork that, after bobbing softly along down a softly-flowing river, is suddenly drawn into a roaring whirlpool. He felt like a firework squib when the gushing sparks are nearly all out of it and it is about to burst. Then gradually the fog in his eyes and the clamour in his ears faded and waned away, and lo and behold, he found himself returned safe and sound into his own skin, shape and appearance again. There he stood in the Lord Fish's fish larder, grinning down out of his cheerful face at the maid who in stature reached not much above his elbow.

'Ah,' she cried, peering up at him out of her small water-clear eyes, and a little dazed and dazzled herself at this

transmogrification. 'So you *were* the other kind, Master
Tench!' And the larder-maid looked at him so sorrowfully
and fondly that poor John could only blush and turn
away. 'And now,' she continued, 'all you will be wanting,
I suppose, is to be gone. I beseech you then make haste
and be off, or my own skin will pay for it.'

John had always been a dullard with words. But he
thanked the larder-maid for all she had done for him as
best he could. And he slipped from off his little finger a
silver ring which had belonged to his father, and put it
into the palm of the larder-maid's hand; for just as when
he had been changed into a fish, all his clothes and everything about him had become fish itself, so now when he
was transformed into human shape again, all that had then
been his returned into its own place, even to the parchment in his breeches' pocket. Such it seems is the law of
enchantment. And he entreated the maid, if ever she
should find herself on the other side of the great wall, to
ask for the village of Tussock, and when she came to
Tussock to ask for Mrs Cobbler.

'That's my mother,' said John, 'is Mrs Cobbler. And
she'll be mighty pleased to see you, I promise you. And
so will I.'

The larder-maid looked at John. Then she took the
ring between finger and thumb, and with a sigh pushed it
into a cranny between the slabs of stone for a hiding-place.
'Stay there,' she whispered to the ring, 'and I'll come back
to 'ee anon.'

Then John, having nothing else handy, and knowing that
for the larder-maid's sake he must leave the pot behind
him, took out of the fob in his breeches' pocket a great silver
watch that had belonged to his grandfather. It was nothing
now but a watch *case*, since he had one day taken out the
works in hopes to make it go better, and had been too

lazy to put them back again. Into this case he smeared as much of the grease out of the pot as it would hold.

'And now, Master Tench, this way,' said the larder-maid, twisting round on him. 'You must be going, and you must be going for good. Follow that wall as far as it leads you, and then cross the garden where the Lord Fish grows his herbs. You will know it by the scent of them in the air. Climb the wall and go on until you come to the river. Swim across that, and turn sunwards while it is morning. The Lord Fish has the nose of a she-wolf. He'd smell 'ee out across a bean field. Get you gone at once then, and meddle with him no more. Ay, and I know it is not on *me* your thoughts will be thinking when you get to safety again.'

John, knowing no other, stooped down and kissed this little wiseacre's lean cold fingers, and casting one helpless and doleful look all about the larder at the fish on hook and slab, and seeing none, he fancied, that could possibly be in the same state as his had been, he hastened out.

There was no missing his way. The Lord Fish's walls and water conduits were all of stone so solid that they might have been built by the Romans, though, truly, they were chiefly of magic, which has nothing to do with time. John hurried along in the morning sunshine, and came at length to the stream. With his silver watch between his teeth for safety he swam to the other side. Here grew very tall rough spiny reeds and grasses, some seven to nine feet high. He pushed his way through them, heedless of their clawing and rasping, and only just in time. For as soon as he was safely hidden in the low bushes beyond them, whom did he now see approaching on the other side of the stream, rod in hand, and creel at his elbow, but the Lord Fish himself – his lank face erected up into the air and his nose sniffing the morning as if it were laden with the spices of Arabia. The larder-maid had told the truth indeed. For at least an hour the Lord Fish stood there motionless on the other side of the stream immediately opposite John's hiding-place. For at least an hour he pried and peeped about him, gently sniffing on. And, though teased by flies and stung with nettles, John dared not stir a finger. At last even the Lord Fish grew weary of watching and waiting, and John, having seen him well out of sight, continued on his way ...

What more is there to tell? Sad and sorrowful had been the maid's waiting for him, sad beyond anything else in the fish-tailed damsel's memory. For, ever since she had so promised him, she had not even been able to sing to keep herself company. But when seventeen days after he had vanished, John plunged in again under the stone arch and climbed the steep stone steps to her chamber, he spent no time in trying to find words and speeches that would not come. Having opened the glass of his watch, he just knelt down beside her, and said, '*Now*, if you please, lady. If you can keep quite still, I will be quick. If only *I* could bear the pain I'd do it three times over, but I promise 'ee it's soon gone.' And with his finger he gently smeared the magic unguent on the maid's tail down at last to the very tip.

Life is full of curiosities, and curious indeed it was that though at one moment John's talk to the enchanted creature had seemed to her little better than Double Dutch, and she could do his bidding only by the signs he had made to her, at the next they were chattering together as merrily as if they had done nothing else all their lives. But they did not talk for long, since of a sudden there came the clatter of oars, and presently a skinny hand was thrust over the window-sill, and her daily portion of bread and fruit and water was laid out on the sill. The sound of the Lord Fish's 'Halloo!' when he had lowered his basket into the boat made the blood run cold again in John's body. He waited only until the rap and grinding of the oars had died away. Then he took the maid by the hand, and they went down the stone steps together. There they plunged into the dark water, and presently found themselves breathless but happy beyond words seated together on the green grass bank in the afternoon sunshine. And there came such a chattering and cawing from the rooks and jackdaws over their heads that it seemed as if they were giving thanks to see them there. And when John had shaken out the coat he had left under the tree seventeen days before, brushed off the mildew, and dried it in the sun, he put it over the maid's shoulders.

It was long after dark when they came to Tussock, and not a soul was to be seen in the village street or on the green. John looked in through the window at his mother. She sat alone by the hearthside, staring into the fire, and it seemed to her that she would never get warm again. When John came in and she was clasped in his arms, first she thought she was going to faint, then she began to cry a little, and then to scold him as she had never scolded him before. John dried her tears and hushed her scoldings. And when he had told her a little of his story, he brought the maid in. And John's mother first bobbed her a curtsey, then kissed her and made her welcome. And she listened to John's story all over again from the beginning to the end before they went to bed – though John's bed that night was an old armchair.

Now before the bells of Tussock church – which was a small one and old – rang out a peal for John's and the fish-maid's wedding, he set off as early as ever one morning to climb the wall again. In their haste to be gone from the Sorcerer's mansion she had left her belongings behind her, and particularly, she told John, a leaden box or casket, stamped with a great A – for Almanara; that being her name.

311

Very warily John stripped again, and, diving quietly, swam in under the stone arch. And lo, safe and sound, in the far corner of the room of all her grief and captivity, stood the leaden casket. But when he stooped to lift it, his troubles began. It was exceedingly heavy, and to swim with it even on his shoulders would be to swim to the bottom! He sat awhile and pondered, and at last climbed up to the stone window, carved curiously with flowers and birds and fish, and looked out. Water lay beneath him in a moat afloat with lilies, though he couldn't tell how deep. But by good fortune a knotted rope hung from a hook in the window-sill – for the use, no doubt, of the Lord Fish in his boat. John hauled the rope in, tied one end of it to the ring in the leaden casket and one to a small wooden stool. At last after long heaving and hoisting he managed to haul the casket on to the sill. He pushed it over, and – as lively as a small pig – away went the stool after it. John clambered up to the window again and again looked out. The stool, still bobbing, floated on the water beneath him. Only a deeper quiet had followed the splash of the casket. So, after he had dragged it out of the moat and on to the bank, John ventured on beyond the walls of the great house in search of the Lord Fish's larder. He dearly wanted to thank the larder-maid again. When at last he found it, it was all shut up and deserted. He climbed up to the window and looked in, but quickly jumped down again, for every fish that hung inside it hung dead as mutton. The little larder-maid was gone. But whether she had first used the magic unguent on the Lord Fish himself and then in dismay of what followed had run away, or whether she had tried it on them both and now was what John couldn't guess, he never knew and could never discover. He grieved not to see her again, and always thought of her with kindness.

Walking and resting, walking and resting, it took him three days, even though he managed to borrow a wheelbarrow for the last two miles, to get the casket home. But it was worth the trouble. When he managed at last to prise the lid open, it was as though lumps of a frozen rainbow had suddenly spilled over in the kitchen, the casket was crammed so full of precious stones. And after the wedding Almanara had a great J punched into the lead of the box immediately after her great A – since now what it held belonged to them both.

But though John was now married, and not only less idle but as happy as a king-fisher, *still* when the sweet south wind came blowing, and the leaves were green on the trees, and the birds in song, he could not keep his thought from hankering after water. So sometimes he made himself a little paste or dug up a few worms, and went off fishing. But he made two rules for himself. First, whenever he hooked anything – and especially a tench – he would always smear a speck or two of the unguent out of his grandfather's silver watch-case on the top of its head; and next, having made sure that his fish was fish, wholly fish, and nothing but fish, he would put it back into the water again. As for the mansion of the Sorcerer, he had made a vow to Almanara and to his mother that he would never go fishing *there*. And he never did.

The Old Lion

There was once a sailor of the name of John Bumps. He had bright blue eyes and wore gold rings in his ears. Although, when this story begins, Mr Bumps was still quite young, he had three children – Topsy, Emmanuel and Kate – who lived with their mother in a nice little house with square windows in Portsmouth, and he had often been round the world. He had sailed into most of its ports in all kinds of weather; and there was scarcely an island of great beauty or marvel that he couldn't tick off on his tarry fingers.

Now one day, a little the right side of the rainy season, he came again to the west coast of Africa. His ship, *The Old Lion*, – and he was her second-mate – had been sailing south down that great coast, past the Canaries and the Green Islands, past the Ivory and the Gold and the Slave Coasts to Banana and the noble Congo; and not long after that Mr Bumps went ashore. He was paddled up the river Quanza, dark and green, past Dondo, to visit an old friend. And there in a village of the black men, for two green-and-red bead necklaces and a jack-knife, he bought a monkey.

Mr Bumps had now and then bought other monkeys, and he knew this was a high price for one in that part of the country. But his friend, the Chief of the Mlango-Nlango tribe, who was exceedingly fat, and wore two blankets besides his beads and ivories, assured Mr Bumps that this was no ordinary monkey.

The Chief's round black face, with its two rows of flashing teeth, broke into an immense smile as he told Mr Bumps this. 'Ee no skittle-skattle monk-ee, no,' he said, for he had often traded with the English. 'Ee ... ,' but instead of finishing the sentence, he shut his eyes and put one black hand on the top of his head, though what exactly he meant Mr Bumps could not tell. At first glimpse of the monkey, however, Mr Bumps had known at once that whatever pleasant things the Chief might say of it they would be true. Besides, the Chief was an old friend of his, and wouldn't tell him lies.

On the other hand, since the hairy little fellow stood an inch or so under the common stature of monkeys of its kind, it was of no great size, and there was nothing else remarkable that showed – not then. As Mr Bumps held it on his arm, in its long-skirted crimson coat, which one of the Chief's wives had made out of the royal cloth, it sat far less heavy indeed than would his younger daughter, Kate. And she herself was very small for her age.

But it had a neat, pretty head, wonderfully slender hands and long thumbs, and as it turned its solemn hazel eyes on Mr Bumps, he suddenly felt acutely homesick. He had been more than once more than half round the world without feeling *that*. 'It's *no good* longing,' he would say, 'when you've got to wait.'

And then something which Mr Bumps had not expected at all happened. It was this. His eyes, as has been said already, were of a particularly bright blue, and as the blue of his blue eyes met the gazing hazel of the monkey's, the creature stirred on his arm, opened its mouth, and made a remark. Mr Bumps had never paid much attention to foreign tongues, and he did not understand what it said. Nevertheless, he knew what it *meant*. He knew for certain that the tiny liquid syllables which had issued from the small mouth were a message from friend to friend.

He bade a cheerful good-bye to the Chief, kissed his hand

to the black lady who had brought the monkey into his hut, and went off again down to the river. He took aboard *The Old Lion* a good store of nuts, bananas, and other fruit; and as that evening he looked back at the coast, shining in the last of the sun – and *The Old Lion* was now some miles out to sea – he turned to his monkey and said, 'How do you like the sound of the name of Jasper, sonny?'

The monkey softly turned to him as if to answer, but this time said nothing.

So Jasper he was called; although this was really due to a mistake on the part of Mr Bumps. What had come into his mind, as he stood at the taffrail looking back at the coast of Africa, were the first two lines of a hymn that had been a favourite of his mother's –

> From Greenland's icy mountains
> To India's coral strand.

But in saying the words over to himself he had got the last but one word wrong. He had said,

> From Greenland's icy mountains
> To India's *jasper* strand.

Still, Jasper, he thought, was a better name than Coral, and Jasper it remained.

There never was a monkey so quick to learn, so grave in the learning, and so quiet and pleasant in manner as Jasper. Mr Bumps could only guess how old he was, and he guessed, 'p'raps five'. And since the famous little son of John Evelyn even before this age could all but talk in Greek, Latin and Hebrew, it may not be so marvellous as it sounds that Jasper soon began to pick up a few words of English. Long before this, however, he had learned to sit at table and say his grace (in his own tongue); to use a knife and fork, and a mug for drink; to bow when spoken to; to swing his own hammock, and little things like that.

He would creep up, too, to watch the man at the wheel or the cook at his cooking in the galley or caboose. He would gaze for minutes at a time at the compass and lamp in the binnacle, and would salute the captain whenever he saw him on the bridge. He knew the Christian names of every jack of the crew, and where each of them slept in the fo'c'sle; he could manage a little rope-splicing, and knew the difference between a granny and a reef knot, a loop and a fisherman's bend. In spite of his red cossack gown, he could scamper up the rigging to the truck or very summit of the mainmast twice as quick as any cabin-boy – and like every cabin-boy he had no tail to help.

Besides all this Mr Bumps taught Jasper much else. Not that he sat him down and *made* him learn. It amused him, and Jasper enjoyed it. It was a long voyage too; *The Old Lion* edged into the Doldrums; and there was plenty of time.

As the days and weeks drew by, Jasper became as much at home on *The Old Lion* with his friend Mr Bumps as if he had been born to the sea. Merely because he was jimp and hairy, had a small flat-nosed face, and showed his teeth when he talked, the sailors at first would tease and laugh at him, treating him only as a pet or a plaything. As soon as he began to talk King's English, however, they teased him no more. He began to say things they remembered.

What Mr Bumps meant to do with him when he was safe home in his little house in Portsmouth he hardly knew. He was sure his wife, whose name was Emma, would be pleased to see his new friend, and there was no doubt at all about Topsy, Emmanuel and Kate. But how could he ever part with Jasper now? Yet how expect him to lead a sea-life? There was, however, no need to decide anything for the present; and meanwhile he took almost as fond a care of him – sought him out dainties, physicked him when sick – as Mrs Bumps was taking of their little Kate.

At last, and Mr Bumps had long since made up his mind that he could never of his own wish be separated from Jasper, *The Old Lion* drew into the English Channel. She was nearly home. And one misty afternoon in November she sailed slowly up the Thames and dropped anchor in the Pool of London. It was bitter cold, but still; and a haze of the colour of copper hung over the mighty city. And there in the midst, like an enormous leaden bee-hive against the sullen sky, rose the dome of St Paul's.

Mr Bumps stepped ashore early next morning, with the monkey hooded upon his arm, some presents for his wife and children in his bag, and set out briskly for his railway station. He had not been in old England for many months, and the first thing in his mind was to get down to Portsmouth as soon as he possibly could. But the haze that had been high over the city the day before had now descended into its streets, and Mr Bumps had to grope on in the direction of the Monument and Pudding Lane through a fog which grew steadily denser.

He knew, at last, that he had lost his bearings. And when presently he came to a little public house, *The Three Swans*, its windows dimly glowing in the fog, he decided to go in and ask his way. But, somehow or other, he didn't like the notion that Jasper should go in too. He glanced into the little face under its hood, and saw how cold and doleful it looked. But he was afraid the thick tobacco smoke and the smell of the beer and spirits in *The Three Swans* might make him ill.

So, 'Sit you here a moment, Jasper,' he said, as he put him down beside his bag beside the lamp-post, 'and don't 'ee stir till I come back.'

The Old Lion

But, alas, Mr Bumps stayed many minutes longer than he had intended to in *The Three Swans*, and when he came back, though his bag was still there where he had left it, Jasper was gone.

Indeed, Jasper had been patiently waiting in the fog in the dim light of the lamp-post for no more than five of those minutes, when there came by a stranger, with a black hat on his head, a black beard, and a coat reaching almost to his heels. If the monkey had not stirred at that moment, all might have been well. But, at sound of these footsteps in the strange cold London street, the solitary creature had lifted his face and put out a hand; for he had made many friends on board ship. And the stranger stooped, and looked at him.

Now, by a chance – whether evil or not it is hard to say – this man with the dark beard was a dealer in all kinds of animals. He had a shop in a narrow alley not far from the river. That shop went back, and every now and then up two or three steps, at least thirty paces. And from end to end of it there were cages of all kinds of birds and small beasts; besides tanks of fish and of rare snakes and lizards, and even gauze-covered cages of butterflies on rows of shelves. His larger animals he kept, though out of the rain, in a stone-flagged yard.

He stooped down, his rusty black coat brushing the paving-stones, and in the foggy gloom looked long into Jasper's face. Then he took the little, narrow hand in his, and gently shook it.

'How d'ye do?' he said, in a wheedling voice, and speaking through his nose. 'Very pleased to meet you, I'm sure.'

And Jasper, with his usual gentle manners, and thinking no harm of him, looked up into his face and chattered a few sounds, which were uncommonly like sea-English.

The stranger shot one swift, thief-like glance over his

shoulder, then, opening a button of his great-coat, gingerly lifted Jasper from where he sat, slipped him in under it, and strode rapidly away.

Before evening, Jasper found himself, with a few monkey nuts and a can of water, squatting alone in a cage, surrounded by other cages in which, beside barking dogs and scrambling puppies, were scores of white rabbits and rats and cats – Manx, tabby and Siamese – squirrels, ferrets, stoats, tortoises, owls, love-birds, canaries, parrots, parakeets and macaws; and in the midst of a din and screaming of voices more deafening by far than he had ever heard in his own west-African forests, or in the middle of a storm at sea. He sat shivering and trembling in his gown, and at last pushed his head in under its furry hood, muttering to himself in small, mournful, monkey accents, 'Mr Bumps. Mr Bumps. Oh, Mr Bumps!'

But Mr Bumps, having in great grief given up his friend for lost, was long since in the train and on his way in spite of the fog to his little square-windowed house in Portsmouth, and back to his Emma, his Topsy, Emmanuel and Kate.

Jasper did not stay long in Mr Moss's animal shop – only for nine days and nine nights. But at the end of them he had already begun to pine and droop, could scarcely eat and seldom opened his eyes. He missed his friend the sailor, and his care and kindness; though whenever Mr Moss himself, or the sharp-nosed, sallow-faced young man that helped in the shop, looked in at his cage, and spoke to him, he looked solemnly back, without showing either his teeth or his temper. He never clutched at his food when it was pushed in through the wire door, nor did he even attempt to make any sound in response to what they said to him. He sat there, his hands folded under his gown, like some small hairy king deprived of his kingdom. Mr

Moss and his young man had never seen his like before; and even in this short time, they had both discovered that they could not face out the little creature's dwelling eyes.

But though Jasper sat for the most part so quiet and motionless in his cage that he might seem, at first sight, to be fast asleep, or even stuffed, all day long his ears and wits (and now and then his eyes) were busy. He would watch the Belgian canary birds which Mr Moss, during their moulting, had fed on special seed and cayenne pepper to brighten their feathers, for hours at a time. There was an enormous python, too, coiled up in straw not far away, and for a long time he hardly dared to look at it. But at last he made himself watch that too; and he never ceased to listen to the talk between Mr Moss and his pale, soft-footed assistant, and the strange human beings that came into the shop. Strange talk in the shop too he heard between his fellow-captives.

Mr Moss himself, though if Jasper had been like other ordinary monkeys he would have soon forgotten it, never felt *wholly* at ease at the thought that he had stolen this one. Odd, unlucky things began to happen in the shop. He himself upset a glass case full of Death's Head Moths. It frightened him – their tiny feet on his skin and the fanning of their sepulchral wings. The python one night, having managed to glide out of her tank, devoured a mandarin duck at one gulp, and escaped into London. And when his assistant, first thing in the morning, tripped over a broom that had been left on the floor of the shop and broke his left leg, his master began to think that it would be as well to get rid of Jasper as soon as he could.

So when that afternoon an acquaintance of his, who had once been a showman and trainer of animals for a circus, stepped into his shop and enquired how much he wanted for Jasper, the price he asked him was so very moderate that his friend paid it down at once, and carried the monkey off with him, there and then. At first sight of Jasper he too had become homesick – for the ring-lights and the tan and the tinsel and the ambling horses – and had determined to begin again.

'And what do you call him?' he asked Mr Moss.

'Call him? Why, what he calls hisself, day in, day out, and even in his sleep! – Jasper.'

'Ah, now, "Jasper"?' repeated his friend.

He too was a dark man, but hollow-cheeked and lean; and he wore his hair long over his ears. His name was Mr J. Smith, but he changed this on the programmes and playbills, when he was showing his animals, to Signor Dolcetto Antonio. Unlike one or two black-hearted miscreants who followed his trade, he believed in kindness and commonsense. 'There are five things,' he would say to his wife, 'all things breathing – buffaloes to bullfinches – *need*; like you and me, Amy: food, shelter, sleep, company and freedom.' And he gave his animals nearly as much as they could wish of them all except the last.

Away from the cold and noise and stench and darkness of Mr Moss's shop, Jasper soon began to be himself again. His appetite returned, his eye brightened, he looked sleek and nimble. He was soon as well as could be expected – his bosom friend Mr Bumps gone, and himself so far from his own land.

In order to take all possible care of his charge, Signor Antonio brought him home to where he lived with his wife – the upper parts of a house in Jay Street, Soho. Part of this house was a shop that sold wine and oil and coffee and macaroni and olives and sausages and other kind of foreign meats and drinks. In the rest, first floor to roof, lived Mr and Mrs Smith. Here, beside the fire in their small parlour, they made Jasper as cosy as they could – in a little chamber to himself.

For two hours every morning, Signor Antonio would talk to Jasper, and teach him tricks. When he was gone out to do his business, Mrs Smith, busy herself over her cooking and housework, would talk to him too. She was a very stout woman, even stouter than the Chief of the Mlango-Nlangoes. And, like the Chief, she was full of good humour, and had a kind heart. She took particular pleasure in children and animals; and at the Zoo would not only cheep to the birds and stroke the gazelles, but nod and smile at the orang-outangs and hippopotami. She treated Jasper as if he were a long-lost son.

Her husband had soon discovered that Jasper was a monkey that had no equal. He was as different from other monkeys as day is from dusk. He learnt everything he was taught with ease and alacrity and could soon chatter away to his friend, almost as if he had known English all his life. If he *looked* five, he could certainly *talk* like two-and-a-half. But, though he was so teachable and sweet-tempered and serious in his manners, there was something about him that never ceased to perplex Mr Smith.

He felt this in particular when, his lessons done, Jasper would sit quietly in his chair, waiting for his mid-day meal. He had an air, at such times, as if he were brooding on something of which Mr Smith had not the least notion. He seemed to be so far away that even Mr Smith never ventured to ask him what he was thinking about, or to summon him back to dark Soho.

Merely to look at, Jasper was a comfort to the eye. Mr Smith, though he was a good-natured man, was as awkward and clumsy as a saucepan with too long a handle to it. He was all angles. Mrs Smith, too, who was even more good-natured than her husband, sat and talked with no more grace than a feather bed. But Jasper, even in the least motion of his small body, turn of the head, of the hand, of the foot, was quiet as flowing water and delicate as the flowers beside it. When he touched, it was as if thistledown had settled at his finger-tips. When he stretched out his fingers to take an apple, it was like the movement of a shadow through the air. He would sidle along Mrs Smith's curtain-rod without stirring a single ring; and if she were near, would be allowed to follow her out on to the roof where she sometimes sat – in spite of smoke and smuts – sewing a hem and looking over London. Jasper would balance himself in his gown on the edge of the tallest of the red chimney-pots, glancing north, south, east and west, and not a finger-tip to keep his balance!

If he was this to look at, what can he then have *been* in his secret mind – with its memories and dreams and sedate ponderings, river and forest, the terrors and dangers and delights of vast dark Africa, or rather of his own particular dark green corner of it?

'What I feel about our friend over there,' Mr Smith said to his wife one day, when Jasper sat asleep in his chair, 'what I feel is, that he could learn me a sight more than I can learn *him* – of what, I mean, *matters*, my love. He's that privy yet polite you don't know where you are. And what I feel *too* is that there's something little short of shameful in letting a mere mob of humans come paying their half-crowns and shillings and sixpences just to stare at him. He talks to us; but, bless you, he only talks to us about what he knows we can understand. He don't tell us his secrets. Never. The truth is, he ought not to have been took away from where he came from, though where *that* was, nobody knows. No Moss ever got such a mystery by rights. Never. He's had a queer past, has that little monk; mark *me*.'

And Mrs Smith, though in her heart she agreed with her husband, thought it would be unwise to say so.

'Don't you fret, Jim,' she replied. 'He has plenty to eat and keep him busy. Worry! Not he! Look at him there, sleeping as peaceful as a babby, as if there wasn't a coconut or a black man in the world. He's as happy as the day is long.'

'Coconuts!' said her husband, but he was not convinced.

At last, one early morning, a happy thought came into Mrs Smith's mind.

'What by and by would be really fair and square, Jim,' she said as she was combing her hair by the glass, 'what by and by would be nice and proper, would be for you to take half of what you make out of Jasper, and him take the other half. Once he began to earn a bit of money, we could teach him what money *means*. After all, Jim, it's only a sort of short cut for bread and cheese and tables and chairs and clothes and houses – not to mention the time and trouble taken in making them; and he would soon pick it up. Then, mebbe, he might like to get a few little things for himself. He might like to set up, with some cash in the bank, as an independent gentleman. Judging from what *I*'ve seen of the world, he has twice as much sense as most such, and not a shadow of any vices; and I don't see *any*thing against it.'

Mr Smith looked at his wife in astonishment. Nor was it merely because she had been speaking with her mouth full of hairpins. It was because she would seem for days together not to agree with a single word he said, and then, of a sudden, like a knife from its sheath, out would come a notion that made everything plain and easy. So it was with what she had said about Jasper.

About nine months after he had brought him home, Mr Smith became perfectly certain that there was nothing else he could teach his charge. Jasper could make a speech; could sing; and draw pictures of forests and ships with a box of coloured chalks. He could scribble down simple sums up to fractions on a blackboard, and find an answer. He could manage everything to the last nicety with his clothes. During the week he was dressed in scarlet breeches and a green coat, with ivory buttons. On Sundays he wore a lightly-starched ruff round his neck, a velvet gown to his heels, made out of an old Sunday dolman of Mrs Smith's, and fine shoes. For out-of-doors he had two or three different kinds of cloak. Not that Mr Smith *kept* him to human clothes, or human ways either. Jasper agreed he must grow used to them. Whenever he so fancied he went bare; and, if he wished, he kept two Sunday-clothes days in one week. But this was very seldom.

He knew many simple rhymes, and Mr Smith had made a little harp for him – rough, of course, but tunable. To this he would sing these rhymes, and other airs, and a curious music also, whose meaning he kept to himself. More than once, indeed, Mr Smith had been awakened early in the morning to hear Jasper playing on his harp in the next room. And *then*, while both the words and tune seemed to be of Jasper's own making or remembering, there sounded a cadence in them that almost made him weep. By good fortune Mrs Smith slept far heavier of nights than he did.

Anyhow, there was no doubt at all, that if Signor Antonio and Dr Jasper – as they were going to call themselves in the play-bills – were ever to get rich, now was the time to begin. Mr Smith had long ago been to see the Manager of the Bank in which he kept his savings, and had arranged with him to open an account in Dr Jasper's

name. Into this each week he afterwards paid Jasper's
share of their takings which mounted up by leaps and
bounds.

'You see,' he had first explained to the Manager, 'it may
be some time before my young friend is able to come and
pay his money in himself. But I want everything open
and aboveboard. When he makes his debboo, which will
be shortly, he will take half the fees and I shall take half.
And when we have made what he thinks is enough, then
he shall choose as he thinks best.'

The Manager, Mr Johnson, who until then had seen
only a few photographs of Dr Jasper, not very good like-
nesses either, smiled at this arrangement. But there was no
doubt that it *was* all open and aboveboard, and he fell in
with Mr Smith's wishes.

It was in the month of December that Dr Jasper made
his first appearance on the stage. This was in London.
There was sleet that Christmas, and a cold wind was blowing in the lamplit London streets, when Signor Antonio
and Mrs Smith set off together in a four-wheeled cab
bound for the *Fortune*, a famous theatre which had been
named after the old *Fortune* in the days of Queen Bess,
and the Merry Wives of Windsor. 'And not much more
than twenty years after it was built,' Mr Smith told
Jasper, 'it was burned down to the very ground – in two
hours.'

'In two hours!' said Jasper.

Still, Mrs Smith, as she reclined quietly but firmly against
the purple velvet of the cab, her back to the horse and her
face to Jasper, and her husband beside her to keep out
the draught, might herself have been one of those merry
wives come to life again!

In the bleak cold north wind, the tiny snowflakes vanishing as they fell through the dark air, and with its multitudes

of people going off about their pleasure in their furs and wraps and winter clothes, London looked as bright as a peep-show.

Jasper trembled a little, and not from cold, as he gazed out of the glass cab-window at the passers-by, while Mr and Mrs Smith talked cheerfully to keep his spirits up, and sometimes made wonderfully good fun together about some over-dressed lady or gentleman they could admire from their little inside gloom in the cab without themselves being seen. For *their* hearts too were beating high. But Jasper himself, in his warm dark corner, said nothing. The crowd of humans and the brightly-lit windows of the shops, reflected in his round dark eyes, the noise and cold, alarmed and frightened him. He longed to be home again; or far, far away from this strange land. The cab trundled along down the Charing Cross Road and into Trafalgar Square. Mr Smith had told the cabman to take this way round to the theatre because he wanted Jasper to see the lions.

'And look, Jasper,' said Mrs Smith, when her husband had pointed them out, '*that* there up there is the great Lord Nelson; and mighty sharp-set he must be in his cocked hat – and only one eye and one arm, pore feller – with all that sleet falling up among them stars.'

Jasper lifted his quiet face and could but faintly detect the great silent granite figure aloft against the sky.

'Sea,' he muttered. 'Seaman.' But, strangely enough, Mrs Smith, who was usually quickness itself at following what he said, supposed he meant to spell the word *see* and not *sea*, and was afraid he must be very nervous indeed of what lay in front of him if he had gone back to his old childish way of speaking – *See ... Man ...* when he had first learnt English. But Jasper had other thoughts.

The cab rolled on along the Strand, and there was still

enough melting sleet in the street almost to silence its iron-tyred wheels. On and on it went, past the great railway-station in its cobbled yard, and on towards Waterloo Bridge; and in a little while drew up in a back street where an iron lamp jutting out over the pavement lit up the 'Stage Door'.

Mr Smith then got out of the cab. He paid the fare, and (as much for his own good luck as for the cabman's) gave him a half-crown over. And he asked him to be waiting for them at eleven. 'Eleven sharp,' he said.

Then, having handed out Mrs Smith, he mounted the three steps, pushed open the door, which clapped to after them with a bang that shook poor Jasper to the heart, and they all three entered the theatre.

'Good evening, Sam,' said Mr Smith to the stout man sitting in a box behind a little open window by the door.

'Good evening,' he replied; but his watery grey eyes were fixed not on Mr Smith but on Jasper. With a turn of his small head and a touch of his fingers, he had shown his friend that he wished to be put down. So, one after the other – Mr Smith, Jasper, Mrs Smith – the three of them ascended the flight of stone steps into the dressing-room that had been set apart for them by the Manager of the theatre. And here Mr Smith helped Jasper to spell out the description of himself that had been printed in large capital letters on the play-bill, a copy of which was pinned to the wall. THE FIRST APPEARANCE OF THE LEARNED AND FAMOUS DR JASPER, he read out slowly, Jasper sagely nodding his head at every word, THAT MINUTE MARVEL OF MONKEYLAND, AND MASTER MIMIC OF MAN!

'There,' said Mrs Smith, 'that's *you*, Jasper! What do you think of that?' But Jasper made no answer. At this moment, trembling a little, he was gazing at the picture of himself underneath the print. It had taken him straight home again – since the artist, though no doubt he had done his best, had made him look very much like a small gorilla!

When with deft fat hands Mrs Smith had put the finishing touches to his toilet, and her husband was ready, they all three went down the stone steps again and made their way to the wings of the stage. There, in shadow and in silence, they waited. Soon it would be Jasper's turn. In this nook of the painted scenery – all flowers and trees and butterflies – the framework of which went up into the blaze of lights above, Jasper peered about him. It was the night after Christmas, and the theatre, from the floor up to its very roof, was packed with human beings of all ages, but particularly human children.

By standing on tiptoe and peering through a tiny hole in the canvas Jasper could see row above row of strange faces mounting higher and higher, their eyes fixed on the five *Exceptionally Elegant Ethiopian Elephants Engaged at Enormous Expense* which were now seated around their trainer on the stage. At sight of all these faces a sigh shook him from head to foot. And he turned away his head – and peered out to see the elephants themselves.

Four of these mighty animals, garlanded with mistletoe, were caparisoned in bright green and silver. The fifth, and the smallest, was dressed up as a clown, his face whitewashed, and one eye surrounded with a diamond in red. They sat on their tubs. They wreathed their proboscises. They greeted their trainer in a chorus that drowned even the blare of the band. They walked on their hind legs; they passed the bottle; they turned the handle of their hurdy-gurdies; and the two senior elephants danced a cumbrous polka, while the two junior sat fanning themselves, and the youngest with a painted poker beat time.

Then, one by one, these sage and monstrous beasts, their tiny eyes alight with excitement, stumpy tails a-swing, trailed off the stage to their own quarters. The curtain descended. It was Jasper's turn.

And soon all was made ready for him. A table, with books upon it, an empty inkstand, some foolscap and a dinner bell; two gilt chairs covered in bright blue satin beside it, and a sofa – this was the only furniture, apart from an umbrella stand, a palm in a pot, and a red and green Axminster rug.

The music stopped. The curtain slowly rose again. And there, in the middle of the stage, was Signor Antonio, dressed up like a lackey in a black tail-coat, and as if engaged in putting the room in order in preparation for the coming home of his master. And while he tidied the books and gave a last flick of his feather-brush over the fleckless satin chairs and the palm in the pot, he kept talking to himself, though loud enough for everybody to hear. He was explaining who he was – the faithful servant of the great Dr Themistocles Marmoset Jasper, the kindest and wisest master manservant ever had, and the most famous medico in Europe. – 'In Europe, did I say?' he cried to himself, slapping his leg with his brush. 'Nay, in the WORLD!'

'*Now*, Jasper,' whispered Mrs Smith, stooping over her small friend's head. '*World*, Jasper: that's your word, that's your cue! On you go, and bless you, Jasper! And if, poor mite,' she breathed to herself, 'you're half as nervous of the business as I am, in spite of my size, well ... *Now*, Jasper!'

Jasper looked up at her; he let go her hand. Out of the shadows he went, and into the light.

In his striped trousers, french-grey waistcoat, long black morning-coat, with his gold watch chain and starched collar, high hat in hand, he minced gently forward. His patent-leather shoes were a little too long for him, but he managed them with ease.

At sight of his master, Jennings at once stepped forward. Dr Jasper gave him his hat, his cane, and his canary-coloured gloves. 'Thank you, sir. Very good, sir,' said Jennings. He hung the hat on a peg, and stood the cane in the stand.

The Doctor lifted his head a little as he came to the low table, and reaching up, laid his hand upon a book. 'It's a fine ssunny morning, Jennings,' he said. 'Who iss my firsst pay-sshent today?'

So dead a silence hung in the theatre at first sound of these small treble words and their soft-hissed esses one could not only have heard a pin drop, but could have declared whether it had fallen on its head or its point! Then a little girl, in a seat high up in the dress circle, began to whimper a little. But she was soon hushed, and Jennings was explaining to his master that his first patient was the Right Honourable the Countess of Crumpet; 'and a very nice lady too, sir, as I have been told; closely related to Lord Muffin, sir, of Teacake Castle.'

Thereupon his master drew his watch from his pocket, and said: 'It iss five minut'ss after ten, Jennings, I fear her ladysshipp iss late.'

'I will see, sir,' said Jennings; 'she may be in the ante-room.' And he retired.

'It's all right, Ma; it's all right,' he whispered to Mrs Smith as, swift and quiet as a shadow, he went whisking by. 'Don't worry. He's *safe*.'

Meanwhile, and while he was gone, Jasper, having taken a chair at the gilded table, drew the long goose-quill pen from out of the dry inkpot, and bending his small head till his flat nose almost touched the paper, pretended to write on it.

'That will be three guine'ss,' he sighed to himself almost like a miser as he scrawled with the pen. 'Three more guine'ss!' But though he said these words *as if* to himself, they were loud enough, like Mr Smith's, for everybody in the theatre to hear; and yet they were said so solemnly that nobody laughed.

At this moment Signor Antonio came on to the stage again, from behind the wings. But while he had been gone he had dressed himself up in a bonnet, a flounced purple skirt and bustle, with a long train, and he carried a green striped parasol. He was now of course the Countess of Crumpet. Dr Jasper bowed to the Countess, and they both sat down. And Dr Jasper said to the Countess, 'It iss a fine morning. Would your ladysship, pleess, kindly put out the tongue?'

Then he stood up on his chair to look at her tongue, and said, 'Ah! excussing me, your lady-sship, a ssorry tongue, a dreadful tongue.' And still nobody laughed. But when the Countess, with a simper, thrust out a great man's hand in a white cotton glove from under her Paisley shawl for Dr Jasper to feel her pulse – then *every*body laughed; and after that – except when Dr Jasper was all alone on the stage – they hardly stopped to take breath.

And so the play went on, Jasper saying his part as if it were as simple and easy a thing to do as it is for other apes and monkeys to crack nuts and skin bananas. But though he seemed to all who watched from high and low in the theatre to be as the Manager had said he was – the Master Mimic of Man – this was not really true. This was only the human way of looking at him.

All the time he was really and truly himself, and only himself – thinking his own thoughts, gazing out of his bright, darting, round, dark-deepened, and now almost amber-coloured eyes over the glare of the footlights at the people beyond, and at Signor Antonio in his shawl and gloves and bonnet and bustle. And though he smiled as he chattered, and even grinned with laughter when owing to a mistake made on purpose the Countess sat down on the floor instead of on her chair, he looked gravity itself underneath, if one could have seen him close.

It was cold to him in London – this wintry weather; and though he liked Mr and Mrs Smith, who had been very kind to him, and though he knew quite well in his own way of thinking what *a pot of money* meant, he had *not* liked the large, fat, black-moustached face of the Manager of the theatre, and had consented to shake hands with him only out of politeness. He took everything in good part. And yet, he pined still for a long-lost friend, and to return again to his own people.

And when the curtain fell at the end of his performance his face shrunk up as into a mask, and his eyes suddenly shut, at sound of the roar of voices that had broken out beyond it. Up went the curtain again – himself and Signor Antonio in the middle of the stage : and yet again and yet again – Dr Jasper alone now; and again and again, now hand in hand with the Manager on one side of him and Mr Smith on the other. It seemed as if the audience would shout themselves to a whisper and clap their hands off!

When at last the curtain came down and stayed down, he walked off a little dizzily and unsteadily, and clutched at Mrs Smith's skirt. 'Bless *me*, you poor poor mite!' was all she could say to him, for there were tears in her eyes, part of rejoicing and part for pity, and she fondled his cold fingers as if he had been a child. But small though he was, even as monkeys of his kind go, he had been a gigantic success, and the Manager's face was one wide, dark, greasy smile when once more he shook hands with him, bowed to the ground, though it was not much more than in mockery, and said good night.

So the money – Jasper's share – poured into the bank until he was by far the richest monkey in the world, even though he was also the only monkey in the world that knew it. Mr and Mrs Smith in all their dealings with him were as honest as the day, and they of course were soon rich too.

Now one day John Bumps came home again from sailing round the world, as he had sailed many times before, though never without pleasure. And even though he lived so far away from London as Portsmouth is, he had not been two days with his family before in large print in his newspaper he saw the name of Dr Jasper, and read of what he had done.

'Jasper,' he repeated to himself, 'why that's queer, now, *that* is! *Jasper!*' He read it again, and slapped his leg. 'The same name, right enough,' he said to himself. 'And, Solomon Davy, surely there can't be two Jaspers, not like this! And if there are *not* two Jaspers, then this Jasper must be my Jasper!'

And there and then, he'd made up his mind, for he still had a good deal of money in his pocket after his voyage, that he would take Mrs Bumps and Topsy and Emmanuel and Kate right up to London so that they could go to the *Fortune*, and see this Jasper with their own eyes. Even if he were not his old friend of the Mlango-Nlangoes and only a coincidence, it would be a Treat. And Mr Bumps always gave his family a Treat when he came home from sea. He said nothing whatever to the children meanwhile about his friend Jasper in case it should prove a disappointment, though he told Mrs Bumps. The following Saturday morning, having locked up the house, they all set out together

336

in their best clothes, and caught an early train.

Emmanuel and Kate had never been to London before. They sat, each of them in a corner, staring out of the carriage window so intently at the fields and meadows and villages and churches and hills and farms gliding by that they both of them had only just finished the buns Mrs Bumps had bought for them to eat on the journey when the train steamed into the great glass-roofed cavern of a station called Waterloo – after (as Mr Bumps explained) the great Duke of Wellington, the Iron Duke, Old Nosey.

They had the whole day before them, and Mr Bumps, when he gave them a Treat, never wasted a minute. He at once led them all off into an omnibus and they went, first to Westminster Abbey, then to see the soldiers on their horses in Whitehall, then to St Paul's Cathedral. And there Mr Bumps showed them through the brass grating where the body of Lord Nelson reposed in his tomb made of the cannon he had captured from the French. 'He was a great sailor, was Lord Nelson,' said Mr Bumps.

'Do you mean a sailor just like you, Daddy?' piped out Topsy.

'Ssh! Topsy!' whispered Mrs Bumps. 'You mustn't call out like that. It's a church.'

In St Paul's churchyard, on a seat in the open – for the sun was shining, though it was rather cold – they ate the lunch which Mrs Bumps had packed into her wicker basket. Then, after seeing where the two little Princes had slept for the last time in the Tower of London, they had tea in a tea-shop. The three children had a boiled egg each, but Mr and Mrs Bumps preferred theirs poached. After that they had some Bath buns and plenty of cake. Then they all went out again; and after letting them look for a little while into the shop windows in Cheapside, and especially a toy-shop bowered in with a great plane tree like an immense umbrella, Mr Bumps – as if he had suddenly made up his mind – packed them all into a hackney cab and off they went to the *Fortune*.

Though Mr Bumps was now first-mate of *The Old Lion*, he was not yet a rich man, so he could not afford to take tickets for the seats downstairs, except in what is called the Pit. And he did not take tickets for the Pit because Mrs Bumps said she always liked to look down when she went to a theatre. They were extremely early and by good luck there were five seats available in the Upper Circle, and these in the very middle of the front row. Very pleased they were to be able to sit quietly in these stuffed easy seats and to rest and watch the people, after walking about such a long time in London. Indeed, they had hardly settled themselves in, when little Kate, who was only five and tired out, fell fast asleep in her chair.

Topsy and Emmanuel however stayed wide awake, sucking their peardrops (because Mrs Bumps had thought the seats too dear for bull's-eyes), and whispered and chattering and watching everything that went on. They had never in all their lives seen so many fine ladies with bare shoulders, and diamonds in their hair, or so many gentlemen in long black coats and tall collars.

One by one the members of the band, some carrying their instruments, came edging their way to their seats in front of the stage, and began to tune up or softly tootle on their oboes and trombones. The drummer too thumped softly on his drums, but not on his triangle or cymbals. And last came the conductor with his ivory wand.

'What's that for?' chirped Emmanuel.

'That,' said Mrs Bumps, 'is to do the music with.'

The conductor sat down on his little velvet seat and waited.

Mr Bumps took out his silver watch. 'Sharp on the

hour,' he whispered to Mrs Bumps; 'I wonder what they are waiting for.'

He had no need to wonder long. For suddenly at a signal the conductor with white-gloved hand lifted his wand, and to a crash of music that nearly startled poor little Kate out of her wits, everybody in the theatre stood up and the band played the National Anthem. Sure enough, in a moment or two there came into a great box beside the stage which had been trimmed up with holly and mistletoe, first the King of England himself, then the Queen, then their son, the Prince of Wales, and then a little foreign princess with black ringlets and a tiny fan. They were followed by a few nice-looking but splendid ladies and gentlemen; and the King stood in front of the box, in the middle of it, while the anthem went on.

'That's the King,' whispered Mr Bumps to Emmanuel.

'And that's the Queen,' said Mrs Bumps. 'And there, see, Topsy, see, Manny, see, Kitty, that's the Prince of Wales!'

It was a long time before little Kate could see at all, she had been so dead asleep. When the last note had been played, they all five cheered as loud as they could, and so did the other people in the theatre. The King bowed. They cheered again. Then he sat down; and slowly, quietly, in heavy folds, the curtain ascended and the performance began.

First came acrobats, in tights and spangles. Next came a juggler and his small daughter. It looked as if the balls and hoops and dinner-plates they juggled with were things alive. After the juggling there came a man who sang 'The Bay of Biscay', though Mr Bumps knew a good deal more about the Bay than he did. And after him the five silent-footed Ethiopian Elephants debouched one after the other on to the stage.

The Old Lion

At the sight of them, though the three children opened their mouths like O's and clapped till it hurt, Mr Bumps himself could scarcely breathe. But not, of course, because he had never seen elephants before. Far from that. He had seen quantities of elephants – either walking about, wild and tranquil, in the black man's swamps in Africa, or lying caked with mud in the heat of the tropic sun, or fountaining one another with cascades of silvery water at the close of day. And even though these Five did clever tricks, he had watched others at far more useful ones in their own country. Not that he despised the elephants, he was only used to them.

No; Mr Bumps was waiting for Dr Jasper and could scarcely endure the delay. He was waiting for Dr Jasper in his 'Grand New Act' – as the play-bills said, an act 'especially invented for the August Amusement of Royalty; and patronized by the Shah of Persia, the Emperor of Abyssinia, and other all-powerful Potentates'. And he knew now that before he could count fifty it would begin.

The huge ponderous beasts, having bowed, kneeling in their green and silver, to express their thanks for the applause, were shuffling towards the back of the stage. There, as the lights dimmed, they stood in a row, their trunks uplifted above their heads. There came a pause; and then a slender shaft of pearly light struck down from on high towards the wings. A sudden shawm-like trumpeting broke out from the elephants' throats, a trumpeting loud enough to drown the strains of twenty orchestras.

And into the beam of light – it moving with him as he went – there came tripping softly forward – a trailing cloak of crimson velvet edged with gold lace upon his shoulders, a tall cap of sable surmounted by a plume of *aracatan* feathers pinned with a diamond in front of it upon his head, a little silver-gilt sceptre in his right hand – Jasper.

No longer now a medico of fashion, prescribing pills for the Countess of Crumpet, but himself *Almighty Emperor of All the Ethiopians*, the All-Excellent Ammanabi Nana Dah.

Following in his train came two small fuzz-wigged pygmy blackamoors in ostrich feathers and in robes of silk – of yellow and vermilion. One of these was carrying the Emperor's royal sunshade, and the other (for it was very light in weight) his gilded throne. And these were followed by Signor Antonio (Mr Smith), no longer either a manservant or a countess, but one of the Emperor's tallest and lankiest wives!

When the trumpeting of the elephants had died down and the cymbals and drums had ceased to sound, there went up such a roar of voices in the theatre from the people in it that it was heard outside for half a mile in all directions. Even the King of England, seated smiling in his Royal Box, could not remember to have been greeted with a louder *Huzza*. And then, almost as if this prodigious noise itself had caused it, an utter quiet fell. The Emperor, having gathered his crimson skirts around him, his scarlet sunshade like a huge mushroom over his head, had taken his seat upon his throne. The royal twelve-whiskered leopard-skins had been laid about his feet.

He sat there a moment – small, upright – perfectly still, and looked on them all. Not a tongue wagged, not a sigh or a cough sounded in all the theatre. The *only* stir, and no one noticed it, was that little Kate, who had never before seen such things or anything like them, ducked down her head out of sight of the stage and hid her face in her mother's lap.

The Emperor Jasper looked around him. He was accustomed now to the glare and the sea of faces, and the plaudits and the laughter. He knew where he was, and he knew too – though he himself alone could tell it – *who* and *what* he was. And perhaps for this reason, as he sat there peering out of his splendour, the host of those who were looking at him felt a peculiar coldness stealing into their blood.

It was not only as if they were uneasy in his presence – the tiny motionless head, the intent eyes – but also as if they were frightened. Even the Queen, in her disquiet, glanced sidelong at the King, but the King was looking at the Emperor. And the Emperor at this moment, having very gently lifted his minute left hand, had opened his lips to speak ...

Perhaps if Mr Bumps had thought all this over for a moment or two he would have remained quietly seated with his family in the front row of the Upper Circle and would have said nothing. He would have waited till the end of the performance, and then found his way round to the Stage Door, and sent in to the Manager his card – his visiting card – which he had printed when he was made first-mate of *The Old Lion*: *Mr John Bumps, First-Mate of* T H E O L D L I O N, *7 The Transoms, Portsmouth*. That would have been the right thing to do. But Mr Bumps, being a seaman and not used to holding himself back when anything that needed was to be done, couldn't wait to think.

Out loud, the only sound in the theatre, except that the Emperor having opened his lips had said, 'W E', he called 'Jasper! ...' And as if on one hinge every face in the theatre and every face even in the Royal Box had turned round to look at him. Moreover the puny Emperor on the stage in his gold and crimson finery had said not a syllable after that first clear 'We' – which he had pronounced as if it were spelt Oo-*ee* – but had looked at him too. All else then but rapture had vanished out of his mind. And, in the twinkling of an eye, without the least haste, or word, or sound, or nod, he had risen from his throne, and was softly pattering towards the footlights, or rather to the side of the footlights opposite the Royal Box.

Now the stage was framed in, top and sides, with a shimmering arch of carved wood and painted plaster. All kinds of knobbly fruits and flowers and little cupids and ribbons and dolphins and birds adorned it, glistening bright with gilt and colours. It was behind this arch that the curtain rolled down, and the *Fortune* was one of the handsomest theatres in London.

In all that quiet, then, slowly and without haste, Jasper began to climb this arch, his royal robes swinging free behind him. They were heavy with their gold lace, and he climbed slowly. But he climbed none the less surely, on and on, and up and up, and watched by every eye, until he had reached to where Mr Bump's gallery began. Here there ran a low wooden wall to keep the people from falling out of the gallery. Those in the front row of this gallery sat in their seats with their knees bent, looking over this low wall at the stage, and – to make it comfortable for their elbows as well as to look nice – the top of it had been padded with horsehair and covered with a maroon-coloured stuff called plush.

So it was with no sound at all from his small five-toed feet that Jasper came – hastening, now – alone along this wall in front of the people seated there, their faces in the reflected glow of the footlights looking as white as china. Straight along this dizzy path he silently tippeted until he reached the place where Mr Bumps was sitting. There he stopped. He looked at Mr Bumps and bowed his head. Then he said something that few heard and nobody understood. He put out his hands towards Mr Bumps. And the two friends were restored to one another.

Now all this time the people had sat perfectly still,

343

watching. But when they witnessed what had happened –
and these two there, Jasper and Mr Bumps – though they
didn't really know what to say or think, they all began
to talk, and some to shout, even to hoot. They were angry.
They were being cheated. *This* was not what they had paid
all that money to see! Poor Mrs Bumps could even hear
what those near by were saying. She was growing more and
more hot and discomfited. 'Oh, John! Oh John!' she kept
repeating.

And now the Manager, whom Jasper had come to like
even less and less as his nights had gone by, appeared,
marching on to the stage. He bowed to the King, he bowed
to the Queen, he bowed to the Prince of Wales, and he called
out in a loud voice that he was very sorry for what had
happened. He said he was very sorry to them all. He said
that he had paid pounds and pounds of money for Jasper
to come and amuse them, and now here was this man up
there enticing him away. He bawled out, 'Emperor Jasper,
Emperor Jasper, come down, sir!'

Then some voices in the back parts of the theatre shouted,
'Turn him out!' and a great clamour began, some yelling
this and some that, and the Manager standing alone, fat and
black and helpless in the middle of the stage, cajoling in
vain Jasper to come back. As for Mr Smith – since he was
dressed up as one of the Emperor's wives, and was a born
actor, he felt that it was not his place to speak; especially
before Royalty. His eyes rolled in his black-dyed face, but
he said nothing.

Meanwhile, safe with his Mr Bumps again, Jasper had
made not the faintest sign that he had even heard the
Manager's call. And now, louder and louder, many voices
were shouting, 'Send him back!' and some were bellowing,
'Let him stay!' and the uproar grew worse and worse.

At last the King himself stood up in the Royal Box and

raised his hand. There was at once a great hush in the theatre. Everybody fell silent. The King said, 'Whose monkey is this marvel?'

With a frowning countenance he looked down upon the Manager. And the Manager answered not a word. Then the King turned his eyes towards Mr Bumps. He said, 'Let that man stand up.'

And Mr Bumps stood up.

'Who are you?' said the King.

'I am John Bumps, may it please your Majesty,' said Mr Bumps simply. 'First-mate of *The Old Lion*, now lying at Portsmouth.'

'What are you doing here?' said the King.

'I came, your Majesty – and this is Mrs Bumps beside me with the children – I came in hopes of seeing an old friend again.'

'Who?' said the King.

Mrs Bumps was now clutching tight her husband's hand, since it was hidden by the plush-topped wooden wall. His voice faltered. He touched with his other hand Jasper's sable cap.

'This, sir,' he said.

'You mean,' said the King, smiling, 'his Serene Mightiness, the All-Excellent Ammanabi Nana Dah? Beseech his Mightiness to stand forth.'

This good-humour of the King greatly pleased all the people present, and every eye was now fixed on Mr Bumps.

'*Now*, Jasper,' whispered he, 'the King of England is speaking to 'ee.'

Jasper blinked but once at his old friend, pressed the finger clasped tight in his hand, and stood up on the plush parapet, before them all.

And the King, his eye twinkling, said, 'Is it your wish, cousin, that you remain with our loyal subject, Mr Bumps, or' – and he swept his hand towards the Manager and the footlights.

An instant's silence followed.

And then, 'Thissee Misster Bumpss, ssir,' piped Jasper, for he had never quite mastered his s's, 'thissee Misster Bumpss, ssir, iss my *firsst* friend. Mr Ssmith iss my o-ther friend. My *firsst* iss ...' But the next word which was *firsst* was almost drowned by the shout of delight from a thousand throats that went up to the roof of the theatre like the roar of an avalanche. It was fortunate for the Manager that he had already left the stage and gone into the back parts of the theatre.

And then and there Mr Bumps and Mrs Bumps and the three children and Jasper were conducted down to the Royal Box and were presented to His Majesty. And first the King and then the Queen and then the Prince of Wales and then the little foreign princess shook hands with Jasper, and he spoke to them. And the King slipped a ring off his own finger and hung it round the neck of the Ethiopian Emperor. They met, one might say, as equals.

But Mr Bumps being a sailor and an honest man, when the theatre was empty and the lights were out and the people gone away, sat down in a little back room behind the stage with the Manager and Mr and Mrs Smith, while Mrs Bumps and the children waited for them in Jasper's dressing-room. Here, the four of them, over a bottle of port wine, made a bargain together, so that the Manager should not lose too much money. The bargain was that for the whole of the next three days, except when it was time for Dinner or Tea, Jasper should sit on the stage of the *Fortune* in his gold and crimson, the King's ring dangling round his neck, his cap of sable on his head, while every man, woman or child who wished and could pay to see him, passed along – in at one door out at another – before his throne. And of the cash they might take at the doors, it was agreed that the Manager should keep half, Mr Smith a quarter, and Jasper a quarter. Mr Bumps would take nothing. In those three days the Manager made more profit than he had ever made before in a whole month!

When the three days were over, Mr Bumps's leave from his ship was over too, and they all went down to Portsmouth. By the kindness of the captain of *The Old Lion*, it had been arranged that Jasper should come aboard – it was his wish – and return to Africa. He might, if he had so chosen, have stayed in England and lived in a palace for the rest of his life. His fame had run like wildfire through the Kingdom, and far beyond it. Telegrams had come from Paris and Rome and Vienna and Budapest, and all parts of America, entreating him to visit them.

Apart from telegrams, the postman brought Jasper a small sack of letters every morning – from old ladies in the country who wished to adopt him, from learned professors of Oxford and Cambridge who wished to share his wisdom, from cunning men who hoped to make money out of him, and from all kinds of people grown-up and otherwise who asked him to put his name in their birthday books. And the King did not forget him. But Jasper refused everything – except the birthday books; he pined only for home.

In the meantime he himself made many presents to all his friends, and especially to little Kate, according to what he thought they would like best. The rest of his money – after he had said good-bye to Mr Johnson – had been packed in the cellar at the Bank into twenty-eight small chests or coffers. These were piled up in the cabin that had been prepared for him on *The Old Lion*. And a nice pile they made.

Besides this, with the captain's consent, Jasper and Mr

and Mrs Bumps had bought a large quantity of all kinds of trinkets, toys, linen and silk, dainties and beverages that would not rust or tarnish or go bad upon the voyage, whatever weather they might encounter. Jasper had thought of everything that his own people round about Dondo might fancy and enjoy. And the King had commanded that on this voyage *The Old Lion* should fly not the red ensign but at the main truck the Royal Standard.

A crowd of people so vast thronged the quay and the windows and the roofs of the houses near by to see Jasper off that some of those in the front were tumbled into the water. All except one had nothing worse than a sousing and were picked up by row-boats. But the Manager unfortunately, who had pushed past some small boys for a better view, was drowned.

The best brass band in Portsmouth played *Rule Britannia*, and to the strains of *Rio Grande* the men of *The Old Lion* weighed anchor.

> *Oh* say, *were you ever in Rio Grande?*
> Awa-ay, Rio!
> *It's there that the rivers run down golden sand –*
> And we're bound for the Rio Grande.
> And awa-ay, Rio! – away, Rio!
> Sing, fare you well, my bonny young gal,
> We're bound for the Rio Grande!

She shook, she stirred. Softly a gentle breeze between the blue sky and the sparkling water bellied out the sails of the ship. She drew away upon the water, past Nomansland Fort, where a gun puffed out to greet her, and smalled more and more. By the time Mrs Bumps and the three children sat down to tea, she was out of sight of land.

Mr Bumps had many a quiet and private talk with Jasper in his cabin as the days went by. Never had the old ship seen fairer weather. The two friends were sad at heart, for Mr Bumps knew that nothing he could say now would dissuade Jasper from returning to his own people. That, Jasper assured him, as well as what words he had could do so, was his *one* wish; and Mr Bumps could say no more.

Now the head village where Mr Bumps's friend the Chief of the Mlango-Nlangoes lived was a mile or more from the banks of the Quanza. It lay beyond a swamp where there is a forest of mangroves, the abode of countless crocodiles, though the two-horned rhinoceroses keep to the river. Between the river and the swamp (where, if there were hundreds of crocodiles there must have been thousands of monkeys!) was a stretch of sand and green.

In this spot, out of sight of the river, but well in reach of the trees, the black men whom Mr Bumps's friend, the Chief of the Mlango-Nlango tribe, had very kindly lent him for the purpose, brought up not only Jasper's crates and tubs and boxes and barrels of rare nuts and fruits, fruits in syrup, biscuits, beads and gewgaws, etc., but also his money chests crammed tight with sovereigns and silver. For nothing that Mr Bumps or Mr Johnson or Mr and Mrs Smith could say, could persuade Jasper that all this money of his was just that and nothing more, and would be of no more use to his friends in their treetops, except perhaps for the beauty of it, than nut-shells or pebble-stones. It had been given to him, he kept saying, for what he had done; and therefore he would like to take it all back to his people – except of course what he wished to spend on the presents he had given to Mr Bumps and his other friends.

Since, then, Jasper, however much they argued, still wished to take back his money with him, Mr Bumps had said of course, 'Let it be so.' Just as the King had said.

When all Jasper's possessions had been piled up in the open space between the hidden river and the forest which he had chosen for his camping-place, and when a small bell-tent had been pitched for him beside them, it was evening. Strange voices of all manner of animals and birds sounded in their ears when Mr Bumps bade his friend good night.

'I hope, Jasper,' he said, 'ay, and more than hope, that your kith and kin over there will be pleased to see you. I hope so. But they have been keeping mighty quiet.'

He said it with a faint heart, smiling at his little friend dressed up, as he had himself decided, in his robes of gold and crimson, his sable cap on his head. Still, since Mr Bumps had promised to come back in the morning, this was not good-bye. It was only good night.

When Mr Bumps did come back in the morning, Jasper greeted him sadly enough. Though he had heard in the night faint chattering and shufflings, not a single friend of all he had known in past times – not one – had come near him. So at Mr Bumps's advice they unpacked some of the boxes and crates containing the dainties that smelt sweetest and strongest and strewed them about in enticing piles some little distance away from Jasper's tent and nearer the forest.

Next morning these had vanished; and yet Jasper had remained solitary and unvisited in his tent all the night long. He had not slept a wink. Never mind, he told Mr Bumps; his friends were no doubt shy and timid. He was sure they would be pleased to see him and longed to speak to him and welcome him back.

But morning after morning the piles grew less and less; the food was all gone; the toys and trinkets were scattered out of the boxes; only the money, the sovereigns and the silver, were left. And these the monkeys, having smelt and fingered them, left disowned.

Jasper thought at last it must be his royal robes, his antelope slippers, his cap and his colours that kept his people from knowing who he was. He said this smiling, to his friend Mr Bumps, but not as if he quite believed it.

That evening when they parted again, the air over Africa was heavy and stagnant and the sky lowering. Silent lightnings gleamed ever and again above the distant forests, and they could hear the tom-toms of the Mlango-Nlangoes sullenly drumming from their hidden dancing-places. Jasper had stripped himself of all his finery, and stood up beside his tent only in his own fur – a little monkey, as he was before. Mr Bumps shook him by the hand.

'Good night, old friend,' he said, 'and God-speed.'

But when he came back the next morning after the storm, the cap and the robes and the slippers and the gilded sceptre were gone. The tent had been blown away. And Jasper was gone too. Mr Bumps called and called and called. He came back in the evening and called again. No voice answered him. The forest lay dark and silent. Three days, by the kindness of the captain, to whom he had sent a black man as messenger, he waited and waited. But he waited in vain. And on the fourth *The Old Lion* sailed away.

Broomsticks

Miss Chauncey's cat, Sam, had been with her many years before she noticed anything unusual, anything *disturbing*, in his conduct. Like most cats who live under the same roof with but one or two humans, he had always been more sagacious than cats of a common household. He had learned Miss Chauncey's ways. He acted, that is, as nearly like a small mortal dressed up in a hairy coat as one could expect a cat to act. He was what is called an 'intelligent' cat.

But though Sam had learned much from Miss Chauncey, I am bound to say that Miss Chauncey had learned very little from Sam. She was a kind, indulgent mistress; she could sew, and cook, and crochet, and make a bed, and read and write and cipher a little. And when she was a girl she used to sing 'Kathleen Mavourneen' to the piano. Sam, of course, could do nothing of this kind.

But then, Miss Chauncey could no more have caught and killed a mouse or a blackbird with her five naked fingers than she could have been Pope of Rome. Nor could she run up a six-foot brick wall, or leap clean from the hearthmat in her parlour on to the shelf of her chimneypiece without disturbing a single ornament, or even tinkling one crystal lustre against another. Unlike Sam, too, she could not find her way in the dark, or by her sense of smell; or keep in good health by merely nibbling grass in the garden. If, moreover, she had been carefully held up by her feet and hands two or three feet above the ground and then dropped, she would have at once fallen plump on her back; whereas when Sam was only three months old he could have managed to twist clean about in the air in twelve inches and come down on his four feet, as firm as a table.

While then Sam had learned a good deal from Miss Chauncey, she had learned nothing from him. And even if she had been willing to be taught, and he to teach her, it is doubtful if she would have proved a promising pupil. What is more, she knew much less about Sam than he knew about his mistress – until, at least, that afternoon when she was doing her hair in the glass. And then she could hardly believe her own eyes. It was a moment that completely changed her views about Sam – and nothing after that experience was ever quite the same again ...

Sam had always been a fine upstanding creature, his fur jet-black and silky, his eyes a lambent gold, even in sunshine, and at night aglow like green topazes. He was now full five years of age, and had an unusually powerful miaou. Living as he did quite alone with Miss Chauncey at Post Houses, it was natural that he should become her constant companion. For Post Houses was a singularly solitary house, standing almost in the middle of Haggurds-don Moor, just where two wandering byways cross each other like the half-closed blades of a pair of shears or scissors.

She was well over a mile from her nearest neighbour, Mr Cullings, the carrier; and yet another mile from the straggling old village of Haggurdsdon itself. Its road were extremely ancient. They had been sheep-tracks long before the Romans came to England and had cut *their* roads from shore to shore. But for many years few travellers on horse or foot, or even sheep with their shepherd had come Miss Chauncey's way. You could have gazed from her windows for days together without seeing so much as a tinker's barrow or a gipsy's van.

Post Houses too was perhaps the ugliest house there ever was. Its four corners stood straight up on the moor like a pile of nursery bricks. From its flat roof on a clear day the eye could see for miles and miles across the moor, Mr Cullings's cottage being out of sight in a shallow hollow. It had belonged to Miss Chauncey's respectable ancestors for generations. Many people in Haggurdsdon indeed called it Chauncey's. And though in a blustering wind it was as full of noises as an organ, though it was cold as a barn in winter, and though another branch of the family had as far back as the 'seventies gone to live in the Isle of Wight, Miss Chauncey still remained faithful to the old walls. In fact she loved the ugly old place. Had she not lived in it ever since she was a little girl, with knickerbockers showing under her skirts, and pale-blue ribbon rosettes at her shoulders.

This fact alone made Sam's conduct the more reprehensible, for never cat had kinder mistress. Miss Chauncey herself was now about sixty years of age – fifty-five years older than Sam. She was tall and gaunt, and straight as a ramrod. On weekdays she wore black alpaca, and on Sundays a watered silk. Her large round steel spectacles straddling across her high nose gave her a look of being keen as well as cold. But truly she was neither. For even so stupid a man as Mr Cullings could take her in over the cartage charge for a parcel – just by looking tired, or sighing as he glanced at his rough-haired, knock-kneed mare. And there was the warmest of hearts under her stiff bodice.

Post Houses being so far from the village, milk and cream were a little difficult. But Miss Chauncey could deny Sam nothing – in reason. She paid a whole sixpence a week to a little girl called Susan Ard, who brought these dainties from the nearest farm. They were dainties indeed, for though the grasses on Haggurdsdon Moor were of a dark sour green, the cows that grazed on it gave an uncommonly rich milk, and Sam flourished on it. Mr Cullings called once a week on his round, and had a standing order to bring with him a few sprats or fresh herrings, or any toothsome fish that was in season, Miss Chauncey would not even withhold her purse from whitebait, if no other cheaper wholesome fish were procurable. And Mr Cullings would eye Sam fawning about his cartwheel, or gloating up at his dish, and say, ' 'Ee be a queer animal, Mum, shure enough; 'ee be a wunnerful queer animal, 'ee be.'

As for Miss Chauncey herself, she was a niggardly eater, though much attached to her tea. She made her own bread and cookies. On Saturday a butcher-boy drove up in a striped apron with her Sunday joint; but she was no meat-lover. Her cupboards were full of home-made jams and bottled fruits and dried herbs – everything of that kind, for Post Houses had a nice long strip of garden behind it, surrounded by a high old yellow brick wall.

Quite early in life Sam, of course, had learned to know his meal-times – though how he 'told' them was known only to himself, for he never appeared even to glance at the face of the grandfather's clock on the staircase. He was punctual, a dandy in his toilet, and a prodigious sleeper. He had learned to pull down the latch of the back door, if, in the months when an open window was not to be found, he wished to go out. Indeed, he often seemed to prefer the latch. He never slept on Miss Chauncey's patchwork quilt unless his own had been placed over it. He was fastidious almost to a foppish degree in his habits, and he was no thief. He had a mew on one note to show when he wanted something to eat; a mew a semitone or two higher if he wanted drink (that is, cold water, for which he had a natural taste); and yet another mew – gentle and sustained

– when he wished, so to speak, to converse with his mistress.

Not, of course, that the creature talked *English*. He liked to sit up on one chair by the fireside, especially in the kitchen – for he was no born parlour cat – and to look up at the glinting glasses of Miss Chauncey's spectacles, and then down a while at the fire-flames (drawing his claws in and out as he did so, and purring the while), almost as if he might be preaching a sermon, or reciting a poem.

But this was in the happy days when all seemed well. This was in the days when Miss Chauncey's mind was innocent of doubts and suspicions.

Like others of his kind, too, Sam had delighted in his youth to lie in the window and idly watch the birds in the apple-trees – tits, thrushes, blackbirds, bullfinches – or to crouch over a mousehole, for hours together. Such were his house amusements (he never ate his mice), while Miss Chauncey with cap and broom, duster and dish-clout, went about her work. But he also had a way of examining things in which cats are not generally interested. He as good as told Miss Chauncey one afternoon that moths were at work in her parlour carpet. For he walked to and fro and back and forth with his tail up, until she attended to him. And he certainly warned her, with a yelp like an Amazonian monkey, when a red-hot coal had set her kitchen mat on fire.

He would lie or sit with his whiskers to the north before noonday, and due south afterwards. In general his manners were perfection. But occasionally, when she called him, his face would appear to knot itself into a frown – at any rate to assume a low sullen look, as if he expostulated: 'Why must you be interrupting me, Madam, when I was attending to something else?' And now and then, Miss Chauncey fancied, he would deliberately secrete himself or steal out of (and into) Post Houses unbeknown.

Miss Chauncey too would sometimes find him trotting from room to room as if on a visit of inspection. On his second birthday he had carried in an immense mouse and laid it beside the shiny toecap of her boot as she sat knitting by the fire. She smiled and nodded merrily at him, as usual, but on this occasion he looked at her intently, and then deliberately shook his head. After that he never paid the smallest attention to mouse or mousehole or mousery, and Miss Chauncey was obliged to purchase a cheese-bait trap, else she would have been overrun.

Almost any domestic cat may do things of this nature, and all this of course was solely on Sam's domestic side. For he shared house with Miss Chauncey and, like any two beings that live together, he was bound to keep up certain appearances. He met her half-way, as the saying goes. When, however, he was 'on his own', he was no longer Miss Chauncey's Sam, he was no longer merely the cat at Post Houses, but just *himself*. He went back, that is, to his own free independent life; to his own private habits.

Then the moor on which he roved was his own country, and the 'humans' and their houses on it were no more to him in his wild privy existence than mole-hills or badgers' earths or rabbit warrens are to ourselves. Of this side of his life his mistress knew practically nothing. She did not consider it. She supposed that Sam behaved like other cats, though it was evident that at times he went far afield, for he now and again brought home a young Cochin China pullet, and the nearest Cochin China fowls were at the vicarage, a good four miles off. Sometimes of an evening, too, when Miss Chauncey was taking a little walk herself, she would see him – a swiftly moving black speck – far along the road, hastening home. And there was more purpose expressed in his gait and appearance than ever Mr Cullings or even the vicar showed!

It was pleasant to observe, too, when he came within miaouing distance, how his manner changed. He turned at once from being a Cat into being a Domestic Cat. He was instantaneously no longer the Feline Adventurer, the Nocturnal Marauder and Haunter of Haggurdsdon Moor (though Miss Chauncey would not have so expressed it), but simply his mistress's spoiled pet, Sam. She loved him dearly. But, as again with human beings who are accustomed to live together, she did not *think* very much about him. It could not but be a shock then that late evening, when without the slightest warning Miss Chauncey discovered that Sam was deliberately deceiving her.

She was brushing her thin brown front hair before her looking-glass. At this moment it hung down over her face like a fine loose veil. And as she always mused of other things when she was brushing her hair, she was somewhat absent-minded the while. On raising her eyes from her reverie behind this screen of hair, she perceived not only that Sam's reflection was in sight in the looking-glass, but also that something a little mysterious was happening. Sam was sitting up as if to beg. There was nothing in that. It had been a customary feat of his since he was a few months old. Still, for what might he be begging, no one by?

Now the window to the right of the chintz-valanced dressing-table was open at the top. Outside, it was beginning to grow dark. All Haggurdsdon Moor lay hushed and still in the evening's thickening gloom. And apart from begging when there was nothing to beg for, Sam seemed, so to speak, to be gesticulating with his paws. He appeared, that is, to be making signs, just as if there were someone or something looking in at the window at him from out of the air – which was quite impossible. And there was a look upon his face that certainly Miss Chauncey had never seen before.

She stayed a moment with hair-brush uplifted, her long lean arm at an angle with her head. On seeing this, Sam had instantly desisted from these motions. He had dropped to his fours again, and was now apparently composing himself for another nap. No; this too was a pretence; for presently as she watched, he turned restlessly about so that his whiskers were once again due south. His backward parts towards the window, he was now gazing fixedly in front of him out of a far from friendly face. Far indeed from friendly for a creature that had lived with her ever since he opened the eyes of his blind kittenhood.

As if he had read her thoughts, Sam at that moment lifted his head to look at his mistress; she withdrew her eyes to the glass only in the nick of time, and when she turned from her toilet there sat he – so serene in appearance, so puss-like, so ordinary once more that Miss Chauncey could scarcely believe anything whatever had been amiss. Had her eyes deluded her – glass? Was that peculiar motion of Sam's fore-paws (almost as if he were knitting), was that wide excited stare due only to the fact that he was catching what was, to her, an invisible fly?

Miss Chauncey having now neatly arranged her 'window-curtains' – the sleek loops of hair she wore on either side her high forehead – glanced yet again out of the window. Nothing there but the silence of the Moor; nothing there but the faint pricking of a star as the evening darkened.

Sam's supper cream was waiting on the hearthrug in the parlour as usual that evening. The lamp was lit. The red blinds were drawn. The fire crackled in the grate. There they sat, these two; the walls of the four-cornered house beside the crossroads rising up above them like a huge oblong box under the immense starry sky that saucered in the wide darkness of the Moor.

And while she sat so – with Sam there, seemingly fast asleep – Miss Chauncey was thinking. What had occurred in the bedroom that early evening had reminded her of other odd little bygone happenings. Trifles she had scarcely noticed, but which now returned clearly to memory. How often in the past, for example, Sam at this hour would be sitting as if fast asleep (as now) his paws tucked neatly in, looking very much like a stout alderman after dinner. And then suddenly, without warning, as if a distant voice had called him, he would leap to his feet and run straight out of the room. And somewhere in the house – door ajar or window agape, he would find his egress and be up and away into the night. This had been a common thing to happen.

Once, too, Miss Chauncey had found him squatting on his hindquarters on the window-ledge of a little room that had been entirely disused since, years ago, Cousin Milly had stayed at Post Houses when Miss Chauncey was a child of eight. She had cried out at sight of him, 'You foolish Sam, you; come in, sir! You will be tumbling out of the window next!' And she remembered as though it were yesterday that though at this he had stepped gingerly in at once from his dizzy perch, he had not looked at her. He had passed her without a sign.

On moonlight evenings, too – why, you could never be sure *where* he was! You could never be sure from what errand he had *returned*. Was she sure indeed where he was on *any* night? The longer she reflected, the gloomier grew her doubts and misgivings. This night, at any rate, Miss Chauncey determined to keep watch. But she was not happy in doing so. She hated all manner of spying. They were old companions, Sam and she; and she, without him

in bleak Post Houses, would be sadly desolate. She loved
Sam dearly. None the less, what she had witnessed that
evening had stayed in her mind, and it would be wiser to
know all that there was to be known, even if for Sam's
sake only.

Now Miss Chauncey always slept with her bedroom
door ajar. She had slept so ever since her nursery days.
Being a rather timid little girl, she liked in those far-away
times to hear the grown-up voices downstairs and the
spoons and forks clinking. As for Sam, he always slept
in his basket beside her fireplace. Every morning there he
would be, though on some mornings Miss Chauncey's eyes
would open gently to find herself gazing steadily into his
pale green ones as he stood on his hind paws, resting his
front ones on her bedside, and looking into her face. 'Time
for breakfast, Sam?' his mistress would murmur. And
Sam would mew, as distantly almost as a seagull in the
heights of the sky.

Tonight, however, Miss Chauncey only pretended to be
asleep. It was difficult, however, to keep wholly awake,
and she was all but drowsing off when there came a faint
squeak from the hinge of her door, and she realized
that Sam was gone out. After waiting a moment or two,
she struck a match. Yes, there was his empty basket in
the dark silent room, and presently from far away – from
the steeple at Haggurdsdon Village – came the knolling
of the hour.

Miss Chauncey placed the dead end of the match in the
saucer of her candlestick, and at that moment fancied she
heard a faint *whssh* at her window, as of a sudden gust or
scurry of wind, or the wings of a fast-flying bird – of a
wild goose. It even reminded Miss Chauncey of half-
forgotten Guy Fawkes days and of the sound the stick
or a rocket makes as it slips down through the air – while

its green and ruby lights die out in the immense vacancy above. Miss Chauncey gathered up her long legs in the bed, got up, drew on the blue flannel dressing-gown that always hung on her bedrail, and lifting back the blind an inch or two, looked out of the window.

It was a high starry night; and a brightening in the sky above the roof seemed to betoken there must be a moon over the backward parts of the house. Even as she watched, a streak of pale silver descended swiftly out of the far spaces of the heavens, and fading into the darkness dwindled and vanished away. It was a meteorite; and at that very instant Miss Chauncey fancied she heard again a faint remote dwindling *whssh* in the air. Was *that* the meteorite too? Could she have been deceived? Was she being deceived in everything? She drew back.

And then, as if in deliberate and defiant answer, out of the distance and from what appeared to be the extreme end of her long garden where grew a tangle of sloe bushes, there followed a prolonged and as if half-secret caterwaul: very low – contralto, one might say – *Meearou-rou-rou-rou-rou!*

Heaven forbid! Was *that* Sam's tongue? The cater- wauling ceased. Yet still Miss Chauncey could not suppress a shudder. She knew Sam's voice of old. But surely not that! Surely not that!

Strange and immodest though it was to hear herself, too, in that solitary place calling out in the dead of night, she nevertheless at once opened the window and summoned Sam by name. There was no response. The trees and bushes of the garden stood motionless; their faint shadows on the ground revealing how small a moon was actually in the sky, and how low it hung towards its setting. The vague undulations of the Moor stretched into the distance. Not a light to be seen except those of the firmament. Again, and yet again, Miss Chauncey cried 'Sam, Sam! Come away

in! Come away in, sir, you bad creature!' Not a sound.
Not the least stir of leaf or blade of grass.

When, after so broken a night, Miss Chauncey awoke a
little late the next morning, the first thing her eyes beheld
when she sat up in bed was Sam – couched as usual in
his basket. It was a mystery, and an uneasy one. After
supping up his morning bowl, he slept steadily on until
noonday. This happened to be the day of the week when
Miss Chauncey made bread. On and on she steadily
kneaded the dough with her knuckled hands, glancing
ever and again towards the motionless creature. With
fingers clotted from the great earthenware bowl, she stood
over him at last for a few moments, and eyed him closely.

He was lying curled round with his whiskered face to
one side towards the fire. And it seemed to Miss Chauncey
that she had never noticed before that faint peculiar grin
on his face. 'Sam!' she cried sharply. An eye instantly
opened, wide and ferocious, as if a mouse had squeaked.
He stared at her for an instant; then the lid narrowed. The
gaze slunk away a little, but Sam began to purr.

The truth of it is, all this was making Miss Chauncey exceedingly unhappy. Mr Cullings called that afternoon, with
a basket of some fresh comely young sprats. 'Them'll wake
his Royal Highness up,' he said. 'They'm fresh as daisies.
Lor, m'm, what a Nero that beast be!'

'Cats *are* strange creatures, Mr Cullings,' replied Miss
Chauncey reflectively; complacently supposing that Mr Cullings had misplaced an *h* and had meant to say, *an hero*.
And Sam himself, with uplifted tail, and as if of the same
opinion, was rubbing his head gently against her boot.

Mr Cullings eyed her closely. 'Why, yes, they be,' he said.
'What I says is is that as soon as they're out of sight, you
are out of their mind. There's no more gratitood nor affection in a cat than in a pump. Though so far as the pump is

concerned, the gratitood should be on our side. I knew a
family of cats once what fairly druv their mistress out of
house and home.'

'But you wouldn't have a cat *only* a pet?' said Miss
Chauncey faintly; afraid to ask for further particulars of
this peculiar occurrence.

'Why, no, m'm,' said the carrier. 'As the Lord made 'em,
of they be. But I'll be bound they could tell some knotty
stories is they had a human tongue to their heads!'

Sam had ceased caressing his mistress's foot, and was
looking steadily at Mr Cullings, his hair roughed a little
about the neck and shoulders. And the carrier looked back.

'No, m'm. We wouldn't keep 'em,' he said at last, 'if they
was *four* times that size. Or, not for long!'

Having watched Mr Cullings's little cart bowl away into
the distance, Miss Chauncey returned into the house, more
disturbed than ever. Nor did her uneasiness abate when
Sam refused even to sniff at his sprats. Instead, he crawled
in under a low table in the kitchen, behind the old seaman's chest in which Miss Chauncey kept her kindling
wood. She fancied she heard his claws working in the wood
now and again, and once he seemed to be expressing his
natural feelings in what vulgar people with little sympathy
for animals describe as 'swearing'.

Her caressing 'Sam's, at any rate, were all in vain. His
only reply was a kind of sneeze which uncomfortably resembled 'spitting'. Miss Chauncey's feelings had already
been hurt. It was now her mind that suffered. Something
the carrier had said, or the way he had said it, or the
peculiar look she had noticed on his face when he was returning Sam's stare in the porch, haunted her thoughts.
She was no longer young, was she becoming fanciful? Or
must she indeed conclude that for weeks past Sam had been
steadily circumventing her, or at any rate concealing his

wanderings and his interests? What nonsense. Worse still:
was she now so credulous as to believe that Sam had in
actual fact been making signals – and secretly, behind her
back – to some confederate that must either have been up
in the sky, or in the moon!

Whether or not, Miss Chauncey determined to keep a
sharper eye on him. Their future was at stake. She would
at least make sure that he did not leave the house that
night. But then: why not? she asked herself. Why shouldn't
the creature chose his own hour and season? Cats, like
owls, *see* best in the dark. They go best a-mousing in the
dark, and may prefer the dark for their private, social, and
even public affairs. Post Houses, after all, was only rather
more than two miles from Haggurdsdon Village, and
there were cats there in plenty. Poor fellow, her own dumb
human company must sometimes be dull enough!

Such were Miss Chauncey's reflections; and as if to reassure her, Sam himself at that moment serenely entered the
room and leapt up on to the empty chair beside her
tea-table. As if, too, to prove that he had thought better of
his evil temper, or to insinuate that there had been nothing
amiss between himself and Mr Cullings, he was licking
his chops, and there was no mistaking the odour of fish
which he brought in with him from his saucer.

'So you have thought better of it, my boy?' thought
Miss Chauncey, though she did not utter the words aloud.
And yet as she returned his steady feline gaze, she realized
how difficult it was to read the intelligence behind those
eyes. You might say that, Sam being only a cat, there was
no meaning in them at all. But Miss Chauncey knew better.
There could be meaning enough if such eyes had looked
out of *human* shape at her.

Unfortunately, and almost as if Sam had overheard his
mistress's speculations regarding possible cat friends in the

village, there came at that moment a faint wambling mew beneath the open window. In a flash Sam was out of his chair and over the window-ledge, and Miss Chauncey rose only just in time to see him in infuriated pursuit of a slim sleek tortoiseshell creature that had evidently come to Post Houses in hope of a friendlier reception, and was now fleeing in positive fear of its life.

Sam returned from his chase as fresh as paint, and Miss Chauncey was horrified to detect – caught up between the claws of his right forefoot – a tuft or two of tortoiseshell fur, which, having composed himself by the fire, he promptly removed by licking.

Still pondering on these disquieting events, Miss Chauncey took her usual evening walk in the garden. Candytuft and virginia stock were seeding along the shell-lined path, and late roses were already beginning to blow on the high brick wall which shut off her narrow strip of land from the vast lap of the Moor. Having come to the end of the path, Miss Chauncey pushed on a little further than usual, to where the grasses grew more rampant, and where wild headlong weeds raised their heads beneath her few lichenous apple-trees. Still further down, for hers was a long, though narrow, garden – there grew straggling bushes of sloe and spiny whitethorn. These had blossomed indeed in the moor's bleak springs long before Post Houses had raised its chimney pots into the sky. Here, too, flourished a frowning drift of nettles – their sour odour haunting the air.

It was in this forlorn spot that – just like Robinson Crusoe, before her – Miss Chauncey was suddenly brought to a standstill by the appearance of what might be nothing other than a footprint in the mould. But not only this. A few inches away there showed what might be the mark of a walking-cane or even of something stouter and heavier

– a crutch. Could she be deceived? The footprint, it was true, was of a peculiar kind. 'A queer shoe that!' thought Miss Chauncey. Could the resemblance be accidental? *Was* it a footprint?

Miss Chauncey glanced furtively across the bushes towards the house. It loomed gaunt and forbidding in the moorland dusk. And she fancied she could see, though the evening light might be deluding her, the cowering shape of Sam looking out at her from the kitchen window. To be watched! To be herself spied upon – and watched!

But then, of course, Sam was always watching her. What oddity was there in that? Where else would his sprats come from, his cream, his saucer of milk, his bowl of fresh well-water? Nevertheless, Miss Chauncey returned to her parlour gravely discomposed.

It was an uncommonly calm evening, and as she went from room to room locking the windows, she noticed there was already a moon in the sky. She eyed it with misgiving. And at last bedtime came; and when Sam, as usual, after a lick or two, had composed himself in his basket, Miss Chauncey, holding the key almost challengingly within view, deliberately locked her own bedroom door.

When she awoke next morning Sam was asleep in his basket as usual, and during the day-time he kept pretty closely to the house. So, too, on the Wednesday and the Thursday. It was not until the following Friday that having occasion to go into an upper bedroom that had no fireplace, and being followed as usual by Sam, Miss Chauncey detected the faint rank smell of soot in the room. No chimney, and a smell of soot! She turned rapidly on her companion: he had already left the room.

And when that afternoon she discovered a black sooty smear upon her own patchwork quilt, she realized not only that her suspicions had been justified, but that for the first time in his life Sam had deliberately laid himself down there in her absence. At this act of sheer defiance she was no longer so much hurt as exceedingly angry. There could be no doubt. Sam was now openly defying her. No two companions could share a house on such terms as these. He must be taught a lesson.

That evening, in full sight of the creature, having locked her bedroom door, she stuffed a large piece of mattress ticking into the mouth of her chimney and pulled down the register. Having watched these proceedings, Sam rose from his basket, and with an easy spring, leapt up on to the dressing-table. Beyond the window, the Moor lay almost as bright as day. Ignoring Miss Chauncey, the creature crouched there, steadily and sullenly staring into the empty skies, for a vast gulf of them was visible from where he sat.

Miss Chauncey proceeded to make her toilet for the night, trying in vain to pretend that she was entirely uninterested in what the animal was at. A faint sound – not exactly mewings or growlings – but a kind of low inward caterwauling, hardly audible, was proceeding from his throat. But whatever these sounds might imply, Sam himself can have been the only listener. There was not a sign of movement at the window or in the world without. And then Miss Chauncey promptly drew down the blind. At this Sam at once raised his paw for all the world as if he were about to protest, and then, apparently thinking better of it, he pretended instead that the action had been only for the purpose of beginning his nightly wash.

Long after her candle had been extinguished, Miss Chauncey lay listening. Every stir and movement in the quiet darkness could be easily understood. First there came a furtive footing and tapping at the register of the fireplace, so clearly showing what was happening that Miss

368

Chauncey could positively see in her imagination Sam on the hearthstone, erecting himself there upon his hind legs, vainly attempting to push the obstacle back.

This being in vain, he appeared to have dropped back on to his fours. There came a pause. Had he given up his intention? No: now he was at the door, pawing, gently scratching. Then a leap, even, towards the latch: but only one – the door was locked. Retiring from the door, he now sprang lightly again on to the dressing-table. What now was he at? By covertly raising her head a little from her pillow, Miss Chauncey could see him with paw thrust out, gently drawing back the blind from the moon-flooded window-pane. And even while she listened and watched, she heard yet again – and yet again – the faint *whssh* as of a wild swan cleaving the air; and then what might have been the night-cry of a bird, but which to Miss Chauncey's ears resembled a thin shrill pealing cackle of laughter. At this Sam hastily turned from the window, and without the least attempt at concealment pounced clean from the dressing-table on to the lower rail of her bed.

This unmannerly conduct could be ignored no longer. Poor Miss Chauncey raised herself in her sheets, pulled her nightcap a little closer down over her ears, and thrusting out her hand towards the chair beside the bed, struck a match and relit her candle. It was with a real effort that she then turned her head and faced her night-companion. His hair was bristling about his body as if he had had an electric shock. His whiskers stood out at stiff angles with his jaws. He looked at least twice his usual size, and his eyes blazed in his head, as averting his face from her regard he gave vent to a low sustained *Miariou-rou-rou-rou!*

'I say you shall *not*,' cried Miss Chauncey at the creature. At the sound of her words, he turned slowly and confronted her. And it seemed that until that moment Miss Chauncey had never actually seen Sam's countenance as in actual fact it really was. It was not so much the grinning tigerish look it wore, but the morose assurance in it not only of what he wanted but that he meant to get it.

All thought of sleep was now out of the question. Miss Chauncey could be obstinate too. The creature seemed to shed an influence on the very air which she could hardly resist. She rose from her bed and thrusting on her slippers made her way to the window. Once more a peculiar inward cry broke out from the bedrail. She raised the blind and the light of the moon from over the moor swept in upon her little apartment. And when she turned to remonstrate with her pet at his ingratitude, and at all this unseemliness and the deceit of his ways, there was something so menacing and stubborn and ferocious in his aspect that Miss Chauncey hesitated no more.

'Well, mark me!' she cried in a trembling voice, 'go out of the *door* you shan't. But if you enjoy soot, soot it shall be.'

With that she thrust back the register with the poker and drew down the bundle of ticking with the tongs. Before the fit of coughing caused by the smotheration that followed had ceased, the lithe black shape had sprung from the bedrail, and with a scramble was into the hearth, over the firebars, up the chimney, and away.

Trembling from head to foot, Miss Chauncey sat down on a cane rocking-chair that stood handy to reflect what next she must be doing. *Wh-ssh! Wh-ssh!* Again at the window came that mysterious rushing sound; but now, the flurrying murmur as of a rocket shooting up with its fiery train of sparks thinning into space, rather than the sound of its descending stick. And then in the hush that followed, there sounded yet again like a yell of triumph from the foot of the garden, a caterwauling piercing and sonorous enough

to arouse every sleeping cock in the Haggurdsdon hen-roosts, and for miles around. Out of the distance their chanticleering broke shrill on the night air; to be followed a moment afterwards by the tardy clang of midnight from the church steeple. Then once more, silence; utter quiet. Miss Chauncey returned to her bed, but that night slept no more.

Her mind overflowed with unhappy thoughts. Her faith in Sam was gone. Far worse, she had lost faith even in her affection for him. To have wasted that! All the sprats, all the whitebait in the wide, wide seas were as nothing by comparison. That Sam had wearied of her company was at last beyond question. It shamed her to think how much this meant to her – a mere animal! But she knew what was gone; knew how dull and spiritless the day's round would seem – the rising, the housework, the meals, her toilet in the afternoon, her evening slippers, book or knitting, a dish of tea, her candle, prayers, bed. On and on. In what wild company was her cat, Sam, now? At her own refusal to answer this horrid question, it was as if she had heard the hollow clanging slam of an immense iron door.

Next morning – still ruminating on these strange events, grieved to the heart at this dreadful rift between herself and one who had been her trusted companion for so many years; ashamed too that Sam should have had his way with her when she had determined not to allow him to go out during the night – next morning Miss Chauncey, as if merely to take a little exercise, once again ventured down to the foot of her garden. A faint, blurred mark (such as she had seen on the previous evening) in the black mould of what *might* be a footprint is nothing very much. But now – in the neglected patch beyond the bushes of whitethorn and bramble – there could be no doubt in the world – appeared many strange marks. And surely no cats' paw-prints these!

Of what use, indeed, to a cat could a crutch or a staff be? A staff or a crutch which – to judge from the impression it had left in the mould – must have been at least as thick as a broomstick.

More disquieted and alarmed than ever over this fresh mystery, Miss Chauncey glanced up and back towards the chimney-pots of the house clearly and sharply fretted against the morning light of the eastern skies. And she realized what perils even so sure-footed a creature as Sam had faced when he skirred up out of the chimney in his wild effort to emerge into the night. Having thus astonishingly reached the rim of the chimney – the wild burning stars above and the wilderness of the Moor spread out far beneath and around him – he must have leaped from the top of the low pot to a narrow brick ledge not three inches wide. Thence on to the peak of the roof and thence down a steep, slippery slope of slates to a leaden gutter.

And how then? The thick tod of ivy, matting the walls of the house, reached hardly more than half-way up. Could Sam actually have plunged from gutter to tod? The very thought of such peril drew Miss Chauncey's steps towards the house again, in the sharpest anxiety to assure herself that he was still in the land of the living.

And lo and behold, when she was but half-way on her journey, she heard a succession of frenzied yelps and cat-calls in the air from over the Moor. Hastily placing a flower-pot by the wall, she stood on tiptoe and peered over. And even now, at this very moment, in full flight across the nearer slope of the Moor, she descried her Sam, not now in chase of a foolishly trustful visitor, but hotly pursued by what appeared to be the complete rabblement of Haggurdsdon's cats. Sore spent though he showed himself to be, Sam was keeping his distance. Only a few lank tabby cats, and what appeared to be a grey-ginger Manx (unless he was an ordinary cat with his tail chopped off) were close behind.

'Sam! Sam!' Miss Chauncey cried, and yet again, 'Sam!' but in her excitement and anxiety her foot slipped on the flower-pot and in an instant the feline chase had fallen out of sight. Gathering herself together again, she clutched a long besom or garden broom that was leaning against the wall, and rushed down to the point at which she judged Sam would make his entrance into the garden. She was not mistaken, nor an instant too soon. With a bound he was up and over, and in three seconds the rabble had followed, in vehement pursuit.

What came after Miss Chauncey could never very clearly recall. She could but remember plying her besom with might and main amid this rabble and mellay of animals, while Sam, no longer a fugitive, turned on his enemies and fought them man to man. None the less, it was by no means an easy victory. And had not the over-fatted cur from the butcher's in Haggurdsdon – which had long since started in pursuit of this congregation of his enemies – had he not at last managed to overtake them, the contest might very well have had a tragic ending. But at sound of his baying, and at sight of teeth fiercely snapping at them as he vainly attempted to surmount the wall, Sam's enemies turned and fled in all directions. And faint and panting, Miss Chauncey was able to fling down her besom and to lean for a brief respite against the trunk of a tree.

At last she opened her eyes again. 'Well, Sam,' she managed to mutter at last, 'we got the best of them, then?'

But to her amazement she found herself uttering these friendly words into a complete vacancy. The creature was nowhere to be seen. His cream disappeared during the day, however, and by an occasional rasping sound Miss Chauncey knew that he once more lay hidden in his dingy resort behind the kindling-wood box. There she did not disturb him.

Not until tea-time of the following day did Sam re-appear. And then – after attending to his hurts – it was merely to sit with face towards the fire, sluggish and sullen and dumb as a dog. It was not Miss Chauncey's 'place' to make advances, she thought. She took no notice of the beast except to rub in a little hog's-fat on the raw places of his wounds. She was rejoiced to find, however, that he kept steadily to Post Houses for the next few days, though her dismay was reawakened at hearing on the third night a more dismal wailing and wauling than ever from the sloe-bushes, even though Sam himself sat motionless beside the fire. His ears twitched; his fur bristled; he sneezed or spat but other-wise remained motionless.

When Mr Cullings called again, Sam at once hid him-self in the coal cellar, but gradually his manners towards Miss Chauncey began to recover their usual suavity. And within a fortnight after the full moon, the two of them had almost returned to their old friendly companionship. He was healed, sleek, confident and punctual. No intruder of his species had appeared from Haggurdsdon. The night noises had ceased. Post Houses to all appearance – apart from its strange ugliness – was as peaceful and calm as any other solitary domicile in the United Kingdom.

But alas and alas. With the very first peeping of the crescent moon, Sam's mood and habits began to change again. He mouched about with a sly and furtive eye. And when he fawned on his mistress, purring and clawing, the whole look of him was a picture of deceit. If Miss Chauncey chanced to enter the room wherein he sat, he would at once leap down from the window at which he had been perched as if in the attempt to prove that he had *not* been looking out of it. And once, towards evening, though she was no

spy, she could not but pause at the parlour door. She
had peeped through its crack as it stood ajar. And there
on the hard sharp back of an old prie-Dieu chair that
had belonged to her pious great-aunt Miranda, sat Sam
on his hind quarters. And without the least doubt in the
world he was vigorously signalling to some observer outside with his forepaws. Miss Chauncey turned away sick at
heart.

From that hour on Sam more and more steadily ignored
and flouted his mistress, was openly insolent, shockingly
audacious. Mr Cullings gave her small help indeed. 'If I
had a cat, m'm, what had manners like that, after all your
kindness, fresh fish and all every week, and cream, as I
understand, not skim, I'd – I'd *give* him away.'

'To whom?' said poor Miss Chauncey.

'Well,' said the carrier, 'I don't know as how I'd much
mind to who. Beggars can't be choosers, m'm.'

'He seems to have no friends in the village,' said Miss
Chauncey, in as light a tone as she could manage.

'When they're as black as that, with them saucer eyes,
you can never tell,' said Mr Cullings. 'There's that old
trollimog what lives in Hogges Bottom. She've got a cat
that might be your Sam's twin.'

'Indeed no, he has the mange,' said Miss Chauncey,
loyal to the end. The carrier shrugged his shoulders, climbed
into his cart, and bowled away off over the Moor. And
Miss Chauncey, returning to the house, laid the platter
of silvery sprats on the table, sat down, and burst into
tears.

It was, then, in most ways a fortunate thing that the
very next morning – five complete days, that is, before the
next full-moon-tide – she received a letter from her sister-
in-law in Shanklin, in the Isle of Wight, entreating her to
pay them a long visit.

'My dear Emma. You must sometimes be feeling very lonely [it ran] shut up in that grate house so far from any neighbours. We often think of you, and particularly these last few days. It's very nice to have that Sam of yours for company, but after all, as George says, a pet's only a pet. And we do all think it's high time you took a little holiday with us. I am looking out of my window at this very moment. The sea is as calm as a mill-pond, a sollem beautiful blue. The fishing boats are coming in with their brown sails. This is the best time of the year with us, because the *tripper* season is drawing to a close and there are fewer of those horrid visitors to be seen, and no crowds. George says you *must* come. He joins with me in his love as would Maria if she weren't out shoping, and will meet you at the station in the trap. And we shall all be looking forward to seeing you in a few days. Emmie is now free of her cough – only hooping when the memory takes her, and never sick. Yours affec., (Mrs) Gertrude Chauncey.'

At this kindness, and with all her anxieties, Miss Chauncey all but broke down. When the butcher drove up in his cart an hour or two afterwards, he took a telegram for her back to the village, and on the Monday her box was packed, and all that remained was to put Sam in his basket in preparation for the journey. But I am bound to say it took more than the persuasions of his old protectress to accomplish this. Indeed Mr Cullings had actually to hold the creature down with gloved hands and none too gently, while Miss Chauncey pressed down the lid and pushed the skewer in to hold it close. 'What's done's durned done,' said the carrier, as he rubbed a pinch of earth into his scratches. 'And what *I* say is, better done for ever. Mark my words, m'm!'

Miss Chauncey took a shilling out of her large leather purse; but made no reply.

Indeed, all this trouble proved at last in vain. Thirty miles distant from Haggurdsdon, at Blackmoor Junction, Miss Chauncey had to change trains. Her box and Sam's basket were placed together on the station platform beside half a dozen empty milk-cans and some fowls in a crate, and Miss Chauncey went to make inquiries of the station-master in order to make sure of her platform.

It was the furious panic-stricken cackling of these fowls that brought her hastily back to her belongings, only to find that by hook or by crook Sam had managed to push the skewer of the basket out of its cane loops. The wicker lid gaped open – the basket was empty. Indeed one poor gasping hen, its life fluttering away from its helpless body, was proof enough not only of Sam's prowess but of his pitiless ferocity.

A few days afterwards, as Miss Chauncey sat in the very room to which her sister-in-law had referred in her invitation, looking over the placid surface of the English Channel, the sun gently shining in the sky, there came a letter from Mr Cullings. It was in pencil and written upon the back of a baker's bag.

'Dear madam i take the libberty of riteing you in reference to the Animall as how i helped put in is bawskit which has cum back returned empty agenn by rail me having okashun to cart sum hop powles from Haggurdsden late at nite ov Sunday. I seez him squattin at the parlour windy grimasin out at me fit to curdle your blood in your vanes and lights at the upper windies and a yowling and screetching as i never hopes to hear agen in a Christian lokalety. And that ole wumman from Hogges Botom sitting in the porch mi own vew being that there is no good in the place and the Animall be bewhitched. Mister flint the boutcher agrees with me as how now only last mesures is of any use and as i have said afore i am willing to take over the house the rent if so be being low and moddrit considering of the bad name it as in these parts around haggurdsden. I remain dear madam waitin your orders and oblige yours truely William Cullings.'

To look at Miss Chauncey you might have supposed she was a strong-minded woman. You might have supposed that this uncivil reference to the bad name her family house had won for itself would have mortified her beyond words. Whether or not, she neither showed this letter to her sister-in-law nor for many days together did she attempt to answer it. Sitting on the esplanade, and looking out to sea, she brooded on and on in the warm, salt, yet balmy air. It was a distressing problem. But 'No, he must go his own way,' she sighed to herself at last; 'I have done my best for him.'

What is more, Miss Chauncey never returned to Post Houses. She sold it at last, house and garden, and for a pitiful sum, to the carrier, Mr Cullings. By that time Sam had vanished, had never been seen again. He had gone his way.

Not that Miss Chauncey was faithless to his memory. Whenever the faint swish of a seagull's wing whispered through the air above her head; or the crackling of an ascending rocket for the amusement of visitors broke the silence of the nearer heavens over the sea; whenever even she became conscious of the rustling frou-frou of her Sunday watered-silk gown as she sallied out to church from the neat little villa she now rented on the Shanklin Esplanade – she never noticed such things without being instantly transported in imagination to her old bedroom at Post Houses, and seeing again that strange deluded animal, once her Sam, squatting there on her bed, and as it were knitting with his fore-paws the while he stood erect upon his hind.

Alice's Godmother

Though Alice sat steadily looking out of the small square pane of glass in the railway carriage, she was not really seeing the green and hilly country through which the train now clattered on its way. While everything near – quickening hedges, grazing cattle, galloping calves, wood, farm and stony foaming brook – swept past far too swiftly for more than a darting glance; everything in the distance – hill, tree and spire – seemed to be stealthily wheeling forward, as if to waylay the puffing engine and prevent it from reaching her journey's end.

'If only it would!' sighed Alice to herself. 'How much – much happier I should be!' Her blue eyes widened at the fancy. Then once more a frown of anxiety drew her eyebrows together; but she said nothing aloud. She sat on in her corner gently clasping her mother's hand and pondering in dismay on what might happen to her in the next few hours.

Alice and her mother a little prided themselves on being just 'two quiet ordinary people', happy in each other's company, and very seldom going out or paying calls and visits. And the particular visit that Alice was about to make when they reached the little country station of Freshing, she was to make alone. It was this that alarmed her. The invitation in that queer scrabbling handwriting had been to herself only. So though her mother was with her now, soon they would be parting. And every now and again Alice would give the hand she held in hers a gentle squeeze of self-reassurance. It was the Good-bye – though it would be only for a few hours – that she dreaded.

And yet their plans had all been talked over and settled again and again. Alice must, of course, take a fly from the station – whatever the expense. After telling the cabman when she would need him again, she would get into it and her mother would wait for her in a room at the village Inn until she herself returned in the early evening from her visit. Then everything would be safely over. And to imagine the joy of seeing all these fields and woods come racing back the other way round almost made Alice ill.

It was absurd to be so nervous. Alice had told herself that a hundred times. But it was no use. The very thought of her great-great-great-great-great-great-great-great-grandmother filled her heart with a continuous foreboding. If only she were a little stronger-minded; if only this old old lady, who was also her godmother, had asked her mother to come with her; if only her heart would stop beating so fast; if only a wheel would come off the engine!

But then, after all, Alice had never before so much as seen her godmother. Even now she could not be quite certain that she had the number of 'greats' to the 'grandmama' quite right. Not even strong-minded people, she supposed, are often suddenly invited to tea with relatives aged three-hundred-and-forty-nine. And not only that either; for this day – this very Saturday – was her godmother's birthday: her three-hundred-and-fiftieth!

Whenever Alice remembered this, a faint smile stole into her face. At seventeen a birthday is a real 'event'. Life is galloping on. You are sprouting up like a beanstalk. Your hair is 'put up' (or at least it was when Alice was a girl), your skirts 'come down', and you're soon to 'come out'. In other words you are beginning to be really and truly 'grown-up'. But three-hundred-and-fifty! Surely by that time ... It must be difficult even to be certain you have the total right. Surely there can't be *any* kind of a change by then! Surely not!

Still, Alice thought, it is perhaps the *name* of the number that chiefly counts. She herself had known what an odd shock it had been to slip into her teens, and could guess what the shivers would be like of the plunge into her twenties. Yet even if it were only the name of the number – why, at the end of three centuries you must be beginning to be getting accustomed to birthdays.

It was a little odd that her godmother had never asked to see her before. Years ago she had sent her a squat parcel-gilt mug – a mug that her godmother herself used to drink her beer out of when she was a child of ten in Queen Elizabeth's reign. A little sheepskin, illuminated Prayer Book, too, that had once been given to her godmother by Charles the First, and a few exquisite little old gold trinkets had come too. But receiving presents is not the same thing as actually meeting and talking with the mysterious giver of them. It is one thing to imagine the unknown; another thing altogether to meet it face to face. What would her godmother look like? What *could* she look like? Alice hadn't the faintest notion. Old ladies of eighty and upwards are not unusual; but you can't just multiply eighty by four as if growing older were merely a sum in arithmetic.

Perhaps when you are very old indeed, Alice suspected, you have no wish to sit for a portrait or to be photographed. It is a petrifying experience even when you are young. When you are – well, very old indeed, you may prefer to well, to keep yourself *to* yourself. *She* would.

'Mamma dear,' she suddenly twisted round on her hard seat, her straight ribboned straw-coloured hair slipping

over in one smooth ripple on her shoulder as she did so;
'Mamma dear, I can't think even now what I ought to
do when I go into the room. Will there be anybody there,
do you think? Do I shake hands? I suppose she won't
kiss me? I simply can't think what I ought to do. I shall
just hate leaving you – being left, I mean.'

She stroked hard with her fingers the hand that was in
her own, and as she gazed at her mother's face in this
increasing anxiety, she knew that the smile on it was just
like a pretty blind over a window, and that her mother's
self within was almost as much perturbed over this visit
as she was herself.

'It's getting nearer, darling, at any rate, isn't it?' her
mother whispered. 'So it will sooner be over.' Whereupon
the fat old farmer in the further corner of the carriage
emitted yet another grunt. He was fast asleep. 'I *think*,'
her mother continued softly, 'I should first enquire of
the maid if she is quite well – your godmother, I mean, my
dear. Say, "Do you think Miss Cheyney is well enough
to see me?" She will know what you ought to do. I am
not even certain whether the poor old lady can speak:
though her handwriting is simply marvellous.'

'But, Mummie darling, how are we to know that there
will be a maid? Didn't they, in godmother's time, always
have "retainers"? Supposing there are rows of them in the
hall! And when ought I to get up to say Good-bye? If
she is deaf and blind *and* dumb I really don't know what
I *shall* do!'

A dozen questions at least like this had been asked but
not answered during the last few days, and although
Alice's cheek, with that light hair, was naturally pale,
her mother watched it grow paler yet as the uncomfortable
old-fashioned railway-carriage they sat in jogged steadily
on its way.

'Whenever I am in any difficulty, sweetheart,' she whispered close up to her daughter's ear, 'I always say a little prayer.'

'Yes, yes, dear dearest,' said Alice, gazing at the fat old farmer, fast asleep. 'But if only I weren't going quite alone! I don't think, you know, she can be a very good godmother: she never said a word in her letter about my Confirmation. She's at least old enough to know better.' Once more the ghost of a smile stole softly over her face. But she clasped her mother's fingers even a little tighter, and the hedges and meadows continued to sidle by.

They said Good-bye to one another actually inside the cab, so as to be out of sight of the Inn and the cabman.

'I expect, my sweet,' breathed Alice's mother, in the midst of this long embrace, 'we shall both soon be smiling away like two turtledoves at the thought of all our worry. We can't tell what kind of things she may not be thinking of, can we? And don't forget, I shall be waiting for you in the "Red Lion" – there's the sign, my dear, as you see. And if there is time, perhaps we will have a little supper there all to ourselves – a little soup, if they have it; or at any rate, an egg. I don't suppose you will have a very *substantial* tea. Not in the circumstances. But still, your godmother wouldn't have asked you to visit her if she had not really wanted to see you. We mustn't forget that, darling.'

Alice craned her head out of the window till her mother was out of sight behind the hedge. And the fly rolled gently on and on and on along the dusty lanes in the direction of The Grange. On and on and on. Surely, thought Alice at last, we must have gone miles and miles. At this she sprang up and thrust her head out of the window, and called up to the cabman, 'The Grange, you know, please.'

'That's it, Miss, The Grange,' he shouted back, with a

flourish of his whip. 'Not as how I can take you into the Park, Miss. It ain't allowed.'

'Mercy me,' sighed Alice as she sank back on the fusty blue cushions. 'Supposing there are miles of avenue, and the front door's at the back!'

It was a pleasant sunny afternoon. The trim hedgerows were all in their earliest green; and the flowers of spring – primrose, violets, jack-in-the-hedge, stitchwort – in palest blossom starred the banks. It was only half-past three by Alice's little silver watch. She would be in good time, then. In a few minutes, indeed, the fly drew up beside immense rusty wrought-iron gates on the four posts of which stood heavy birds in stone, with lowered heads, brooding with outstretched wings.

'And you will be sure to come back for me at six?' Alice implored the cabman, though she tried to keep her voice natural and formal. 'Not a minute later than six, please. And then wait here until I come.'

The cabman ducked his head and touched his hat; drew his old horse round in the hafts, and off he went. Alice was alone.

With one last longing look at the strange though friendly country lane – and there was not a house in sight – Alice pushed open the little gate at the side of the two large ones. It emitted a faint, mocking squeal as it turned slowly upon its hinges. Beyond it rose a hedge of yew at least twenty feet high, and in a nook there stood a small square lodge, its windows shuttered, a scurry of dead leaves in its ancient porch. Alice came to a standstill. This was a difficulty neither she nor her mother had foreseen. Ought she to knock or to go straight on? The house looked as blind as a bat. She stepped back, and glanced up at the chimneys. Not the faintest plume of smoke was visible against the dark foliage of the ilex behind the house. Some unseen bird flew into the shadows with a cry of alarm.

Surely the lodge was empty. None the less it might be good manners to make sure, so she stepped into the porch and knocked – but knocked in vain. After pausing a minute or two, and scanning once more the lifeless windows, in a silence broken only by the distant laughing of a wood-pecker, Alice determined to go on.

So thick and close were the tufted mosses in the gravel of the narrow avenue that her footsteps made no sound. So deep was the shade cast by the immense trees that grew on either side she could have fancied evening was already come, though it was yet early afternoon. Mammoth beeches lifted their vast boughs into the air; the dark hollows in their ancient boles capacious enough for the dwelling-house of a complete family of humans. In the distance Alice could see between their branches gigantic cedars, and others still further, beneath which grazed what she supposed was a herd of deer, though it was impossible to be quite certain from so far.

The few wild creatures which had long ago detected her in these haunts were strangely tame. They did not trouble to run away; but turned aside and watched her as she passed, the birds hopping a little further out of her reach while yet continuing on their errands. In sheer curiosity indeed Alice made an attempt to get as near as she possibly could to a large buck rabbit that sat nibbling under the broken rail of the fence. With such success that he actually allowed her to scratch his furry head and stroke his long lopping ears.

'Well,' thought she with a sigh as she straightened herself, 'there can't be very much to be afraid of in great-great-great-great-great-great-great-great-grandmother's house if the rabbits are as tame as all that. *Au revoir*,' she whispered

to the creature; 'I hope to see you again very very soon.'
And on she went.

Now and then a hunchbacked thorn-tree came into view,
and now and then a holly. Alice had heard long ago that
hollies are wise enough not to grow prickles where no animal can damage their leaves by browsing on them. These
hollies seemed to have no prickles at all, and the hawthorns,
in spite of their bright green coats, speckled with tight
buds, were almost as twisted out of shape as if mischievous
little boys had tied knots in them when they were saplings.
But how sweet was the tranquil air. So sweet indeed that
this quiet avenue with its towering branches and the childlike blue of the skies overhead pacified her mind, and she
had almost forgotten her godmother when, suddenly, at a
break between the trees there came into view a coach.

Not exactly a coach, perhaps, but a large painted carriage
of a faded vermilion and yellow, drawn by two cream-
coloured horses – a coachman on the box in a mulberry
livery, and a footman beside him. What was really strange,
this conveyance was being noiselessly driven round a circular track so overgrown with moss and weeds that it was
hardly discernible against the green of the grass. Alice
could not but watch it come nearer and nearer – as she
stood drawn up close to the furrowed bark of an oak that
branched overhead. This must be her godmother's carriage. She must be taking her daily drive in concealment
from the wide wide world. But no: it had drawn near;
and now, with a glimpse of the faded red morocco within,
it had passed; it was empty. Only the backs of coachman
and footman now showed above its sun-bleached panels –
their powdered hair, their cockaded hats.

All Alice's misgivings winged back into her mind at
sight of this unusual spectacle. She tiptoed out of her hiding-
place, and hastened on. Her one wish now was to reach

her journey's end. Presently after, indeed, the house itself appeared in sight. The shorn flowerless sward gently sloped towards its dark low walls and grey chimneys. To the right of it lay a pool as flat as a huge looking-glass in the frame of its trees. Behind it rose a smooth green hill.

Alice paused again behind yet another of the huge grey boles to scan it more closely before she herself could be spied out from any of its many windows. It looked as if it had stood there for ever. It looked as if its massive stones had of their own weight been sinking imperceptibly, century after century, into the ground. Not a blossoming shrub, not a flower near by – except only a powder of daisies and a few yellow dandelions.

Only green turf and trees, and the ancient avenue on which she stood, sweeping gently towards its low-porched entrance. 'Well,' she sighed to herself, 'I'm thankful I don't live *there*, that's all – not even if I were a thousand-and-one!' She drew herself up, glanced at her shoes, gave a little push to her ribboned straw hat, and, with as much dignity as she could manage, proceeded straight onwards.

A hoarse bell responded, after a whole second's pause, to the gentle tug she had given the iron pull that hung in the porch. It cried 'Ay, ay!' and fell silent. And Alice continued to look at the immense iron knocker which she hadn't the courage to use.

Without a sound the door opened at last, and there, as she had feared, stood, not a friendly parlour-maid with a neat laundered cap, but an old man in a black tail-coat who looked at her out of his pale grey eyes as if she were a stuffed bird in a glass case. Either he had been shrinking for some little time, or he must surely have put on somebody else's clothes, they hung so loosely on his shoulders.

'I am Miss Alice Cheyney – Miss Alice Cheyney,' she said. 'I think my great-great ... Miss Cheyney is expecting me – that is, of course, if she is quite well.' These few words had used up the whole of one breath, and her godmother's old butler continued to gaze at her, while they sank into his mind.

'Will you please to walk in,' he said at last. 'Miss Cheyney bade me express the wish that you will make yourself at home. She hopes to be with you immediately.' Whereupon he led the way, and Alice followed him – across a wide hall, lit with low, greenish, stone-mullioned windows. On either side stood suits of burnished armour, with lifted visors. But where the glittering eyes of their long-gone owners once had gleamed, nothing now showed but a little narrow darkness. After a hasty glance or two to either side, Alice kept her eyes fixed on the humped back of the little old butler. Up three polished stairs, under a hanging tapestry, he led her on, and at length, at the end of a long gallery, ushered her into what she supposed was her godmother's sitting-room. There, with a bow, he left her. Alice breathed one long deep sigh, and then, having unbuttoned and buttoned up again one of her grey silk gloves, she sat down on the edge of a chair near the door.

It was a long, low-pitched, but not very wide room, with a coffered ceiling and panelled walls, and never before had Alice seen such furniture. In spite of the dreadful shyness that seemed to fill her to the very brim, at thought of her mother's little pink-and-muslin drawing-room compared with this, she almost burst out laughing.

Make herself at home! Why, any one of those chests would hide her away for ever, like the poor lovely lost one in 'The Mistletoe Bough'. As for the hanging portraits in their great faded frames, though she guessed at once they must be by 'old masters', and therefore eyed them as solemnly as she could, she had never supposed human beings could look so odd and so unfriendly. It was not so much their clothes : their stomachers, their slashed doublets and wide velvet caps, but their faces. Ladies with high bald foreheads and tapering fingers and thumb-rings, and men sour and dour and glowering.

'Oho! Miss Nobody!' they seemed to be saying. 'And pray, what are *you* doing here?'

The one single exception was the drawing of a girl of about her own age. A dainty cap with flaps all but concealed her yellow hair; a necklet dangled at her breast; the primrose-coloured bodice sloped sharply to the waist. So delicate were the lines of this drawing and so faint the tinted chalk, they hardly stained the paper. Yet the eyes that gazed out across the low room at Alice seemed to be alight with life. A smile half-mocking, half-serious lingered in their depths. See, I am lovely, it seemed to be hinting, and yet how soon to be gone! And even though Alice had never before seen a face so enchanting, she could not but confess it bore a remote resemblance to herself. Why this should have a little restored her confidence she could not tell. None the less, she deliberately smiled back at the drawing as if to say, 'Well, my dear, I shall have *you* on my side, whatever happens.'

The lagging minutes ticked solemnly by. Not a sound to be heard in the great house; not a footfall. But at last a door at the further end of the room softly opened, and in the greenish light of the deep mullioned window appeared what Alice knew was She.

She was leaning smally on the arm of the butler who had admitted Alice to the house. Quiet as shadows they entered the room; then paused for a moment, while yet another man-servant arranged a chair for his mistress. Meanwhile the old lady was peering steadily in search of her visitor. She must once have been as tall as Alice herself, but now time had shrunken her up into the stature of a child, and though her small head was set firmly on the narrow shoulders, these stooped like the wings of the morose stone birds upon her gates.

'Ah, is that you, my dear?' cried a voice; but so minute was the sound of these words that Alice went suddenly hot all over lest she had merely imagined them.

'I say, is that you, my dear?' repeated the voice. There was no mistaking now. Alice ventured a pace forward into the light, her knees trembling beneath her, and the old lady groped out a hand – its shrunken fingers closed one upon another like the cold claws of a bird.

For an instant Alice hesitated. The dreadful moment was come. Then she advanced, made the old lady a curtsy, and lifted the icy fingers to her lips.

'All I can say *is*,' she confided to her mother when they met again, 'all I can say *is*, Mamma, if it had been the Pope, I suppose I should have kissed his toe. And really, I would have very much rather.'

None the less, Alice's godmother had evidently taken no offence at this gesture. Indeed what Alice thought might be a smile crinkled, as it were, across the exquisite web of wrinkles on her face. On her acorn-shaped head rose a high lace and silver cap resembling the gown she wore; and silk mittens concealed her wrists. She was so small that Alice had to bend almost double over her fingers. And when she was seated in her chair it was as if a large doll sat there – but a marvellous doll that had voice, thought, senses and motion beyond any human artificer's wildest fancy. The eyes in this dry wizened-up countenance – of a much fainter blue than the palest forget-me-not – steadily continued to look at Alice, the while the butler and foot-man with head inclined stood watching their mistress. Then, as if at a secret signal, they both bowed and retired.

'Be seated, my dear,' the tinkling voice began when they had withdrawn. And there fell a horrifying pause. Alice gazed at the old lady, and like half-transparent glass the aged eyes remained fixed on herself, the bird-like hands crossed daintily over the square lace handkerchief held in the narrow lap. Alice grew hotter and hotter. 'What a very beautiful old house this is, great grandmamma,' she sud-denly blurted out. 'And those wonderful trees!'

No flicker of expression showed that Miss Cheyney had heard what she had said. And yet Alice could not help thinking that she *had* heard, and that for some reason she had disapproved of her remark.

'Now come,' piped the tiny voice, 'now come; tell me what you have been doing this long time. And how is your mother? I think I faintly remember seeing her, my dear, soon after she married your father, Mr James Beaton.'

'Mr Beaton, I *think*, was my great-grandfather, great-grandmamma,' Alice breathed softly. 'My father's name, you know, was John – John Cheyney.'

'Ah well, your great-*grand*father, to be sure,' said the old lady. 'I never pay much attention to dates. And has anything been happening lately?'

'Happening, great-grandmamma?' echoed Alice.

'Beyond?' said the old lady. 'In the world?'

Poor Alice; she knew well the experience of nibbling a pen over impossible questions in history examinations, but this was far worse than any she had ever encountered.

'There, you see!' continued her godmother. 'I hear of the wonderful things they are doing, and yet when I ask a simple question like that no one has anything to say. Have you travelled on one of these steam railway trains yet? Locomotives?'

'I came that way this afternoon, great-grandmamma.'

'Ah, I thought you looked a little flushed. The smoke must be most disagreeable.'

Alice smiled. 'No, thank you,' she said kindly.

'And how is Queen Victoria?' said the old lady. 'She is still alive?'

'Oh yes, great-grandmamma. And that is just, of course, what *has* been happening. It's her Diamond Jubilee this year – sixty years – you know.'

'H'm,' said the old lady. 'Sixty. George III reigned sixty-three. But they all go in time. I remember my dear father coming up to my nursery after the funeral of poor young Edward VI. He was one of the Court pages, you know – that is, when Henry VIII was King. Such a handsome lad – there is his portrait ... somewhere.'

For a moment Alice's mind was a whirlpool of vague memories – memories of what she had read in her history-books.

But Miss Cheyney's bead-like notes had hardly paused. 'You must understand that I have not asked you to come this long way by one of those horrid new-fangled steam-engines just to gossip about my childhood. Kings and Queens come and go like the rest of things. And though I have seen many changes, it seems to me the world is pretty much the same as ever. Nor can I believe that the newspaper is a beneficial novelty. When I was a girl we managed well enough without, and even in Mr Addison's day one small sheet twice a week was enough. But there, complaint is useless. And you cannot exactly be held responsible for all that. There were changes in my girlhood, too – great changes. The world was not so crowded then. There was nobility and beauty. Yes.' Her eyes wandered, to rest a moment on the portrait of the young woman in the primrose gown. 'The truth is, my dear,' she continued, 'I have to tell you something, and I wish you to listen.'

Once more she remained silent a moment, clutching the handkerchief she held between her fingers. 'What I desire you to tell *me*,' she said at last, leaning stealthily forward in her great chair, 'what I am anxious that you should tell me is, How long do you wish to live?'

For a few moments Alice sat cold and motionless. It was as if an icy breath straight from the North Pole had swept across the room, congealing with its horror the very air. Her eyes wandered vacantly from picture to picture, from ancient object to ancient object – aged, mute and lifeless – to rest at last on a flowering weed that reared its head beyond one of the diamond-shaped panes of glass in the window.

'I have never thought of that, great-grandmamma,' her dry lips whispered. 'I don't think I know.'

'Well, I am not expecting an old head on young shoulders,' retorted the old lady. 'Perhaps if King Charles had realized that – so learned, so generous, so faithful a monarch – I doubt if that vulgar creature Oliver Cromwell would ever have succeeded in having his off.'

The acorn chin drew down into its laces like a snail into its shell. Until this moment Alice might have been conversing with an exquisite image, or an automaton – the glittering eyes, the crooked fingers, the voice from afar. But now it seemed a new life was stirring in it. The tiny yet piercing tones sank almost to a whisper, the head stirred furtively from side to side as if to be sure no eavesdropper were within earshot.

'Now listen close to me, my child: I have a secret. A secret which I wish to share only with you. You would suppose, wouldn't you, that this being the three-hundred-and-fiftieth anniversary of my natal day' – and at this the dreadful realization suddenly swept over Alice that she had quite forgotten to wish her godmother 'Many happy returns' – 'you might suppose that you are about to meet a gay numerous company here – young and happy creatures like yourself. But no: not so. Even your dear mother is, of course, only my great-great-great-great-great-great-great-granddaughter-*in-law*. She was a Miss Wilmot, I believe.'

'Yes, Woodcot, great-grandmamma,' said Alice softly.

'Well, Woodcot,' said the old lady; 'it is no matter. It is you, my child, whom I have made, to be precise, my chosen. In mere men I take no interest. Not only that, but you must now be of the age I was when the portrait you see on yonder wall was painted. It is the work of a pupil of Hans Holbein's. Hans Holbein himself, I believe, was dead at the time. Dear me, child, I remember sitting for that portrait in this very room – as if it were yesterday. It was much admired by Sir Walter Raleigh, who, you may remember, came to so unhappy an end. That was, I recollect, in my early seventies. My father and his father were boys together in Devonshire.'

Alice blinked a little – she could not turn her eyes away from her godmother's – that mammet-like face, those minute motionless hands.

'Now glance at that picture, please!' the old lady bade her, pointing a tiny crooked-up forefinger towards the further wall. 'Do you see any resemblance?'

Alice looked long and steadily at the portrait. But she had neither the courage nor vanity to deny that the fair smiling features were at least a *little* like her own. 'To whom, great-grandmamma?' Alice whispered.

' "To whom?" Well, well, well!' came the reply, the words sounding like the chiming of a distant silver bell. 'I see it. I see it ... But never mind that now. Did you perhaps look at this *house* as you made your way up the avenue?'

'Oh yes, great-grandmamma – though I couldn't, of course, look close, you know,' Alice managed to say.

'Did you *enjoy* its appearance?'

'I don't think I thought of that,' said Alice. 'The trees and park were very lovely. I have never seen such – *mature* trees, great-grandmamma. And yet all their leaves were budding and some were fully out. Isn't it wonderful for trees so – so long in the world to – why, to come out at all?'

'I was referring to the house,' said the old lady. '*Springs* nowadays are not what they used to be. They have vanished

397

from the England I once knew. I remember once an April
when angels were seen on the hilltops above London. But
that is no matter for us now: not now. The house?'

Once again Alice's gaze wandered – to come to rest
again on the green, nodding weed at the window.

'It is a very very quiet house,' she said.

The childlike tones died between the thick stone walls;
and a profound silence followed them, like that of water
in a well. Meanwhile, as Alice fully realized, her godmother
had been fixedly searching her face with her remote but
intent eyes. It was as if Time itself were only a child and
that of this aged face he had made his little secret gazebo.

'Now please listen to me very carefully,' she continued
at last. 'Such a countenance as yours – one bearing the least
resemblance to that portrait over there, must be the possessor of a fair share of wits. I am old enough, my child,
not to be charged, I hope, with the folly of vanity. In
my girlhood I enjoyed a due share of admiration. And
I have a proposal to make to you which will need all the
sagacity you are capable of. Don't be alarmed. I have every
faith in you. But first, I want you to go into the next room,
where you will find a meal prepared. Young people nowadays, I hear, need continuous nourishment. What wonder!
Since they have forgotten all the manners of a lady as *I*
know them, and are never still for a moment together. What
wonder! With all these dreadful machines I hear of, the dis-
content, the ignorance and folly, the noises and unrest and
confusion. In my young days the poor were the poor and
the humble the humble, my child; and knew their place.
In my young days I would sit contented for hours at a time
over a simple piece of embroidery. And if I needed it, my
mother never deigned to spare the rod. But there, I didn't
invite you to visit an old woman merely to listen to a
sermon. When you have refreshed yourself you are to take

a little walk through the house. Go wherever you please; look well about you; no one will disturb you. And in an hour's time come back to me here again. Nowadays I take a little sleep in the afternoon. I shall be ready for you then . . .'

Alice, with a relief beyond words, rose from her chair. She curtsied again towards the small, motionless figure in the distance, and retired through the dark oak door.

The room in which she at once found herself was small, hexagonal, and panelled with the blackest of old oak. A copper candelabrum hung from the dark moulded ceiling, and beyond the leaded panes she could see the gigantic trees in the park. To her dismay the footman who had accompanied the butler into the room when her godmother had first made her appearance, was stationed behind the chair at the table. Never had Alice supposed that it was proper for men-servants, except perhaps gardeners, to wear long grey beards. But there he was, with his dim sidling eyes. And she must needs turn her back on him to seat herself at the table. She nibbled the fruit and bread, the rich cake and the sweetmeats which he presented in their heavy silver dishes, and she sipped her sweet drink. But it was a hasty and nervous meal, and she tasted nothing of what she had eaten.

As soon as it was over, the servant opened the door for her, and she began her voyage of discovery through the great, deserted house. It was as if her very ghost were her only company. Never had solitude so oppressed her, never before had she been so intensely aware of being wide awake and yet dreaming. The long corridors, the low and crooked lintelled doors, the dark uneven floors, their Persian mats, their tapestries and hangings, only the lovelier in that their colours had been dimmed by so many suns,

the angled flights of stairs, the solemn air that brooded
between the walls, the multitude of pictures, the huge beds,
the endless succession of superannuated coffers, daybeds,
cabinets – all this in but a few minutes had tired and fatigued
Alice far more even than the long journey from the home
of her childhood that morning. Upstairs and downstairs,
on she wandered for all the world like the goosey-goosey-
gander of the old nursery rhyme.

And when at last with a sigh she glanced at the
bright little silver watch which had been her mother's
birthday gift, its slender hands told her that she had
still a full quarter-of-an-hour before she need return
to her great-great-great-great-great-great-great-great-grandmother's room.

That into which she had now admitted herself seemed
to be a small library. Its walls were ranged from ceiling
to floor with old leather and lambskin folios and quartos
and squat duodecimos, while between them hung portraits and the loveliest miniatures and medallions of scores
upon scores of persons who she guessed must be her
ancestors and ancestresses of goodness knows how many
monarchs ago.

One or two of the pictures, indeed, as the crabbed in-
scriptions showed, had been gifts to the family from those
monarchs themselves. In their various costumes, wigs,
turbans and furbelows they looked as if they must have
been the guests at an immense fancy-dress ball.

> What tho Felicitie befal?
> Time makyth shadowes of us all.

In this room a low recess filled the shallow bow window
and on this lay a strip of tapestry. The leaded pane of
the window was open. The sun was already westering,

its beams slanting in on the gilt and ebony and ivory of
the frames suspended from their nails. Alice knelt down
at the window; and her mind slipped into a daydream, and
her gaze wandered far away over the golden budding tops of
the enormous oaks, the flat dark outstretched motionless
palms of the cedars – perhaps descendants of those which
Sir Philip Sidney had brought home to his beloved England from the East.

The thoughts that had all day been skittering in her
mind like midges over a pool gradually fell still, and she
sank deeper and deeper into the hush that lay over the
ancient house. It was as if its walls were those of an enormous diving-bell sunken beyond measure in an unfathom-
able ocean of Time. So tranquil was the sweet April air
beyond the window that she could actually detect the
sound of the browsing of the herd of fallow deer that had
now closely approached the lawns of the house itself.

And as, lost in this reverie, she sat entranced, she became
conscious that a small living animal – the like of which
she had never seen before – had crept up within a pace or
two of her on the window-sill, and was now steadily regarding her with its clear bead-brown eyes. In size it was
rather larger than a mole, its dark thick fur was soft as a
beaver's, and it had a short, furry, and tufted tail. Its ears
were cocked on its head, its silvery whiskers turned downwards above its jaws, and Alice could see its tiny ivory
claws as it sat there erect on its haunches like a tame cat
or a dog begging for a titbit of meat. Alice, alas, had nothing
to offer her visitor, not even a cherry-stone, not even a
crumb.

'Well, you pretty thing,' she whispered, 'what is it?'

The creature's whiskers moved ever so slightly, its eyes
fixed more intently than ever on the face of this strange
visitor. Very very delicately Alice thrust out her finger,

401

and to her astonishment found herself gently caressing the furry nose. 'It was as if I was in Wonderland, myself,' she explained long afterwards to her mother. Perfectly mute and still, the owner of it seemed to enjoy this little courtesy. And when she had withdrawn her finger, it looked at her more closely and searchingly than ever, as if bidding her take heed. It then tapped repeatedly with its ivory-clawed paw on the oak casement, glanced searchingly at her yet again, then shook its furry head vehemently three times, paused, turned swiftly about and pattered away into hiding behind a huge carved Moorish cabinet before Alice could so much as bid it adieu.

Quiet little events in this life, even though we cannot understand what exactly they mean, are apt to *seem* to mean a great deal. So with this small animal and Alice. It was as if – though she was not aware of it – she had been brooding over a problem in Algebra or a proposition in Euclid, and it had ventured out of its living-place to tell her the answer. How fantastic a notion! – when Alice knew neither the problem nor what its solution was.

She glanced at her watch once more; her fair cheeks pinking all over at realizing that she was now ten minutes late for her assignation with her grandmother. She must be gone. None the less, she had time to look her farewell at the huge dreaming park before she set out on her return journey.

Before at last finding her way, however, she irretrievably lost it. For the house was a silent maze of deceptive passages and corridors. Every fresh attempt only increased her confusion, and then suddenly she found herself looking into a room utterly different from any she had yet seen. Its low walls were of stone, its dusty windows shuttered; it contained nothing but a chair. And in that chair sat what appeared to be the life-size image of the smiling lovely creature she had seen in the portrait – eyes shut, cheeks a faint rose, hair still shimmering with gold, the hands laid idly in her lap, the fingers of one of them clutching what seemed to be the dried-up fragments of a bunch of roses. What there was to alarm her in this harmless image she could not tell; but she gazed awhile at it in horror, closed-to the door and ran off as if pursued by a nightmare, down one corridor and up another, to find herself at last by good fortune once more in the room where she had had her meal. It seemed, as she stood there, her hand upon her breast, as if she would never again recover her breath. She was no longer nervous; no longer merely timid : she was afraid. 'If only, if only I had never come to this house!' was her one terrified thought.

She discovered with relief on re-entering Miss Cheyney's presence that her godmother was still asleep. Alice could see awhile without being seen.

Now one of her mother's brothers – one of Alice's uncles, that is – was an old bachelor who delighted in birthday gifts. Alice had therefore been richer in dolls than most children : wooden, wax, china, Dutch, French, Russian, and even one from the Andaman Islands. But no single one of them had shown a face so utterly still and placid as that now leaning gently aside in its lace and silver cap and mantle. There was no expression whatever on its features. No faintest smile; no shadow of a frown. And yet the tiny wrinkles all over it, crooking down even from the brows over the eyelids, gave it the appearance of an exquisitely figured map.

And Alice was still surveying it as closely as some old treasure-hunter might the chart of his secret island, when the minute eyes reopened and her godmother was instantly awake and intent.

'Ah,' whispered she, 'I have myself been on a long

journey, but I heard you calling. What happens, I wonder,' and the tones sank lower, 'what happens when one has ventured on too far to hear any such rumours? Answer me that, eh? But no matter. There is a more important question first. Tell me now, if you please, what you think of my house.'

Alice moistened her lips. 'That, great-grandmamma,' she managed to reply at last, 'that would take *ages*. It is marvellous: but oh, so very still.'

'What should there be to disturb it?' asked the old lady. Alice shook her head.

'Tell me,' and her voice tinkled across the air with a peculiar little tang, 'would you like this house for your own?'

'This house – for my own?' breathed the young girl.

'Ay, for your own, and for always – humanly speaking.'

'I don't quite understand,' said Alice.

The little head leaned sidelong like an inquisitive bird's.

'Naturally, my child. You *cannot* until I have gone a little further. The gift I am now offering you is one that few human beings in this world conceive to be possible. It is not merely this house, my child, with all that it contains – much as that may be. It is life. My father, you must understand, was a traveller; and in days when danger was a man's constant companion. In this very room on his return from a many years' journey, he told me as a girl of a dismal mountainous region of snow and ice and precipices that lies *there* – West of China, I believe. It was from hence that he brought back his secret. It was one that for grievous and tragical reasons he could not follow himself. And I, my child, was his only choice. You will realize there may come a day when the wish to live on may have somewhat dimmed in my mind. I confess to feeling a little weariness at times. But before I go, it is my privilege – my obligation

– to confer the secret on another. Look at me!' The voice rose a little; it was as though a wren had uttered its shrill song in the low resounding room. 'I am offering this inestimable benefit to *you*.'

Alice sat straight as a dart in her chair, not venturing to turn her eyes aside even for a moment.

'The secret, great-grandmamma?'

'Ay,' continued the old woman, closing her eyes, 'you heard me aright. I will presently whisper it into your ear. Imagine my child, the wonder of infinite time! Imagine a life in such surroundings as these, far from all the follies and vexations of the world – and one fear – the most terrible of all fears – gone, or at any rate so remote as to be of no consequence. Imagine that, I say.'

For an instant Alice's gaze wavered. Her eyes glanced swiftly towards the window where shone the swiftly changing colours of the sunset; where sang the wild birds, and Spring was fleeting on its way.

'Take your own time: and do not be afraid of me. I shall make few conditions. Only that you must vow silence, to breathe not one syllable of what I shall tell you – not even to your own mother. All else will be easy – comparatively easy. All else. You will come here and live with me. Rooms are prepared for you – books, music, horses to ride, servants to wait on you, all that you need. And in due season this house, this accumulation of things precious and old and beautiful, this wide park stretching for many more miles than you can see from my topmost windows, will be yours alone. You may pine for a while for old friends. It is an unhappy thing to say good-bye, as I have heard. But all fades, all goes. And in time you will not wish for company. Servants as aged as mine are not difficult to find; they are discreet, and have need to remain faithful. We shall have many a quiet talk together. I have much to tell you. I long,

my dear child, to share memories with you that I have
never breathed to a living soul. There are wings to this house
into which you cannot have penetrated, simply because
they are shut off by bolts and bars. They contain much
to see: much to linger over; much to wonder at. Yes,
and my dear child, in you I should live on – our two minds
... two lives. Tell me now, what do you think of my proposal? And remember this: – Not even Solomon in all
his glory could have conferred on you what I now offer.'

The aged head was nodding – as if with fatigue. The
cramped fingers fumbled aimlessly with the lace handkerchief, and Alice's poor wits were once more in a desperate
confusion. The room swam dizzily before her eyes. She shut
them a moment; endeavouring in vain to consider calmly
what that remote unhuman voice had been saying to her.
She might as well have struggled in sleep to shake off the
veils and nets of a dream, the snares of a nightmare. One
thing only was audible to her now, a bird singing in the
garden and the sound of her shoe tapping on the floor. She
listened – and came back.

'You mean,' she whispered, 'on and on and on – like you,
great-grandmamma?'

The old lady made no reply.

'May I, do you think, then, if you would be so kind, may
I have time to think it over?'

'Think what over?' said her godmother. 'Are you supposing a child of your age can think over three complete
centuries before a single moment of them has come into
view?'

'No,' said Alice, her courage returning a little, 'I meant,
think over what you have said. It is so very difficult to
realize what it means.'

'It means,' said the old lady, 'an immeasurable sea,
infinite space, an endless vista – of time. It means freedom

from the cares and anxieties and follies that are the lot of the poor creatures in the world beyond – living out their few days in brutish stupidity. You are still young, but who knows? It means, my child, postponing a visit to a certain old friend of ours – whose name is Death.'

She breathed the word as if in begrudged pleasure at its sound. Alice shuddered, and yet it gave her fresh resolution. She rose from her chair.

'I am young and stupid, I know, great-grandmamma; and I would do anything in the world not to – not to hurt your feelings. And of course, of course I know that most people have a very hard time and that most of us are not very sharp-witted. But you said *death*; and I think, if you will forgive my saying so, I would rather I should have to die when – just when, I mean, I *must* die. You see, it would be a very sorrowful thing for me if it came after my mother had – if, I mean, she cannot share the secret too? And even then . . . Why cannot we all share it? I do see, indeed I do, there is very little time in this world in which to grow wise. But when you think of the men who have –'

'You are here, my child,' Miss Cheyney interrupted her, 'to answer questions – not to ask them. I must not be fatigued. Then I should have no sleep. But surely you are old enough to know that there is not a human creature in a thousand, nay, not one in a hundred thousand, who has any hope of growing wise, not if he lived till Doomsday.'

She edged forward an inch in her chair. 'Suppose, my child, your refusal means that this secret will perish with – with *me*? Unless,' the voice sank to a muttering, 'unless *you* consent to share it? Eh, what then?'

Alice found her eyes fixed on the old lady like a bird's on a serpent, and the only answer she could make was a violent shake of the head. 'Oh,' she cried, suddenly bursting into tears, 'I simply can't tell you how grateful I am for all your kindness, and how miserable I seem to myself to be saying this. But please, Miss Cheyney, may I go now? I feel a dreadful thing might happen if I stay here a minute longer.'

The old lady seemed to be struggling in her chair, as if in the effort to rise out of it; but her strength failed her. She lifted her claw-like mittened hand into the air.

'Begone at once, then,' she whispered, 'at once. Even my patience is limited. And when the day comes that will remind you of my kindness, may you wish you had ... Oh, oh! ...' The frail voice rose shrill as a gnat's, then ceased. At sound of it the old butler came hastening in at the further door; and Alice slipped out of the other ...

Not until the house had vanished from sight behind the leaping branches of its forest-trees did she slacken her pace to recover her breath. She had run wildly on, not daring to pause or even glance over her shoulder, as if her guardian angel were at her heels, lending wings to her feet to save her from danger.

That evening she and her mother – seated in the cosy red-curtained coffee-room of the 'Red Lion' – actually sipped together a brimming glass of the landlord's old Madeira. Alice had never before kept any secret from her mother. Yet though she was able to tell her most of what had happened that afternoon, she could not persuade herself to utter a syllable about the purpose which had prompted Miss Cheyney to send her so improbable an invitation. Not then, nor ever afterwards.

'Do you really mean, my own dearest,' her mother repeated more than once, pressing her hand as they sat in the chill spring night under the old oil-lamp-post awaiting their train in the little country railway station; 'do you mean she never gave you a single little keepsake; never offered you *anything* out of all those wonderful treasures in that dreadful old house?'

'She asked me, mother dear,' said Alice, turning her face away towards the dark mouthed tunnel through which they would soon be venturing – 'she asked me if I would like ever to be as old as she was. And honestly, I said I would much prefer to stay just the silly green creature I am, so long as I can be with you.'

It was an odd thing to do – if the station-master had been watching them – but, however odd, it is certainly true that at this moment mother and daughter turned and flung their arms about each other's necks and kissed each other in such a transport as if they had met again for the first time after an enormous journey.

Not that Alice had been quite accurate in saying that her godmother had made her no gift. For a day or two afterwards there came by post a package; and enwrapped in its folds of old Chinese paper Alice found the very portrait she had seen on the wall on that already seemingly far-off day – the drawing, I mean, made by a pupil of the famous Hans Holbein, depicting her great-great-great-great-great-great-great-great-grandmother in the year of grace 1564, when she was just turned seventeen.

Maria-Fly

Little Maria that morning – and this is a good many years ago now – was dressed in a black and white frock with a flounce to it. Her hair was tied back over her small ears with a white ribbon, and she was sitting in the drawing-room on a low armchair with a blue-cushioned seat; her stockinged legs dangling down in front of her. She was all by herself. She had wandered in there – nobody by; and after walking about for a little while looking at the things in the room, and sniffing at a bowl of red damask roses, she had sat down, looking so sleek and demure you might have supposed that company was present and she was 'behaving'.

But she was not; she was only thinking. It was a quiet morning. The room, with its two square-paned bow windows, was rather long. There was sunshine in it, and it was still, and though, as it appeared, there was no other living thing between its walls except herself, it seemed to be happy too. And Maria had begun to think – or rather not exactly to think and not exactly to dream, but (if that is possible) to do both together; though she could not have told anyone what she was thinking and dreaming about.

She had had a bowl of bread and milk for breakfast, half an apple, and two slices of bread and jam. She felt comfortable. Her piano practice in the old room by the nursery was over, and now she was alone. But she was alone more than usual. It was as if she were not only sitting there in her blue-cushioned armchair with her legs dangling down,

410

but that she could see herself sitting there. It startled her a little when that notion occurred to her. It was almost as if at that moment she must have really slipped into a dream. And she glanced up quickly with her rather round face and clear, darting eyes to make sure. And on the white paint at the side of the door, not very far away, she saw a fly.

It was just a fly. But simply because at that moment everything was so quiet in the world, and because, maybe, unlike the chairs and tables around her, it was alive, Maria fixed her eyes on the fly. It was nevertheless a perfectly ordinary fly – a housefly. It stood there alone on its six brushy legs and clawed feet, their small, nimble pads adhering to the white gloss of the paint. But, though ordinary, it was conspicuous – just in the same way as a man in black clothes with immense boots and a high cap on the enormous dazzling snow-slopes of a mountain is conspicuous – and Maria seemed to be seeing the fly much more clearly and minutely than you would have supposed possible, considering the distance between herself and it.

On the other hand, the fly was not standing there doing nothing, as Maria was sitting there doing nothing. It was not, for example, merely standing on the paint in *its* drawing-room and looking across at another fly infinitely tinier on the white paint of the minute door to that draw-ing-room. It was busy as flies usually are in the warm, sunny months.

Maria had been up and had dressed herself hours and hours ago; but flies seem to be dressing, or at least to be toileting and titivating themselves all the time when they are not prowling about on a table in search of food, or roving about, or sucking up water, or standing like mock flies asleep, or angling to and fro in the air under a chandelier or a fly-charm in one another's company.

Not that Maria was by any means fond of flies. She shooed them away with her spoon when they came buzzing about her blancmange or red-currant-and-raspberry tart, or alighted on her bare arms, or walked rapidly about over her bedclothes. Once she had pulled off the wings of a fly, and had never forgotten how suffocatingly fusty and hot she had felt after doing so.

And if there was one thing Maria couldn't abide, it was a fly floating in her bath. It was extraordinary that though its carcass was such a minute thing you could at such a moment see absolutely nothing else. It was extraordinary that the whole of the water at such a moment seemed like fly-water.

She would ask her nurse to take the ill-happed creature's corpse out of the bath and put it on the window-sill in case it was not quite dead and might come-to again.

And if she remembered to look next morning, maybe it was not, or maybe it *was*, there still – just its body. She had more than once, too, heard the dismal languishing drone a fly utters when it has been decoyed into a web and sees the spider come sallying out of its round, silken lair in the corner. It had filled her with horror and hatred and a miserable pity. Yet it had not made her any fonder of flies just for their own sakes alone. But then, one doesn't always feel exactly the same about anything. It depends on where you are, and what kind of mood you are in, and where the other thing is, and what kind of mood *that* is in.

So it was this morning. For some reason, this particular fly was different; and Maria sat watching it with the closest attention. It seemed to be that just as Maria herself was one particular little girl, so this was one particular fly. A fly by itself. A fly living its own life; confident, alert, alone in its own Fly World.

To judge from its solitude, and the easy, careless, busy

way in which it was spending its time, it might be supposed indeed that it had the whole universe to itself. It might be supposed it was Sirius – and not another star in the sky. And after a while, so intent did Maria become that she seemed to be doing a great deal more than merely watching the fly. She became engrossed.

She was now stooping together in her chair almost as if she were a pin-cushion and her eyes were black-headed pins in it. She seemed almost to have *become* the fly – Maria-Fly. If it is possible, that is, she had become two things at once, or one thing at twice. It was an odd experience – and it lasted at least three minutes by the little gold clock, with the gilt goggling fish on either side its dial under the glass-case on the chimney-piece. Three minutes, that is, of ordinary clock-time.

For when Maria herself came-to, it seemed she had been away for at least three centuries – as if, like the stranger in the rhyme, she had been with her candle all the way to Babylon; aye, and back again: as if she had gone away Maria, come back Maria-Fly and now was just Maria again. But yet, when she came-to, everything was a little different.

She could not possibly have explained why, but she felt surprisingly gay and joyful. It was as if a voice, sweet and shrill as the angel Israfel's, had been singing in her mind from a very long way off. She looked about her in sheer astonishment. If anything, the things in the room were stiller than ever, and yet she would almost have supposed that up to a moment ago they had been alive and watching her, and were now merely pretending to be not-alive again.

She looked at the roses in the bowl: they were floating there filled with their fragrance and beauty as a dew-drop is with light. The fishes on either side the little clock seemed to be made of flames rather than gilded plaster.

There was a patch of sunshine, too – just an oblong patch resting on the carpet and part of a chair. It seemed to be lovelier than words could tell and to be resting there as if in adoration of its own beauty. Maria saw all this with her young eyes, and could not realize what had happened to her. She was glad she was alone. She had never felt like it before. It was as if she had ceased to be herself altogether in her black and white frock and had become just a tied-up parcel marked 'Pure Happiness', with the date on it.

And as she gradually became aware how very still the room was, almost stealthy – and all quiet things, of course, seem in a way a little watchful – she felt she must go out of it. She felt she must go out of it at once. So she scrambled down off her chair. On purpose, she didn't even glance again at her friend the fly. She most particularly (though she didn't know why) wished not to see it again. So she walked sidelong a little, her head turned to one side, so that no part of her eye should see the fly again even by accident.

She went out of the room, walked along down the hall, and went down the rather dark side-stairs into the kitchen. There was a fire burning in the great burnished range. A green tree showed at the window, and a glass jar half-full of beer and wasps was twinkling on its sill. Mrs Poulton, the cook, was rolling a piece of dough on her pastry or dough-board, with an apron tied with all its tape round her waist. There was an immense flour dredger like a pepper-pot beside the board, and a hare, its fur soft as wool, cinnamon and snow-white, lay at the farther end of the table. Its long white teeth gleamed like ivory between its parted lips.

'Mrs Poulton,' Maria said, 'I have seen a fly.'

'Now, *have* you?' said the cook. And the 'have' was like

a valley or a meadow that slopes up and down with wild flowers all over it. 'And did the fly see you?'

That hadn't occurred to Maria. She frowned a little. 'It's got lots of kind of eyes, you know,' she said. 'But what I mean is, I *sawn* it.'

'And that was a queer thing, too,' said cook, deftly lifting up the dough and arranging its limp folds over the fat, dark, sugary plums in the shallow pie-dish, with an inverted egg-cup in the middle. She gave a look at it; and then took up her kitchen knife and, deft as a barber, whipped the knife clean round the edge of the dish to cut away what dough hung over. 'Would you like a dolly, dear?' she said.

'No, thank you,' said Maria, a little primly, not wishing to have the subject changed. 'I have told you about the fly,' she repeated, 'and you don't seem to take a bit of notice of it.'

The cook lifted her doughy knife, turned her round face and looked at the little girl. She had small, lively, light blue eyes and the hair under her cap was as fair and light in colour as new straw. It was a plump face, and yet sharp. 'And what do you mean by that, may I ask?' she said, eyeing Maria.

'I mean,' said Maria stubbornly, 'I *sawn* a fly. It was on the paint of the door of the droring-room, and it was all by itself.'

'Whereabouts?' said Mrs Poulton, trying to think of something else to say.

'I said,' said Maria, 'on the door.'

'Yes; but whereabouts on the door?' persisted the cook.

'On the side where it's cut in and the other part comes.'

'Oh, on the jamb,' said Mrs Poulton.

'Jam!' said Maria. 'How could there be jam on the door?'

415

'Well, I'm not so sure about that, Miss Sticky-fingers,' said the cook. 'But by jamb I meant *door*-jamb, though it's spelt different – leastwise, I think so. And what was the fly doing? – nasty creatures.'

Maria looked at her. 'That's what everybody says,' she said. '*My* fly – wasn't doing anything.' This was not exactly the truth; and feeling a little uneasy about it, Maria remarked in a little voice, 'But I am going now, thank you.'

'That's right,' said the cook. 'And be sure and mind them steep stairs, my precious.'

Maria glanced at the wasps hovering over the bottle, she glanced at Mrs Poulton, at the fire in the range, at the dish-covers on the walls – and then she went out of the door.

She minded the steep kitchen stairs just as much as usual, though she was a little indignant after her talk with the cook. When she reached the top of them, she went on along the slippery hall, past the grandfather's clock, with the white moon's-face in the blue over its hands, past the table with the pink-flowering pelargonium on it, and climbed on up the wide, shallow staircase, taking hold of the balusters one by one, but treading as near as possible in the middle of the soft, rose-patterned stair carpet.

And when she got to the top she came to a room where she knew she would find a guest who was staying in the house. His name was Mr Kittleson; he was a clergyman, and this Saturday morning he was writing his sermon for Sunday, and his text was 'Consider the lilies of the field ... They toil not neither do they spin.'

After fumbling with the handle a little Maria pushed the door open and looked in. And there sat the old gentleman in a round leather chair, with his silvery-grey beard spreading down over his chest, his sermon-paper on the blotting book in front of him, and a brass inkstand beyond that. His lips were moving as he wrote. But on hearing the door open he stayed his writing, and with stooping head looked round over his gold spectacles at Maria.

'Well, well, my dear, this is a very pleasant sight, and what can I do for you?' he said, being one of those peculiar old gentlemen who don't mind being interrupted even when they are writing sermons.

'I,' said Maria, edging a little into the room, 'I have just seen a fly! It was standing all by itself on the – the jamb of the door in the droring-room.'

'In the drawing-room? Indeed!' said the old gentleman, still peering over his gold spectacles. 'And a very fortunate fly it was, to be in your company, my dear. And how very kind of you to come and tell me.'

Maria was almost as little pleased by the old gentleman's politeness as she had been with her talk with the cook. 'Yes,' she said, 'but this was not a norinary fly. It was all by itself, and I looked at it.'

The old gentleman peeped down a little absently at his clear, sloping handwriting on the paper. 'Is that *so*?' he said. 'But then, my dear little Maria, no fly is really ordinary. They are remarkable creatures if you look at them attentively. And especially through a microscope. What does the Book say: "fearfully and wonderfully made"? They have what is called a proboscis – trunks, you know, just like elephants. And they can walk upside down. Eh? How about that?'

At that moment, out of its shadowy lair a silvery clothes-moth came flitting across the sunlight over his table. The old gentleman threw up his hands at it, but it wavered, soared, and escaped out of his clutches.

'Cook says flies are nasty creatures,' said Maria.

'Ah,' said the old clergyman, 'and I've no doubt cook avoids them in our food. But they have their ways, which may not please us, just as we have our ways, which may not please somebody else. But even a fly, my dear, enjoys its own small life and does what it is intended to do in it. "Little busy, thirsty fly",' he began, but Maria, who was looking at him as attentively as she had looked at the insect itself (before, that is, it had actually become a Maria-Fly), at once interrupted him. 'It's a *beau*tiful rhyme,' she said, nodding her head. 'I know it very well, thank you. But that was all I wanted to say. Just that I had sawn it – seen it. I don't think I could tell you anything else – so, I mean, that it would be 'xplained to you.'

The old gentleman, pen in hand, continued to smile at his visitor over his beard in the same bland cautious way he always did, until she had slid round the door out of his sight, and had firmly closed it after her.

On her way back along the corridor Maria passed the door of the workroom; it was ajar, and she peeped in. Miss Salmon, in her black stuff dress, sat there beside a table on which stood a sewing-machine. At this moment she was at work with her needle. She always smelt fresh, but a little faint; though also of camphor. She had an immensely long white face – high forehead and pointed chin – with rather protruding eyes and elbows; and she and Maria were old friends.

'And what can I do for you, madam, this morning?' she cried in a deep voice like a man's.

'Well, I just looked in, madam, to tell you I seen a fly.'

'If you was to look through the eye of the smallest needle in that work-basket you would see the gates of Paradise,' said Miss Salmon, stitching away again with a click that sounded almost as loud as if a carpenter were at work in the room.

'Give it me,' said Maria.

'Ah ha!' cried Miss Salmon, 'such things need looking for.'

'Ah ha!' chirped Maria, 'and that means tidying all the basket up.'

'Nothing seek, nothing find,' cried Miss Salmon, 'as the cat said to the stickleback, which is far better than Latin, madam. And what, may I ask, was the name of Mr Jasper Fly Esquire? If you would kindly ask the gentleman to step this way I will make him a paper house with bars to it, and we'll feed him on strawberries and cream.'

Maria's spirits seemed to sink into her shoes. 'It was not that kind of fly at all,' she said, 'and – and I don't wish to tell you the name, thank you very much.'

'*Good* morning,' said Miss Salmon lifting her needle and opening wide her eyes, 'and don't forget closing time's at seven.'

It was strange that Maria should feel so dismal at this turn of the conversation, considering that she and Miss Salmon were such very old friends and always had their little bit of fun together. Maria looked at her sitting bolt upright there in her high-collared black stuff dress, with her high head.

'*Good* morning, madam,' said Miss Salmon.

And Maria withdrew.

Opposite the workroom there was a portrait hanging on the landing in a large gilt frame. Maria looked at the lady painted in it, in her queer clothes, with a dome of muslin draped on high over her head, and she said, under her breath, though not out loud, 'Mm, *you* don't know I've seen a fly.' And then she ran off downstairs again and met her father at that moment issuing out of his den with the topmost joint of a fishing-rod in his hand. He had on his ugly brown suit and thick-soled brown shoes.

'Daddy,' she called at him, 'I've just been telling him I have seen a fly.'

'Oh, have you,' said he, 'you black-eyed young ragamuffin. And what business had you to be mousing into his room this time of morning, I should like to know? And talking of flies, Miss Black-and-White, what would you recommend for this afternoon, so as to make quite sure of a certain Mrs Fat Trout I wot of?'

'You see, Daddy,' said Maria stiffly, 'you always turn things off like that. And it was something so very special I wanted to tell you.'

'Now see here,' said her father, flicking with the tip of his tapering rod-piece, 'what we'll do is this, we will. You shall tell me all about that fly of yours when I come in to say good night tonight. And perhaps by then you will have seen lots of other things. And you shall have a penny for every one that begins with a Q. There's plenty of flies,' he added.

'I don't think I shall *care* to see lots of other things,' said Maria – 'but I'll see.' And she walked off, more sedately even than little old Queen Victoria, into the garden.

Up till then it had been a morning like a blue-framed looking-glass, but now a fleece of cloud was spread over the immense sky. Far away in the kitchen-garden she came across the gardener, Mr Pratt. With his striped cotton shirt-sleeves turned up over his elbows, he was spraying a rose-tree on which that day's sun even if it came out in full splendour again would shine no more. Maria watched him.

'What are you doing that for?' she said. 'Let me!'

'Steady, steady, my dear,' said Mr Pratt – 'you can't manage the great thing all by yourself.' But he put the syringe with a little drop of the liquid left in its brass cylinder into her hands. 'Now, push!' he said, 'all your might.'

Maria pushed hard, till her knuckles on her fat hands

went white, and she was plum-red in the face. But nothing came. So Mr Pratt put his thick brown hands over hers, clutched the tube, and they pushed together. And an exquisite little puff of water jetted like a tiny cloud out of the nozzle.

'It came out then,' said Maria triumphantly. 'I could do it if I tried really hard. What, please, are you doing it *for*?'

'Ah,' said Mr Pratt, 'them's secrets.'

'Ah,' said Maria imitating him, 'and I've got a secret, too.'

'What's that?' said the gardener.

She held up her finger at him. 'I – have – just – seen – a – fly. It had wings like as you see oil on water, and a red face with straight silver eyes, and it wasn't buzzing or nothing, but it was scraping with its front legs over its wings, then rubbing them like corkscrews. Then it took its head off and on, and then it began again – but I don't mean all that. I mean I sawn the fly – saw it, I mean.'

'Ah,' said Mr Pratt, the perspiration glistening on his brown face, and his eyes at least two shades a paler blue than Mrs Poulton's, as though the sun and the jealous skies had bleached most of the colour out of them. 'Ah,' he said. 'A fly now? And that's something to see too. But what about them pretty little Meadow Browns over there, and that Painted Lady – quiet, now, see – on that there mallow-bloom! There's a beauty! And look at all them yaller ragamuffins over the winter cabbage yonder. We won't get much greens, Missie, if you can underconstumble, if *they* have their little way.'

Maria could perfectly underconstumble. But she hated greens. She hated them as much as if she had eaten them on cold plates in another world. It was odd too that nobody had the smallest notion of what she wanted to say about the Fly. No one. How stupid. But she looked at the Painted

Lady none the less. It was limply perched on the pale paper-like flower of the mallow, with its ball-tipped antennae, and sucking up its secret nectar for all the world like the Queen in her parlour enjoying her thick slice of bread and honey. And then the sunshine stole out again into the heavens above them, and drew itself like a pale golden veil over the shimmering garden. The Painted Lady's wings, all ribbed and dappled orange and black and white, trembled a little in its gentle heat, as if with inexpressible happiness and desire.

But though Maria admired the creature in its flaunting beauty more than she could say, this was not her Fly – this, at least, was no *Maria*-Fly. It was merely a butterfly – lovely as light, lovely as a coloured floating vapour, exquisitely stirring, its bended legs clutching the gauzy platform beneath it and supporting its lightly poised frail plumy body on this swaying pedestal as if the world it knew were solid as marble and without any change; even though it now appeared as gentle as a dream.

Maria was not even thinking as she watched the butterfly, except that she was saying over to herself, though not using any words, that she did not want to go into the drawing-room any more just now; that she had no wish to see her fly again; that she didn't want ever to be grown-up; that grown-ups never could underconstumble in the very least what you were really saying; that if only they wouldn't try to be smiling and patient as though the least cold puff of breath might blow you away, you might prove you were grown-up too and much older than they – even though you had to eat greens and do what you were told and not interrupt old gentlemen writing sermons, and must wait for bed-time – *no*, she was not really thinking any of these things. But her small bosom rose and fell with a prolonged deep sigh as she once more glanced up at Mr Pratt.

He was hard at work again with his syringe, and now, because the sun was shining between herself and its watery vapour, it had formed a marvellous little rainbow in the air, almost circular, with the green in it fully as vivid as that of the myriad aphides clustering like animated beads round the stems of the rosebuds.

'I told you,' she quavered a little sorrowfully, though she was trying to speak as usual, 'I told you about something and you didn't take any notice.'

'Well, well, well,' said the gardener. But he hadn't time to finish his sentence before Maria was already stalking down the path, and in a moment had disappeared round the corner of the green-house.

And there, a moment or two afterwards, she happened to come across patient Job, the gardener's boy. Job was an oaf to look at, with his scrub of hair and his snub nose and silly mouth. He was little short of what the village people called a half-wit or natural. He laughed at whatever you said to him, even when you frowned double-daggers at him. But there was no gardener's boy like him; the very roots of the flowers he handled seemed to want to net themselves about his clumsy fingers, and he was 'a fair magician' with bees. Three little steel mole-traps lay on the gravel beside him where he knelt, and he was scouring flower-pots with a scrubbling-brush, and as Maria appeared he looked up with a face like a good-humoured pumpkin, and he grinned at her with all his teeth.

'Marning, missie,' he said.

'Good morning, Job,' said Maria. She stood looking at him, looking at his tiny pig-like eyes in the great expanse of his good-humoured face, and hesitated. Then she stooped a little and all but whispered at him.

'Have you ever seen a fly?'

'Oi, miss, seen a floi?' he replied, opening his mouth.

'Oi, missie, oive seed a floi.'

'But have you,' and Maria all but let all her breath go –
over just those first three words, 'But have you, Job, ever
seen the only teeny tiny fly there ever was: *your* Fly?'

Job scratched his head and looked so serious for an
instant that Maria feared he was going to burst out crying.
'Oi, missie,' he suddenly shouted at last with a great
guffaw of laughter, 'that oi 'ave, and avore I could catch
un ee was gawn loike a knoifejack clean down Red Lane
ee wor. Oi and ee *wor* a floi, ee wor.'

Maria burst out laughing: they laughed in chorus; and
then she found tears were standing in her eyes and she suddenly felt silent and mournful. 'And now,' she said, 'you
had better get on with your pots.'

She turned away, her small head filled as if with a tune
ages old, and as sorrowful as the sounds of the tide of the
unvisited shores of the ocean. There was a little old ear-
wiggy arbour not far away that always smelt damp even
after weeks of fine hot weather – though then it smelt dry-
damp.

Maria went into its shadow and stood there by herself a
moment. Why she had gone in she didn't know. It was very
still. But mustily, stuffily, gloomily still – quite different
from the sunny coloured stillness of the drawing-room.
There was a wide droning in the air outside. Millions of
minute voices were sounding in concert like the twangling
of the strings of an enormous viol. A bird hopped on to
the roof of the arbour; she could hear its claws on the
wood. Its impact dislodged a tiny clot of dust. It fell into
the yet finer dust at her feet. The arbour's corners were
festooned with cobwebs.

Maria gave yet another deep sigh, and then looked up
around her almost as if in hopes of somebody else to whom
she might tell her secret tale – about the fly – about Maria-

Fly. She paused – staring. And then, as if at a signal, she hopped down suddenly out of the arbour, almost as lightly as a thin-legged bird herself, and was off flying over the emerald green grass into the burning delightful sunshine without in the least knowing why, or where to.

Visitors

One of the very last things that Tom Nevis was to think about in this world was a sight he had seen when he was a child of about ten. Years and years were to pass by after that March morning; and at the last Tom was far away from home and England in the heat and glare of the tropics. Yet this one far-away memory floated up into his imagination to rest there in its peace and strangeness as serenely as a planet shining in its silver above the snows of remote hills. It had just stayed on in the quiet depths of his mind – like the small insects that may be seen imprisoned in lumps of amber, their wings still glistening ages after they were used in flitting hither-thither in their world as it was then.

Most human beings have little experiences similar to Tom's. But they come more frequently to rather solitary people – people who enjoy being alone, and who have daydreams. If they occur at other times, they may leave little impression, because perhaps one is talking or laughing or busy, working away at what has to be done, or perhaps reading or thinking. And then they may pass unnoticed.

But Tom had always been a funny solitary creature. Even as a child he enjoyed being alone. He would sit on a gate or a stile for an hour at a time just staring idly into a field, following with his eyes the shadows of the clouds as they swept silently over its greenness, or the wandering wind, now here, now there, stooping upon the taller weeds

and grasses. It was a pleasure to him merely even to watch
a cow browsing her way among the buttercups, swinging
the tuft of her tail and occasionally rubbing her cinnamon-
coloured shoulder with her soft nose. It seemed to Tom at
such times – though he never actually put the feeling into
words – almost as if the world were only in his mind;
almost as if it were the panorama of a dream.

So too Tom particularly enjoyed looking out of his window when the moon was shining. Not only in winter when
there is snow on the ground, and clotting hoar-frost, but
in May and summer too, the light the moon sheds in her
quiet rests on the trees and the grass and the fields like a
silver tissue. And she is for ever changing: now a crescent
slenderly shining – a loop of silver or copper wire in the
western after-glow of sunset; and now a mere ghost of
herself, lingering in the blue of morning like a lantern
burning long after the party is over which it was meant to
make gay.

Tom was more likely to be left alone than most boys,
owing to a fall he had had when he was three. He had a
nurse then, named Alice Jenkins. One morning she sat
him up as usual close to the nursery table and his bowl
of bread and milk; and had then turned round an instant
at the sound of something heard at the window. And he, in
that instant, to see perhaps what she was looking at, had
jumped up in his chair, the bar had slipped out, and he
had fallen sprawling on to the floor.

The fall had injured his left arm. And try as the doctors
might, they had never been able to make it grow like his
right arm. It was lean and shrunken and almost useless,
and the fingers of the hand were drawn up a little so that
it could be used only for simple easy things. He was very
little good at games in consequence, and didn't see much
of other boys of his own age. Alice had cried half the

night after that miserable hour; but the two of them loved each other the more dearly for it afterwards. Even now that she was married and kept a small greengrocer's shop in a neighbouring town, Tom went to see her whenever he could, and munched her apples and pears and talked about everything under the sun.

This accident had happened so long ago that he had almost forgotten he had ever at all had the full use of his arm. He grew as much accustomed to its hanging limply from his shoulder as one may become accustomed to having a crooked nose, prominent ears or a squint. And though he realized that it kept him out of things like climbing trees or playing such games as other boys could do with ease, though it had made a kind of scarecrow of him, it was simply because of this that he was left more to himself and his own devices than most boys. And though he never confessed it to himself, and certainly not to anybody else, he immensely enjoyed being in his own company. It was not a bit – as it well might be – like being in an empty house, but rather in an enchanted one; wherein you never knew what might not happen next, even though everything was still and quiet – the sun at the windows, the faint shadows in the corridors, the water in the green fishpond and the tangled branches in the orchard.

Tom, too, beside being for this reason rather odd in his body – small for his age, with narrow shoulders, a bony face, light grey-blue eyes and a stiff shock of yellow hair standing up on his high head – was also a little odd in mind. He was continually making up stories, even when there was no one to listen to them. For his black-eyebrowed elder sister very seldom had time to do so; and the nurse he had after Alice was married had not much patience with such things. But he almost as much enjoyed telling them to himself. And when his sister Emily died he seemed to get into the habit of mooning and daydreaming more than ever.

He had other queer little habits too. Whenever he went downstairs from his bedroom – unless he was in a violent hurry or his father had called him – he always sat down for a few moments on a narrow stair from which he looked out from a tall landing window over the garden. It seemed to him you could never tell what you might *not* see at such a moment; though as a matter of fact he never saw anything very unusual : just the grass and the lawn and the currant-bushes and the monkey-puzzle; perhaps a cat walking gingerly on its errand, and the usual thrushes and blackbirds, tits and robins, and the light of the sun on the red-brick wall. And what you don't actually see you cannot put a name to.

Another fancy of his was, whenever he passed it, to stoop down and peer through the keyhole of a cellar that spread out underneath the old Parsonage. He might just as well have looked up a chimney for there was even less light to be seen through the keyhole. And nothing was stowed away in the cellar except a few old discarded pieces of furniture, some bottles of wine, empty hampers, an old broken rocking-horse and such things as that. None the less, whenever he passed that door, Tom almost invariably stooped on his knees, puckered up one eye and peered through its keyhole with the other, and smelt the fusty smell.

There was no end to his cranky comicalities. Long ago, for example, he had made a rule of always doing certain things on certain days. He cared no more for washing in those early days than most boys : but he always had a 'thorough good wash' on Fridays; even though it was 'bath night' on Saturdays. He went certain walks on certain evenings, that is, evenings after it had been raining, or maybe when some flower or tree was just out. **And he** always went to see his sister Emily's grave once a month. She had died on the twelfth of April; and apart from her birthday, he always kept her month day – all the

twelfths throughout the year. If he could, and if he had time, he would take a bunch of flowers along with him, choosing those which Emily had liked the best or those he liked the best, or both together. The churchyard was not far away, as the crow flies, but it was yet another of his odd habits not to go there direct – as if that might be too easy – but to go round by a meadow path that was at least three-quarters of a mile further than the way by the village lane.

Except when he happened to be by himself at evenings just after the sun was set, Tom always felt more alone on these monthly journeys than at any other time. And for as long a time as he could spare he would sit on an old bench under the churchyard yew. At first he had been exceedingly wretched and miserable on these visits. The whole Parsonage, his father and his sister and the maids – it was just as if a kind of thick cold mist had come over them all when Emily died. Everything that was familiar in the house had suddenly stood up strange and exclamatory, as if to remind them something was gone that would never come back again. And though none of the others, of course, really forgot what had happened, though he often actually noticed his father desisting from what he was just about to say simply because he could not bear the grief of mentioning Emily's name, as time went on, things began to be much as ever again.

In the early days Tom's black-haired elder sister, Esther, used to come with him to the churchyard now and then; but she soon had so many things to think about and to amuse herself with that there was very little time to spend with him. Besides, they agreed about nothing and spent most of the time arguing and wrangling. So for a good many months Tom had gone alone. He knew his own particular monthly walk to the churchyard as well as he knew his own clothes or anything else in the world. He never set out on it without wishing he could see his sister Emily again, and he never came home again to the Parsonage without thinking to himself that it was better perhaps he could *not* bring her back. For he was somehow sure, wherever her body might be, that she herself was perfectly happy, and, as it were, always to be young. Now and then, indeed, it seemed as if some wraith of herself had actually whispered this into his ear as he sat on his bench looking out across the tombstones, and sometimes wondering how long it would be before he was dead to. But then Tom's little moperies came very near at times to being a little mad.

That was another odd thing about Tom. He enjoyed thinking and puzzling over everything that came into his head, whereas most people will not allow hard or disagreeable thoughts to stay in their minds. They drive them out like strange dogs out of a garden, or wasps out of a sunny room. Tom thought of them, however, in the most practical way possible. He knew, for example, as much about grave-digging when he was ten as the old sexton could tell him at sixty. The thought of the bones beneath the turf did not frighten him a bit. Surely, he thought to himself, nothing could be as ugly as all that if it were just the truth. And if it was, why, then it *was*.

Not that he did not enjoy being alive in this world. He fairly ached sometimes with delight in it. He had talked to Alice about it, and to Emily too, sitting on a green bank in the sunshine or in the hayfields, or by the banks of their secret pond in the woods. He loved also to brood on what might happen to him in the future; though he never had the faintest notion in those days that he was going to travel, that he was going to leave England when he was still a young man, for good and all, and never come back. He had no notion of that at all until there came a talk one afternoon in her husband's shop with his nurse Alice. After that he knew he had been born to be a traveller in spite of his arm and his cranky meagre body. And what led up to the talk was what happened to him that March morning as he came back from his customary visit to the church-yard.

A faint but bleak east wind was blowing. Except for a light silvery ridge of cloud in the south the sky was blue all over, and the sunlight was as bright as if a huge crystal reflector behind it were casting back its beams from the heavens upon the earth. A few daffodils were out in the fields, and the celandine with its shovel-shaped glossy leaves too; and the hedges were beginning to quicken, looking from a distance as if a faint green mist hung over them. The grass was already growing after its winter's rest, and the birds of the countryside were busy flying hither and thither as if time were something that melted in the sun. Instead of returning from the churchyard to the house by the way he had come, Tom had turned in through a wicket gate into a straggling wood of birch and hazel, and so came out at the corner of a large meadow which lay over against the Old Farm.

There had been heavy rains during the previous week, and as Tom – absent-minded as ever – came edging along the path of the meadow, he lifted his eyes and was aston-ished to see a pool of water in the green hollow of the meadow beneath him, where none had lain before. Its waters were evidently of the rains that had fallen in the past few days. They stretched there grey and sparkling, glassing the sky, and the budding trees which grew not far from their margin. And floating upon this new wild water he saw two strange birds. Never had he seen their like be-fore, though he guessed they might be straying sea-birds. They were white as snow, and were disporting themselves gently in this chance pool, as if it were a haven of refuge or meeting-place which they had been seeking from the first moment they had come out of their shells.

Tom watched them, fixed motionless where he stood, afraid almost to blink lest he should disturb their happy play. But at last he took courage, and gradually, inch by inch, he approached stealthily nearer until at last he could see their very eyes shining in their heads, and the marvellous snow of their wings and their coral beaks reflected in the shallow wind-rippled pool. They appeared to be companions of all time. They preened their feathers, uttering faint cries as if of delight, as if they were telling secrets one to the other. And now and again they would desist from their preening and float there quietly together on the surface of the water, in the silvery sunshine. And still Tom continued to gaze at them with such greedy eagerness it was a marvel this alone did not scare the wild creatures away. It seemed to Tom as if he had been looking at them for ages and ages under the huge shallow bowl of the March sky. He dreaded every instant they would lift their wings and fly away. That would be as if something had gone out of his own inmost self.

He was whispering too under his breath, as if to persuade them to remain there always, and let there be no change. Indeed they might be human creatures, they floated there on the water so naturally and happily in their devotion to one another's company. And it seemed once more to Tom as if the whole world and his own small life had floated off into a dream, and that he had stood watching their movements and their beauty for as many centuries as the huge oak that towered above the farm had stood with outflung boughs, bearing its flowers and its acorns from spring on to spring, and from autumn to autumn until this very morning.

What was curious too, the two strange birds seemed at last to have no fear of his being there, even though the bright shallow basin of rain on which they rested in the

meadow was not more than eleven paces wide. They eyed
him indeed with a curious sharp brightness, almost as if
they wished to be sharing their secret with him, one brought
from the remote haunts from which they had set out overnight; as if this was the end of their journey. The drops
they flung with their bills over their snowy plumage gleamed
like little balls of changing silver or crystal, though not
brighter than their eyes. The red of their webbed feet
showed vividly beneath the grey clear water. And the faint
soft cries uttered in their throats rather than with open
bills were not sweet or shrill as a peewit or a linnet singing,
but were yet wonderfully gentle and tender to listen to.

And Tom's odd mind slipped once more into a deep
daydream as he stood there – in his buttoned-up jacket,
with his cap over his short springy hair – in the light but
bleak east wind that swept out of the clouds across the
meadow and the roof and chimneys of the old red-brick
farm ... In the middle of that night he woke up: as suddenly almost as if a voice had called him. And the scene
was still as sharp and fresh in his imagination as if he
were looking at it again spread out in actuality in the
morning light before his very eyes.

It was just like ridiculous Tom not to visit the meadow
again for many days afterwards. Once or twice he actually
set out in that direction, but turned off before the farmyard
came into view. And when at last he did go back again,
towards evening, the whole scene had changed. No longer
was the wind from the east, but from the south. Lofty
clouds towered up into the intense blue of the sky, like
snow-topped mountains. The air was sweet with spring.
The tight dark buds had burst in the hedges into their first
pale-green leaf; thrushes were singing among the higher
branches of the elms. But the pool of rainwater had sunk
out of sight in its hollow, had been carried up by the wind

and sun into the heavens, leaving only the greener and fresher grass behind it. The birds were flown ...

One day in the following July, Tom went off to see his old nurse, Alice Hubbard. She had grown a good deal stouter after her marriage, and Tom sat with her in the cramped parlour behind the shop, looking out into the street across the bins of green peas and potatoes, carrots and turnips, lettuces and cabbages and mint, the baskets of gooseberries and currants and strawberries and the last cherries. And while Alice was picking out for him a saucerful of strawberries, he told her all about himself: what he had been doing and thinking, and about the new maid, and about the Parsonage. And she would say as she paused with finger and thumb over her basket, 'Lor, Master Tom!' or 'Did you ever, now, Master Tom!' or 'There now, Master Tom!' And all of a sudden the memory of the pool of water and the two strange birds flitted back into his mind and he fell silent. Alice put down before him the saucer of strawberries, with a little blue-and-white jug of cream, and she glanced a little curiously into his narrow, ugly face.

'And what might you be thinking of now, I wonder?' she said.

An old woman in a black bonnet and shawl who had been peering about at the fruit from the pavement close to the window outside, at this moment came into the shop, and Alice went out to serve her with what she wanted. Tom watched the two of them; watched the potatoes weighed and the sprig of mint thrown into the scale; watched a huge dapple-grey cart-horse go by, dragging its cartload of bricks, with its snuff-coloured driver sitting on a sack on top. And then Alice had come back into the little parlour again, and he was telling her all about the birds and the pool.

'Lor now, that *was* queer, Master Tom,' said Alice. 'And where might you have been that morning?'

And Tom told her he had been to the churchyard.

'Now you know, my dear soul,' she said in a hushed voice as if somebody might be listening; 'you know you didn't ought to go there too often. It isn't good for you. You think too much already. And Joe says – and you wouldn't believe how happy I am, Master Tom, living here in this little shop, though I never never forget the old Parsonage and the kindness of your dear mother – but Joe he says that one didn't ought to keep on thinking about such things. Not keep on, he means. How would the world go round, he says, if we was all of us up in the clouds all day. It looks to me as if you were more a bag of bones than ever, though p'raps you have been growing – sprouting up a good deal.'

'But wasn't it funny about the birds?' said Tom.

'Why,' said Alice, 'what was funny?'

'Why,' said Tom, 'they weren't just ordinary birds. I am not sure now they were even quite live birds – real birds I mean, though they might have come from the sea. And why didn't they fly away when I got near? They saw me right enough. And why, do you think, do I keep on thinking about them?'

'Lor bless me!' said Alice. 'The questions he asks! And all them whys! You ain't much changed at that, Master Tom.'

'Yes, but why?' Tom persisted, spoon in hand, looking up at her over his saucer of strawberries and cream.

Alice stood on the other side of the table, resting the knuckles of one hand upon it, and as she looked out across the shop a vacancy came into her blue eyes, just as if, like Tom himself, she too at times fell into daydreams. 'Well, I suppose – I suppose,' she said at last in a low far-away voice, 'you keep on thinking about them because you can't get them out of your head.'

'Oh that's all right,' said Tom a little impatiently; 'but what I want to know is why they stay there?'

'Well,' said Alice, 'some things do. I can see those birds meself. And of course they were real, Master Tom. Of course they were real. Or else' – she gave a little gentle laugh – 'or else, why you and me would be just talking about ghost birds. What I mean is that it doesn't follow even if they *was* real that they didn't mean something else too. I don't mean exactly that such things do mean anything else, but only, so to speak, it *seems* that they do. All depends, I suppose, in a manner of speaking, on what they are to us, Master Tom. Bless me, when I stand here in this shop sometimes, looking out at the people in the street and seeing customers come in – even serving them, too – I sometimes wonder if the whole *thing* mayn't mean something else. How was I to know that I was ever going to get married to my Joe and keep a greengrocer's shop too? And yet, believe *me*, Master Tom, it seems just as ordinary and natural now as if I had been meant to do it from my very cradle.'

Tom looked at her curiously. 'Then what do you think the birds *mean*?' he repeated.

The soft lids with their light lashes closed down a little further over her blue eyes as Alice stood pondering over the same old question. 'Why,' she whispered almost as if she were talking in her sleep, 'if you ask me, it means that you are going to travel. That's what *I* think the birds mean. But then I couldn't say where.'

And suddenly she came back again, as it were – came out of her momentary reverie or daydream, and looked sharply round at him as if he might be in danger of something. She was frowning, as though she were frightened.

'You know, Master Tom,' she went on in a solemn voice, 'I can never never forgive myself for that poor arm of yours. Why you might by now ... But there! life *is* a mystery, isn't it? I suppose in a sort of a way – though Joe would say we oughtn't to brood on it – life itself is a kind of a journey. That goes on too.'

'Goes on where?' said Tom.

'Ah, that we can't rightly say,' said Alice, smiling at him. 'But I expect if them birds of yours could find their way from over the sea, there is no particular reason why human beings should not find theirs.'

'You mean Emily found hers?' said Tom.

Alice nodded two or three times. 'That I do,' she said.

'Well, all I can say is,' said Tom, 'I wish they'd come back, and the water too. They were more – more – well, I don't know *what*, than anything I have ever seen in the whole of my life.'

'And that's a tidy-sized one too!' said Alice, smiling at him again. And they exchanged a long still look.

And what she had said about his travelling came perfectly true. Quite early in his twenties Tom had pushed on up the gangway and into the bowels of the ship that was to take him across the sea to that far-away country from which he was never to come back. And though green peas and mint and the last of the cherries may not be quite such magical things in the memory as the sight of two strange sea-birds disporting themselves in a pool of rain-water on a bleak silvery March morning far from their natural haunts, these too when they came round each year always reminded Alice of that talk with Tom. Indeed she loved him very dearly, for Tom was of course – and especially after his accident – a kind of foster son. And when she heard of his going abroad she remembered the birds as well.

Sambo and the Snow Mountains

Sambo's *great*-grandfather had been a king in his own country, though it was only a small country. Sambo's *grand*-father was brought to the White Man's Land by a missionary, whose name was Grimble, the Rev. Silas Makepeace Grimble. He had been born in Aberdeen. Sambo's *father*, after being Mr Grimble's eldest son's valet *and* coachman, set up in business as a barber. But though he merrily did his best, he couldn't get enough customers, either for haircutting, singeing, shampooing or shaving. He would sometimes sit for hours in his empty shop beside the basin, staring out into the sunny street. So at last he was compelled to pull down the blind, put up the shutters, and take down his pole; and he soon afterwards died; and was laid to rest beside his beloved Dinah.

That leaves Sambo. Sambo was *Dr* Grimble's pageboy – Dr Grimble being the Rev. Silas's great-nephew. The doctor lived in a tall brown house made of wood. It had three Lombardy poplar trees in front of it and honeysuckle grew over the porch. Sambo had many duties. With his twenty-one little silver buttons in front of his tunic, and a little peak behind over his tight trousers, he used to open the door to his master's patients and show them into his waiting-room. It was a small but cheerful room with mosquito-screens at the windows, black and white oilcloth on the floor, a picture over the fireplace, and a lovely fall of coloured horse-hair piled up in the grate beneath, all through the summer. This cascade hid the ugly bars of the grate. So in summer there was no need for Sambo to blacklead them.

Sambo also helped his master to mix his medicines. When the doctor had put the drugs into the bottle, Sambo added the water; when the doctor had rolled out his pills, Sambo put them into the pill-boxes. By means of a large stick of red sealing-wax and a little blue gas-jet, he used to seal down the paper after he had wrapped up the bottles and boxes. He enjoyed the sealing-wax part of his work far better than the bottle-washing – in a small square leaden sink under a tiny brass tap.

All this was in the early afternoon. When the bottles had been neatly wrapped and numbered, Sambo used to put them into his basket and carry them off to his master's patients. Sometimes he had to walk one mile, sometimes three, sometimes even five – and right into the country. The times so taken depended on how many candy shops, other boys, performing animals, street musicians, dog-fights and other pleasures or dangers he encountered on his way to and fro. So long as he was home again at his master's house by six, all was well. In the evening he waited on the doctor while he ate his supper, and this the doctor did very quickly. Sambo brought him his grog about nine, and then went to bed.

On the whole, Sambo was happy, though until he became *un*happy he had not noticed it much. Though he scampered with beating heart at sound of his master's call, he admired the reddish hair that stood in a little wall above his forehead, his gold spectacles and handsome watch-chain. He had enough to eat, time to be lazy in, and a truckle bed with a flock pillow in a little box-room under the roof. There was only one thing against him. He was black. He was as black as all his ancestors. He was as black as a bale of velvet, as a cellar with no windows in it, as a chimney full of soot.

He might not himself have much noticed this if the pale-faced boys of the town were not always reminding him of it – particularly a pug-nosed little rascal called William who was page to a dentist of the odd name of Tooth: Mr Tooth. This William, whenever he met Sambo – partly because he was jealous of his buttons (which were silver), and even of his two-lidded basket (which was covered with mottled American cloth), but mostly because he knew no better – would yell at sight of him, 'Yah! Blackamoor! Yah! tar-face! Yah! you little grinning bandy-legged monkey-jibbed lump of ebony! Off the streets with you! Streets is for white men!'

At this Sambo, pretending not to have heard him, would at once cross the road. White or black or coffee-coloured, it was beneath him, he told himself, to be seen fighting with a dentist's boy. But he knew in his heart he was afraid of William, and he crossed the road. Still, it was chiefly his black skin that was now on Sambo's mind. And *now* it troubled him not only because of his enemies, the street boys, but for his own private sake also. After all, he knew that the rest of him, what was inside, was little different even from his master's. And even his skin was not his fault. Yet the more intently he pored over his young face in his bedroom scrap of looking-glass, the blacker he seemed to get.

This could not have been so in his own country. There, to be black was bliss. His great-grandfather, as he knew, had been a king in that country and it was white boys who would be laughable there. Indeed, when first the Rev. Silas Grimble appeared in Poojooboo, the black women and children laughed so much among themselves at his tall hat, pale face and silvery whiskers – supposing that his clothes were as much a part of him as its spots are part of a leopard –

that at last they became quite friendly with him. They liked him because he looked so amusing. But not even they – not even the piccaninnies – laughed at him to his face. That was not their manners. If, then, William the dentist's boy had taken ship to Poojooboo to find Sambo on the throne, the boys in the streets under the bread-fruit trees would have yelled their *Yahs* at *him* – but not out loud.

Sambo knew enough of all this, mused on it when he was alone, to make him feel not only unhappy but homesick. It was not, then, that he pined merely to be a white boy. There were white boys he knew by sight he wouldn't have pined to be for anything in the wide world. No, he only saddened more and more at having to stay black. He wanted to be *all* white and yet himself. This sorrowfulness came over him in curious ways.

On getting up in the morning, for example, he would remember again – if there had been any light to see him by – how black he must have looked between his sheets. Or again, after blowing out his candle on going to bed – and Dr Grimble gave him only an inch at a time so that he should not undersleep himself – he would realize that without his nightshirt he could not be seen in the dark. There was nothing sad or dreadful in either of these facts – not really; but they stayed in Sambo's mind. They haunted him as a spectre might a copse.

Perhaps if Sambo had not been so slow in his mind he might soon have learned to be less vain. But he had never been told that to grieve over what one is not may be as vain as to simper at what one is. He had been told very little. So night and morning, Sambo stared at himself in the scrap of looking-glass he treasured. Round, glossy, solemn, his young face stared back at him; and alas, as black as jet!

But though Sambo was slow by nature, though his

master always told him things twice over to make sure, though on his rounds he always walked much further than he needed to walk because he made mistakes in arranging the houses he had to walk to, Sambo was persevering, even stubborn. What he began he finished. If mere trying could have blanched him, he would soon have become as fair in aspect as an albino. He took the greatest pains.

First he prayed to be made white, and almost sobbed in his bed, watching in vain for the angel he had hoped might come down through the starry night at once in answer. Then he gave up the kitchen black bread that by rights was his, and lived on the white scraps of French rolls left over from his master's table. The doctor's livery was a dark green, with yellow edging. But Sambo was allowed to wear a white drill waiting-jacket in the mornings – after eleven o'clock. This he himself washed and ironed three times a week and wore in private whenever his master was out, particularly on the days when the doctor went to see his Aunt Clara and spent the night at her house. Often in fear Sambo slept with his head under his bedclothes lest the night itself darkened even the dark. But all such efforts were in vain.

At last one morning – but by no means for the first time – he heard the doctor mention scarlet fever, and that very afternoon he himself carried round a large bottle of medicine to the patient who was suffering from this sad malady. This gentleman lived in a square house covered with vines and creepers, and Sambo could see the shutters drawn close across the windows behind which he lay in bed – bright red, as Sambo supposed, from head to foot.

This reminded him of another patient of the doctor's – a lady who was from Mexico and whose fever had been yellow; and of a little girl with auburn curls who had been

445

at death's door with yellow jaundice, and whose small brother was afterwards brought to the doctor suffering from pink eye. His master too had once had for cook a negro mammy who at full moon was always oppressed with what she called 'de blue debbles'. And what but the doctor's medicines had cured them all? Surely, pondered Sambo, if physic could take away scarlet, yellow, blue and pink, it could wash out black?

Sambo cast his eye towards his master's shelves of bottles and jars and could scarcely wait in patience until he was alone again. He had often been warned not to meddle with them. But then, what a happy surprise it would be for the doctor if one morning Sambo appeared in his bedroom to pull up his blinds as white as himself. He might double his wages.

So one by one Sambo tried every kind of medicine on the shelves in turn, except the poisons which were kept locked up in a small cupboard. Of each he took no more than the least sip and only one sip at a time. If, after removing the glass stopper, the medicine had a very pungent or nauseous smell, he took even less. As with the bottles, full of essences and tinctures, so with the powders and the pastes and the pills. Of every powder he took no more than half a saltspoonful; enough to cover the tip of his little finger of every paste; and half a pill of every kind and size.

Most of these medicines made no difference at all – but then, being little more than a child, Sambo did not at first venture to taste more than one of them at a time. Others made him giddy, or hot, or breathless, or limp, or excited, or silly, or talkative, or thirsty, or hungry – or just the reverse; and one or two of them made him sick. After these his face looked a little green, but even then it was only a black-green and soon passed away. In spite of all this pain and trouble, Sambo remained precisely as black as ever, then, if not a little blacker.

It was odd perhaps that the doctor never noticed either that any of his medicines were dwindling, or that Sambo sometimes looked peculiar. But then he was not an observant man, and he was short-sighted. Besides, though Sambo did not know it, it would have made no difference to his master if he were grey or brown, striped, dappled or piebald. So long, that is, as he did his work well. On the other hand, the doctor was quick enough to notice when Sambo made a mistake – let his little leaden tank run over, delivered a medicine at the wrong house, packed the wrong pills in the right box or *vice versa*. And then Sambo noticed *him*. But Sambo always made it a rule to take very little indeed from any jar or pot that was less than half full.

When Sambo had tasted every kind of physic in his master's dispensing-room – sweet, sour, salt, bitter, dry, oily, thick or thin, including even one or two little remedies that were kept for the doctor's best patients' pet or lap-dogs, stuff to make the eyes bright, or the hair grow, or the teeth clean, or the nails lustrous, and nothing was of any avail, he became sadder than ever. Still, he did not despair, and this was a blessing, for if he had, his poor heart might have become almost as black as his face. Instead of despairing, he began to read the doctor's books. But since of the words on every page he had to look into a dictionary to find the meanings of at least 20 up to 100, and then forgot them, he did not get on very fast or far.

And then one day – he had just brought in the doctor's grog on his salver – Sambo dared to ask him a question.

'If you please, Massa Doc'r,' he said, 's'posin' you'm wanted to be ebber so black like Sambo what fijjick would Massa take?'

Unfortunately the doctor was a little deaf as well as short-sighted, and all he said was, 'No, no; that will be all tonight.'

On hearing this, Sambo rejoiced. He thought his master meant that this very evening, after he himself was gone to bed, he would try to turn himself black: '*That* – the taking of the physic – will be all to*night*!' It seems almost impossible, but Sambo did. And he waited up until he fell asleep about three in the morning kneeling at the doctor's keyhole in the hope of seeing it happen.

He asked his master only one more question, and this was the last question he had ever need to ask. He had thought it over and over for three whole days before. It was a much bolder and braver thing to do even than to call back at the dentist's boy, 'Yah! Chalk-face! Yah! Mammy's milkysop! Off of de streets wid you! Streets am for gentlemen!'

At nine o'clock as usual the following evening he went into the doctor's room with the silver grog-tray in his hand – but nothing on it. It so chanced the doctor was asleep in his chair with his mouth open. So Sambo had to clank with his salver on the table to wake him up. That made the doctor vexed.

Then he noticed the tray was empty, and he said, 'What's that for?'

And Sambo said, 'Dere isn't no rum left, Massa Doc'r' – for rum was the doctor's fancy.

'Where is it gone?' said the doctor.

'*Me* had it, Massa Doc'r,' said Sambo.

'You!' shouted the doctor. 'What for?'

'Oh, Massa,' said Sambo, falling on his knees, 'to make pore Sambo lose his black. To wash him grey, Massa Doc'r, then white like the little lambs, like Massa Doc'r himsel'. Oh, sir, begorra, I wash and wash and wash, and scrub

and scrub and scrub, and rum only polish Sambo's nose and
smart his eyes.

> A pill, a pill, is all he ask,
> Dat take away his ink-black mask,
> And make him quicker at his task.'

Sambo had spent exactly eight hours and a half in making
up and learning this piteous rhyme. He thought his master
could not but understand that if he had taken so much
trouble he *must* be in earnest. He thought that the instant
his master knew the rum had made no difference to Sambo's
black he would tell him what would. Instead, the doctor,
who, disappointed of his grog, was now very angry, lifted
Sambo up in one hand, boxed each of his ears in turn
with the other, opened the door, and dropped him on the
mat outside it. And so poor Sambo had failed again.

Still, the doctor was not an unkind-hearted man, and
next morning he had forgotten all about the rum. In fear
that he might remember, however, Sambo had been wise
enough to smear a little blacking on the polish which so
much rubbing had made of the tip of his broad nose. But
there had been no real need to do this. The doctor had
quite forgotten, and the same day a whole keg of the best
Jamaica rum went down into his cellar.

So the days and even weeks went by. Sambo did not dare
to dream even of asking his master any more questions.
Instead with a faint heart he tried mixing together one or
two and even three of the different drugs and powders, and,
thumb and finger clutching his nose, he swallowed these.
On his annual half-holiday he even went so far as to swallow a pill which he had mixed with sal volatile and pare-
goric and then dried into a larger pill with some of the
doctor's medical soap and a pinch of senna. It was a very

big pill and he nearly choked in the effort, as he sat in the doctor's garden under a blossoming pear-tree. But though a sort of dusky pallor crept over his cheek, it was at least twenty tints away from being as white as the myriad flowers over his head : and by the evening, when he was better, Sambo was wholly his natural black again.

Last of all, his rolling eye glanced along the row of locked-up medicines called Poisons in the doctor's cabinet. *Could* some of them be poisons simply because they would turn a white man into a blackamoor, he wondered? And was the doctor afraid of taking one himself by mistake? *Could* they? But Sambo dared not tamper with the lock.

And still he pined. Lying awake sometimes between his white sheets, the full moon silvering his fuzzy head and gleaming in his treacle-black eyes, he would gaze at her till they ached in his head. Up there, he thought, perhaps ... But before he could follow this fancy far, he was usually fast asleep.

One afternoon, out on his rounds, he met the dentist's boy again. His heart all but choking him, he set down his basket on the 'sidewalk', put his fingers into his ears to keep out the hated *Yahs*, and waited until William had come up with him. Then, trembling all over, he asked the pug-nosed urchin in a shrill quavering voice what was the matter with being black.

'What's the matter?' squeaked the urchin, mimicking him; 'why, dat,' slapping him on one cheek, 'and *dat*!' slapping him on the other. And with redoubled *Yahs* off he went.

So Sambo grew sadder and sadder. Yet by this time he was sure that he knew almost as much about doctoring and physicking, pilling and draughting as his master. And he had all but worn out the dictionary. One of his jobs every day – after whitening the three steps on to the street, polishing up the knocker and the bell-handle, sweeping out the waiting-room, and making the doctor's coffee, was to arrange his master's letters (that had been brought by the postman) on a tray. These he carried in, after thumping at the doctor's bedroom door, with his coffee.

And there came one morning a letter addressed to his master in a most beautiful handwriting. Sambo had never seen such spidery letters, such exquisite curves. Besides this, a most delicious perfume and odour eddied up from the speckless paper to his nose. He lifted the envelope and sniffed and sniffed again. What valerian is to a cat, so was the scent of this envelope to Sambo. He longed to have it for his own.

It seems indeed that Sambo's Satan must have been by at this moment, though he himself could not imagine how Satan could spare the time to tempt so small a darkey. Sambo's night-dark oily eyes glanced around him. He *saw* no one near. And instead of taking up the letter at once to his master, he undid three of his round silver buttons and pushed it in under his tunic. There it remained throughout the morning – the unhappiest he ever had. When he came in the afternoon to a high wall under some bushy linden trees, he sat down beside his basket in the sunshine and shadow, opened the letter, and set to spelling it out.

First came the address from which it had been written: *White Slopes, The Snow Mountains*. And this, after half an hour's patient endeavour, was what Sambo read:

The last Miss Bleech presents her compliments to Dr Grimble and wishes to say that she is a very old woman now and ill in bed. She would be much obliged if the doctor would bring physic and come and see her as soon as he can.

In ten minutes Sambo had spelled it through again. He could not understand why this letter began not with 'Dear',

as all the few other letters he had ever seen began, but
in this strange fashion: *The last Miss Bleech*. Yet perhaps
it was her very name that made him in his small mind's
eye *see* this old lady; as plainly as if she lay in her bed
before him under the linden trees! Her face wore the
kindest of smiles. But it was her address still more that
fascinated him. It was like the stare of a snake at a
canary. That sudden sweep of frosty whiteness – it shone
in on his sorrowful spirit with a radiance he could hardly
bear. If only he had wings! Here, the streets were often
dark with rain and wind, the doctor's house was at best
a gloomy abode, and the white faces of everyone he saw
seldom met him with any but the blackest of looks. There
was neither help nor hope anywhere to bring the change
he pined for. If only his master would send *him* on this
journey, tell him what to do, and what physic and juleps
and lotions to take with him in his stead!

Sambo knew well this was impossible. He should have
driven the very thought of it out of his head. But even
under the green lime trees the Satan he feared must have
been there beside him. He pushed back the letter under his
tunic, hooked his basket over his arm, and finished his
afternoon's round. He had made up his mind. He would say
nothing about the letter. He would pack up the physics
himself. When he got to where the letter said, he would
tell this old lady, the last Miss Bleech, that the doctor had
sent him. And there, surely, would be the end of all his
troubles. This sinful plan had grown up within him as quick
as Jonah's gourd. He went home on fire with it; and waited
only until the next time the doctor went off, to visit his
Aunt Clara, to carry it out.

Poor Sambo. His master had told him little about his
oughts; and though he knew that borrowing money without leave was wrong, he did not know that it was almost

as wicked as *stealing*. He had been kept 'in the dark'. But he did know that it might be a very long way to the Snow Mountains, that he would have to travel there in a train, and that to travel in a train you must go to the railway station and buy a ticket. In the middle of that night, then – and the doctor had gone off with his little black bag about three in the afternoon – Sambo crept downstairs, opened his master's drawer, and took out from it in green-backs and silver dollars about half of the money he found in the little tin box inside it. For a moment he stood listening, his bulging eyes ashine in the candlelight, his pale-palmed hands trembling. But no sound at all came out of the empty night. If in his dreams his master *was* watching him, he had not uttered a word.

The money safe in his pocket, he stole up to a room where the doctor's old mother used to sleep when she was alive. He had sometimes glanced sharply in here before, in dread of her ghost, and once in curiosity and in the bright light of day, he had peeped too into the wardrobe that stood facing the empty bed. His lighted candle in his hand, his black feet bare, his small ivory-white teeth chattering, he crept soundlessly and more darkly than a shadow into this chamber. He opened the great wardrobe door. From every hook there hung limp and lifeless the old clothes of the doctor's old mother – gowns and shawls and mantles; puce and violet, mauve and purple; and on a hook all to itself a little satin bodice, lovelier than any and of a faded vermilion, which must have been worn by her when she was young. Sambo gasped for delight at sight of all these colours, these silks and satins. He gently put out his finger as if to touch them. For Sambo's master, even though he had a quick temper, had been very fond of his mother, and so could not bear to part with her clothes.

Else, Sambo perhaps would never have reached the Snow

Mountains. For among them there hung a cloak made only of ermine. This had been a present from the doctor to his mother on her seventieth birthday, and must have cost a mint of money. For love of her son and for pride in it she always wore it after that when she went out at night to hear music or to sup with her friends, though this was seldom.

Sambo carefully placed his candlestick on the dressing-table in front of the large dark looking-glass, and standing on a chair took down the cloak from its hook. He not only took it down, he put it on. Then he got up on to a stool, and by the flickering beam of his candle surveyed himself in the glass. Out of its quiet depths showed his round black fuzzy head, his dark liquid eyes, gleaming teeth, small black hands – and from chin to heel flowed down this silken, silvery, soft white fur – except for the little black tufts on it.

Sambo had never seen so marvellous a thing before. He could hardly even sigh for wonder. This it was then to be the great-grandson of a king! There was but one small trouble in his mind – the tufts. And lo and behold, on the dressing-table there lay a pair of the old lady's embroidery scissors, of silver and mother-of-pearl, and with tapering steel points. Sambo sat down on the floor, and heedless of how the cold hours glided away, snipped out with the scissors every single tuft of black he found in the cloak. He gathered them up, opened a bandbox, put them in, huddled up the cloak into a bundle, took his candle and went back to his master's room.

There, for his candle was now guttering out, he lit the gas and turned it low. From the shelves above his head, since he could not borrow from all, he took down the third and seventh bottles of the powders from every shelf – his small heart being dark with superstitions – and he put a little of each of their contents into some pill-boxes. He took only powders because he was afraid on a long journey that bottles might break. Now Dr Grimble served up his pills in boxes of different colours, according to what ailment the pills were for. So Sambo had ten boxes in all, two of which were of the same colour, as there were five shelves. These ten boxes he put into his basket. In other boxes he put some of his favourite pills, and he could not resist one bottle of Nicey-Nicey, as the doctor called it. It was this nicey-nicey that he mixed with his medicines to make them go down sweeter. Sambo also put into his basket one or two little shiny knives, some long scissors, a slim wooden pipe with a cup at the end of it for listening to hearts with, and a pair of dark-glassed tortoiseshell spectacles: and that was all.

When he had finished packing his basket the grey of dawn was showing through the cracks of the window shutters. His cheek almost as grey itself, though he did not know it, he stole downstairs. His basket on one side of him, and a bundle – containing his money, both his nightshirts and two old bandana handkerchiefs – on the other, he sat down to breakfast. It was still early morning when, having eaten the doctor's breakfast as well as his own, Sambo let himself out of the house, crept past the whispering poplar trees, and ran off.

It was a bad thing to do, but perhaps if the dentist's boy had told Sambo what was the matter with being black, he might never have gone at all. But go he did; and all that day until evening fell, he hid in one of the mangers in the stables of an old empty house that he had often noticed on his rounds – its rambling garden deep with grass and busy with birds. Part of the time he nodded off to sleep, but most of it he sat with clammy hands and open mouth listening in dread of the baying of the bloodhounds sniffing him out; of Satan; but far more, of never reaching the Snow Mountains. Only once he ventured from his hiding-place to see if any of last year's apples were still moulder-ing in the grass. He found none, and had to go hungry.

In the dusk, his basket and ermine cloak over his arm, he skulked off to the railway station and asked for a ticket to the nearest station to the Snow Mountains.

'Who wants it?' said the man.

'Massa, sir,' said Sambo.

'If he wants a ticket for the Snow Mountains, why doesn't he say so?' said the man.

'Me no know,' said Sambo, and the man gave him a ticket. Sambo dared ask nobody any other questions, but spied about until he saw a tall wooden pole surmounted with a finger-board. On this was scrawled in charcoal: 'To the Snow Mountains'. It pointed to a train – standing empty in the murky gloom of a siding – and an ancient, faded, blistered, ramshackle train it looked.

There was not a human soul to be seen here, or even sign of any, not even of the engine-driver. And when Sambo at last sidled up to enquire of a huddled shape sitting in the dark in how many hours' time the train would be starting, no tongue answered, and he found he had been whispering to a huge sack of bran! So without more ado he climbed up into one of the carriages – and very dark and musty it was inside – lay down on the hard wooden seat, covered himself with his ermine cloak, and in less than no time he fell asleep.

He awoke in a dreadful nightmare, not knowing where he was, and supposing there had been an earthquake. When he scrambled to his knees and looked out of the window, he found that the train was jerking and jolting along over a very narrow track in the light of the moon, and on either side of the track was nothing but the wide glare and glitter and whiteness of ice and snow. The scene stretched on into the distance, a waste of frozen snow. It was a strange thing that any train could have gone rambling off so quick into the north like this. But then Sambo had been fast asleep, nor knew how long. And but one glance at the glory of the snow did him more good than if he had swallowed the whole of his master's medicines, including the poisons.

The train went on, clanking and clattering – Sambo could even hear the tinkle of the broken ice, and still the moon shone down, and now it began to snow again, but very sparsely. Sambo hung as far as he could out of the narrow window to peep into the carriages ahead of and behind him. Both it seemed were empty. Now and again he saw a house, but it was always only a little house and far away. And once the track made so sharp a curve that he could see even the twinkle of the fire in the engine-cabin and what looked like a black man crouching there, though he couldn't be sure. And as they were scuttling along as fast as ever, and Sambo was soon drowsy again with watching the snow, he lay down on his hard seat in the warmth of the cloak and once more fell asleep.

When he awoke, the train was at a standstill. Sambo heard a bell ringing, and looked out of the window. It was bright full morning. And there he saw a low narrow platform crusted thick with snow, and an open shed. Above the shed were the words: 'The Snow Mountains. *Change!*' He had only time enough to take out his basket and his bundle and his cloak before there came a long mournful hoot from the engine, and in a moment the train was gone.

And still there was no one to be seen. So Sambo, who was cold, put on his cloak, and, with his basket under it on one arm, and his bundle in his hand, he came to the

wicket gate of the station. An old man with a beard was standing there, a lighted lantern in his hand, though the sun had risen. This old man asked Sambo for his ticket. And Sambo, having given him the ticket, asked the old man where the last Miss Bleech lived. '*White* Slopes am de name,' he said.

'You go along and along there,' mumbled the old man, pointing to a winding narrow road beyond the station, 'until you begin to go up and up. Then up and up you go and follow the trees.'

Sambo thanked him and went on his way. In spite of his long and heavy sleep in the train, his leg bones ached and he was very weary. His basket grew heavier, his cloak hotter, the path steeper. The sun shone down on the whiteness and dazzled his eyes. The pine trees by the wayside had hours ago gone far beyond his counting. He could not even guess how many miles he had tramped scrunching on through the snow when of a sudden he came round a bluff in the hills and saw with joy indeed what he felt sure must be White Slopes. For *there* was the strangest house in all the world. Peaked and sloping, wide and narrow, and clotted with snow, its shining roofs stood high above its walls and windows. It was not a house but a great Mansion. Up, up, into the solitary mountains Sambo had climbed, following the pine trees that marked his narrow path, and here at last was where he longed to be. What should he do next?

Before he started he had thought he would tell the old lady that his master had sent him. 'Massa Doc'r ill in bed, he say: *he* sent Sambo.' These would be the words he would use. Then he would mix a little of the powder from each of his coloured boxes in turn with some of the nicey-nicey and a little water, and would give her one teaspoonful of each of them every day. He knew his physics now by heart; and though they had done him no good, not at any rate the kind of good he longed for, they had done him no harm.

As long as the medicines lasted, he felt sure the old lady would let him stay with her. When she was better again, perhaps she might ask him to be her house-boy. How happy that would be! For if only, poor Sambo felt certain, he could remain long enough in this white shining mansion among the mountains, and in these radiant wastes of snow, surely, surely, his black would slowly vanish away. Had not his master's window curtains, even in sunlight incomparably less fair and bright than this, turned from blue to faded grey?

The faintest of breezes came sighing through the air, so faint that it scarcely stirred the glittering crystals at Sambo's feet. He shivered. And his thoughts grew darker. Supposing the old lady, when he appeared before her great bed, did not believe that his master had sent him? Supposing she asked him questions, discovered that he had stolen his medicines; that he was a little black cheat? What then?

He eyed again the strange house, rising in solitude under the blue sky among the slopes of the mountains. He fancied that in the distance he saw living shapes, moving on the terraces beneath it, though he could not detect what they were. What then? he asked himself again, and began to be afraid. And though even Sambo himself could not have believed that Satan would ever venture into a place so full of light and peace as this, an even wickeder thought had stolen into his mind. Why should he not pretend that he himself was his master, that *he* was the Doctor? There had been not a word in the letter to say that the last Miss Bleech knew his master. Not one word. That was perhaps why she hadn't begun her letter with the word 'dear'. Perhaps then, if he himself gave her only half the doses he had intended to give her, she would get better only half as quickly. Then he might stay on and on and on – and never go back. No, never.

As he sat there in his ermine in the snow with this thought in his mind, there suddenly sprang into view beneath him a wild white buck rabbit, with eyes like burning coals. At least Sambo thought it was a rabbit, though it was much bigger than any he had ever seen before. Stiff as a post in the snow and for the best part of a minute, it glared at Sambo – not fiercely but because its eyes were so full of light. Then, as if assured he meant it no harm, it made a little noise that was almost like laughter, and scuffled its hind legs rapidly in the snow. Other creatures like it answered. And soon the whole expanse beneath Sambo – and there was a dark lake of ice encircled with frosted trees at its foot – was alive with rabbits – hundreds and hundreds of rabbits, large and small. They paid no heed to Sambo, no more than if he had been as spotlessly white as they were themselves. Perhaps, thought he, they had not noticed his hands or his face. But the old lady would. When she saw he was black, she would not only not believe he was a doctor, but might tremble with scorn and hatred. What then?

He was so tired and hungry he could think no more. So, his basket on his arm, he set off again, and presently came to the back parts of the house. Apart from the faint-coloured shadows cast by the sunlight on its roofs and walls, it was white all over. Here there were many little outhouses like beehives capped with snow, and they seemed to have been all of them freshly whitened. Peeping about Sambo saw in a corner under the house a large tub or butt, put there as if to catch the rain. He stole over and lifting himself by his hands to its edge, peeped in. The butt was half full of a thick white liquid, like whitewash. He hauled himself up, and stooping over, broke the thin sheet of ice that wrinkled its surface and dipped in his finger. It came out white as milk. If the tip of a finger, why not his whole body? Surely here was the end of all his troubles!

He hesitated no more. He stripped off his ermine cloak, his silver-buttoned tunic, his black trousers, his shirt, his shoes, everything he had on. And there and then, naked and shuddering with the cold, he climbed up over the edge of the butt, let himself down, and three times over dipped himself head to foot in the creamy ice-cold water – face, hands, woolly hair and all. Once safely out, he ran about until he was caked dry. Then he put on his clothes again. No one, it seemed, had heard his splashing; no one had seen him. But as he was snapping-to the silver clasp of the cloak at his throat, having put on his master's goggles from out of his basket, he heard a little noise. Out of its dark shining eyes a gentle deer stood watching him in the snow. It was hornless and as white as he himself; nor did it start back or hasten away when he came near. He put out his white crudded hand and stroked its gentle head. And because of the friendliness of the deer, he was afraid no more. Cloaked and peering, he went round to the front of the house, and mounting the steps, knocked solemnly on the great door.

It was opened by the butler. At least Sambo guessed him to be the butler, for he had seen many butlers. But he had had never seen one so old or so odd to look at. Over a long starched waistcoat his spotless swallow-tailed coat almost brushed the floor. His nose was even broader and flatter than Sambo's, his lips as thick and his hair as woolly and, except for his face, he was almost as white. He looked sorrowful, too, and full of care. And though Sambo's lips were stiff, partly with the whitewash and partly because he was telling a lie, Sambo told him not who he was but who he was *not*. He then asked him how his mistress did, and if she were well enough to see the doctor.

'Ah, massa, massa,' replied the old butler, lifting his hands in grief; 'worser and worser!' And without another word he led Sambo up the wide white staircase and along a corridor whose windows looked out upon the mountains; and then he tapped at a door.

When Sambo saw the last Miss Bleech in her great bed, her high, narrow, silvery head reclining on the pillows, her far-away blue eyes fixed on the window in front of her, he knew that she was not long for this world. And he wept inside to think it. It seemed she must be at least ninety-eight, if not even ninety-nine. Her voice was so small and low he could scarcely hear what she said to him. But when the butler told her who this visitor was, she smiled at Sambo. She was rejoiced to see him, even though she could see him but dimly. Not too dimly, however, to realize that this was not only the whitest of doctors that had ever come to do her good, but the whitest of human beings. All her other doctors, though she had needed few since her child-hood, had been dressed up in solemn long black coats to match their hats and trousers; and of all things in the world she liked black least. Or rather, she loved white best; though Sambo did not know this, then.

But first, she thought only of *his* comfort. She bade the butler show him to his room. It had been specially prepared against the coming of the visitor whom she had been pining so much to see, and it was next to her own. She told Sambo, as he stood there – small, staring, and motionless at the foot of her bed – that she knew how cold and wearisome a journey his had been. Nor did the old lady so much as sigh when she said she would not be troubling him for long. Her one hope was that he would stay with her as many days as he could spare.

Sambo, who had often mimicked his master's speech and manners behind his back, imitated them, as well as he could, now. He told the old lady that he thought she was looking a little better, and that he would do his best to make her quite well again. So long as there is breath in the body, he said, there is hope. 'Care, fijjick, sleep,' he said, lifting a finger. But he kept his dark spectacles turned away from the light of the window as he spoke, in terror lest she should look close into his white-washed face and know him for a cheat.

When Sambo was alone in the lofty room that had been made ready, when he looked round him at the tall bed canopied with white velvet, the sofa, the carpet – deep and thick as moss, but white too itself as snow – he sat down on a stool, and burst out crying. He was young, he was alone, he was weary; but it was his villainy that weighed heaviest. Still, he cried only for a few moments, and at once hastened over to the great glass on the dressing-table, to see if his tears had left their traces on his cheek. No; he had dipped deep in the whitewash, and stains there were none. Indeed, at first glimpse of himself – that sheeted face, small hoary hands, a dwarf in ermine – terror seized him. It was as if he had met his own ghost. And then he sighed. He was whiter even than his master! He eased the buckle at his throat, turned his head, and looked out of the window.

Beneath him the mountain fell away in snowy terraces towards the valley far below. Trees and bushes heaped in snow and glistening in the sun of evening met his wondering gaze. The sweet yet sorrowful 'cry of winter curlews wafting their way through the windless air came to his ear. And beneath them strayed strange creatures he had neither seen before nor knew the name of. Some were antlered, some were small and nimble, and all of so pale a colouring that they could scarcely be seen against the snow. And though, so vast was the view from his window, they were scattered far apart, they seemed to be at peace with one another. Not a voice yelled *Yah*, no cry of wrath or pain pierced the air. It was as if, gazing out over these snow mountains and valleys, smooth and radiant beneath the blue, Sambo had been transported into the place called *Nowhere*. And for a while he forgot that he was black.

Day after day he tended the old lady, putting so in- finitesimal a pinch of his master's powders into her physic- bottles and so much nicey-nicey that she enjoyed taking her medicine, and would even sip instead of merely swallowing. Sambo would sit for hours in silence at her bedside, touch- ing her hand now and again with his rough-washed fingers, not in order to tell if she were feverish but merely to comfort her, and to prove that he was there. And the longer he stayed with her the more she came to find ease and com- fort in his company, and the sadder Sambo grew : first, to think that she was now too old ever to be young again, and next, that he was deceiving her. But try as he might, and though he often lay long hours awake brooding on this, he could not find words to tell the old lady, whom he now loved dearly, what a dreadful net of falsehood he was in.

Once when the black was beginning to dim his whitewash he had to steal down to the outhouses for another coat. And though this time the sudden shock of cold from his tub brought on a hacking cough, fortunately, packed up in his basket, he had brought with him a powder good for coughs, and as his patient did not need it, he took it himself.

When his cough was better, he would sometimes sing to her, in his shrill falsetto, songs of his own people that he

had heard as a child. Among her favourites, and his, was
the lament beginning, 'Weep no more, my lady!' And as he
sang it, the black rolling eyes of the child would meet the
faded blue of his friend's, and it was as if by the mere grace
of the music they shared an unsearchable secret.

> Weep no more, my lady,
>   O, weep no more today!
> We will sing one song for the old Kentucky home,
> For the old Kentucky home, far away ...

And then, for better cheer, Sambo would warble up, 'Shine,
shine, Moon!' or, 'So Early in the Morning'; though at the
words –

> When I was young, I used to wait,
> On Massa's table lay the plate,
> Pass the bottle when him dry,
> Brush away the blue-tail fly ...

his memory ran back in a flash to his master, and his voice
shook.

At length, one afternoon, after a long silence, as he sat
on his customary stool by the great bed, he asked the old
lady if she minded things *looking* what they are *not*. And
he turned his face full into the light as he said it.

'Why, but no, my dear kind doctor,' she replied to him.
'It is not what things *look* like that matters *most*; but what
they are.' When she was young, she went on – almost as
if, without knowing it, she were reading his thoughts –
once, when she was young, she had loved colours – every
faintest colour and hue and tint visible in the rainbow;
though some of them of course were her favourites. But all
colours, her father had explained to her, even when she was
a little girl with short pigtails dangling round her head, lie
hidden in *white*. 'White,' her father had told her, 'is not a
colour at all; it is *all* colours.' She had never forgotten that.

And the longer she lived, she told Sambo, the more she had come to delight in white : snowdrops, anemones, the convolvulus; dew before the sun rises; hoarfrost; foam of falling water; the sea's spray. So at last she had come to live in these mountains where there was snow nearly all the year round, and all living creatures shared in its splendour.

'Listen, doctor, is it not the voice of birds I hear? Look out, now, at their wings of light!'

Sambo lifted his heavy head and looked out of the window. But the birds must have been in the old lady's mind. There were none in the heavens.

He asked her then if she had ever travelled in the Black Man's Land, in the country of the Darkeys. Was it not a dreadful thing, he entreated her, to be born like that? Black?

'Why, no, dear doctor,' she assured him eagerly. 'Never to me. That again is what my father used to tell me. White gives back all colours; black welcomes them in. What is the centre of every seeing human eye, he would say; *black*. Besides all things on earth have an out and an in. Even an apple hangs there on its twig for the sake of its seeds. A black man whose mind is free from darkness and his heart from cruelty is in truth whiter than *any* one whose soul is in the shades.' And she smiled to herself after listening to this little sermon to one so learned as a doctor; but she had seen that Sambo was in some trouble of mind.

'Ay,' said Sambo in a lamentable voice. 'And de blackest ob all dings, lady, *dat* is a lie!' And he hastened out of the room.

It was curious perhaps that one so young as he, and with so little royal blood left in him by now, should have wept as he did at the thought of a lie. But weep he did.

That night, after he had given the old lady her physic, and it was all but all of it nicey-nicey, for most of his powders were gone; when he had seen that she was in comfort, and had lit her wax candle in the silver candlestick beside her bed, he bade her good night, and locked himself into his room.

A shallow tin white bath lay underneath his bed. He dragged it out in front of his dressing-table and emptied the cold water out of his jug into it. There was no more than an inch or two of water in the shallow bath, and he was three coats thick with whitewash. So that it took him a long time to sponge and rub and scrape himself black again, or as nearly black as he could manage. When he had finished and was dry, he lay down on the sofa to rest awhile, for he wished to rise at daybreak. Then he would tell the old lady all he was, his one fear being that it might make her worse. But it was impossible the next morning to make the last Miss Bleech worse, for when Sambo, having unlocked his door, went in at daybreak, she was dead.

He stood at the foot of the bed, gazing out of his blackness at the placid face upon the pillow, at the birdlike hands on the counterpane. And he nodded his woolly head, in his grief, as if to say, Too late! At last he stole nearer and ventured to put out his ink-black fingers and touch her ice-cold hand.

'*Sambo* am here, lady,' he whispered.

But there was no look in his friend's fixed eyes to show that she had heard. And as in his misery he stood there, he saw beside the candlestick a slip of paper folded in two. 'My last wishes' was written on it and beside it was a long envelope, sealed down. Sambo took the slip of paper to the window, and though the handwriting was very spidery and shaky he had learned it long since under the linden trees, and in a few minutes he had read the message within.

'Dear friend, and far more than Doctor,' it said, 'after your kindness and goodness to me, beyond any physic, I wish to leave you all I have. You will see that my butler and the others shall never want. Take care of the animals, and never put on anything but white for me. And may heaven bless you. *Emily Bleech*.'

Sambo read this over and over; then put it back where he had found it. His grief and love were almost greater than he could bear, but there was only one thing he could *do*. Having emptied his bath-water out of the window, he hastened downstairs. Not a soul was stirring. It was as if the strangers of night had but a moment before left the round beehive outhouses to their daily solitude. Three times Sambo dipped himself from crown to sole in the great tub; and came out like chalk. He was doing what his friend wished him to do.

After a few days had gone by, and Sambo's heart was less troubled, he did one or two things that he wished for himself. When he ran off from his master he had no thought of money except what would take him to the Mountains. It was only time he pined for in which to grow white. And now time stretched out before him like the sands of the desert, the face of the sea. And he thought again of what was past. He made up a parcel of money – containing twice as much as he had borrowed from his master; one single Stars-and-Stripes bank-note with a great many noughts on it to pay for the ermine cloak; and a hundred dollars over for the missing medicine. This parcel he despatched secretly to the doctor, with *From Sambo* written inside the paper but no address. At the same time he sent fifty dollars to the most famous candy shop in the doctor's town, telling them to deliver to Mr Tooth-the-Dentist's boy a large jar of Maple Sugar, a keg of dates, a cake of black dainty made of molasses called brandy-bread, and a blue-and-white pot of the finest Chinese ginger.

After all, Sambo thought, he might never have come to the Snow Mountains if it had not been for this cater-wauling young vagabond, and he would know by this that Sambo was 'off the streets'! As for the butler and the other servants, they could never even have hoped for a kinder master. 'Of all de massas he was best.'

And yet, in the years that followed, as he lived on at peace in his mansion in the Snow Mountains, gazing out of his window – a thing he never wearied of – a strange craving at times would creep into Sambo's mind. And the fear would take him that Satan was nearing again. At this he would steal to his looking-glass, and confront, on and on, that speckless face of chalk from eyes as motionless and dark as basalt.

'O but for a moment,' a voice would cry out on him as if from the very recesses of his being. 'O but for a moment, to be black again!' And always, to silence the voice, Sambo would pick a few snowflowers and go down and lay them on his old friend's grave. There he would stay for a few moments, alone in the valley, looking up at the tranquil hills; and then, slowly and solemnly shaking his whitewashed head, would return again – comforted.

The Riddle

So these seven children, Ann and Matilda, James, William and Henry, Harriet and Dorothea, came to live with their grandmother. The house in which their grandmother had lived since her childhood was built in the time of the Georges. It was not a pretty house, but roomy, substantial, and square; and a great cedar tree outstretched its branches almost to the windows.

When the children were come out of the cab (five sitting inside and two beside the driver), they were shown into their grandmother's presence. They stood in a little black group before the old lady, seated in her bow-window. And she asked them each their names, and repeated each name in her kind, quavering voice. Then to one she gave a work-box, to William a jack-knife, to Dorothea a painted ball; to each a present according to age. And she kissed all her grand-children to the youngest.

'My dears,' she said, 'I wish to see all of you bright and gay in my house. I am an old woman, so that I cannot romp with you; but Ann must look to you, and Mrs Fenn too. And every morning and every evening you must all come in to see your granny; and bring me smiling faces, that call back to my mind my own son Harry. But all the rest of the day, when school is done, you shall do just as you please, my dears. And there is only one thing, just one, I would have you remember. In the large spare bedroom that looks out on the slate roof there stands in the corner an old oak chest; ay, older than I, my dears, a great deal older; older than my grandmother. Play anywhere else in the house, but not there.' She spoke kindly to them all, smiling at them; but she was very old, and her eyes seemed to see nothing of this world.

And the seven children, though at first they were gloomy and strange, soon began to be happy and at home in the great house. There was much to interest and to amuse them there; all was new to them. Twice every day, morning and evening, they came in to see their grandmother, who every day seemed more feeble; and she spoke pleasantly to them of her mother, and her childhood, but never forgetting to visit her store of sugar-plums. And so the weeks passed by ...

It was evening twilight when Henry went upstairs from the nursery by himself to look at the oak chest. He pressed his fingers into the carved fruit and flowers, and spoke to the dark-smiling heads at the corners; and then, with a glance over his shoulder, he opened the lid and looked in. But the chest concealed no treasure, neither gold nor baubles, nor was there anything to alarm the eye. The chest was empty, except that it was lined with silk of old-rose, seeming darker in the dusk, and smelling sweet of pot-pourri. And while Henry was looking in, he heard the softened laughter and the clinking of the cups downstairs in the nursery; and out at the window he saw the day darkening. These things brought strangely to his memory his mother who in her glimmering white dress used to read to him in the dusk; and he climbed into the chest; and the lid closed gently down over him.

When the other six children were tired with their playing, they filed into their grandmother's room for her good night and her sugar-plums. She looked out between the candles at them as if she were uncertain of something in her thoughts. The next day Ann told her grandmother that

The Riddle

Henry was not anywhere to be found.

'Dearie me, child. Then he must be gone away for a time,' said the old lady. She paused. 'But remember, all of you, do not meddle with the oak chest.'

But Matilda could not forget her brother Henry, finding no pleasure in playing without him. So she would loiter in the house thinking where he might be. And she carried her wooden doll in her bare arms, singing under her breath all she could make up about it. And when one bright morning she peeped in on the chest, so sweet-scented and secret it seemed that she took her doll with her into it – just as Henry himself had done.

So Ann, and James, and William, Harriet and Dorothea were left at home to play together. 'Some day maybe they will come back to you, my dears,' said their grandmother, 'or maybe you will go to them. Heed my warning as best you may.'

Now Harriet and William were friends together, pretending to be sweethearts; while James and Dorothea liked wild games of hunting, and fishing, and battles.

On a silent afternoon in October, Harriet and William were talking softly together, looking out over the slate roof at the green fields, and they heard the squeak and frisking of a mouse behind them in the room. They went together and searched for the small, dark hole from whence it had come out. But finding no hole, they began to finger the carving of the chest, and to give names to the dark-smiling heads, just as Henry had done. '*I* know! let's pretend you are Sleeping Beauty, Harriet,' said William, 'and I'll be the Prince that squeezes through the thorns and comes in.' Harriet looked gently and strangely at her brother but she got into the box and lay down, pretending to be fast asleep, and on tiptoe William leaned over, and seeing how big was the chest, he stepped in to kiss the Sleeping Beauty and to wake her from her quiet sleep. Slowly the carved lid turned on its noiseless hinges. And only the clatter of James and Dorothea came in sometimes to recall Ann from her book.

But their old grandmother was very feeble, and her sight dim, and her hearing extremely difficult.

Snow was falling through the still air upon the roof; and Dorothea was a fish in the oak chest, and James stood over the hole in the ice, brandishing a walking-stick for a harpoon, pretending to be an Esquimau. Dorothea's face was red, and her wild eyes sparkled through her tousled hair. And James had a crooked scratch upon his cheek. 'You must struggle, Dorothea, and then I shall swim back and drag you out. Be quick now!' He shouted with laughter as he was drawn into the open chest. And the lid closed softly and gently down as before.

Ann, left to herself, was too old to care overmuch for sugar-plums, but she would go solitary to bid her grandmother good night; and the old lady looked wistfully at her over her spectacles. 'Well, my dear,' she said with trembling head; and she squeezed Ann's fingers between her own knuckled finger and thumb. 'What lonely old people, we two are, to be sure!' Ann kissed her grandmother's soft, loose cheek. She left the old lady sitting in her easy chair, her hands upon her knees, and her head turned sidelong towards her.

When Ann was gone to bed she used to sit reading her book by candlelight. She drew up her knees under the sheets, resting her book upon them. Her story was about fairies and gnomes, and the gently-flowing moonlight of the narrative seemed to illumine the white pages, and she could hear in fancy fairy voices, so silent was the great many-roomed house, and so mellifluent were the words of the story. Presently she put out her candle, and, with a confused babel of voices close to her ear, and faint swift

pictures before her eyes, she fell asleep.

And in the dead of night she rose out of her bed in dream, and with eyes wide open yet seeing nothing of reality, moved silently through the vacant house. Past the room where her grandmother was snoring in brief, heavy slumber, she stepped lightly and surely, and down the wide staircase. And Vega the far-shining stood over against the window above the slate roof. Ann walked into the strange room beneath as if she were being guided by the hand towards the oak chest. There, just as if she were dreaming it was her bed, she laid herself down in the old rose silk, in the fragrant place. But it was so dark in the room that the movement of the lid was indistinguishable.

Through the long day, the grandmother sat in her bow-window. Her lips were pursed, and she looked with dim, inquisitive scrutiny upon the street where people passed to and fro, and vehicles rolled by. At evening she climbed the stair and stood in the doorway of the large spare bedroom. The ascent had shortened her breath. Her magnifying spectacles rested upon her nose. Leaning her hand on the doorpost she peered in towards the glimmering square of window in the quiet gloom. But she could not see far, because her sight was dim and the light of day feeble. Nor could she detect the faint fragrance as of autumnal leaves. But in her mind was a tangled skein of memories – laughter and tears, and children long ago become old-fashioned, and the advent of friends, and last farewells. And gossiping fitfully, inarticulately, with herself, the old lady went down again to her window-seat.

SECRET LAUGHTER

Walter de la Mare

'These poems . . . which are offered especially to the young, are poems to remember all your lives.' – Eleanor Graham, who made the selection. Illustrated by Margery Gill.

COME HITHER

Walter de la Mare

A classic anthology of poetry in two volumes, enriched by de la Mare's own comments and interpretations of each poem. Wood engravings by Diana Bloomfield.

I'LL TELL YOU A TALE

Ian Serraillier

Long before most people could read and write, wandering minstrels were the news reporters of their time, broadcasting reports of great battles, heroic deeds, runaway lovers and foul murders. Today the poet is still reporter and storyteller and in this book will be found all manner of tales to intrigue and amuse you.

AUTHORS' CHOICE II

A really special, rich, colourful, utterly engrossing collection of favourite short stories, chosen by sixteen of the most distinguished present-day writers for children.